Born in the UK, **Becky Wicks** has suffered interminable wanderlust from an early age. She's lived and worked all over the world, from London to Dubai, Sydney, Bali, NYC and Amsterdam. She's written for the likes of *GQ*, *Hello!*, *Fabulous* and *Time Out*, a host of YA romance, plus three travel memoirs—*Burqalicious*, *Balilicious* and *Latinalicious* (HarperCollins, Australia). Now she blends travel with romance for Mills & Boon and loves every minute! Tweet her @bex_wicks.

Lifelong romance addict **JC Harroway** took a break from her career as a junior doctor to raise a family and found her calling as a Mills & Boon author instead. She now lives in New Zealand and finds that writing feeds her very real obsession with happy endings and the endorphin rush they create. You can follow her at jcharroway.com, and on Facebook, Twitter and Instagram.

**Also by Becky Wicks**

*South African Escape to Heal Her*
*Finding Forever with the Single Dad*
*Melting the Surgeon's Heart*
*A Marriage Healed in Hawaii*

**Also by JC Harroway**

*Her Secret Valentine's Baby*
*Nurse's Secret Royal Fling*

**A Sydney Central Reunion miniseries**

*Phoebe's Baby Bombshell*

**Gulf Harbour ER miniseries**

*Tempted by the Rebel Surgeon*
*Breaking the Single Mum's Rules*

Discover more at millsandboon.co.uk.

# DARING TO FALL FOR THE SINGLE DAD

BECKY WICKS

# SECRETLY DATING THE BABY DOC

JC HARROWAY

MILLS & BOON

First published in Great Britain 2024
by Mills & Boon, an imprint of HarperCollins*Publishers* Ltd,
1 London Bridge Street, London, SE1 9GF

www.harpercollins.co.uk

HarperCollins*Publishers* Macken House, 39/40 Mayor Street Upper,
Dublin 1, D01 C9W8, Ireland



Special thanks and acknowledgement are given to Becky Wicks
for her contribution to the Buenos Aires Docs miniseries.

Special thanks and acknowledgement are given to JC Harroway
for her contribution to the Buenos Aires Docs miniseries.

ISBN: 978-0-263-32164-7

07/24

This book contains FSC™ certified paper
and other controlled sources to ensure responsible forest management.

For more information visit www.harpercollins.co.uk/green.

Printed and Bound in the UK using 100% Renewable Electricity
at CPI Group (UK) Ltd, Croydon, CR0 4YY

# DARING TO FALL FOR THE SINGLE DAD

BECKY WICKS

MILLS & BOON

To my lovely dad, Ray Wicks, who is definitely not single, and will probably never read this.

You'll always be my number one anyway.

# CHAPTER ONE

HOLDING UP A HAND, Dr Ana Mendez waved at the post boy, smiling at his pink feathered headdress as he zoomed past her windows on his bicycle.

'I guess everyone's getting in the spirit already,' she said to her vase of fresh marigolds. It was early now, and relatively peaceful on the streets, but in just a few hours her city would be pumping with a thousand kinds of music, dancing groups and musicians in every side street. The crowds would be shuffling in colourful costumes through the blocks and barrios, and her ears would be assaulted from all angles as every speaker tried its best to compete with the rest. The first day of Carnival was always fun in Buenos Aires—*unless you worked in A&E*, she thought to herself. The staff at the hospital were always run off their feet at this time of year. Luckily this clinic wasn't opening till Monday, so she had the perfect excuse to hide away from the mayhem.

Ah, this clinic—*her* new clinic! Steering her wheelchair expertly to the desk, breathing in the smell of the fresh paint, Ana glanced at the plaque on the wall above her MD certificate. Her lips twitched with a proud smile at the sight of her name glistening in silver: Dr Ana Mendez. She had her own practice…finally!

She and her small but excited team had decided to get the madness of Carnival over with first, but every day had dawned with a new set of tasks to complete in the run up to opening. She'd been coming here every day with new additions in preparation, or to assist the workmen with new equipment, new lighting or new posters. Any excuse would do, because this was all so exciting. So…not what people had expected someone like her to go and do.

Turning her chair back towards her consulting room, she noted how at home the snake plant she'd brought in today looked already. 'Very nice, *mijo*, I think this place is ideal for you,' she said to it. Its sword-like leaves with bold stripy patterns suited the corner of her desk, she decided, and, best of all, it could survive with little help—just like her.

After years of working her way up and around hospitals all over Argentina, she had finally taken over the barrio's clinic round the corner from the home she'd grown up in, and moved into her new wheelchair-adapted apartment too. Dr Azaban, the old GP, had hung up her coat and retired just a few months ago. The call had come in while Ana was on a break from a shift at the Medical Medicina Privada in Bariloche, where she'd been for the best part of five years.

'The time is now, Ana,' she'd said, in the phone call that would change the direction of her life. 'Are you ready to come home and take over?'

It had taken a while, a lot of prep, a lot of money and a lot of documentation but she'd sailed through it all with one goal on the horizon—a home from home, a place to call hers and a new, refreshed clinic for the community to call theirs. She'd always said, when she came home, it would be for something worthwhile. Dr Azaban was an old family friend who'd been preparing Ana for this since she'd completed her studies. Not that it wasn't going to take a while to readjust—she was still bumping into people she'd forgotten to tell she was even back in Recoleta!

Ana adjusted a bright-red truck on the colourful mat in the children's section of the waiting room, then sat up straighter a soft blue teddy bear on his tiny stool. It had been decided years ago, and even laid out on her vision board, that *her* clinic would possess none of the drabness she'd encountered in other GP practices over the years. The process of getting well began in the mind, in cheery surroundings with positive vibes, she reminded herself, plucking a colourful marigold from another vase on the magazine stand and placing it behind her ear.

This was something she'd taken on board as a child, when the kind staff at the children's ward at Hospital General de Buenos Aires had sat her down and explained how she would likely never walk again. At just six years old, she'd lain there after the car accident, wondering how on earth she'd get by without the use of her legs. She'd been too young to fathom how hard it would be, not just on her going forward but also on her parents, Juan and Martina. She'd been too young to understand anything then, except the kindness and good intentions of the people around her and the way the bright colours had made her feel.

In those dark times she'd grown to find a sense of hope in the cheery flowers and toys, the pretty fabrics of the blankets and the reassuring faces on the posters on the walls. Everything ever since had been about colour, she thought now, catching a glimpse of herself in the window. She didn't need Carnival as an excuse to dress up as though she'd wheeled her chair through a rainbow and come out draped in it on the other side. Her bright-yellow polka-dot headscarf held back her long mass of raven black curls and matched her shoes. She always matched her headscarves to her shoes wherever possible.

A banging on the door made her start. 'We're not open yet!' she called. But the banging continued, this time louder. *What the...?*

Ana sped for the door, only to find a white-haired man doubled over on the pavement, clutching his chest. 'Mr Acosta!' she cried, recognising in shock the seventy-something man from the shop over the road.

'I think I'm having a heart attack, Ana,' he managed, his face creased in pain. No soon had she flung open the doors than he was lurching forward, practically landing on her lap in the wheelchair.

'Come in, we'll get you help!' Her words were reassuring, even as she swiftly lowered her chair as far down as it would go. Bundling him inside across the threshold onto the cool floor, she loosened his collar with one hand and called for an ambulance with the other, praying the streets weren't yet too packed with Carnival revellers for it to reach them. Pressing an ear to his chest, the rhythm of his heart was evident, which would buy some time, but she carefully tilted back his head on the tiles, keeping his airways clear. 'You're going to be OK, Mr Acosta.'

Thankfully, the sound of a siren in the distance soon gave her comfort, and within minutes she was watching two men leap expertly from the vehicle outside, Ambu bags bouncing on their hips. Then she realised who was wearing the first paramedic's uniform.

*Oh, my God.*

'Gabriel Romero,' she mouthed in surprise as the world stopped.

He pulled up short in front of her. 'Ana?'

Her old friend looked at her wide-eyed, and she took in the full extent of his dashing looks in a fraction of a second: the piercing yet warm brown eyes that had steadied her as a child and teenager into adulthood; the thick chocolate-brown hair that matched his beautiful dark skin; his sculpted face; and those adorable dimples that had always made him seem more boy than man. Now at thirty-two, as was she, he was just all man. Their locked gaze left her breathless, before any surprise at seeing him was quickly overshadowed by the severity of Mr Acosta's condition.

His partner, Bruno Gomez—whom admittedly she hadn't known as well as Gabriel had over the years—dropped to his knees beside the man. He swiftly assessed the situation. 'Pulse is weak, respirations are shallow,' he murmured to Gabriel, his gloved hand checking for signs of life. Mr Acosta wasn't moving now and dread pooled in her stomach.

Gabriel looked up. 'Possible myocardial infarction. Get the AED ready, Bruno.'

Bruno nodded and reached for the automated external defibrillator from their medical bag. 'AED's ready, Gabe.'

Bruno attached the AED pads to Mr Acosta's chest as Gabriel continued monitoring his vital signs. 'Analysing,' the AED's automated voice announced. They both stepped back as it assessed the situation. Ana held her breath. 'Shock advised. Stand clear.'

A surge of anxiety gripped her, and she fought to stop herself gripping Gabriel's arm. She had seen her share of medical emergencies, of course, but the urgency of this moment in her as yet unopened clinic seemed different for some reason. She glanced at Gabriel, who nodded, his face determined.

'Clear,' he declared as the AED administered the shock. The man's body jolted briefly as the electric current coursed through him.

Bruno leaned in, listening to the man's chest with a stethoscope. The man's face made her want to cry suddenly. No! She could not have a man die here, not now, not ever! Her clinic would be a big failure before it even launched, and as for poor Mr Acosta…

'We've got him!' came Gabriel's relieved announcement. 'OK, we're good, let's get him to hospital.'

The two men talked coolly and calmly to Mr Acosta, and fixed him with the breathing apparatus. Ana remained calm and collected, making a call to Mr Acosta's wife to tell her what was happening.

At the same time, she couldn't help the way her mind was reeling, not just with the adrenaline of the moment, but with the rapid-fire memories coming at her the more she watched Gabriel in action. He had done a lot to help bring her to this point… Actually, did he even know this was now her clinic? He had always wanted more for her. He was the one who'd encouraged her to apply for medical school in the first place!

In minutes, they had Mr Acosta on the stretcher,

breathing heavily but stable. Ana held the door open for the two paramedics, and grabbed her own car keys.

'I'll follow you,' she said on the street, motioning to her wheelchair-adapted vehicle outside.

'Are you sure? It's getting pretty crazy out here already.' Gabriel held her eyes for a second over the stretcher as he heaved it up into the back of the ambulance with Bruno. Her breath caught in her throat as he leaned out through the doorway, reached for her face and adjusted something in her hair. She had clean forgotten the marigold was still there, sticking out from behind her ear.

'They were always your favourite flowers,' he said, just before Bruno called to him, offering her an apologetic look over Gabriel's shoulder. Ana fought the flush warming her cheeks.

'I'll meet you in A&E,' she said quickly, sweeping past him, surprised and marginally annoyed by the fluttering in her belly at a time when she could have done with staying calm.

As she drove behind the ambulance in the blare of its siren, her cheek tingled with the lingering feeling of him rearranging flower in her hair after all this time. Of course, the city was big, but the medical scene was small, so it had always been just a matter of time before their paths crossed again.

Still, now she couldn't stop thinking about their history together. Five years was a long time to go without seeing her friend, maybe even too long to pick up where they'd left off without it being a little weird, she thought, taking in a crowd of teens in feathers and sequins drinking soda by a pulsating speaker. Ana being in Bariloche for the last five years had cemented the divide, but they'd fallen out of touch even before that. She supposed he'd been too busy to check in as much, just as she had. He was a dad now; Dads were always busy. Or maybe those were just the excuses she'd been telling herself to trick her mind into falling out of love with him…

'Mr Acosta is going to be fine; he's stable, and his wife is on her way,' Gabriel said later, closing the door to the treatment room and motioning Ana to accompany him down the hall. 'Coffee?'

With the elderly man settled in recovery, Ana thought, what was another thirty minutes? Especially if it meant finding out what Gabriel Romero had been up to all this time.

Her heartbeat intensified yet again as she motored her chair alongside him through the labyrinth of corridors. Silly, she scorned herself. Once, maybe years ago, she'd had a hard crush on Gabriel, but that had been stomped out pretty fast once she'd realised he definitely did not feel the same way about her. The fact that he'd had a child with a relative stranger proved she'd hardly known him at all, really!

*He looks beyond handsome in his uniform, though*, she thought to herself as they made for the cafeteria. And Ana didn't miss the way he kept shooting her sideways glances as he stopped briefly to discuss something with a tall, muscular man whose name tag read 'Dr Carlos Cabrera'. She'd never seen Carlos before.

A&E was a hubbub of activity as usual. Nurses called out names, another ambulance arrived in a blare of sirens outside and Ana wheeled her chair alongside Gabriel, noting the acrid, astringent smell in the air and the lack of colour. Her clinic would always smell fresh, if she could help it, such as using flowers, she decided. It would always be a place of calm…at least, compared to this. It was more than a little strange just being here in the giant, hectic Hospital General de Buenos Aires, after all the time she'd spent in quieter, smaller establishments, let alone being with Gabriel.

'You look really well,' Gabriel said, holding open the cafeteria door for her. 'I see you're still as colourful as I remember. Nice shoes, by the way.'

'Why, thank you!' He was such a charmer. That hadn't changed, then. Gabriel had always complimented her choice of clothing, unlike her mother, who'd suggested on more than one occasion that it was unprofessional. Ana disagreed, of course. Mama was always trying to help in ways Ana didn't need her to; besides, she could do her job in any size, shape or colour of clothing, as long as she was always sitting down. Not everyone knew how to approach a GP in a wheelchair, so she'd learned over the years to hit them with the real her before they could imagine her as someone else in their own heads.

Gabriel sat her down in a quiet corner of the cafeteria, undisturbed. Soon they were sipping their coffees. His dark hair was still short, almost shaved to the scalp, which only intensified his liquid brown eyes as they talked.

Her stomach twisted with guilt as he talked about Javi. The little boy was already five—how had that even happened? Maybe he thought she was a terrible friend for not reaching out sooner…but he'd have been so busy, being a father to baby Javi, and she'd felt bad taking up his time. He had always wanted to be there for her, so maybe a part of her had felt that, if she wasn't around, he wouldn't be able to and she'd free him somehow. The distance had also been a pretty convenient way to get over her unrequited crush, seeing as never in a million years would he feel the same way about her.

'How are your parents? I see Martina quite a lot in the grocery store; she always says you take ages to return her calls.' He grinned even as Ana flinched.

'Well, now, my mother can just walk down the street to me, like old times,' she said with a wry smile. 'Lucky me.'

He stifled a laugh and she felt her eye twitch. Gabriel knew how overbearing both Juan and Martina had always been. She'd been lucky, she supposed. Well, as lucky as a girl with a spinal cord injury could be, in that she'd never let other people's impressions of her, or her condition, stand in her way. Not that people hadn't tried. Her own parents, as well-meaning as they were, had never abandoned their tendency to try and wrap her up safe and tight in cotton wool. There'd been a decade when they'd barely let her leave the house alone. She'd had to battle every cousin, aunt, uncle and grandparent over the years to be able to do anything independently at all.

But Gabriel…he'd always been different. Consequently, her crush on him had grown and grown, until she'd almost been bursting with her secret feelings. Gabriel had been the ever-present friend, platonic, and completely oblivious to the fact that, upon reaching their teenage years, and with the two of them being pretty much inseparable, Ana had wanted more.

The cafeteria was filled with people, and the sound of voices talking filled the air, along with the strong smell of coffee. It should have been quite comfortable talking to him, despite her old feelings, which had probably started around the time she'd turned twelve or thirteen. They'd grown up together after, all, the two of them and their families. He'd been the first one to jump in front of her whenever one of the mean kids had tried to bully her because of her wheelchair—her hero! But he'd never known about her massive crush on him. How could he? She'd feared his rejection so much that she'd never told him. And, besides, how could she tell him that, hear him say, 'Er, no thanks, Ana' and *then* go back to being friends? There was just no way!

There had been one point when he'd asked to see her, all serious and nervous-looking, and she'd freaked out inside, thinking, finally, he was going to tell her he *knew* how she felt about him, and that he had feelings for her too. Her heart had swelled to the size of a balloon as she'd sat there opposite him in the park, watching him wringing his hands together.

*Just kiss me*, she'd willed him. *Just do it before I burst!*

Then of course he'd told her about Ines being pregnant and that they were going to make it work because she wanted to keep the baby. Talk about being blindsided.

'So…tell me about this clinic,' he said now, gesturing with his cup. 'I saw the plaque on the wall, Ana. I know it's what you always wanted. Look at you, taking over from the barrio's favourite GP. Dr Az only ever had you in mind for that. When does it reopen?'

Ana breathed a harried sigh through her lips. 'I know, crazy, right? It opens officially on Monday.' She told him how she'd been so worried that things wouldn't come together in time, but soon her usual excitement was shining through as she told him all about her plans—from hiring the staff and finding donations from local businesses for the toys and furnishings, to decorating the interior and selecting medical equipment—it felt as if no detail was too small for her to go into. He listened intently, as he always did.

'It all sounds very impressive.' He smiled warmly. There were those butterflies again, she thought. They flapped even harder in her chest as he added softly, 'You were missed around here, you know.'

She flushed again, readjusting her yellow headscarf. 'By who, your mother? How is she?'

Gabriel laughed softly. 'She's well.'

Ana looked away for a moment, suddenly not sure what to say all over again. 'It must have been different in Bariloche,' he continued into the awkward silence that had just descended. 'Wasn't it cold in the foothills of the Andes?'

'Sometimes, but I loved my work, and that's where I spent most of my time. It was a pretty small clinic, not unlike the one I'm opening.'

Gabriel eyes narrowed indecipherably as he studied her, and he sat back in his seat. 'But you took yourself somewhere different; you embraced the challenge. I'm proud of you, Ana.'

Ana bit her lip, wishing the stupid butterflies would calm down—this was Gabriel, her friend! 'You helped give me the courage, remember? You cheered me on.'

'Maybe so, but you still would have done it without me. You always just did everything you set your mind to. You've seen so much more than I ever will. You've travelled…'

'You can still travel,' she told him, noticing the flecks

of gold around his pupils that she'd always thought made his eyes look like marigolds shimmering in deep, dark pools. For so long, she'd been living life on her own—away from family and old friends—so it was kind of hard to fathom how anyone wouldn't want that experience, even if it wasn't for long. A few years, or even months away, doing things by oneself, and *for* oneself, could do wonders for the self-esteem.

'I can't go far, can I? I have my family, Javi and his dog…'

'Oh, I know!' She nodded, realising how naive and idealistic she must sound. Fathers of five-year-old kids didn't just uproot themselves and go work on the other side of the country.

'How is Javi liking school?' she asked now. 'I assume you share custody with Ines?'

In that moment, something seemed to shift between them. Gabriel pressed his palms together.

'Things are a little different now, yes,' he said quietly. The tension was rising by the second. He hunched his shoulders suddenly, gripping his coffee cup so hard it looked about ready to break. Surely he wasn't still upset about the separation with Ines? Ana knew they'd tried hard to make it work for the sake of the baby, but the baby had been the result of a quick fling over five *years* ago!

Ana was just about to ask what was wrong when someone called his name. They turned to see a heavily pregnant medic hurrying over to them as best she could, scraping back chairs to fit herself and her belly through, muttering apologies to people as she moved.

'There you are.' Ana studied her name badge: Dr Isabella Lopez. Isabella blew a long, shiny black curl from her face as she stopped in front of them, squinting her dark eyes a moment. Gabriel shot up and helped her into a chair, and she pressed two hands to her belly. 'Sorry guys; hi.' She huffed, introducing herself quickly to Ana. 'I'm glad I caught you, Gabe, I have a huge favour to ask you.'

Gabriel nodded in understanding as Isabella explained how she wasn't feeling very well, how her pregnancy was doing a number on her sleep patterns and that she didn't think she could handle the medical post at Carnival tonight. She was expecting triplets!

'I'm so sorry to ask at such short notice,' she said now, her tired brown eyes pleading. Isabella pressed a hand over his and rubbed another over her sweating forehead in a way that made Ana wonder what on earth it must feel like, having a tiny human inhabiting you, let alone three of them throwing your internal systems all out of whack. She had parts that didn't work as they should herself, namely her legs, but being pregnant must be something else entirely.

'No need to apologise, Bella. Of course I'll cover for you; you go home and rest,' Gabriel said kindly. Ana realised she was staring at him over the table now, and that her heart was melting at his kindness. And Isabella was looking between them with some interest.

'My parents are taking Javi tonight anyway; they'll probably take his dog too, seeing as they adore him,' Gabriel added, glancing at Ana, as if knowing full well she'd ask, *what dog?* 'Actually, they might leave the dog behind. Carnival is no place for canines. He's a rescue dog called Savio, a terrier mix—super-smart. He lives with Ines and Pedro but we're teaching him tricks when he visits. Pedro—that's Ines's new husband—picked him up from a farm. Savio killed a chicken, so they were about to put him to sleep for it, but the poor thing was starving. They hadn't fed him in a week, can you believe that?'

Ana's mouth had fallen open, but not just because of the chicken-killing dog and his troubled life on the farm. Ines had remarried; when on earth had that happened? Usually she got all the gossip from her mother. Maybe she *should* have returned more of Mama's calls.

OK, so there was a lot she didn't know about Gabriel's life these days, she mused despondently. Before she had even thought about what the heck she was doing, she turned to Isabella.

'I can help him this evening.' She smiled broadly. 'If that's OK?'

'Really?' Gabriel looked surprised and the fluttering started back up in Ana's stomach lining. 'You have so much to do before the clinic's opening; you should take tonight to relax!'

Isabella reached out and took Ana's hand in her own slightly clammy one, squeezing it gently before letting go. 'You're opening a clinic?'

Ana answered all of the sweet Isabella's questions, feeling Gabriel's eyes on her face the whole time. She wasn't quite sure, as later she made her way back out to her car, whether it was the clinic's impending opening that kept the butterflies soaring around her internal pathways or the thought of having Gabriel back in her world after all this time.

# CHAPTER TWO

THE CROWDS THRONGED and bulged in the boulevards beyond their makeshift medical tent, and the music threatened to deafen Ana as she welcomed in a teenage boy.

'I think I sprained my wrist.' He winced at them as Gabriel pulled out a chair, his name tag swinging from his uniform top. The boy's face was ghostly white against his neon-yellow headdress as Gabriel ushered him into the chair and dropped to his haunches in front of him.

Meanwhile, someone else stuck in their head. Ana kindly asked the woman, who looked to be in her late thirties, to take another seat, reminding her to bend down first, so her peacock hat with all its turquoise feathers wouldn't break against the canvas ceiling. 'I'll be with you soon,' she said, noting her grazed knees. Maybe she'd fallen off her stilts.

'It's getting crazier by the minute,' Gabriel whispered as he hurried past Ana's wheelchair for more gauze. In the three hours since they'd set up in the medical tent, they'd already tended to three cases of fainting, thanks to the suffocating crowds; one food poisoning, thanks to endless empanadas and other fried snacks that had been left out in the sun all day; and even an elderly lady in her eighties who'd tripped on some steps in her high heels.

Still, Ana thought, glancing at Gabriel with the teenage boy, she probably wouldn't want to be here with anyone else. If she hadn't been working here, she'd have been hiding out at home, prepping for the clinic's opening on Monday, as if she wasn't ready by now—the last time she'd been in, it had been to tend to her snake plant, for goodness' sake. Although, it was lucky she had, otherwise what would have happened to poor Mr Acosta?

She wouldn't have been reunited with Gabriel, and she wouldn't be here now, checking out his cute butt in his uniform trousers every chance she got. It wasn't as if the carnival got her pumped as it did most people in Buenos Aires, even though she'd missed a few while working away from big cities. Her wheelchair wasn't best suited for squeezing through crowds.

'Remember that time you got stuck out there on Pinamar beach?' Gabriel said later when they finally found themselves with a moment to themselves. They were standing in the doorway to the tent, watching a kaleidoscope of colourful crimson tailored suits shimmy past, the men's fedoras tilted at rakish angles under the twilight sky.

'How could I forget?' Ana grimaced as a marching band of women followed, shimmering in sequinned dresses like gems. In fact, she was blushing now, just thinking about how she'd called everyone in their friendship group for help, and only Gabriel had been paying enough attention in the height of Carnival's chaos to realise she was missing and to answer. They'd gone as a group to the *balneários* and rented a wheelchair-friendly apartment, at Gabriel's insistence.

'You came to get me.' She smiled to herself, and he grinned, nodding slowly.

'I got you out of that sand pile and away from those drunks pretty fast. They were determined to dress you and your chair up in the Brazilian flag.'

Ana bit back a smile. 'My hero,' she said, remembering how she'd been on the verge of a panic attack when he'd raced across the sand and rescued her. He'd given the guys a massive telling off, then had forced them to apologise, which they had done sheepishly.

'Ines wasn't impressed. We were gone for hours, remember?' he said. Ana's stomach dropped like a sack of lead. Of course, he'd been trying to get back to Ines. She'd been pregnant then, and Ana had been trying her best to keep him to herself whilst simultaneously trying to get over her crush on him. It hadn't helped either cause to have him rushing off the minute Ines had called with another demand.

Just then, they were forced apart in the doorway by the arrival of a young man in a green hat covered in purple balloons. He limped towards them and proceeded to drop to his haunches at Gabriel's feet.

'I ran out of water; can you help me?' he slurred at them, and a balloon popped on his chest as he made to grab for Ana's knees. Gabriel held him back as she steered herself away quickly for the oxygen and some water.

'What are you supposed to be?' she heard Gabriel ask the guy.

'Sour grapes.' The man grunted. Despite himself and his drunken situation, he laughed. Ana bit back a smile and saw Gabriel do the same as the human sour grapes gulped down the water and breathed a sigh of relief so hard, she thought the tent might blow over.

*Gosh, Gabriel's smile.* He'd always lit up every room with that. His family adored him, and he them. In fact, they were the reason he'd said he'd never go anywhere else, even before he'd become a dad. The Romeros had never been the wealthiest family in the neighbourhood, but they'd never been lacking in love for each other. He was so good to them, just as now he was probably so good to his son Javi. He looked incredibly handsome in his uniform, too. And his cheekbones…

Ana had to look away before he caught her staring again. She just hadn't seen him in a while, and her old self was still acting on autopilot around him, that was all. The mild crush she'd had on him was all water under the bridge; thank heavens he'd never had a clue! But she could see the impression he made on everyone who came in here. His warmth radiated and instantly made everything better.

'You know,' she said, raising her voice above the blaring music from the passing parade, 'You're pretty good at all this. Maybe I should be hiring you to work for me at the clinic!'

Gabriel smirked, and suddenly Ana was flooded by paranoia. Shoot, she shouldn't have said that. Had that sounded as if she wanted him there with her? As if she needed him? That was the last impression she wanted to give him. He'd spent enough of his childhood, and his adult life, coming to her rescue.

As the hours went on and the patients rolled in, Ana found herself thinking more and more about that day at the beach—how they'd piled into a friend's giant van and driven the four hours south, laughing the whole way—well, the others had been laughing. She'd been trying to keep the scowl off her face at the way Ines had kept raking her long fingers through Gabriel's hair in the seat in front of hers. The job in Bariloche had been on the horizon then, but she hadn't told anyone yet. In truth, she'd wanted to tell Gabriel first, maybe just to gauge his reaction. He had been her champion, of course, and had told her to go for it. So, bolstered by the fact that she'd already lost him, and feeling as though she'd only be getting in the way if she stayed, she'd gone for it.

They'd drifted apart after that. The baby had arrived. The texts and emails had dried up. Looking at him now, she couldn't help wondering about his life now. They hadn't really gone into it too much beyond work stuff… and maybe she'd talked more than him, no thanks to her nerves. He was a single dad, and she assumed was living alone, seeing as he hadn't mentioned having a partner. And Ines had a new husband. The questions had been hovering on her tongue all day but the timing had just never felt right. Well, that and the fact that between them they could barely finish a sentence before someone blasted reggae, drum and bass or yelled over a microphone right outside the tent.

Finally, their tent was clear again. She wheeled back to the doorway, but Gabriel seemed glued to his phone now. Maybe he was chatting to a date, she thought idly, surprised at the pinpricks of jealousy that rose on the back of her neck. It had been weird enough when he'd admitted he'd had slept with Ines, let alone that he'd got her pregnant. Funny how she'd always kind of thought of him as hers.

'Check him out,' Gabriel said, walking over to her and handing her his phone. 'Doesn't he look great in that costume? I helped him pick it out at the fancy dress shop.'

Ana studied the photo of Javier. He was dressed as a ladybird in a bright-red fuzzy suit with huge black polka dots. He was so cute it almost hurt her eyes, and he was the spitting image of Gabriel when he'd been that age.

'Where are they?' she asked.

'Out and about somewhere. My parents would have taken him to all the kids' stuff. There's a children's parade soon; it'll be his first time taking part in it.'

'And you're missing it; that's a shame,' Ana said before she could think. A look of mild remorse fell across his handsome face, just as four people brushed past them, twirling around each other in some version of a tango, and almost sent them flying into each other. Gabriel caught her chair from behind and twirled her himself. Then he danced with her a moment on the pavement outside the tent, making her laugh as she spun her chair round and round. A group of women in antlers waving glow sticks stopped to cheer and whoop.

Gabriel used to do that a lot, back when she'd been feeling sorry for herself at being stuck in the stupid chair. Most of the time she'd been the picture of strength and determination… Well, that was what other people had seen. Gabriel had always known better. He'd seemed to instinctively know whenever she'd needed a reminder that she could do anything she put her mind to.

'You're still an excellent dancer, *chica*,' he told her, and she rolled her eyes, not quite managing to hide her laugh as one of the women removed her glittery antlers and placed them on his head. Gabriel went along with this new deer headpiece, performing another twirl to rapturous applause. He looked so ridiculous, she thought, smiling. Why would those butterflies not go away?

Gabriel was just doing a few quick steps of his own strange tango in front of her, making her laugh more and more with every exaggerated move, when another message came in on his phone. Soon, the headpiece and the onlookers were gone, and he was showing her a video. This time Javier was waving at him between his grandparents, whom she recognised, of course. Gabriel's ever-enthusiastic, ever the life of the party, parents were wearing matching bumble bee outfits, looking the epitome of the perfect grandparents.

'Hi, Papa!' Javier called out to the camera.

A jolt struck Ana's heart. Mixed emotions flooded through her as he stood behind her. She felt nothing but empathy for what he was missing, being here devoting his time to others; then a little guilt, and maybe a little envy too at just hearing the child's voice! She'd never heard it, she thought now with a frown, but it resonated somehow. The look on Gabriel's face was one of pure adoration and pride. He was a good father; she'd always known he would be, even if he hadn't exactly planned for that part of his life to start with Ines and an accidental pregnancy. His beautiful heart had propelled him on that journey with Ines anyway.

Why had Ana not made more of an effort to keep in touch with him, to try and meet the person who meant most to him in the whole world? They used to be so close!

'He really is adorable.' She sighed to herself. 'When do you get to hang out with him next?'

'Next weekend, I suppose,' he said. 'He spends half the time with Ines now.'

'And her new husband Pedro,' she added thoughtfully. She could hear in his voice that it bothered him, being away from his son so much.

Gabriel cleared his throat, taking the phone from her hands. 'What about you?' he asked now. 'Is there anyone special in your life, Miss Independent?'

It was her turn to smirk. 'Me? I don't think so. Too busy,' she said. As the words left her mouth, she knew it was a lie. Yes, she was busy, but she had always *made* herself busy, too determined to prove she could be something more than what she assumed people expected her to be, being stuck in a wheelchair.

Gabriel was cocking his head at her now, looking at her in interest, his brown eyes piercing her the way they always had. She laughed. 'What?'

'Nothing,' he said quickly, just as a flashback of them cuddled on the couch hit her from out of nowhere. She felt herself flushing. The feeling of comfort and safety she had always associated with Gabriel growing up was morphing into images of things that had never happened. She'd done that with her last serious boyfriend, Alberto, not Gabriel—never. She'd have to rein those thoughts in, if they were going to bump into each other more now, she thought.

'There was Alberto,' she admitted now. 'In Bariloche. But he wanted me to move out to the hills with him and have his babies…'

'Even further out into the hills?' He looked amused now, and she grimaced.

'I couldn't do it. He was nice but…no. What would

someone like me do in the middle of nowhere?' More than that, she found herself thinking now, Alberto had not been 'the one'. They'd barely had a thing in common besides their location.

'You'd find something; you always do,' he chided playfully, and she shrugged. Maybe he thought so, but being a parent was tough enough; she couldn't even imagine how someone in a wheelchair would deal with all that without more of a support system around. Gabriel was so lucky having that here. Besides, she *was* busy. All she'd ever wanted was her own clinic. Nothing was going to mess that up now.

Before long, the medical tent was bulging again. At one point they even had a queue outside. All the while, as they worked together and around each other to tend to all manner of minor injuries, and finally to release their rehydrated sour grapes back out into the cacophony of music and merriment, Ana couldn't help thinking she had been a bad friend the last five years. She'd gone off and busied herself in all those other places while Gabriel had been going through so much with Javi and Ines.

Working here with Gabriel was great, but the music—the heartbeat of the Carnival—pulsed through the night and only seemed to intensify her guilt. He'd always been there for her and then she'd just disappeared and hooked up with Alberto—probably to take her mind off the whole thing with Gabriel and Ines, now that she really thought about it.

She'd even avoided Gabriel's family on her return visits—out of jealousy, she thought, annoyed with herself. That was the truth of it, really. She hadn't been able to stand seeing him set up home with someone else, let alone with someone he barely knew. Why on earth would she have wanted to watch the whole neighbourhood and all his friends and family coo over them? Yes, she and Gabriel had only ever been friends, but part of her had often thought maybe…*maybe*…something might happen between them, eventually.

'It's getting late; I'm starving,' Gabriel announced when they found themselves alone yet again. Ana was starting to get a bit of a headache from the loud music, but she realised her stomach was growling like a caged monster too. 'I can go get us some snacks, if you don't mind holding the fort.'

'Please,' she said, tidying the last of the gauzes and iodine back into their box. 'Vegan empanada for me,' she added, and he threw her a look.

'Vegan?' He play-gasped. 'Ana, you're breaking my heart!'

She smirked and tutted. He was so dramatic. 'I just don't want to risk eating any meat that's been sitting round all day.'

'That's smart, actually. I'll be straight back.'

Gabriel wasn't even gone three minutes when a shadow appeared in the doorway and two people called her name in unison. She spun round in surprise and felt her eyebrows disappear into her hair as two human bumble bees stepped into the tent, their glittery wings brushing the canvas sides as they shuffled someone else through with them—a little boy dressed as a ladybird.

'It is you, isn't it? Ana! Gabriel said you'd be here tonight. Oh, it's so good to see you! We kind of need your help… Where is Gabriel?'

Ana could hardly believe it. It was Gabriel's mum and

dad, sprightly as ever, standing here after all this time. And between them, nursing a grazed knee, was little ladybird Javi.

'I'm so sorry, Gabriel went out for snacks,' she explained, motioning for them to sit the little boy down. 'What's happened here, *mijo?*'

'I fell.'

Quickly she got the gauze back out and told him to sit still as she wiped his wounds gently with antiseptic. All the while, she couldn't help thinking how much he looked like Gabriel: the same mussed black hair fell wildly across his face, like his father's used to when it had been longer, and he'd the same soulful brown eyes. His little brow was furrowed, his eyes screwed up with concentration. He gasped when Ana dabbed the disinfectant onto his skin, then breathed bravely through the sting, blowing bursts of air through his mouth as if he was blowing up an invisible balloon—dramatic, just like Gabriel.

He was looking up at her now, sussing her out, as if realising for the first time that she was different. 'Why are you in a wheelchair?' he asked.

# CHAPTER THREE

GABRIEL HAD TAKEN longer than expected getting the snacks, thanks to Carlos Cabrera and his captivating capoeira group. That had taken him completely by surprise—he'd had no idea that the stoic trauma surgeon from the hospital had been so into capoeira, but there he'd been just now, on the side street by the snack stand with his group, drumming up interest for his gym. That had been pretty cool. He could have sworn he'd seen his friend Sofia in the crowd too, too far away for him to call to or reach, but suffice to say it had all been all going on out there and he was later getting back than he'd intended. Was that his parents he could hear…?

Their enthusiasm meant they'd always had the loudest voices of anyone around, but the gap in the blaring music confirmed it was definitely them that he could hear. His heart sped up as he hurried for the doorway of the tent, but when he saw Javi sitting on the chair, talking to Ana, something made him stop and stand back for a second. He couldn't hear what they were saying but Ana seemed to be explaining something about her wheelchair. To his shock, Javi put his arms around Ana, and he watched as she pulled him into a sweet embrace, as if they'd already become firm friends.

'What happened *mijo*?' he demanded, dropping the snacks onto a table and making straight for Javi. His parents stood up from their seats, said his name in unison and he did a double take at their ridiculous outfits.

'I fell, and Ana was just helping me,' his son said, wriggling his knees from his chair, both of which were covered in plasters.

'Nothing too terrible; he'll live,' Ana said, steering her chair back to make more room for him. Gabriel was already on his knees in front of Javi.

'Good thing you knew to come here. We wouldn't want a trail of blood in the parade; it's not Halloween,' he said, making Javi giggle and Ana smirk. He mouthed, 'Thank you!' at her then he pulled his son into a hug, breathing in the familiar scent of his hair, grateful as he always was after a scrape that his son was fine.

He tried never to show it—his son should grow up confident, strong and fearless—but he himself feared something new every day when it came to Javi, especially now the boy lived with Ines and Pedro most of the time. He thought a lot about that cosy family unit. It was something Gabriel had never been able to give him. Javi wouldn't exactly grow up remembering the short year or so after his birth when he and Ines had bunked up together, trying to make things work for his sake.

'I was on the way to the children's parade when I fell, Papa,' Javi said now, pouting and crossing his arms. The action made a huge dent in the front of his ladybird outfit. 'I'll never get to join the parade now.'

'I'm sorry, *guapo*,' Gabriel sympathised. 'But you had a good time with Grandma and Grandpa, right?'

He nodded a little despondently, and Ana pulled up

beside him again. 'Why don't you go?' she suggested to Gabriel, touching his arm. Her slender fingers lingered there for just fraction of a second, but it was long enough for heat to shoot up his forearm and start pumping fresh, hot, new blood to his heart. It was the same as when her eyes had locked on his over Mr Acosta—he hadn't been able to shake how attractive he found her, even more so now that she'd helped Javi.

Gabriel stood up as his mother took to comforting Javier and promising him a story before bed time. 'Go, enjoy what you can of Carnival with him before bed time,' Ana said. 'I'll be fine here, and I should have help soon…'

Just as she said it, Sebastián Lopez, the A&E clinical lead, poked his head round the door, ready for his shift. 'Just in time!' She beamed.

'You have snacks!' Sebastián grinned, high-fiving Gabriel and Javi respectively, before checking out the array of food items on the table.

'Help yourself,' Gabriel offered, still composing himself regarding the strange new heat that had settled around his chest. 'But I'm warning you, there's a vegan item in there.'

Sebastián pulled a face, and Gabriel swung round to Ana. 'Are you sure it's OK if I go?' He studied her deep brown eyes. For some reason, even though he was thrilled to spend at least an hour with Javi before bed time, he was a little reluctant to leave Ana…and it had nothing to do with the fact that he didn't think she could handle things. She could handle anything; it was the thing he admired most about her. It had felt like old times just then, just the two of them dancing on the street, like before she'd left for Bariloche.

'I'm sure. Go.'

Gabriel gathered his things and changed out of his uniform behind the screen, listening to them talking. He remembered more about that night she'd got herself stuck on the beach in Pinamar. That was the night she'd told him she had a job offer in Bariloche.

He'd been crushed. Ines was pregnant and he was losing his best friend at the time he needed her most. He'd had no idea how to be a father! But then, how could he have asked her to stay? That would have been so selfish. Instead he'd missed her madly, all on his own. Maybe he'd even realised what she'd meant to him, how he'd taken her friendship for granted. He felt so guilty that he'd stopped contacting her once Javi had come along—it wouldn't have been fair to burden her with his problems, not when he'd landed himself in the situation in the first place.

She'd been everywhere before that anyway—or, it seemed like everywhere—while he'd always stayed with his family, where he belonged. It was his place to look out for them and always had been. The Romeros looked out for each other; it was just what they did.

'Go!' Ana laughed now as he hovered around the cabinet, about to put a few more things away.

'OK, OK…bossy as you ever were!' She was practically shooing him out of the door. His parents fussed around her behind him as he took Javi outside. He heard them gushing over how nice it was to have her back after all this time, and how they'd missed seeing her around. Everyone loved Ana. He'd had a pretty hard crush on her once, he mused to himself before shaking it off. No point going there. It wasn't as if he'd ever told his best friend that in the first place. She'd only have rejected him, what with all her plans for global domination.

'Enjoy!' she called to him now, waving at them all, just as he saw Sebastián gag and almost spit something out into his hand.

'He *told* you not to eat the vegan thing,' he heard Ana reprimand him playfully as he, his parents and Javi were swallowed by the crowd again.

The carnival was as crazy as usual as they manoeuvred through a block party, swung past the capoeira demo again and moved out the other end to the kid's carnival. Luckily, Javi seemed to have forgotten the fact that he'd hurt his knees. While they didn't catch the kid's parade, they did forge a path to the funfair for a few games.

'Grandpa, Papa, I want that one!' Javi cried now, jabbing his finger towards a giant stuffed panda hanging above the man behind the mini basketball hoops.

Gabriel and his father exchanged glances. 'Maybe later, Javi,' his father suggested, eyeing his watch. It was almost his bed time, but Gabriel knew that look in his son's eyes. When he wanted something, he wanted it now—a trait he'd inherited from Ines.

The man behind the stand handed Javi a basketball, while pointing towards the hoop at the other side of the booth. Javi missed twice at first, but soon got into a rhythm, and to Gabriel's surprise it wasn't long before he landed three shots in quick succession.

'You're a pro player. Nice one, *mijo*!' He offered a high five, making Javi's ladybird wings knock the hat off a lady nearby, and Javi jumped up and down with excitement as he was handed the large stuffed panda. Javi walked ahead with his grandfather, but Gabriel's mother took his arm, whispering conspiratorially.

'It's so lovely that Ana's back, don't you think?' she said with a sideways smile. 'She was so good with Javi, and she's as pretty as ever. You know, I remember you two running around together before her accident. Such a shame, what happened to her…' She trailed off, shaking her head, and Gabriel frowned.

'It hasn't stopped her doing everything she's always wanted to do,' he found himself saying, as Javi stopped abruptly near the fishing stand and turned to them expectantly. His father promptly handed over the cash for the fishing rod, and Javi went about trying to fish for plastic turtles in an inflatable pond.

'I know, she's always been ambitious,' his mother agreed as they looked at Javi, who was tossing the rod over and over into the water until finally it knocked a small turtle out of the pond completely. 'That new clinic of hers is going to be a lot of work.'

'She has a great team,' Gabriel told her, wondering why he felt obliged to defend her. They were adults now. They weren't on the playground any more, facing the bullies. 'You just watch her, Ma. Dr Az wouldn't have sought her out to take over if she didn't think she could handle it. She always had Ana in mind to run the place after her.'

'I know. Don't you worry; the doctor put in a good word with us too, before she retired. Your father already suggested we keep our medical files with Ana, what with my hernia and his bad knee. It's always been our clinic, but with our family's history maybe now we'll get extra-special attention, huh?'

Gabriel nodded as she spoke about the Romeros' long running friendship with the Mendezes, unable to stop his mind casting back over this evening, working so closely with Ana in the medical tent. He could have sworn he'd felt her eyes on him a lot today, watching him closer than you'd usually watch a work colleague. But things had been pretty hectic, and he hadn't seen her in so long; maybe his mind was playing tricks on him. He might have had a crush on her once, but they'd practically been kids. There was nothing there now, not on her side anyway. She'd been off experiencing the world and was now finally realising her dream of opening her own clinic. The last thing on her mind was hooking up with a childhood friend and single dad from the same barrio!

His mother was still going on about the time Ana had brought a pot of chicken soup to their door one time she'd been recovering from a cold, when Javi squealed in fresh delight and swung around with a turtle dangling from his fishing line. 'Papa, I caught one!'

'Well done, *mijo*! Now, bed time!' He laughed as Javi skipped ahead with his agile grandfather. Luckily Gabriel's dad was still young enough to keep up with his grandson's enthusiastic endeavours. Javi clutched the panda in his arms tightly, as if it might fly away at any moment, and Gabriel looked on fondly, committing this moment of his young son to memory.

How quickly they grew up. Would Javi even remember the times he spent with him like this, or would he remember his home as being wherever his new family unit was—Ines, Pedro and him? Sometimes he wished he could have made things work with her for his son's sake, but no… Ines and Pedro were perfect for each other.

He and Ines had been a completely different story—they were different people.

Somehow, thoughts of Ana kept creeping back in as he took in the colours of the carnival all around them. Maybe it was the colourful way she still dressed… She was a moving rainbow, nothing like the way most other GPs looked, and he admired her for it, breaking the mould under her white coat, and out of it too. Why did healthcare always have to be so dull? She was who she was, at work and at home. Did she consider this her home, now that she was back? Would she stay? Did she want a family some day?

*Why are you even thinking all this, Gabriel?*

He couldn't get her out of his head now—her colourful presence, her reassuring smile and her easy manner with Javi. Today it had hit home just how much he'd missed being around her all this time. And she really had seemed to hit it off with Javi.

As he tucked Javi up in bed, the little boy asked him about Ana.

'She said she had a car accident and that's why she's on wheels,' he said, frowning.

'It's a wheelchair, Javi,' Gabriel corrected him, listening to his parents shuffling around downstairs, still wearing their bumble bee outfits and making each other laugh.

'She said I must always wear a seatbelt.'

'And she's right,' he said with a sigh, getting back to the book he was reading. How could he help the fact that his mind was only half on the book now? He was thinking about the accident, the car wreck that had torn Ana's life to shreds when she'd been a kid and had damaged her spinal cord beyond repair. His parents had taken him to visit her in hospital, and he hadn't been able to comprehend it at the time, the fact that his best friend might not be able to walk again. She'd always been a faster runner than him: racing ahead on the track during sports class; sprinting for the school bus at his side before hopping on first every time, always in a hurry to get somewhere—always in a hurry to get *everywhere*, with or without him.

Two months after the accident, when she'd finally come home from hospital for good, his whole family had gone to her house to welcome her back. The first time they'd seen her pale face and frail frame, being lifted from the ambulance and lowered into the wheelchair outside her house, his mother had started sniffing behind her bouquet of peonies, and it had only really hit him then exactly what had happened to Ana. He'd felt it like a switch. The gravity had been sucked out from all around him and, when he'd met her eyes, he'd seen only a shadow of his friend.

The younger him had never showed how shocked, sad and sorry for her he really was, though. He'd known enough then to know that wasn't what she needed. Instead, from that very day, when he'd taken the flowers from his mother's hands and marched ahead of them all up to the front door, he'd made it his job to make her life easier in any way he could.

Only, Ana had never really needed him to do that for her. She'd made it a point not to need *anyone* over the years, to do everything herself that any able-bodied person could do and more. She'd never stopped running, really. There was always some place she had to be, with him or without him—mostly without him. And he'd always let her go. More than that, he'd encouraged her!

In later years, he'd sometimes wondered if his one-man best-friend support system had been an act, a cover up, some kind of disguise he'd just kept putting on every day so she wouldn't see the real him. The real him, who had sometimes looked at her as more than a friend—as *his*, somehow—but she would never have felt the same way about him.

Turning out the light on a sleepy Javi's nightstand, he had a sudden flashback of doing the same thing to Ana's light the night he'd taken her home blind drunk after she'd graduated medical school. She still didn't know how long he'd stayed there, watching over her while she'd slept, wishing he could just curl up beside her and go to sleep instead of being the gentleman and making his way home.

Sometimes he'd been so confused about his feelings for Ana, and so certain she'd reject him if he tried anything at all, that he'd hooked up with other people right in front of her just to cover the tracks of his crush.

Maybe that was why he'd slept with Ines in the first place, he considered now. It was hard to remember, exactly—it had all been such a whirlwind—but, thinking back, the look on Ana's face in the car the whole way to the Pinamar that day had not been one of excitement… and hadn't that been the first time she'd met Ines? He could remember being acutely aware of Ana there, watching them. Could remember the way his heart had sped up at the notion that she might be…jealous. What could he have done by that point, though? Ines had already been pregnant and his hands were tied.

And on that same trip, Ana had announced she was

leaving for Bariloche. It was funny—and kind of troubling at the same time—that even now, even after spending the last five years apart, Ana was having the same effect on his heart.

The sound of slow, romantic love songs crept up the stairs as he left Javi's room. Deciding that his parents were probably doing something cute, such as dancing together in their bumble bee costumes, he called goodnight to them, went into his own room and lay down on the bed, picking up his book. They would let themselves out the way they always did—his family were used to coming and going as they pleased.

But Gabriel didn't even get to finish one chapter before he was fast asleep and dreaming of being back in Ana's bedroom. This time, however, he was very much in the bed with her. He was not just keeping an eye on his sleeping friend from the doorway. And Ana was very much awake and doing wicked things to him in return.

# CHAPTER FOUR

GABRIEL WAS JOLTED awake by his phone trilling from the nightstand. He blinked, eyes adjusting to the darkness, and glanced at the clock: four-forty-five. 'So early,' he mumbled to himself, groping for the phone with one hand and swinging his legs over the side of the bed. His dreams about Ana played on in his head as he said a sleepy hello. Blinking again, his heart jolted into his throat as an unmistakeable Ana replied.

'Gabriel?' She sounded frantic and spoke so fast he could barely keep up. 'I'm sorry, I know it's so early—I wouldn't have called, except it's an emergency. My healthcare assistant was knocked out by an octopus…'

'An octopus?' he blurted, trying not to laugh despite the hour *and* the unwelcome thoughts about this very woman that he still couldn't shake, especially as she spoke to him while he was still in bed.

'Someone dressed as an octopus, last night at Carnival,' she explained. 'Swept her off her feet in all the wrong ways—she's dislocated her arm. We don't know how long she'll be out of action.'

He raked a hand through his dishevelled hair, catching sight of himself in the long mirror by the wardrobe. 'And you need me to cover?'

'We open tomorrow, Gabriel, and my appointment book is full. I can't go cancelling on people in my first week, but I need a locum. It'll take some time to find one, but in the meantime, didn't you say something about having some time off while Bruno trains the new recruits?'

Gabriel paused and crossed to the window. He probably had; they'd spoken about all kinds of things in the medical tent between tending to all those minor casualties. Except what he'd wanted to say, of course: the fact that she was still one of the most bewitching people he'd ever had the fortune to stand beside. Oh, Lord, those dreams had got to him more than he'd thought!

'That's right.'

'You know I wouldn't ask unless I needed you.'

He bit back a smile, studying the street outside. It was empty, except for one solo dog-walker illuminated under a streetlamp. He didn't know whether to be happy she'd thought of him first, or annoyed, because now, of course, he couldn't say no. With no ambulance shifts for the week, he'd thought maybe he would take his camper van out to Playa Varese, one of the most well-known beaches along the Mar del Plata waterfront, and maybe do a little fishing. Or see if he couldn't wrangle some more time with Javi, if Ines would allow it outside of his allocated weekends… But now Ana needed him.

'Gabe?'

'OK!' A surge of adrenaline rocketed through him, waking him up properly as his brain attempted to process the enormity of the request, on top of the fact that he'd said OK on autopilot. What the…? 'Yes,' he said groggily. 'Yes, of course I'll help you, Ana.'

Ana breathed a sigh of relief that he felt though to

his core, and immediately he knew he'd made the right choice. Ana had never found it easy asking for help. She always had to do everything by herself or she labelled herself a failure, somehow, she'd told him one night before he'd met Ines.

'Thank you so much,' she said. 'I knew I could count on you. I'll make it up to you, I promise.'

There was a pause. Gabriel shuffled barefoot as the details of his dream came flooding back. She'd already made it up to him in his subconscious and she didn't even know—should he feel *guilty* for the fact that his dream self had just had sex with his friend?

'I'll text you the details later this morning,' she said finally. 'We'll make it work.'

'Get some sleep,' he told her, realising suddenly that she must not have slept all night, panicking before deciding to call him.

'You know me—I don't sleep when I've got something on my mind.' Gabriel nodded, smiling to himself. He still knew her so well, even after all this time.

When they'd hung up, he reckoned it was pointless trying to go back to sleep. Besides, he couldn't get the very intricate, highly intimate details of his dreams to leave his mind. They played on persistently as he flipped on the coffee pot, and swiped up the newspaper just as it was shoved through his letterbox. So much for his time off, he thought, dropping to the seat at the dining table and staring unseeingly at the paper. Still, at least Javi would be taken care of while he acted as locum for Ana at the new clinic. He was meant to be with Ines all week anyway—and Pedro, he thought begrudgingly, sloshing coffee into his well-loved *Happy Birthday* mug.

Ines and Pedro would have all kinds of adventures lined up for him already. She rarely told him what they were, exactly, until after the fact, although she frequently demanded to know exactly what *he* had planned for Javi's visits with *him*. She'd always struggled to leave Javi with his parents and him, even though she knew he was perfectly safe and content with them. She was the doting mother he'd always known she would be, ever since she'd looked at that positive pregnancy test and had told him flat out she was keeping the baby.

Every time he thought of the day she might demand full custody of their son was enough to make him shudder. Ever since she'd blown up that time when she'd bumped into Javi with his grandparents in the toy shop, he'd been petrified of putting a foot wrong. Oh, she had not been impressed that day! But it hadn't been his fault—it wasn't as if he'd asked for that family's car to crash outside the church gates…

Gabriel had been supposed to look after Javi that afternoon, and they'd been having a great time, but car crashes were the worst—not least because they always reminded him of what had happened to Ana. What was he supposed to have done except ask his parents to step in while he raced to the scene to join Bruno? His parents never minded stepping in at short notice. They lived for spending time with their grandson. But Ines hadn't seemed to understand that. She said the boy needed stability…which was true.

Every time he thought of his sweet little son in that tight, happy, stable family unit of three, in flooded the river of remorse at not being able to offer him the same thing. Ines deserved happiness—she was a great woman and an excellent mother—but all he wanted was to be a great father too. And, right now, he couldn't help fearing that Javi might grow up *wanting* to be with Ines and Pedro full-time.

At least his mind would be taken off that worry all this week working with Ana, he thought, swigging his coffee before realising with a sigh that he might have a whole new set of worries to contend with, now that Ana was back in his life. If those dreams were anything to go by, she'd stirred something up in his subconscious that was very much pleasure-related, not business.

Gabriel couldn't read one paragraph of the newspaper now. Now that he'd entertained the notion that he found Ana attractive, it was almost impossible to stop his mind wandering. But wondering if that connection would ever make it from his dreams into reality was pointless—Ana was far too much of a free spirit ever to be with someone so tied down! He would just have to keep his dream self in check, and make sure she never got wind of this unfortunate attraction.

The clinic was buzzing with energy on the first Monday of opening, and the staff was rushed off its feet on the new, squeaky-clean floors. It was only mid-morning, but to Ana it felt as if they'd been going for hours already. Still, without Gabriel she would have been way more stressed by now, she thought, casting her eye to where he was on the phone. He'd taken a short break to answer a call. He seemed quite pleased about something, from what she could hear, and his smile was contagious.

'What's going on?' she asked, intrigued.

'Sofia and Carlos, two friends from the hospital, that's

what.' He grinned and she cocked her head, confused. 'Trauma loves trauma, what more can I say?' he added with a mischievous smirk. 'Rumour has it they got together at the carnival, but she's not letting on to *me*. That's so Fia! I'm having to hear it from Bruno. He says good luck, by the way.'

'Good luck?' Ana was distracted now.

He looked so cute when he was energised and excited, like the teenage Gabe who'd pushed her chair through the crowds of Defensa Street that time she'd been hell-bent on buying the perfect painting from one of her favourite street artists.

Ana was about to ask more about this rumoured new couple when an elderly man swung through the door and almost stumbled. Gabriel was there in a flash and, as she sprang into action beside him, she tried her best not to think about the way she'd felt in that medical tent, meeting Javi. She'd been almost jealous! It had stunned her, being jealous of Gabriel being a parent, of having something so wonderful, stable and joyous in his life as a much-loved child. He deserved it, but she realised she'd missed a lot while she'd been away.

Still, thank goodness he'd agreed to help out at the clinic. They would have more chances to catch up, maybe rebuild some of the friendship that had broken down. Her assistant Carla would be out for a while with her injuries, but he'd been so cool about covering. His calm, kind and compassionate assistance was a godsend in this frenetic environment, and he'd already helped quite a few patients feel more relaxed both before and during their appointments. She'd almost forgotten, until today, that he had a special ability to explain medical concepts in layman's terms. It made even the most nervous patient feel as if they could trust him implicitly.

Just then, something caught her eye. Ana noticed a woman in her mid-twenties looking uncharacteristically anxious, biting on her nails and fidgeting in her seat. The young brunette was alone, and Ana knew she was waiting for her appointment. She quickly made her way over to her, noting she was looking so anxious, she probably wanted nothing more than to run away.

'Are you all right?' Ana asked gently. The woman, a local called Catalina, looked up at her with an almost desperate expression.

'I thought I could do this,' Catalina told her, her voice coming out choked. 'I thought it would be easy for me to get through the check-up, but now I'm here, I think I'm too scared.'

'That's totally understandable,' said Gabriel, appearing behind her with a smile, a clipboard tucked under his arm. 'It can be hard when you don't know what to expect.'

Ana released a breath. His deep voice had a soothing quality that not only calmed *her* on the spot, it instantly seemed to put Catalina at ease too.

Ana's receptionist, Maria, called her to tend to another patient, but she couldn't help glancing over in admiration as Gabriel began talking to Catalina in earnest about her worries, asking what he could do to help alleviate all her concerns about having her first set of tests done at the clinic. She was here to see if they could determine what was causing her excruciating stomach pains, and she'd already self-diagnosed herself on the Internet, which had only ended up exacerbating her anxiety.

He was listening attentively without judgement or criticism, nodding encouragingly when Catalina shared what Ana knew must have been uncomfortable thoughts or feelings about being there. Eventually, she wheeled back over, just in time to hear him conclude their conversation with one final, friendly remark. 'Remember—we are here for you, all of us, no matter what happens.'

'I'm so glad I was referred to this clinic,' Catalina told him warmly in response. 'I can tell you have an amazing team.'

Ana felt her heart swell and her cheeks flushed when Gabriel caught her watching him. It was just that he was so handsome, and even more so now that his gentle manner seemed to have erased any doubt from this patient's panicked mind. Even later in the private consultation room, when Ana informed her that it looked like endometriosis and further tests from a specialist would confirm it, Catalina seemed calm and in control, and accepting of the fact that she was in good hands, no matter what.

The afternoon went by quickly, and Ana found herself looking forward to the times she and Gabriel were alone with the patients. He was proving himself to be just as helpful as she'd initially suspected he would be, but she was a little annoyed at how her heart seemed to beat just that little bit faster every time he walked by or threw a smile her way. *Cut out this crush—nothing can come of it,* she reminded herself sternly for what felt like the hundredth time that very hour. Gabriel was out of her league. He went for artistic, designer-clothes-clad women like Ines…or at least, he used to, she thought now. Something hadn't worked out between them or they'd still be together, raising Javi.

Javi was *everything* to him, she thought as she welcomed a male patient in his sixties into the consultation room. Gabriel was already there, studying the man's medical chart, just transferred over from his last clinic.

Gabriel had a lot going on, juggling his career with being Javi's doting dad, and he didn't need a romance complicating his life, especially not with her. He needed a friend, not some busy woman with a demanding new position in the community, with barely enough time to do her laundry, let alone arrange a date. They had always been just friends anyway, she thought sadly, remembering Ines's hands in his hair on that car ride to the beach. Ana was his friend—that was all he'd ever seen her as.

Ana steered her chair behind the desk. Gabriel helped her adjust it quietly, then stepped back quickly, as if he'd intruded. 'It's OK,' she mouthed at him, touched as their patient looked between them for a moment with a wry smile on his thin lips. What were these feelings?

Suddenly the man bent over in obvious pain, and Gabriel hurried to help him into a chair.

'Mr Hernandez,' she began gently, once he was settled in the char, still wincing almost apologetically, 'I can see you're in a lot of discomfort; does your back hurt?'

'A lot…' The poor man breathed, producing a polka-dotted handkerchief from his pocket and mopping his brow with it.

'We're here to help you, and we'll do our best to find out what's going on,' she said.

Mr Hernandez nodded, his face etched with pain. 'It's my age, doctor, that's what's going on,' he mumbled, and she ordered him to lie down so Gabriel could examine him. She watched his warm, brown eyes crinkle at the edges. Javi had exactly the same eyes.

'Let's work out what's causing this pain, shall we, sir?' he said now, and Ana couldn't help but steal more than a few glances at him as he ran the stethoscope over the older man's chest and felt about his lower abdomen for any swellings. Whenever their eyes briefly locked, the flutter in her chest took her by surprise again, a sensation she did her best to try and ignore, but totally failed to. This was already getting uncomfortable. Where was the off button for this attraction?

'Based on your symptoms,' he continued minutes later, 'It seems likely that your pain is musculoskeletal, particularly related to your lower back muscles. Doctor, what do you think?'

Ana nodded. 'Small, specific exercises will help, and we can certainly have our expert put a programme together.'

Ana wheeled to the store cabinet she had ensured was at just the right height to enable her to reach everything alone from her wheelchair. 'We'll start you on a physical therapy regimen, Mr Hernandez,' she said as Gabriel offered his assistance to her. She brushed him off, gathering some pain medication, letting him know she didn't need his help. 'Our nurse will provide you with exercises to do at home. In the meantime, we'll give you something to alleviate your pain, how about that?'

When she turned, Gabriel was standing back again, as if he was wholly embarrassed to have tried to help her. She apologised by way of a look and he sighed, frowning to himself. Shoot, had she just been too defensive? He *knew* she hated people feeling that they had to help her, but the tension between them was palpable now. What was happening? This was in no way an emergency case, the likes of which he dealt with every day on paramedic duty, but her heart continued to thrash at her ribs like a wind-ravaged branch as she explained the kind of low-key physical exercises the nurse was likely to suggest, and she could've sworn Gabriel could hear it.

He saw Mr Hernandez out while she swept the sheet from the bed, ready to replace it for the next patient. She mumbled softly to herself the whole time, 'What is wrong with you, Ana?' This was so confusing. Moments later, Gabriel was back in the room, closing the door behind him softly. Her chest heaved with the sudden wild dance of her heart.

'I'm sorry, Ana,' he said quietly, fixing his eyes on hers. 'I remember how annoyed you always used to get when people tried to help you. I shouldn't…'

'It's OK.'

'It's really not,' he said, stepping closer so that only the empty bed was between them. Her heart was trying to escape through her throat. 'You had this whole place specially designed so you could manage it yourself.'

'I never intended to handle *everything* alone, Gabriel,' she snapped back.

He narrowed his soulful eyes and dashed a hand along his jaw just as the door opened behind them. The severity of her own words and tone shocked her as she cleared her throat self-consciously.

Maria stuck her head in. 'Should I send your next patient in, Ana?' she said, looking between them with interest.

Ana caught the flicker of a knowing smile on her receptionist's face as Gabriel walked past her, saying he'd get the patient from the waiting room.

'What's going on with you two?' Maria asked when Gabriel was gone.

'Who, Gabriel? Nothing.' Ana's pulse quickened as she said it, turning her back to Maria in the chair so she couldn't see her reddening cheeks.

'You make a good team. Does that sizzling chemistry extend beyond these walls?'

*Sizzling chemistry?* Ana rolled her eyes.

'We're just friends,' she said loudly, just to make her point crystal clear to herself, as well as Maria. This had to stop; it was already getting ridiculous!

The next thing she knew, Maria had closed the door behind her, and Ana was left wondering how on earth she'd get through the week like this.

# CHAPTER FIVE

THINGS HAD CHANGED so quickly in the city after Carnival, Gabriel thought, locking his front door behind him. The streets that had been bustling with life and snap-happy tourists were now empty at this early hour, apart from the occasional late-night reveller who hadn't made it home before sunrise. Rising above the stillness of the streets, the sound of blaring sirens hit his ears as he walked past the cemetery. It made him picture Bruno out there, training his new intake of paramedics. He'd been talking to Sofia about the drama at the hospital over Carnival, and about her blossoming love for Carlos—good for her! While he'd missed the action sometimes, the slower pace of the clinic and its significant lack of emergency patients and trauma was kind of refreshing.

He was just thinking how quickly this week had gone, in the presence of Ana and all these new clients of hers, when a noise from up ahead caught his ears. The clinic wasn't even open yet, but someone was outside, and a frantic cry cut through the peaceful morning air.

'Help! Somebody, please help!' a young woman's voice cried out, her desperation piercing his heart as he sprinted faster towards the locked clinic. Ana got there at the exact same time, the coffee she'd been balancing between her knees wobbling precariously as she stopped her chair short in front of the woman. Gabriel exchanged a quick glance with her before the young woman with dishevelled chestnut hair started gasping wildly for breath.

'Anaphylactic shock,' he said in sync with Ana, whose eyes widened before narrowing sharply. Her coffee fell to the floor, splattering the pavement with brown liquid.

'Help!' The girl clutched at her throat, her face twisted in panic as she struggled to breathe. Her skin had paled to an eerie shade of blue in the last two seconds, and her eyes pleaded for salvation. Gabriel caught her just as she was about to hit the pavement. He and Ana were right—he'd seen this reaction before.

Ana fumbled for her keys and her phone at the same time while he held the woman on his lap on the ground. 'I'm a paramedic. My name's Gabriel. What's your name?'

The girl's voice, weak and trembling, managed to stammer out, 'M-Melissa…'

Ana was already on her phone, dialling for an ambulance. Maria arrived now, early for her shift. She raced ahead into the clinic to fetch blankets as Ana held the phone to her ear. 'We need an ambulance at City Clinic, a possible anaphylactic shock. Send it right away!'

'Please, help me,' Melissa begged, her voice rasping as her breathing grew more laboured.

'Melissa, we're going to help you,' Ana said quickly as Gabriel patted her down and checked her purse quickly for an epi-pen. 'We think you're having a severe allergic reaction. Try to stay calm. Do you have anything on you for these reactions?'

'I don't see anything,' Gabriel answered for her. With a

nod to Ana to stay with her and keep her calm, he rushed inside for an epinephrine auto-injector. On his return, Ana held Melissa steady while he got to his knees and carefully administered the life-saving medication into her thigh. The tension was palpable as they waited for the epinephrine to take effect and Ana's eyes were hard and focused even as a small crowd gathered round on the street, looking on at them.

Seconds stretched into agonising minutes, but finally Melissa's breathing started to ease. The bluish tint to her skin began to recede, and her desperate gasps turned into shuddering sobs of relief, just as the ambulance screeched round the corner. Bruno and one of his new recruits jumped out.

Ana was still laser-focused on the girl. 'Better?' she asked, her voice gentle and reassuring as Gabriel joined her.

Melissa nodded, tears streaming down her face. 'Thank you, thank you so much. It came on so fast… I couldn't find my phone, I just stumbled straight here, I wasn't thinking…'

Gabriel updated Bruno and his co-dispatcher on Melissa's condition. 'The epinephrine seems to be helping. But you should take her anyway, give her a proper check-up. Poor girl's in shock.'

Melissa's grip on Ana's hand remained tight as she struggled to regain her composure. 'I… I've never had a reaction like this before. I don't even know what triggered it.'

'They'll find out at the hospital,' Ana said, and Gabriel nodded, helping the girl to her feet with Bruno.

Ana offered a comforting smile from her wheelchair.

'Sometimes, allergies can develop suddenly. The most important thing is that you got help in time.'

'Thanks to you two,' she said, her voice laden with relief as she looked between them in gratitude.

Melissa, now in even more capable hands, was quickly loaded into the ambulance, where Bruno's assistant fitted an oxygen mask. Bruno took Gabriel aside. 'Good thing you were there, and Ana too. Who'd have thought the clinic would have you on your toes as much as being out with me?'

Gabriel smirked, glancing back at Ana, who was shooing away the crowds as politely as she could. 'I know, right?'

'So, how long before you ask her out?' Bruno asked quietly.

'What?' Gabriel frowned.

'Oh, come on, we all know that's why you agreed to help her out—you like her! I always knew you two had a connection. Are you…you know…exploring it now, finally?'

Gabriel shook his head at his old friend, hoping Ana hadn't heard. 'We're just friends, Bruno.'

Bruno slapped his shoulder playfully before hopping back into the ambulance. Gabriel watched as the vehicle sped away, pondering his colleague's words. *Exploring* it? As if: Ana only saw him as a friend!

'I hope she'll be okay,' Ana murmured behind him.

Gabriel put a reassuring hand on her shoulder, then removed it quickly. 'We did everything we could. She'll get the care she needs now. As for you, I think you need a new coffee!'

He went for their coffees in the adrenaline-charged

aftermath, his mind racing, remembering the look on Bruno's face just now, and the tone of Ana's voice that first day: *we're just friends.*

She'd spoken so loudly to Maria that the whole waiting room could have heard, if they'd been interested. Thankfully they hadn't been; he was quite sure of that. No one had ever been as interested in Ana and him as *he* had, not that anything had ever happened. She'd always been so invested in her career and maintaining her fierce independence, and she was no different now. He'd always been the guy who'd never leave the city, who'd never crave adventure the way she did, who was happy to stay close in the loving embrace of his happy family circle.

Then he'd grown the biggest roots of all, stronger roots than his family had ever given him: he'd become a dad.

Stopping for their coffees at his usual street vendor, he couldn't help thinking about how Javi had reacted to Ana the first time he'd met her. He had asked about her since, on last night's video call: 'Where's that nice lady in the wheelchair?'

Funny, he had never really focused on Ana's chair at all, maybe because he'd known her before her accident, but even afterwards, when she'd become the bubbly, popular kid in the barrio, always dancing round the tables with him at the endless *asados.*

Back at the clinic, Gabriel watched her for a moment through the glass doors, noting the way her red flowery headband caught the sun, like her matching flats, as she busied herself with rearranging the leaves on a fern on a shelf and adjusting a chair in alignment with the rest. She looked anxious now. Maybe she was waiting for the next patient, or thinking about something else.

Spotting him, she waved and he stepped inside. 'Hi,' he said, handing over one of the *café con leches*.

'You're so thoughtful,' she said with a broad smile, though he could tell she was still a little anxious about something—most likely Melissa, he thought. He pulled out a bag of sweet *alfajors* next— a crumbly cookie made with flour, oozing *dulce de leche*—and watched her eyes widen as he gave her one in a napkin.

'This is new,' she said, eyebrows raised at the offering.

'Well, it's Friday,' he reasoned.

She cocked her head and studied him a moment as he stood in front of her, and he felt her weighing something up. 'I can't thank you enough for helping me out this week. I know you probably had other things to do, places to be.'

He shrugged, walking past her to drop his bag behind Reception. He'd used some of his holiday allowance to be here, not that he'd told her that. She might not have allowed him to come otherwise. 'You know Bruno didn't need me this week; he has that whole new intake of paramedics to order around. I thought it might be nice for *you* to order me around instead.'

'It was. It is,' she said, and she laughed nervously. 'Can you spare some more time for me?' she asked.

Aha! So that was it….

'My assistant is still out injured, and we don't know when she'll be able to return. I'm looking for another locum but…'

'I can stay a little longer,' he said, probably too quickly, now that he thought about it. What was a few more leave days anyway? He had loads of them to use up, and he'd still have plenty left to spend with Javi another time. It wasn't as though he ever went very far.

'You're a life saver. Literally.'

'I know you'll make it up to me.' He watched her smile, just as he smirked, remembering his dream. She was still making it up to him at times in their nightly rendezvous! What would she say if he told her?

For a second he wanted to tell her, to see if she'd laugh and call him an idiot, or remind him tartly that he was her friend, and now colleague, and that he shouldn't go there. Instead he just watched her rosy-red lips as she took a small, bird-like bite of the *alfajor*. In his dreams he had nibbled her bottom lip and woken up still tasting it…wanting it for real. Wanting her, all of her.

Suddenly having the reception desk between them felt safer. Ana seemed to sense the tension that he felt rising and she put down her *alfajor*, patting at her lips self-consciously.

'So, how's Javi doing?' she asked, glancing at the clock. Trust it to be a quiet morning, now that the action of their earlier shock patient was over. He squared his shoulders, still fighting off the desire to lick the taste of *alfajor* from her bottom lip.

'He's great. He's been with Ines and his stepdad all week, and he will be most of next week too.' As he said it, the familiar twinge of annoyance took hold. Their home had become Javi's base instead of his. He had him tomorrow, though, which he told Ana.

'Does Javi call Ines's partner his stepdad?' Ana asked curiously.

Gabriel studied her a moment. That red headband really suited her. 'I don't think Javi refers to him as that, no,' he admitted. 'But that's what Pedro is—they're married, after all. And Javi spends a lot of time with them.'

'More than with you?'

He shuffled on his feet. 'Some weeks, yes. Pedro works from home as a software engineer, so he can be a lot more flexible with his schedule than me. He's building Javi a treehouse in the yard.'

Ana chewed her lip, staring at him. Gabriel realised a little bitterness might have escaped with his words. He probably wouldn't know the first thing about building a treehouse. He used his hands to help sick people, which he'd take over having carpentry skills any day, but it didn't exactly do much to excite a little boy.

Thankfully the door opened behind him then. In walked their first official patient of the day, a girl who looked about ten years old, accompanied by her worried-looking mother. They learned her name was Lily, and her eyes and nose held the tell-tale redness indicative of a cold.

'Hello, Lily,' Gabriel said, offering a warm smile as Ana welcomed them straight into the consultation room, discreetly placing her *alfajor* behind the reception desk on the way past.

In the room, Lily sniffed and looked up at them both, while her mother took the comfy leather chair by the window. Her head was haloed immediately by a vase of fresh marigolds.

'She says her throat hurts, and she can't stop coughing,' the woman explained. At that, the young girl started hacking wildly, banging on her chest.

'It's like there's something stuck in there,' she gasped between coughs.

Ana, with her usual comforting presence, pulled up beside Lily and pressed the stethoscope to her chest. Gabriel itched to swipe an illicit crumb that had landed quietly on the lapel of her white coat. 'We're here to help you, sweetie. How long has this been bothering you?'

Lily started to speak, but her voice was raspy and her mother cut in again. 'I had a fever last week, then her brother got sick; it's been going around their school.'

Ana threw him a look over the girl's head. He could tell she was thinking, if that was the case, they might soon have quite a few sick children coming in. Already his mind was churning. If Javi caught it, would he even be able to see him at the weekend, or would Ines keep him with her, as she'd tried to the last time he'd got sick? Javi had asked for his papa, but apparently Ines had told the little boy that he had to stay put with Pedro and her until he was better. Gabriel had felt so guilty for not being able to offer him the same amount of creature comforts, that he'd shown up unannounced with a toy robot. Ines had let him in, of course, albeit reluctantly.

'My chest feels so tight,' Lily managed. Gabriel could relate. If Javi was ever sick again he'd want to be there, but would he even be told about it? Ines wasn't cruel but she just wouldn't think to involve him. She would probably assume he was too busy, that she and Pedro could manage, and that was what bothered him the most.

Ana was still holding the stethoscope to Lily's chest, assessing her shallow breaths. 'Well, I can tell there's some congestion in your lungs,' she said, her soft hand resting on Lily's shoulder. 'Gabriel here will do a throat swab, and we'll run some tests to confirm, but it seems like you have a respiratory infection. It's nothing to worry about.'

As Lily coughed and winced, Ana exchanged another glance with Gabriel before he turned to prepare the swab, accidentally knocking a file to the floor. Swiping it up, he could feel her eyes on him, even as she talked with Lily's mother. Did she know something was bothering him? Maybe he'd opened up too much before about Ines and Pedro. It wasn't her problem—she had enough going on her own life.

But, despite that, this chemistry between them was building by the second, even with patients in the same room. They'd been doing a silent dance of shared glances and unspoken words all week and he wasn't quite sure how to feel about it. It wasn't exactly professional…but, despite that, he liked working with her. They made a good team. And, now that he'd willingly extended his time as her assistant, he would have to try even harder to keep this attraction hidden, he thought to himself, crinkling up his nose.

*Way to go, Gabe!*

Together, they completed the examination, he doing the swab, she taking notes and discussing possible medications Lily could collect without a prescription from the pharmacy. They saw Lily and her mother out at the front door and Ana turned to him.

'We make a good team, don't we, you and I?' he got out quickly, because he'd just been thinking it. She smiled in the sunlight and adjusted her headband self-consciously.

'I was thinking the same thing,' she replied. He could have sworn he saw a flush starting to spread across her cheeks before she hid it behind her hair. The same kind of look he'd probably had on his face, talking to her on the phone just after that dream about her. Had she also been feeling that this was somehow…different this time? No. He was reading too much into it.

Ana put a hand on his arm. 'You looked a bit… I don't know…distant in there, when she said there was something going around the school. Were you worried about Javi?'

He stared at her, thrown. *How did she know?* Her large brown eyes sparkled with a warmth he suddenly wanted to keep on sinking into. 'I… I don't even know if they go to the same school, but yes, I was thinking about him,' he admitted with a sigh. 'If he gets sick, I'm not able to be there for him the way Ines and Pedro are.'

'That's not your fault, is it? You work hard doing irregular hours, it's the nature of your job. And they're a *couple*, whereas you're…'

'I'm just a single dad,' he finished for her.

Ana screwed up her nose. 'That's not what I meant… I mean, it's not a bad thing being a single dad, is it?'

Maria's eyes were on them again from behind the desk. If only he could stroll to the door and gulp in some fresh air. She'd touched a sore point, not that she knew it. Well, she hadn't till now.

Ana's fingers were still pressed to his arm, holding him in place. 'Javi knows you're a great papa,' she told him, eyeing him in a way that made him ache to sweep back from her face the stray strand of hair that had escaped from her headband. 'I've met him, remember.'

Of course he remembered. Javi still talked about her. But Gabriel just nodded, feeling more than a little uncomfortable all of a sudden, and not just because Maria was watching this all play out whilst tapping at the keyboard with audible efficiency. The last thing he wanted was for Ana to feel bad for him in any way or, heaven forbid, sorry for him. He was doing fine for the most part, and he was here to help *her*, not the other way around!

Besides, she'd made it clear to Maria what she thought of him—they were just friends. He would do well to remember that, he told himself, even if she appeared to see him, really *see* him, for once. This was something new and intriguing, and which he'd never really experienced with anyone else. Most women he'd tried to date after Ines had either been uninterested in Javi, or indifferent to Gabriel's chosen career—or both—so any chemistry he might have felt had always fizzled out after a few encounters.

Was that chemistry he could feel now, sending heatwaves up his arm at Ana's touch? He withdrew his arm quickly and raked his hair back, avoiding her questioning gaze. Maybe it was, maybe it wasn't, but this was getting out of hand. How much longer could he keep this up, resisting the urge to make a move? Welcome relief flooded through him again when their next appointment walked through the door.

A bad case of heartburn, a sprained wrist and a plastic brick getting stuck somewhere it shouldn't have been consumed the rest of the day and afternoon. Ana couldn't help feel a slight pang of excitement that Gabriel had agreed to work at the clinic for a few more days; they really did work so well together, and there wasn't a patient who entered the building who didn't like him. He was charming, kind and affable to the point of adorable, but there was something else about him that drew her in, and kept on drawing her in, the more she was around him—a kind of sadness that seeped through that cheerful exterior and shone in his warm brown eyes when he talked about Javi.

Maybe he felt a little helpless that he couldn't give Javi what Ines could, she thought, watching him now with a ten-year-old boy who was waiting for his mother, reading a comic.

Maybe he genuinely thought it wasn't an attractive quality, being a single dad, which was ridiculous! Not only was he the most handsome man around for miles, he was also a great father. How could he think he wasn't, just because he wasn't married, as Ines was? A thought struck her. Maybe he didn't *want* to be single. Frowning to herself, she realised the thought of him with anyone made her feel quite nauseous. Thinking about it, she'd been too chicken to ask about his love life after Ines in case he admitted he'd had feelings for someone else.

Stupid! They were friends and that was that. He'd seemed a little down about that treehouse, though, she pondered as the child's face lit up. Gabriel had handed him another comic and told him he could keep it. She wondered what Pedro was like. Maybe he'd taken on the stepdad role with such gusto that Gabriel truly thought he couldn't keep up.

Still, it wasn't a matter for her to get involved in, she thought suddenly, catching herself getting flustered on his behalf; there was enough going on in her own life. She didn't have the time to get involved in his, even if she was now wondering what she could do to make him feel special, in case he didn't realise it himself. She'd made him feel pretty special in her dream last night… But then, her dream self was often a wanton sex goddess—probably because she hadn't seen any action in a long time! If it hadn't been Gabriel in her dream, it would have been someone else, she reminded herself. It was only him because he was on her mind, and at her side all the time after having been apart for so long.

She hadn't had dreams like that in a long time, though. No one else had ruffled her this much and got her mind churning. Her subconscious was really doing a number on her!

When the last patient was out of the door, Ana made a point to lock it quickly and turn back to her team.

'Well, that was a successful first week, everyone! I think we deserve a night out to celebrate. What do you say?'

She looked expectantly between Maria and Gabriel, hoping they'd see her enthusiasm and agree. Obviously they were all tired, herself included, but she wanted to treat them all, now more than ever. Secretly she wasn't ready for the day to be over, or to go home alone to her apartment and another box of her mum's leftovers. When was the last time she'd eaten anywhere but her apartment? Hard to remember; there was always some new file or document to read at the dinner table. Most of the time she barely remembered eating, as she did it so often on autopilot.

Gabriel looked a little reluctant. A shiver of disappointment travelled through her bones, though she didn't let it show on her face. Thankfully, Maria was waving her phone in the air enthusiastically.

'How about the Mexican place? I can call them right now.'

'The one with the amazing margaritas?' someone else piped up.

'Exactly. Leave it to me.'

Soon they were gathering up their belongings, chatting away about what food they would order and how much fun they were going to have. Ana sneaked away to the bathroom and applied more lipstick, which matched her hair band and shoes. It was most inappropriate that she thought of Gabriel again as she smacked her lips together.

She'd caught him looking at her lips several times today. If he wanted a brief respite from his single dad routine, maybe she could offer to re-enact the dream he didn't even know she'd had, the one where her legs worked, as they often did in her dreams. She'd straddled him on the examination table and he'd held her tightly by the hips and made wild, passionate love to her so furiously, they'd broken the table. He'd run his fingers through her hair and told her she was beautiful and… well… It was a shame she'd woken up too soon from that one. Though not so soon that she hadn't flushed the next time she'd set eyes on him in real life…

'Come on, Ana! What are you doing in there?' Maria was calling her.

'Coming!' Tutting to her reflection, she realised she was hot under the collar. Of course, she would suggest nothing of the sort to Gabriel. Why would she go and ruin their friendship with something so transient as sex? He was just making her feel validated and important and people making her feel that way, especially hot guys, made her horny, that was all.

She would keep her hands, and her thoughts about her friend, to herself. Tonight, though, she decided as Gabriel shot her a look that sent her pulse racing, she *was* going to have some fun. She deserved it.

# CHAPTER SIX

THE MEXICAN RESTAURANT in San Telmo was already bustling when their group arrived, and the waiter hurried to get them all seated. Ana was pleasantly surprised when Gabriel made a visible effort to place himself in the seat next to hers. His smouldering gaze threatened to set her cheeks on fire as he watched her while she pretended to read the menu. Did he feel her watching him too, as he pondered the burrito and fajita choices in front of him?

'It all looks delicious,' she said, licking her lips and tasting her lipstick. Had she put too much on? Why did she care? He was her *friend*. And he didn't have a clue how attracted she was to him right now. Or did he?

'What are you going to have?' he asked, leaning in, brushing her shoulder with his and wafting his manly, musky scent right up her nose. Ana cleared her throat. He might as well just have asked her if she wanted a naked massage for the effect his closeness was having on her.

When had this happened? Now she just couldn't ignore it. He also looked so handsome in his fitted white shirt and tailored navy trousers. His dark skin gleamed under the lighting, and she couldn't shake the burning need to get closer to him physically and emotionally. She'd been AWOL too long. The fact that he was a single dad with a whole other life just intrigued and enchanted her more now and, combined with her dream…no. She'd have to rein it in! They were working together, for goodness' sake.

'I… I'm… Maybe the chicken,' she managed around her parched throat, and he threw her a sideways smile.

'So you're only a part-time vegan, then?'

'I'm a carnival vegan; I told you.'

'A carnival non-carnivore?'

Suppressing a nervous laugh, she made to pick up her margarita just as the waiter placed a basket of corn cobs down in her path. 'Oh, shoot!' Her drink went flying. A gasp echoed around the table as the liquid pooled and settled in a slushy wet splodge on her shirt, rendering the left side of the white cotton totally see-through, right down to her blue lacy bra. Groaning, she went for the napkins just as Gabriel did.

'You're not having much luck with your drinks today,' he quipped, stopping just short of mopping her breast. For a second he looked more horrified than she did, but somehow, for reasons she couldn't explain other than her general mortification in this moment, she burst out laughing until the whole table was killing themselves.

'It's just a shirt!' Maria giggled, standing up so Anna could wheel her chair past. 'We've all seen worse.'

Gabriel stood up too, dropping the cloth napkin. He made as though he was about to help with her wheelchair, but she expertly manoeuvred herself past, throwing him a look to say, *thanks anyway.* She wasn't laughing any more by the time she reached the bathroom. Her shirt was soaked. Somehow she'd have to do her best to forget it, though; fun was on the agenda, and nothing was going to ruin this rare night out.

It was sweet that he still wanted to help her out after all this time, like he used to do at school in the months after her accident, back when she'd still been trying to work out how on earth she'd get through this thing called life when she couldn't even walk. He seemed to see she had worked it out by now but, back at the table, when his arm brushed hers again reaching for his own drink, she wasn't so quick to move away. At one point, she couldn't stop her fingers from reaching out to the corner of his mouth and wiping a tiny bit of red sauce away. He thanked her, chocolate eyes shining in the low lights, and in her mind he kissed her again, as he had done in her dream, as though it was just the two of them and they were on a date.

They'd never been on a date in real life. *And you never will*, she reminded herself. *Friends don't date!*

Somehow the atmosphere in the restaurant made her feel tipsy without having drunk much at all. Everyone in her small team seemed to be enjoying this reprieve from the stresses of the past week, and she allowed the sudden rush of pride that consumed her and almost brought a tear to her eye. OK, maybe she had drunk a little more than she'd thought.

'What are you thinking?' Gabriel whispered suddenly in her ear, causing a flurry of sparks to travel from her earlobe through to her belly. Her heart thundered like a racehorse on course to the moon as she concentrated on the heat radiating from his body in the small, bustling, candlelit space. Why was her throat constricting—because she hadn't been this close to him physically in years? Oh, gosh, did he feel it too—this growing whatever-it-was that she could almost reach out and grab from the air between them?

She still hadn't spoken. 'I was thinking how proud I am of everyone here,' she told him, putting down her margarita. No more drinks for her.

'And yourself, I hope.' He smiled softly. 'You should also be proud of yourself, Ana.'

He said it so sincerely that the tears really did threaten to fall this time. She released a breath, nodding slowly, focusing back on the flickering candle flame so as not to reveal how his proximity was making her feel. It was more than his good looks, it was the way he looked at her—as though he was taking in every single, miniscule detail, adding it to some sort of mental checklist, memorising ways to please her, help her or make her laugh.

Gabriel had always done this, she realised now. She'd just usually been annoyed by it more than flattered, growing up. She hadn't wanted to be noticed for a long time, in case all people saw was her disability.

The weight of his forearm touching hers as he leaned in to read the dessert menu, the physical nature of him, his presence, the way he looked, his skin, the way he smelled and his touch… Oh, boy. Neither of them had time for this…inconvenient attraction.

'Ana?'

'Yes?' She looked up, only to find her whole team, and the waiter, were looking at her expectantly. She cleared her throat, realising the scratch of the waiter's pen on his pad, his low baritone explaining the difference between the chocolate-covered deep-fried specials and the clink of cutlery and glasses had all gone completely over her head. She had been completely lost in Gabriel. No, no, no…this would have to stop. She would eat her dessert and leave, she decided. Her friend was…her friend. Wasn't that what she'd told Maria? Why could she not just convince her stupid brain to believe that was all she still saw him as?

'Um, I'll just have the churros,' she said quickly, hoping no one realised she hadn't even been reading the menu.

The waiter huffed a sigh. 'I did just explain that we don't have any churros left, ma'am.'

She lowered her head and muttered that she'd have the sorbet. They had to have that, right?

Gabriel was smiling softly beside her. To her surprise, he reached out to squeeze her hand lightly. 'You're tired, huh?' he said now. 'I'm exhausted too. Big week.'

Ana blushed so deeply, she could feel it. How embarrassing that he thought she was tired when really she'd been totally distracted, completely caught up in him, that was all. Gosh, if this crush got any worse, people would start to see it…if they hadn't already. 'Big week,' she agreed. 'And thank you, by the way. I wouldn't have as many reasons to feel so proud if you hadn't been at my side all week. People love you.'

'I love…that they love me,' he said, knocking his knee to hers under the table. Their fingers entwined together over the table cloth for just a few seconds longer before he seemed to think better of it and let go. Her hand was instantly colder.

Maria was looking between them over her margarita even while she talked to Sandrine, their part-time physical therapist, and Ana forced herself to start a fresh conversation with someone else. Knowing that her gorgeous best friend believed in her dream as much as she did filled her with the kind of new-found hope for the future that had seemed somewhat impossible until now. She really could do anything. But this attraction had to be stomped out if they were to continue.

Wait a minute… Had he just been *flirting* with her, knocking her knee under the table, squeezing her hand?

Just then, Gabriel slid his chair back and got to his feet. Men and women, couples and friends all around the restaurant, turned from their tables as he clinked a fork to the side of his glass. Ana sat up taller, even though the sudden urge to shrink took hold. Oh no, what on earth was he going to say?

'Ladies and gentlemen, I'd like to raise a toast,' he said. 'To Dr Ana Mendez, who's been working so tirelessly for so long to make this dream come true. She's a true inspiration and I'm honoured to call her one of my friends.'

One of his…*friends*.

Ana sniffed, even as her stomach dropped. Of course, everyone knew they were friends; he was just seizing the chance to reiterate it. He raised his glass and everyone followed suit, clinking their glasses together, but Gabriel wasn't done.

'Her commitment and drive have always been nothing short of incredible, but this week… Wow…' He trailed off a moment and fixed her with a look of such pride and admiration that Ana felt the tears start to prickle persistently behind her eyes. The six familiar faces were smiling, nodding at her and to each other, celebrating her work and achievements. Maria was looking at her with admiration too, while Sandrine nodded in silent approval, but it was Gabriel's gaze that made the fizz begin under her skin. Yes, he'd drawn a line under their friendship, but his warmth was spreading through her, straight to her heart and on through to everywhere else. Her dream came flooding back all over again in full colour till it was all she could do not to lunge for him.

*No.* No, she would not let herself, or their friendship, down.

She would resist. He was a proud friend, an old friend, the best kind of friend. Quickly blinking away the tears before anyone at the table noticed, she drew a breath deep from her jittery lungs before raising her own glass. 'Thank you,' she said softly, feeling an unfamiliar surge of happiness mixed with helplessness take hold of her chest as their eyes met again. This was…too much.

'I should probably get going,' she said.

Gabriel arched his eyebrows and sat back in his chair with a sigh. 'I should go too…' he started, but no sooner were the words out of his mouth than Sandrine and Maria stopped him.

'Oh no, you don't, we're going dancing! Bueno Tango needs your moves, Gabriel.' Maria wiggled her shoulders. 'Yours too, Ana.'

Maria was a little tipsy, and so was Ana, if she was honest. The last thing she needed was to steer her chair into people's ankles on a dance floor. Not that she couldn't 'dance' in it, so to speak, but the thought of making a scene, doing anything else embarrassing in front of this team of people who respected her position, didn't sit right. Her drink was already splotched on her shirt, though thankfully her bra was no longer on display.

'Not tonight,' she said, throwing them an apologetic

look at the same time as signalling for the bill. 'You guys go, though. Have a great time, and keep the receipt—it's on me.'

'You don't have to cover it all,' Gabriel whispered now, a frown on his handsome face. She found herself matching his expression.

'Yes, I do,' she said, removing her red headband and placing it on again. Like her vision, it wasn't entirely straight. Why on earth would he think she wouldn't cover everything for her staff? Then she realised he probably wasn't used to this wealthier Ana who'd made a life for herself away from her overbearing family and could actually afford to treat the people she cared about.

'Well, it's very generous of you,' he said, and she shrugged. More than anything now, she just wanted to escape. If she couldn't have him as more than a friend and colleague, she would have to leave him here as a friend and a colleague. Sliding her shiny new business credit card onto the waiter's tray the second he approached with the bill, she turned to Gabriel.

'Are you staying?' she asked. Her heart was pounding in her ears, louder than the music.

He looked at her thoughtfully for what felt like an eternity then he crossed his arms. 'Do you *want* me to stay?'

Something shiny caught her eye and she gasped, reaching out for his wrist and pulling him closer. 'Your birthday bracelet! You still have this?'

He frowned in surprise. 'Why wouldn't I?'

Ana smiled now, a warmth spreading through her chest as she turned the silver bracelet over on his wrist, taking in the tiny horseshoe engraved into it for good luck. She'd worked hard at a Saturday job in order to pay for it, had chosen and wrapped it carefully and presented it to him for his sixteenth birthday. She couldn't believe he'd kept it.

'Your birthday was right before you were due to play that football match against the Boars, from the barrio over from ours.'

'They were mean.' He grinned now, watching her face. 'I needed that good luck.'

'You beat them, didn't you?'

'Yeah, we did!' He laughed. 'So, I guess it worked.'

'I remember you running to my house to tell me. Where did you find it?'

'What do you mean, where did I find it? I wear it all the time,' he said.

'Liar!' She made to swipe at him playfully and he batted her off until they were play-wrestling like the kids they'd been back then, when he'd raced to her house and recounted the whole story about how he'd scored the winning goal against all odds.

A cough came from across the table. Ana turned to find the girls still there, their mouths twitching.

'So, I suppose you two really aren't coming?' Sandrine said, glancing at Maria, who smirked back at her knowingly. After a few air-kisses, her team of tipsy people made its way out to join the throng of people heading towards Bueno Tango. Ana knew they were all probably talking about Gabriel and her now. Well, so what? They were just two people, reminiscing about silly childhood moments. He was just a friend…

*Who had kept a good luck gift from her this whole time.*

She looked down at her fingers, now intertwined with

his on the table. How had that even happened? Wriggling them free, Ana was suddenly overcome with equal tiredness from the drinks, the long week and the sense that she was growing increasingly confused and out of her depth.

'I really should go,' she said.

Gabriel nodded, then put a hand on her shoulder that sent her heart into overdrive. 'I'll accompany you home, if you like?'

On the way past the restaurant's reception, Gabriel swiped something from a vase and held it behind his back. Out on the street, he produced a marigold, and held it out proudly to her. She laughed, feigning shock. 'Did you just steal that flower from the restaurant?'

'It's not stealing if it had your name on it,' he said, revealing the dimples she adored, and her breath hitched as he moved her hair aside. Slowly and intentionally, he placed the flower gently behind her ear and met her eyes. 'It suits you.'

Ana's heart raced as they made their way onto the moonlit streets. The night was balmy and busy with groups of friends talking excitedly, and couples whispering closely. She could literally feel an electric current pulsing between them, threatening to start a fire in the trees they passed as they walked. The stars above seemed like some timely reminder of their past, when the nights had stretched out in front of them and they'd had no plans, no responsibilities.

They walked and talked, about his shifts with Bruno and her time in Bariloche, but she still couldn't bring herself to ask if there had been anyone else after Ines. Instead she found herself remembering out loud the time when he had put her to bed drunk after graduation.

He just grinned. 'You're a funny drunk,' he said.

'I'm not drunk now,' she iterated. 'In case you think I am.'

'Just tipsy, right?'

'Exactly.' She pulled her chair to a stop and motioned to her front door. 'Well, this is me.'

He shoved his hands into his pockets. She couldn't read the slight smile on his lips as their eyes met and held. He should already be walking away, down the street to the small apartment he had near his parents' place, where he lived alone, except for when Javi and the dog visited. But he was still here with her, and her heart was pounding with anticipation; she was giddy as a schoolgirl. He was looking at her lips, just as she was looking at his. A thrill of excitement coursed through her body like a shockwave as Gabriel leaned closer, his warm breath tickling her skin.

He hovered for just a moment, running his fingers softly over the flower behind her ear before she reached for his shirt and urged him even closer. In that moment, she knew without a doubt that it was too late for either of them to turn back—way too late.

For a split second, the thought crossed her mind: *will this cost us our friendship*? But that thought was quickly silenced as Gabriel's lips touched hers then pressed down harder, engulfing all her senses. Waves of desire flew through her body like wild birds and left her breathless. All she wanted right now was to stay in this moment for ever and let the world fade away. Every fibre of her being wanted this man…

But then he pulled away and took a step back, seemingly gathering his thoughts. 'You know…' He groaned, almost under his breath, as her heart bucked. 'If I come inside with you, Ana, I don't think I'll be able to leave.'

Before she could think straight and let something as stupid as logic get in the way, she spun her chair back round to the street. 'Then I guess we're both going to your place,' she said.

# CHAPTER SEVEN

ANA WATCHED AS Gabriel carefully measured out the lemongrass tea leaves and scooped them into two cups. Then he added hot water, stirring it slowly, almost seductively, in a circular motion. Ana felt her throat tighten as she looked at him in the bright kitchen light. It wasn't the tea she wanted. It was him she wanted, badly, but maybe he'd changed his mind about her and was about to soften the blow by reminding her they were friends.

She wanted to believe it would be beyond foolish to ruin a good thing. But this chemistry between them was like nothing she'd ever experienced before—it was thrilling and intoxicating, and even now she could feel a strange contraction in her heart muscles, pumping blood to places it hadn't been in a long time. That newly awake and fizzing part of her wanted to stay and explore what they could have, while the other part, the sensible part, knew damn well there'd be consequences if she did. But she was here, wasn't she?

The living area was cosy, from the open-plan kitchen to the soft textured couch and colourful rugs across the floor tiles. Ana rolled her chair towards the couch. Traces of his son were everywhere: a stack of toy cars in the corner, a drawing of a superhero tacked up on the wall, a pair of sneakers peeking out from under a chair. But she knew from their discussions that Javi was with Ines and her husband now, and Gabriel didn't have him till tomorrow. There would be no interruptions if she stayed, if he carried her in his arms up the carpet-clad staircase to his bedroom, if he laid her across the sheets and…

'Tea?'

Ana sucked in a breath quietly as he appeared behind her with a steaming cup. 'If it's too hot, let me know.'

'Thanks,' she mumbled as he cleared the sneakers away quickly. He sloshed a little of his tea as he kicked them towards the wall behind some fitness equipment and turned to her with a sheepish shrug. He was clearly nervous. So was she.

'Gabriel…' she said now, putting the tea down on the little glass coffee table and moving her chair closer. He put his cup down too and dropped onto the couch, rubbing his hands across his chin. 'Don't be nervous,' she told him, as she wheeled up closer, so close she could touch his knees with hers. He ran his gaze over her lips and his eyes grew even darker with hunger, and suddenly she knew he *definitely* wanted her. It was everything else he was nervous about: how to navigate her disability, her wheelchair, or how to treat her.

'I have to admit to you, I am a little nervous. Not because I don't want this…' he started.

'I know. It's OK.'

Ana watched him take a deep breath, as if steeling himself, and her heart felt as if it was going to burst right out of her chest as he took her hands and held them tight, then scooped her towards him. His hands felt cool against the back of her neck, and she inched even closer, letting him kiss her again. He had to know that she wanted the same thing he did, all of it. This longing—the heat, the passion, the connection—wasn't something they could just switch off. Even if this turned out to be a one-night-only event, she couldn't back out now. They just had to find a way to work around what she couldn't do so they could both enjoy the things she most definitely could.

It was always the hardest part; it had been the same with her ex in Bariloche. But this felt more intense, more meaningful, more important somehow. Every time Gabriel pulled his lips away and looked at her, his face told her he knew that too.

If only she had the words to tell him that she could handle herself and make sure he was comfortable in all scenarios but, right now, her breath was so taken away by the growing intensity of his kisses that she was starting to think she didn't need to say a word anyway. Before long she was as far out of her chair as she could get. If only she could break free, she thought; if only she could stand up, wrap her legs around him and feel all of him pressed against her.

His breath was hot and deliciously heavy on her neck, and a rush of electricity surged through her core and made her toes tingle. She could tell her chair didn't matter to him as he trailed kisses that made her shiver down to the crook of her shoulder. Then, suddenly, he scooped her up from her wheelchair in one strong motion and held her close against him, pressing more kisses to her lips. Ana felt herself melting into him. She groaned with mounting lust and pure animal desire as he made for the stairs with her in his arms, just as she'd imagined.

His bedroom was surprisingly neat and tidy, which she

somehow managed to notice between kisses...passionate kisses, with so much heat, so much burning desire. 'I knew this would happen,' he said now, carrying her past the huge wooden dresser that took up the length of one wall. The shelves were lined with more books than she'd imagined he'd have. The walls were painted in shades of blue and grey, and the moon was a huge glowing bulb, spilling its pale light through the trees outside and giving everything an ethereal glow.

'You did, did you?'

'Yes, I kind of did, the moment I saw you again that first day when I jumped out of the ambulance.'

A king-sized bed sat in the middle of the room, covered in a soft navy duvet. Still holding her close, he flung it back to reveal crisp, white cotton sheets, before lowering her gently onto the bed.

'You're so beautiful,' he murmured, just as he'd done in her dream. Ana gasped, barely able to suppress her grin as Gabriel slowly leaned over her, bringing his face level with hers—close enough that she could feel each breath he took, hot with an anticipation that matched her own. She drew him into her lungs, reached up, cupped his face and felt herself melting even more as his deep-brown eyes locked onto hers.

'I'm going to be so careful with you,' he whispered. 'We can do this.'

Ana felt her heart swell, tears prickling her eyes all of a sudden. He was so kind, so gentle, with her. But she wanted more. 'You don't have to be gentle, or even a gentleman. I know you, remember?'

Her hands fumbled at her shirt and she undid the buttons, gasping as he pulled off his own shirt, and in seconds they were naked, flesh to flesh. All fear disappeared as he stood before her naked, and she ran her tongue over her lips, seeing nothing but adoration and desire, and muscles she hadn't imagined he'd have. He worked out: she'd seen the treadmill and weights in the living room.

Ana felt her breath hitch as his hands moved down her body, exploring her curves and lingering on her skin. His touch was tender and caring, but in equal measures daring and passionate, making sure she was pleasured while still ensuring she wasn't in pain or uncomfortable.

'Are you OK?' he asked, his voice full of concern.

Ana nodded, feeling the warmth spread through her body. If only he knew she had never felt so loved, so wanted and desired before. She smiled at the rush of happiness that overtook her.

'Yes,' she told him, her voice soft and breathy. 'All I want is you.'

Gabriel's eyes never left her, his gaze turning her insides to liquid before he leaned in and kissed her again, his lips caressing hers as a wave of pleasure coursed through her body, her inhibitions melting away. She just might have discovered a new-found confidence in her body, a confidence she definitely hadn't felt before, despite trying all kinds of positions with her ex.

'Let's take it slow,' Gabriel said, pulling a condom from the drawer by the bed, his voice low and husky as he positioned himself over her again. She moaned in pleasure as he slid inside her, watching her face the whole time, his voice low and gritty, like broken glass in the moonlight, when he asked again if she felt OK. He studied her face intently, tracing his fingertips along the planes of her cheekbones and jaw as if memorising every feature. She assured him she was more than OK by rocking beneath him, every nerve lighting up as they found their rhythm. His eyes burned with such a fierce intensity that she felt as though tears might well up at any second. No, she would not cry, she told herself, squeezing her eyes shut and locking her arms around him.

She felt her heart racing as their bodies moved together, Gabriel's hands exploring her body, his touch arousing her in ways she never thought possible. 'How is this…us…?' she heard herself ask between kisses as his hands found her waist again, then trailed up and down her back, tangling into her hair as he pulled her in. She felt herself melting into his arms against his broad chest, her body trembling as their passion heightened.

Gabriel suddenly pulled away, his breathing heavy. He looked at her, his eyes soft but so full of desire, it made her blood fizz. She felt him pause after a moment, his hands stilling on her body. He looked into her eyes, his gaze searching for something.

'What is it?' she asked, suddenly worried that he wasn't enjoying this as much as she was.

'You're amazing, in every way,' he told her, his voice still loaded with emotion as he swept her hair behind her ear. This time, she really did have to blink back a tear, which she somehow managed to hide by kissing him fiercely and hungrily till his movements sped up and slowed again in response to hers.

Ana realised she had never felt so safe, so cherished, before. Her body was in his hands and he was so aware of that, it was beautiful. She closed her eyes, feeling another surge of joy course through her body as she guided him into another position she knew would feel even more amazing. Every single thing he was doing felt incredible: his hands, his breath tickling her skin, all leaving her the sweetest sensation of being someone's everything, even if it couldn't last; even if this was the only time they'd ever do anything like this.

Gabriel's movements surged in intensity as they chased their mutual climax, and Ana decided that, unlike in some of her previous sexual encounters—when she'd perhaps felt a little embarrassed at times—she was going to make all the noise she felt like making and not hold back any involuntary shudders. As Gabriel collapsed beside her, their bodies exhausted from the exertion, she could barely keep from telling him how that had been far beyond anything she could have expected, better than in her dreams.

'Wow,' was all he said, and they laughed before he propped himself up on one elbow beside her. Gabriel looked down at her, taking in her features, trailing a finger across her bottom lip. His smile made the flock of butterflies re-emerge and whirl into a mad frenzy inside her chest before he kissed her forehead gently and slid out of bed.

Ana could feel the air between them still humming with electricity, even after he left the bedroom. When he came back, he was carrying water in two shiny blue glasses. She glugged hers back appreciatively. All that action had made her thirsty, and she remembered the tea they hadn't drunk going cold downstairs. Not that she ever wanted to leave this bed, now that she was finally in it. Soon, they both fell asleep, and for Ana dreams of Gabriel swirled round in her head and melted away all the doubts.

Morning came round, however, far too soon. She

glanced at his bedside clock, which read six-fifteen. The birds were singing and Gabriel was still fast asleep. For a moment, she studied his sleeping frame: the contours of his muscles and limbs against the crisp white sheets; his darkly handsome face against the crumpled pillowcase.

This was the embarrassing part, she realised now. She could hardly just sneak out and let him have a well-deserved lie-in on a quiet Saturday morning, the way she would surely have done if she'd had the use of her legs. She would have to wake him up to help her get downstairs. Things were already going to be weird anyway, she supposed grimly, nudging him gently.

He stirred and his eyes fluttered open, and Ana prepared herself for a hint of regret on his face, some sign that he might regret putting their friendship on the line. But Gabriel just smiled at her softly, as if he couldn't believe his luck that she was still there. 'Good morning, you.'

Ana couldn't help but smile back, her heart stopping its heavy thud for a second in relief. He seemed to be genuinely happy to see her still there beside him in bed, as if she could be anywhere else. All the same, she was pretty sure they *both* knew this was the awkward 'morning after' moment, and at some point they would have to talk about it and what happened next.

Gabriel just sat up, yawning, and leaned against the headboard, stretching his arms behind him. She studied his broad chest, remembering how he'd cradled her so close to him before they'd fallen asleep. Would they ever do that again, or had it been a one-off? So many questions, but now…

Ana bit her lip nervously. 'I should go,' she said, holding the sheet around her now, slightly more self-conscious of her body in the morning light. He looked at her a moment before he seemed to realise what she was saying.

'Oh, right, yes…' He flung the sheets back quickly and scrambled for his clothes, and she watched in appreciation and amusement as he pulled his boxer briefs and trousers on so fast, he almost tumbled over.

'Sorry,' he said and she laughed. Somehow he'd lightened the mood again. He looked extra-cute in the morning light, eyelids still heavy as he dashed his hands through his tousled hair. She wanted more than anything to be able to tell him how much last night had meant to her, how much she cared about him, and how she'd never before felt so safe and cherished and adored. But maybe she'd come off as too needy, she decided. Still, she let her arms curl around him once he'd passed over her clothes and swept her up again into his arms.

When she finally left, he stood, shirtless, halfway behind the front door as she made her way back to the street. Her heart was doing crazy moves behind her ribs again as she kept on steering her chair away from him, putting more and more distance between them and their night of passion. Already she wanted to turn round and go straight back, but she didn't want to stay so long that it got any more awkward. All the 'what if?'s were piling up in her busy head already: what if he wished they hadn't done that? What if it *had* ruined their friendship for ever? What if…what if he didn't want to do it again?

# CHAPTER EIGHT

'DON'T FORGET HIS JUMPER. He might need it,' Ines reminded Gabriel as Javi made to rush past them both from the house towards Gabriel's car. She kept one eye on her son the whole time, and her arms were crossed, as if she was physically restraining herself from reaching out and making him stay with her.

'I have the jumper, and he'll be fine,' Gabriel said kindly, stepping back from Ines' doorstep. Nothing was going to ruin his good mood today. Not that that was entirely all to do with the fact he was spending the day with Javi. He could taste Ana on his lips and still see her face in his mind's eye, still feel her. What a night.

'What time will you be bringing him back?' Ines asked, catching him before he turned to the car, and handing him Javi's super-hero backpack. No doubt she had already packed it with a ton more stuff that he already had for Javi at his place, but he was used to this pedantic packing by now. It was just Ines's way of showing motherly concern; he couldn't really blame her.

He told her he wasn't sure what time they'd be back from the wildlife park, but that he'd text her, and then he noticed Pedro's shadow through the pane of glass in the study door. Ines's husband hadn't emerged yet. Usually he came to the door to see Gabriel when he arrived to collect Javi.

'What's he working on?' he asked Ines. Ines looked away and crossed her arms.

'I don't know… Something.'

Gabriel knew that tone of voice. She had something on her mind. 'Is everything all right?' he asked, slinging Javi's pack onto his shoulder. Instincts primed, he watched her carefully as she studied her nails a second and blew air through her nose, sending her mass of black curls out around her slanted cheekbones. OK, so everything was not all right. In fact, it looked a lot as though he might have interrupted an argument or something, but it wasn't his place to bring it up.

'Bye, Pedro,' he called to the closed door. Pedro's shadow raised a hand from his chair but still he didn't get up.

Gabriel forgot about it as soon as they were in the car. He was already focused on thoughts of Ana again. She hadn't exactly left his head all morning but now he was wondering…would it be crazy and way too impulsive if he invited her on their day out today? She couldn't be spending all day working, it was too nice outside for that, and Javi would love it if she came. The wildlife park was suitable for wheelchairs, too.

Temaiken was one of his favourite places to explore with Javi. The wildlife sanctuary and conservation centre was home to a pretty impressive collection of habitats, and each one had been fastidiously designed to replicate the native environments of its furry, scaly, or feathered residents. He could already picture them all strolling through the lush, tropical rainforests. Maybe he would steal a kiss from Ana in a desert, or beside one of the ponds or waterfalls. Hell, he could at least ask her to come, right, even if he was getting ahead of himself? he thought as he drove.

Javi was jabbering to himself in the back seat as Gabriel pulled up outside Ana's place. Ines lived on the other side of Recoleto but he'd do a loop for Ana. Standing on her door step, he told his pounding heart to calm down, and it almost took the words from his mouth when she opened the door and looked up at him in surprise.

'Couldn't keep away from me, could you?' she said with a flushed smile, which he was sure he returned, though he was mildly distracted by another colourful headband and bright-blue sneakers that matched the pattern on her T-shirt.

'Javi's in the car. He was wondering if you'd like to join us at the wildlife park?' he asked hopefully. Ana studied him closely from her chair and he wished he could read her mind. Was that a trace of apprehension in her eyes? Was her heart beating as hard as his? He wasn't quite sure he'd ever felt this nervous on a woman's door step before; she was doing strange things to his insides, even fully dressed.

'Javi wants me to come, huh?'

'Absolutely. Me, I don't want you to at all, but I promised him I'd ask.'

Ana laughed softly and rolled her eyes. 'I had a few things to do, you know, but…'

She let her words falter and trail off, then failed to hide a smile behind her hair as she shook her head. 'Let me just grab my bag.'

* * *

They chatted light-heartedly in the car, Ana's wheelchair folded neatly in the back while she sat beside Gabriel in the front. Even though he knew she was making an effort to seem normal in front of Javi, who was delighted she was joining them, Gabriel knew she must be thinking the same kind of things as him. He'd known last night, in the restaurant, that if he walked her home he would end up kissing her; and he'd known, when he'd kissed her, that if he asked her back for tea they wouldn't actually end up drinking any. He'd taken a risk, putting their friendship on the line, but he couldn't have helped it, even if he'd tried. Which he hadn't. Well, not very hard, anyway.

He reckoned, if he'd left it too long before initiating something like this, it might get even weirder. They still had to work together, at least for the next few days until she could find another locum.

The sun hung high in the clear Buenos Aires sky as he flashed their tickets and they walked through the entrance gates of Temaiken. The sound of gently flowing water filled his ears and just ahead the vibrant reds and greens of exotic birds squawking and preening in a giant aviary set the scene for the tropical gardens in one direction. A sign with a lion on it made Javi race in the other direction and Gabriel followed beside Ana's chair, careful not to try and help her.

She hated that. But she hadn't minded him carrying her up and down his stairs last night and, if he was honest, he'd loved that part the most. There'd been something far more intimate about her actually letting him help her, and care for her, than the act of sex itself.

'This place is really something, isn't it? I haven't been

here in years,' Ana said, her eyes wide with amazement as Javi pointed in excitement at the lion enclosure.

His infectious enjoyment spread and soon they found themselves talking and laughing their way around the park, weaving in between other groups of friends and families and taking silly photos around the enclosures: of a llama with its tongue out, a goat chomping on a bale of hay and a snake curled around a branch in the glare of an orange bulb in the reptile house. Sometimes it was as if nothing had happened between them last night, as though they were still just platonic friends having a day out for old times' sake. But every now and then she would catch his eye and he'd feel it in his blood—something was different. An indelible line had been drawn through that friendship status and now he just wanted to kiss her again.

'It tickles!' Javi laughed as a huge red-and-brown-speckled butterfly landed on his outstretched palm.

'Hold still, very still,' Ana told him, grinning in wonder as she tried to take another photo on her phone. They were in the butterfly enclosure now, and the sweet scent of tropical flowers filled the air in the huge greenhouse. Javi was enchanted, reaching out to try and touch them as they fluttered by. He rarely managed; they were so fast they could barely even capture any on camera, though Ana was trying her best, to her credit.

'I remember what it was like to be that carefree,' she said with a small sigh as Javi ran up ahead of them after another butterfly. 'Running around…with you.' She turned to him now, and the sudden sadness in her eyes made him reach for her hand.

'Before your accident,' he said softly.

She nodded in silence, squeezing his fingers against the arm of her chair. 'Everything can change so quickly. You can't let any moments pass you by, Gabriel.'

Her eyes were fixed on Javi now, but when she flicked her gaze back to his he knew she was talking about them, too. Things had changed for *them* pretty much overnight. They hadn't let that moment pass them by, even though they both knew it would have long-reaching consequences.

He knelt in front of her quickly, taking both her hands in his. 'Are you all right, about what happened?' he asked, running his eyes over her mouth as she drew the corner of her bottom lip between her teeth.

'Papa, look!' Javi was calling him again.

'One sec, buddy!' Fixing his eyes on Ana, he ran a thumb over her knuckles and dared to lean closer. Suddenly he was suppressing the need to kiss clean away any doubts she might be having about how much last night had meant to him, because he could see them written all over her face. Filling his lungs, he stepped closer and leaned in towards her mouth. But Ana moved her head, causing his lips to find her cheek instead. He paused for a moment, struggling for equanimity amongst the bustle of the crowds before getting to his feet. She probably wished she hadn't come here with them now.

'We shouldn't,' she whispered, nodding towards Javi, as shame coursed through him. She was right, Javi was here—not that he thought his son would care, but if it got back to Ines that he was going around kissing women in front of him she might have something to say about it… She might think Gabriel was a bad influence on him, and use it as another excuse in her armoury to ask for full custody, if it came to it.

'Sorry, you're right,' he said, wondering now if she *was* just trying not to get too close to him in front of Javi, or if she actually regretted last night. Ana smiled wistfully, watching a giant Blue Morpho butterfly that had landed on her knee. It matched the shade of her shoes. For a few moments they let the silence envelop them, an awkwardness slowly settling between them with the butterflies. It was far too hot in here.

'You know, what happened between us doesn't have to change anything,' he said tightly, walking beside her towards Javi as the humid air closed in and the palms swept his shoulder, as if reminding him to stay away from her.

'I hope it doesn't,' she whispered back, shooting him another apprehensive glance. 'I really, really value your friendship, Gabriel, I always have. I was perhaps a bit… forward.'

He nodded, feeling slightly offended and bruised despite himself. All he'd heard was a reiteration of that word: friendship. Maybe he had been building this up in his head into something it wasn't. This amazing woman had just been excited about the first week at the clinic going so well, and at being surrounded by so many people who admired her and were out to celebrate her achievements. They'd both just got swept up on a wave, and he told her so.

'It was still a great night—all of it, not just the end part,' he added, leaving room for her to agree with him.

Instead she was quiet. 'Are you OK?' she asked after a moment.

Was he? He would just have to be, wouldn't he? No point making a big deal out of it now.

'Of course. And I value what we have too, Ana; I always have done. Maybe we shouldn't have…'

'You're right, we got carried away,' she said quickly, though she wouldn't meet his eyes now. 'We shouldn't have done that, really. Friends don't sleep together.'

'Right.'

*Awkward.*

'But then, maybe it was always going to happen,' she continued thoughtfully. 'You know—*because* we're friends. Sometimes you just have to see if it's going to work or…not.'

He opened his mouth to assure her he'd thought everything had worked pretty well—everything that mattered, anyway—but he closed his mouth quickly. He was probably putting his foot in it more with every word that came out. Now he wasn't quite sure *how* he felt. This was Ana and he would accept her in any way she needed him: as a friend, a colleague or a lover, even if it burned.

'It won't change anything if we don't let it,' she said, sticking out her hand. 'Let's shake on it now.'

Before he could take her hand, a monarch fluttered up and promptly landed on her outstretched hand. Ana stared at it, blinking. Then, just as fast as it had appeared, it flitted away again and she seemed to forget the attempted handshake.

This was still all a little awkward, he thought as they continued their walk. They leaned over the fence to see the ostriches with their big, round, gawky eyes and tiny heads; they hand-fed the pink piglets in the mini-farm and put Javi on a new dinosaur carousel that hadn't been here before. Ana was acting normal enough, but the whole time Javi was on the ride she was quiet, and she also kept pulling her gaze away from him and fixed it on something else…as if he couldn't feel her watching him anyway.

Gabriel watched the carousel spin under the blue sky and saw Javi's eyes light up when he climbed off and Ana handed him some candy floss they'd bought from the nearby stall. She batted Gabriel's hand away when he made to feed her a soft, pink fluffy piece straight from the bag—something anyone would do to a friend—which stung, but he pretended not to make a big deal of it. Last night had changed everything and they both knew it but, if she wasn't going to risk their friendship over a heated night together, then he certainly wasn't going to push for it. Yes, they had crossed a line, and he'd remember for ever the many different ways they'd crossed it, but if it was only going to happen once he would just have to put it behind him, exactly as *she* was.

'Can we go and watch the sea lion show?' Javi asked them now, his brown eyes gleaming. This really was his favourite place.

'If Ana wants to,' Gabriel said.

She nodded warmly. 'That sounds like a great idea,' she told his son, and Javi made to push her wheelchair in the direction of the sea lions. Gabriel was quick to pull him back.

'It doesn't work like that. Ana can do that on her own,' he told him.

Javi pouted. 'I know she can,' he said.

Ana was watching them. Then she leaned over and grinned at Javi. 'You know, maybe if you climb up on here with me, we can both race your dad to the sea lions?'

Gabriel looked at her in surprise. Was she seriously fine with that? She just shrugged and helped Javi up onto her lap. He couldn't help matching his son's infectious grin as Ana sped forward suddenly, holding Javi tight.

'Hey, not fair!' Gabriel yelled out, sprinting after them. Javi screamed with laughter as Ana wove around the people on the path, with him trying his best to catch them up. To be fair, he wasn't trying too hard; he wanted to let Javi think they were winning. By the time he caught them up outside the sea lion exhibition they were both high-fiving each other at beating him. He couldn't help feeling that Ana was even better with Javi than he'd thought. She had a natural way with him that suddenly made him all the more annoyed that he'd crossed that stupid line with her.

Now, instead of looking at her as his friend, as he would have done, he was looking at her as someone very important and influential, whom his son was already coming to like spending time with as much as he did. Women like her didn't come around very often—if ever. And who wouldn't want more than friendship with a woman like that?

# CHAPTER NINE

THE SEA LIONS were putting on a great show. Ana had been able to position her chair on the end of the row with Gabriel to her left, and Javi two rows in front, closer to the feeding session action but where they could still see him. It was so nice, watching the little boy so happy and carefree. Just as she'd thought, Gabriel was a great father. He was better than great: his son adored him! She wished more than anything that she had the ability to lift Javi onto her shoulders and run around with him, as Gabriel had done at various points today. He was the kind of exemplary dad that didn't even realise how excellent he was.

'Woo-hoo, yes, get the fish, get that big one!' Javi was yelling now as the trainer by the huge blue swimming pool tossed another fish for the sea lion to catch and devour for its dinner. When it succeeded and dove into the pool, coming up close to the glass, as if to show off to the audience, Javi spun round to them, grinning from ear to ear. 'Did you see that, Papa, Ana?'

'We saw,' Gabriel assured him, throwing Ana a sideways glance. 'He likes you,' he said to her. 'But what's not to like?' he added next, almost to himself, before sighing and shaking his head. Ana swallowed. OK, so of course it wasn't going to be easy, being friends after….well… that. But she would have to try.

She'd had to come out with him today to see if their friendship could be rescued. What would she do if she'd messed it all up? Gabriel was important in her life! But the tension was palpable now. Why had she pulled away from that attempted kiss in the butterfly house in the first place? It was proof that maybe he didn't just want to be her friend…which sent her stomach flapping with more butterflies than the enclosure could've handled.

But it was more than Javi being there that had freaked her out. It was that she was scared of getting into something she couldn't get out of, or even something she didn't *want* to get out of! How could she possibly give Javi and him the attention they deserved? She was far too busy—she had only just opened the clinic. She'd worked her whole life for this chance to do something amazing on her own, make a name for herself and prove all the naysayers and mollycoddlers wrong. Romance was a big fat no. It would only get in the way.

Friendship was all she had time to offer anyone, and besides, this was Gabriel! He'd broken her heart once without even knowing it; there was no way she could go through that again if he decided this wasn't worth pursuing for whatever reason. They might have agreed that sex wouldn't ruin their friendship, but it already had, and they both knew it. It was imperative they get that back on track, no matter what.

Ana swallowed as her arm brushed his and the crowd let out another cheer for the fishy feeding exhibit in front of them. Friendship…. It was just a word to her now, a word that no longer held the same meaning, not now he'd been inside her and had treated her like the most special, important, cherished person on the planet. Everything felt so different now that she'd slept with him.

Gabriel's phone buzzed. Sliding it out of his pocket, he started scowling at the screen. Ines: she could read it from here. It was impossible not to hear the one-sided conversation between them as they started talking, though she kept her eyes on Javi and the sea lions in front of them. The big, clumsy, slippery creatures were full and happily-fed, swimming around while the staff answered the kids' curious questions.

'I still don't know what time we'll be back, yet, Ines. No, he didn't need the jumper you packed, it's been too warm. It's the swimming pool you can hear… We're watching the sea lions…'

Ana couldn't help notice how stiff his shoulders had become, just talking to Ines. It wasn't her business, whatever was going on between them as they co-parented Javi, but after last night she knew she would feel even more awkward if she ignored the elephant in the room altogether.

'Everything OK?' she asked when he hung up.

Gabriel forced a smile to his face and her heart twisted. 'Fine. That was Ines,' he said, as if Ana didn't already know. 'She just wanted to know when we'll be back.' He sighed deeply and she knew from the sound of it that he had a whole load of pent-up feelings on the matter.

'Sorry,' he apologised, pulling a face. 'It's not your problem, Ana.'

Ana chewed her lip a moment, looking at his hand, close enough to take and hold in her lap in empathy. She wanted to so badly, just as she'd wanted to kiss him again before she'd cruelly turned her cheek to him earlier in a moment of fear and doubt, but she didn't.

'It sounds like she struggles to let him out her sight,' she commented after a moment, as a sea lion honked in response to something resonating from the tannoy. An exotic bird demonstration, in ten minutes. That would be so lovely for Javi to see…

'She does struggle,' Gabriel admitted, dashing a hand over his hair. 'It's almost as if she doesn't trust me with him, or my parents. You know my parents—they love him. They'd do anything for him, but somehow it's never enough.'

'She's probably just concerned he might hurt himself on someone else's watch, like you are. Doesn't it come with the child-raising territory?' she reasoned. His nerves over telling him this were showing all over his face.

Gabriel shrugged, reaching an arm around the back of her chair, then abruptly removing it and sitting forward in his seat. 'I suppose it does. I just wish she would trust me a little more. He always has a great time with us, and he's perfectly safe. But I can't help thinking she's just counting down the days until she can ask for full custody.'

Ana turned to him fully, eyes wide. *What?* 'She wouldn't do that to you—you two aren't on bad terms, are you?'

'She's his mother and she's married. Sometimes I think Javi might *want* to just live with them permanently anyway. They can give him far more than I can.'

'Like what? You're his father! That counts for something. Might you just be worrying about things that won't ever happen?'

He nodded, contemplating her words, and her heart

beat hard in her throat at how emotionally invested she suddenly was when she had been trying to tell herself that she shouldn't be. It wasn't anything she could help now, not after everything that had happened last night—not after he'd treated her with so much tenderness. But who was kind and tender to him, when he had doubts in his head like these? Gosh, she really had been a totally selfish friend to him. Before now, she'd only ever seen Gabriel as the strong one, the one *she* and everyone else could rely on. Gabriel had made a living doing everything for everyone else who needed him, but who took care of *his* needs? Who held his hand and told him when not to worry, and when to focus on what he wanted for a change, instead of what everyone else wanted from him?

'I'd better get him home after this,' he said now, glancing at her apologetically.

'Why? It's still early,' she said, suddenly annoyed on his behalf, and at herself too.

'Ines will just call me again in half an hour and ask me where he is. Trust me, it's better if we just get him home.'

'But he's having so much fun.'

As if on cue, Javi stood in his seat and clapped enthusiastically at one of the sea lions who'd caught another huge fish in its mouth. A kid in the front had thrown it.

'Papa, can we get a sea lion?' Javi called back to them.

'Sure.' Gabriel smirked. 'And let's just see how your dog reacts to that the next time he's with us.'

They continued to watch in silence. When he drove her home, she couldn't help feeling he was embarrassed at having shared so much with her. He didn't accept her offer to come inside with Javi, after he'd helped her back into her wheelchair with just as much care as he'd carried her up the stairs and laid her down on his bed last night.

'Are you sure? I have some great tea,' she teased, before she could remind herself not to.

His face remained expressionless as he turned back to the car, its engine still running. He was so distracted and probably still thinking about rushing back to Ines, who to all intents and purposes was in full control of Javi's *and* his lives.

'Better not,' he said, predictably.

'OK. Well, thank you for a great day. I had fun,' she said, looking up at his distant expression.

'So did I.' Gabriel seemed to be looking anywhere but into her eyes, and she could feel the connection severing right in front of her. 'I should get back to…'

'Yes, you should probably go.'

It was for the best, she thought as she closed the door after him and listened to the car drive away. They'd both been confused and on a high after last night, and this was reality roaring back in to remind her not to get carried away. Gabriel—her *friend* Gabriel—had no space for her in his personal life; his hands were completely tied. He just didn't know how to say it after that one incredible night of passion they'd shared. Well, in that case, she would take the task off his hands and spare him the need. There was no way she was going to suggest any other close encounters, not even a cup of tea at her house, she decided.

Ana found herself staring unseeingly at the TV for the rest of the evening, knowing she should be doing something else, but completely unable to focus on anything. She had spent all her life keeping everyone—including him—at arm's length. Despite her growing real feelings for him all those years ago, she'd always just treated him platonically until she'd lost him altogether. Now, he had no space for her at all, no more than she had for him, realistically. Why then, if neither of them had the time or the space for this, did she feel as if something monumentally huge had just come crashing down around her? It would be better for her heart and whirring brain if she just stayed as far away from him as possible now, she decided. Except for at work—ugh. She could hardly avoid him there. She should step up her search for another locum.

The afternoon's rain only seemed to intensify the mood in the clinic's colourful consultation room as Ana passed Gabriel a file in preparation for their next patient. If only there was a way that he could ease this awful awkward atmosphere that had been hanging like a storm cloud over them all week.

'Who have we got next?' he asked as their fingers brushed across the papers.

'A kitchen victim,' she replied, moving away too quickly and making a thing out of straightening the pen holder on her desk, looking out at the rain pattering against the windows. 'He came in with his fiancé.'

Gabriel nodded, looking over the file. This weirdness between them was a living creature whispering from his shoulder whenever their sleeves or fingers met by accident, which happened a lot; how could it not in a place this size? She'd been looking for another locum since he'd started at the clinic, but so far there wasn't one with time to spare, and he knew despite this awkwardness that she still needed him. They were practically under each other's feet. He or she would make a concerted effort to pull away too fast whenever an accidental brush occurred, and look the other way, and it was getting kind of ridiculous now.

If only he hadn't said all that when they were watching the sea lions about Ines and his fears about her asking for full custody. Poor Ana had enough going on in her life just now—no wonder she'd backed away completely since then. They'd agreed their friendship wouldn't suffer but he couldn't help thinking it had been ruined even more now by his over-sharing. She probably thought he was a fool too, for bending over backwards for Ines and her demands, but what could he do? One foot wrong, and she might have another reason to get her lawyer involved in deciding where Javi lived permanently. That was something he couldn't compromise on, not for anything.

'Hello?' Maria opened the door slowly, peeking inside before, with a smile, sending their male patient in. His fiancé was close behind and the height difference in the two men made Gabriel bite back a smile despite himself.

The 'kitchen victim' was at least a foot shorter than his partner. He offered them both a slightly sheepish smile, cradling his burned hand against his chest as Ana introduced herself. His name was Davit and he spoke in English with an accent as he explained how grateful he was that they could see him at such short notice. He was Dutch, it emerged, the same as his tall, red-headed fiancé, Berend.

'Tell us what happened, Davit,' Gabriel said.

Davit flushed with embarrassment as he recounted the tale. 'I was trying to make a special lunch for Berend in the hostel kitchen—we're on vacation here. I was sautéing some vegetables and the pan just slipped from my hand. I tried to catch it, but…'

'But he forgot that hot pans are so hot,' Berend finished for him, pressing his hand to his fiancé's arm in sympathy, whilst also smiling ruefully at Ana.

Ana nodded sympathetically. 'Sometimes the most romantic gestures just don't work,' she said softly, reaching for Davit's arm at the same time as Gabriel. He caught her eye, as well as the double entendre, and almost tripped on her wheel. She spun away quickly, throwing him a look that was nothing short of annoyance, which he returned, before resuming his professional demeanour. Was everything going to be this difficult now? He would rather have his friend back than endure this weirdness between them.

'It's a second-degree burn with intact blistering,' Ana told Davit. 'Must be pretty painful, but nothing that won't heal up nicely as long as you don't get it wet.'

'And stay out of the kitchen,' Berend added, to which his partner play-slapped him and laughed, just before wincing in pain again.

Gabriel watched Ana work, as she wrapped the gauze carefully around the wound, her eyes devoid of the sparkle they'd held just last week, before their night together. It should've been obvious that working with her would be like this, though this was the first time she'd directed a slight his way. She must really regret that they'd put their friendship on the line…and annoyed that he'd had no time to stay behind after his shifts to try and talk to her properly.

That was his fault, he supposed. He'd been so intent on rushing to Javi, now that it was his week with him, and to relieve his parents of their grandparent duties once he was done with work. It seemed as if Ana had more on her mind than just him, anyway. But of course she did: she'd only recently opened her clinic!

There was also Ines to contend with. He was even more aware of having to keep things sweet with her than before, after she'd told him last weekend he'd returned Javi from the wildlife park later than she'd been expecting … even though he'd texted her! She'd been distracted lately, so maybe she'd forgotten. He still thought it was unusual that Pedro hadn't left the study to see Javi and him off that day either, or when he'd brought the little boy back, but it wasn't his place to pry with personal questions.

Gabriel watched as Ana saw the bandaged-up Davit and Berend out of the room after handing over a prescription for painkillers, and felt her eyes on him as she wheeled past, feeling the weight of his earlier mistake—clumsily impeding her wheelchair. Why did it suddenly feel as if he couldn't do anything right? Or maybe Ines was getting to him more than he realised.

He also still had his mother's invitation floating around in his head. Mama wanted Ana and her parents to come over to their place for dinner tonight. The menu was already all planned out. She was convinced it would be a fun reunion for them all now that Ana was back and the clinic was running smoothly. He hadn't quite managed to ask Ana to attend yet and time was running out. Maybe he should stop getting all up in his head about everything and just ask her, he thought. Their families were friends, after all, and what had happened between them shouldn't get in the way of that.

# CHAPTER TEN

THE FLUORESCENT LIGHTS buzzed overhead as Gabriel ushered his mother Rosa, whom Ana had always called Mama Romero like everyone else, onto the examination table.

'Mama, what's happening?' he enquired in his most concerned tone, and Ana's heart flapped in her chest at the panic in his eyes. He probably hadn't expected his own mother to show up unannounced at the clinic—she had only called a few minutes ago when Gabriel had been seeing to Mr Acosta regarding the heart medication she'd prescribed for him.

'Thankfully you had a free appointment, and your father told me not to wait any longer,' the petite woman told him, clutching at her abdomen near her navel, the source of her discomfort.

'Your hernia again?' Ana heard him say.

'You did the right thing, Mama Romero, coming straight here,' Ana said reassuringly. Rosa's cheeks were flushed and her greying hair was damp from the rain outside.

As Gabriel offered her his arm for support, Ana felt a pang of guilt for being so cold with him lately, mostly out of self-preservation. She already regretted that snarky comment earlier today about romantic gestures going wrong. They had both made a mistake, blurring the lines of their friendship.

Only, she had been thinking about it ever since, letting his touch invade her dreams, craving more, and then firmly telling herself she shouldn't. The fact that he'd apparently been too busy even to talk to her about it any further had hit her harder than it should have, and she'd erected a wall, she supposed, as she'd always done whenever something threatened her equilibrium. He was back to being at arm's length, where nothing he said or did could affect her from ploughing forward as she always did.

Well, that had been her plan, anyway. It wasn't exactly working. And now here was his mother Rosa, in her own clinic, needing both of them.

'I had to leave Javi with your dad as he just got home from school…'

'Don't worry, he'll be OK,' Gabriel reassured her, getting her a cold glass of water from the tap and arranging a cushion behind her.

Rosa sighed, her voice laced with worry as Ana examined her, pressing gently on the skin around her belly and navel while Gabriel pressed a cold towel to her clammy head. 'The pain just started up again a few days ago, but it's getting worse. I was hoping it would go away on its own, but…'

Ana nodded empathetically as Gabriel gently took a blood sample and conducted a vitals examination. She supposed it must be tough, treating his mother like a patient all of a sudden. Her heart went out to him as she assisted, admiring his expertise and patient bedside manner, and how he managed to put his emotions aside, knowing his mother was sick and in pain. Her gaze lingered on his handsome face a moment longer than necessary, till he caught her and she had to look away again, annoyed with herself all over again.

'Will I need surgery?' Rosa asked them now, eyes wide.

Ana leaned in, keeping her voice soft and reassuring. 'We'll see about that. First I'll order some imaging tests and we'll have to see what the blood samples show.'

Gabriel chimed in, concern evident in his eyes. 'Have you experienced any other symptoms, Mama, like nausea?'

As Mama Romero described some occasional nausea, and Ana explained what she could do to curb it in future, Gabriel met her eyes again briefly, an unspoken understanding passing between them. They had both been making things awkward all week, but they were still irrefutably a team when it came to what really mattered.

They discussed Rosa's symptoms and, as they spoke, Ana couldn't help feeling more moved than she wanted to be by the love and respect the Romeros had for each other. Gabriel's family had always been so wonderful and warm; no wonder he had always wanted to base his life here amongst their love and support. Her own parents loved her too, of course, but it had always been easier to relate to Gabriel's, who had never smothered her the way hers had.

Ana performed the ultrasound, taking care not to apply too much extra pressure. Gabriel's eyes never left his mother, and she felt a pang of remorse suddenly at how she still shut her own mother out sometimes whenever she became overly protective and concerned. Ana had never enjoyed the close connection to her parents that Gabriel had forged with his—her fierce independence had seen to that. Their overbearing tendency to wrap her up in cotton wool had done nothing but make her want to run away, but they were all older now, and wiser. Maybe she should make more of an effort to show her parents that what they'd done for her had been appreciated, she thought…for the most part. Look where she was now!

'Thank you, Ana,' Rosa was saying now, straightening out her clothes as Ana helped her sit up on the exam table. 'Look at you, both like this, making such a great team. It's so nice to see. And you've really made this place your own, Ana, I do love all the bright colours.'

'Thank you, Rosa.'

'Everyone loves the colours,' Gabriel said, looking directly at her. 'They're just so… Ana.'

Ana avoided his eyes once more as a vision of her clothing on his bedroom floor swept into her mind. How graceful he had made her feel the whole time, almost as if she had no disability at all. In fact, she'd felt perfect. He had treated her so wonderfully.

*Stop it, brain!*

Dutifully she wheeled the bulky ultrasound machine away again. The hernia had grown a little larger, according to her records, but all they could do at the moment was refer Rosa to a specialist and send her through to Sandrine to discuss how to manage and alleviate her discomfort with some small changes to her lifestyle.

'Did you decide on a time for tonight?' Rosa said to Gabriel as she straightened her light-pink cardigan. 'I mean, we can eat whenever you both like. But let me know when you think you'll arrive, so I can tell Juan and Martina.'

Ana frowned with her back to them. Juan and Martina, her parents? She spun round to find Gabriel was pulling a face, as if he'd been busted.

'He didn't ask you yet, did he?' Rosa said with a harried sigh at Gabriel.

'To dinner, tonight? No, Rosa, he didn't,' Ana responded as he helped his mother towards the door a little more hurriedly than he should have. Her words had come out snippier than she'd intended them to, but why hadn't he asked her yet?

'I guess I didn't get round to it,' he explained with an insouciant shrug. 'We've both been so busy.'

Ana ordered her face not to display how utterly irked she was now. Maybe he didn't want to have dinner with them all and had been planning to wriggle out of it. Well, so much for that plan. Mama Romero had gone and dropped him in it—ha! Ana realised she was scowling at him now, and Gabriel was scowling back.

Rosa shook her head, lips pursed. 'You two! Always too busy,' she scolded them softly. 'Well, I think *both* of you deserve a night off with your families. You will come, it's an order.'

'I'd love to, thank you, Mama Romero,' Ana told her, picturing their old house and kitchen suddenly. The sink was always warm from the sun streaming in through the window. She remembered the moment she hadn't been able to reach the sink any more, when Gabriel had first brought her into his home in the wheelchair. There had been some happy times spent there as children, though, she and Gabriel running around the kitchen, getting in the way under the guise of helping to make dinner. There'd always been the warm, yeasty smell of baking bread, or the cinnamon scent of dark chocolate melting on cakes beside the stove. His grandmother would sing along to her favourite tunes, high-pitched and off-key. Baking on a Sunday was a weekly ritual at the Romeros'. Fridays were usually for family sit-downs.

'That's settled, then,' Rosa said brightly, smoothing down her dress one last time. 'We'll see you both at seven o'clock sharp at our house.' With that, she dropped a kiss on Gabriel's cheek and glanced back at them over her shoulder as she made her way back to reception. Rosa was the sweetest, Ana thought, watching her stop to admire the marigolds on the desk one more time. She'd always been so encouraging and kind, but she'd also always hinted that she'd love to see the two of them together some day, as more than friends. If only she knew…

No. She would never know, Ana decided. It would just make things even more awkward.

'So, were you going to invite me yourself?' she said to Gabriel when they were alone, unable to keep the shadow of a smile from her face now.

Gabriel dropped to the swivel chair and tapped a pen on the desk, unbuttoning his coat at the top, as if he needed more air than the room could offer. Outside the rain was still pattering at the windows.

'Of course I was,' he said, meeting her gaze head on. 'OK, so maybe I waited because I wasn't sure you'd say yes.'

'Why wouldn't I say yes?' She tapped her nails on her knee, matching the rhythm of his pen, and refused to drop his gaze. It felt like a challenge.

'You know why, Ana.'

She feigned nonchalance. 'We said it wouldn't be weird between us.'

'Except it already is. You know it is.'

She screwed up her nose disparagingly. For a moment she almost caved in, almost moved closer and asked him outright if being friends was really such a good idea, and did he even remember how good the sex had been and how that was probably because they'd been friends first?

But then his phone rang, and he cringed, which meant it was Ines again.

'I should get this,' he said. She watched him walk to the window to talk and sighed to herself, pretending to check the schedule. Now she remembered exactly why it was pointless reminding him how good it had been between them. It wouldn't work, going forward, never. He had no time for her. His priority would always be Javi, as it should be. And hers was the clinic, as it should be. They were *both* too busy. Already the door was opening again, and Maria was sending in another patient.

The timing was always wrong for them, and it probably always would be. And now, not only did she have to find the strength to accept that, but she had to endure a whole dinner with both sets of parents present. How had her life suddenly got so complicated and confusing?

The house was just as she remembered it as she came to a stop outside and psyched herself up to go in. Just being here was bringing it all back. Gabriel's childhood home was a pale pink brick house of two levels, with a low roof of whitewashed slate and a funny-looking satellite array on top that his dad had erected some time in the early nineties for TV and radio and had left there even as more modern methods had been introduced. The antennae up there still turned in the wind sometimes, but surprisingly it had never fallen off.

'He'll never get rid of it. I've offered to remove it,' came a familiar voice behind her.

Gabriel stopped beside her chair and looked up at the roof.

'Remember when you carried me up there to watch the shooting stars?' she said, surprised at the way her pulse had quickened instantly the second she'd heard his voice.

'We're lucky nothing happened.' He grinned, and the way he looked at her made her stomach turn with a series of sparks that travelled up her arms. He meant it was lucky they hadn't fallen off the roof or something, but now she remembered how she had kind of wanted something to happen with him, back when they'd been teenagers, way before he'd met Ines.

'I'll help you up the steps,' he said as she wheeled her chair ahead of him, where he couldn't see her cheeks blush. The door was already swinging open, and Rosa was there, arms outstretched. Her parents would be here any minute. She had to let Gabriel help her inside, there was no other way.

First he lifted her gently from her chair, with the utmost care and attention. He carried her up the steps and held her in the doorway while his father—a tall, broad-shouldered man with a deep voice and friendly eyes like Gabriel's—brought her wheelchair past them, and she couldn't help filling her lungs with the scent of him. It was the musky cinnamon smell she had always associated with Gabriel.

It reminded her of a time when they'd been sixteen, and a group of friends had gone to Cerro Tres Picos for a weekend to camp in the forest. Her parents would never have let her go with them unless Gabriel had convinced them he'd take care of her. And he had. He had carried her then, too, from the car to the campsite, where they'd sat out all night under the stars, and then from her chair to the tent, and she'd trusted him implicitly. He was the only guy she'd ever trusted to treat her so carefully, she thought with a pang.

Soon she was nestled in a pile of cushions, being handed a glass of wine. Inside the house was cosy despite its cool, tiled floors. The familiar kitchen just off the open lounge was still the same with yellow walls, peach-coloured floors and little tiles painted with pictures of tropical birds. The scent of empanadas filled the air.

She drew a deep breath and forced her face into a neutral expression as Gabriel sat close beside her. His eyes burned into her cheek every time she spoke or answered one of his father's questions. Rosa, thankfully feeling a lot better now, bustled away in the kitchen, humming to herself, clinking utensils, plates and glasses and occasionally calling out to his father for something she couldn't reach in the pantry. Ana had always loved this happy home. She was just starting to feel comfortable, regaling them with a story about a particularly funny encounter with a neighbour in Bariloche, when the doorbell rang.

In a flurry of greetings, Ana's parents were ushered into the room. Her father looked as smart as usual in his ironed cream chinos, a crisp shirt and a brown leather belt he only wore for special occasions. Her mother had on her most elegant jeans, an embroidered blouse Ana had brought her back from Peru after a conference in Cusco a few years ago, and heeled sandals. They were very fashionable, and fashionably late, as usual. Ana let her mother kiss her cheeks, enduring it when she then wiped a lipstick smear from one and frowned at her choice of head scarf. She'd gone for a bright-blue one this evening, because Gabriel had commented on how much he'd liked it during the week, she realised now.

'It's so lovely to see you, Gabriel, and even nicer to see both of you together again. I've been hearing you're the angel of the clinic, Gabe.' Her mother cooed at him. Gabriel shot Ana a sideways smirk behind his hand as he too endured a kiss to his cheek, whilst Ana continued wiping the lipstick from hers. 'Is it gone?' she whispered.

'It's all gone,' he assured her with a wink.

'Thanks.' Ana felt her cheeks flame. There was nothing worse than feeling reduced to a useless child again by her mother, especially in front of him.

'Let's eat!' Rosa enthused.

Right away, her father sprang into action, wanting to assist Ana with getting back into her wheelchair, as he'd always done. He was nimble for a man in his mid-sixties, but Gabriel was faster. 'I'll help her,' he insisted, holding out a hand to her. 'If Ana's OK with that.'

'Of course.' She smiled gratefully as he lifted her again with ease and helped her back into her chair. Despite the fact he'd left most of her mother's lipstick on his own cheek, she couldn't deny he was an angel at the clinic—a devilishly handsome one. Again she breathed his homely scent and let her arms loop around his shoulders, wishing the act could take longer than thirty seconds. This was the closest she had let herself get to him all week and she'd missed it. Of course, this was all for their parents' benefit, though, so they wouldn't pick up that anything was wrong.

Still, it was hard to miss the look Rosa and her mother gave them as Gabriel helped her gently back into her chair. They sat at the table before the feast that Rosa had prepared: empanadas filled with sautéed beef and vegetables; barbecued short ribs; a hearty, yellow-orange *locro* stew made with white hominy corn; and roasted sweet potatoes topped with criolla sauce, all served on colourful earthenware plates that Rosa had collected over the years from markets all over Argentina.

It became very obvious, suddenly, that their parents had all been speculating about them behind their backs. And the point of the dinner was probably not just to eat all this wonderful food together… Talk about awkward! As much as they might want her to give them something to talk about, she and Gabriel would never be more than friends, and she was starting to think they both knew it. Ana suddenly couldn't wait to get out of there.

# CHAPTER ELEVEN

GABRIEL TOOK THE last mouthful of his barbecued short ribs smothered in chimichurri sauce and caught Ana's mother looking between them with interest. She hadn't stopped with these questioning looks for the last hour and a half. While he and Ana were certainly giving off no hint of what had happened between them, he could tell they were all on the edge of their seats, waiting to hear that they were more than friends and colleagues.

'So, Gabriel, any new love in your life lately?' The question somehow still caught him off-guard. Ana's mother was looking at him intently. 'I haven't seen Javi in a while; is he still living at Ines's place?'

OK, so she'd decided just to come out with all the personal questions at once. He put his fork down and sat back in his chair but, before he could speak, Ana cut in. 'Mama, you don't have to put Gabriel on the spot, you know. There is such a thing as keeping your business private.'

Her mother pretended to pout. 'I was only asking, *cariño*. We're all family here, are we not?'

Ana's father seemed to be trying his best not to laugh at the situation. Gabriel couldn't tell if it was out of nerves or amusement, but his own parents had their mouths hidden by their wine glasses.

'Everything is fine, thank you, Mrs Mendez. Yes, Javi is with Ines a lot. And, well, I don't have much time for romance at the moment.'

Even as he said it, he could feel the air thicken as Ana tensed beside him. He cleared his throat, reached for the wine, filling their glasses, and switched the conversation to the weather, not wanting to cause any more trouble for Ana than he already had. However, before he could even put the cork back into the bottle, Ana's father cut in with a question of his own.

'Ana, are *you* all right? Is there anything we can do to help? You seem tense. Your mother and I were wondering if you need us to come help clean, or cook, or anything while you're at the clinic. We'd be happy to be more involved, now you're back and so busy.'

His offer was gentle and more than kind, as far as Gabriel was concerned, but Ana sat up even straighter in her chair and glared at them both, her eyes flashing with anger and frustration. 'No,' she answered gruffly. 'I don't need your help, thank you. I *don't* need anything. How many more times do I—?'

'What she means,' Gabriel cut in quickly, reaching out and placing a hand on her arm before she all but exploded, 'Is that she's perfectly capable of managing all that. Well, she can't cook, obviously. She over-cooks every vegetable to the point of mush, always has, but she has the right restaurants on speed dial, right, Ana?'

Ana chewed her lip, tapping her nails on the table while their parents all shuffled awkwardly. She had inherited her mother's eyebrows, which were thick and black, and they arched to his favourite blue head scarf the second he nudged her under the table.

'I do—all of the right restaurants—they know me,' she confirmed quickly, throwing him a sideways look that wasn't quite a smile, but wasn't a simmering volcano of a glare either. 'Sorry, Mama, Papa; I'm just…tired.'

'That's OK, *mija*,' Gabriel's mother soothed, starting to gather up empty plates. 'It's important work you do, both of you.'

Gabriel smiled reassuringly at Ana's parents, trying to project a calm confidence, and changed the subject to Javi's dog, Savio, and the upcoming 'pawrents' day' in a few days' time at Parca 3 de Febrero, near Javi's school. He told them about the smart terrier mix Pedro had rescued, who basically stuck to Javi's side wherever he was, and the tricks he and Javi had been teaching him. Ana stayed quiet and withdrawn.

He knew she was counting down the minutes until she could leave. Her parents had always wound her up, simply by loving her and caring about her. But he had to put himself in her shoes. She was doing more than fine on her own. She really didn't need them worrying so much about her any more. It must have felt suffocating, and only made her want to separate herself more out of defiance. Did she even need *him*? he thought, realising he was nervously turning his silver bracelet around on his wrist, and that she was watching. The thought that she might not need him any more than she needed her parents interfering in her life or standing up for her didn't sit right. OK, so the clinic was different—she needed him there—but was that enough?

Gabriel's jaw clenched and a familiar, prickling heat

rose up his neck, just imagining the day she might find someone else to care for her. Someone less complicated than him, with more to offer her than he ever could. He already knew he'd have issues with that person. Deep down in his bones, there would always be a primal impulse to take care of Ana.

On the way home they took a detour. Gabriel walked slowly besides Ana's wheelchair along the winding paths of the cemetery, smiling a little at how tired she looked as she rested her head back against the chair and came to a stop at her grandfather's grave.

'Thanks for walking me home,' she said on a sigh.

'I wanted to.' He'd been here lots of times to lay flowers on her behalf while she'd been away—not that she knew—but he hadn't been here with her in years. It was oddly peaceful in the moonlight—not spooky or eerie in the slightest—and somehow it calmed his racing thoughts from earlier.

A few streetlights dotted the grounds and illuminated their path as they said their respects and moved on. Ana didn't say much but, when Gabriel finally stopped at one of the larger monuments to study the inscription on a couple's gravestone, she spoke softly.

'Imagine loving someone so much that you're actually buried next to them when you die.'

He nodded slowly, raising his eyebrows at her, and said nothing. *Imagine.*

'Thank you for this evening,' she said now, with more than a hint of sadness in her voice. She paused for a moment, adjusting the tie on her headscarf, and added, 'And for defusing that situation with my parents. I'm not so good at dealing with…all that.'

Gabriel nodded gently again and turned to face her, dropping to his knees. 'They love you, you know.'

'I know,' she said, studying his eyes. He was unsure what else to say in the moment, but looking at her now, wanting to sweep her up in his arms again but knowing he shouldn't, was killing him.

'Gabriel…' she started, her eyes weary but also determined, as if she was trying to make a decision that might have far-reaching consequences if she chose wrongly. But he was already leaning in, already cupping her face, and she was responding. He felt an explosion of emotion as his lips met hers, a deep warmth that seemed to travel right through him, radiating from his legs, arms and hands to his heart, till all he could feel was her. She was the total opposite of every other woman he'd been with, and her disability had nothing to do with it, he realised with a groan against her lips. She had a rebellious streak, and an independence that only he seemed to be able to break through to the soft, vulnerable woman inside.

Ana's hands moved up to wrap round the back of his neck as he deepened the kiss and Gabriel's heart raced in his chest as his breathing grew shallow with desire. She made him feel alive and *needed.* Even when her indefatigable ambition and drive for success blinded her to what really mattered, he saw how much she needed him emotionally, more than physically. Ines hadn't needed him at all. In fact, they'd had nothing in common besides one night that had given them both the greatest gift they'd never asked for.

'I like kissing you way too much,' he murmured against

her mouth as the trees whispered overhead. This sense of being needed was something he hadn't felt for a long time. Now that Pedro was on the scene, filling his shoes, even Javi didn't seem to need him as much any more.

*Nope, don't think about that now.*

He felt her mouth part against his again and it made him forget all his insecurities. He focused only on the feel of her skin, soft yet firm beneath his fingers, and the way her lips moved so perfectly with his, just picking up where they'd left off.

Ana sighed against his mouth as he pulled away to look into her eyes. They were heavy with emotion now, but she smiled softly and nodded towards the exit. 'Walk me back?'

That kiss, Ana thought as they entered her apartment. Well, so much for trying to be friends. It had felt as natural as breathing to kiss him back.

It was dark inside. Flicking on the lights, she spotted some dishes still piled in the sink ahead of her in the kitchen. Thinking better of it, she flicked them off again, leaving on just one that lit a less embarrassing pathway up the stairs. That kiss had rendered her powerless to resist him and, even if she had to be brazen about it, or regretted it afterwards, she wasn't just going to stop there.

'Let me,' he said now, as if reading her mind. He motioned to the stairs, then swept her up in his arms again, heavily nudging the front door closed behind him with his foot in a dramatic statement of his intentions.

A chair lift had been installed to help with this part, but why let technicalities get in the way of romance? Suppressing a giggle, she let Gabriel carry her; he was good at it by now, and she enjoyed the way he swept her up with less care this time, letting passion override the need to treat her carefully.

When he lowered her onto the bed this time, she didn't even care about what she might look like, free from her chair and unable to move very much below her waist. It didn't mean she couldn't feel. Contrary to what a lot of people thought, she could still feel everything a man might do to her, and as her nervous giggles dissipated she found she was tingling in places that she'd been longing to feel tingly in since their last encounter. Oh…gosh.

'Oh, Gabe…'

Ana closed her eyes and melted into him, giving in to all the feelings flooding through her as Gabriel explored every inch of her body with his hands and tongue, lips and teeth. He was more than happy to help her. He seemed to move intuitively after just a few minutes, as if he'd been paying close attention before, memorising what made her most comfortable, which positions meant they could go further and deeper.

Kissing him, making love to him in her bed, was everything she'd been replaying in her head since they'd made love the first time, and more. How could she even have tried to forget the way he'd made her feel—as if everything else just melted away?

'You feel so good,' he mumbled against her into her hair, pressing deeper. The deeper he went, the more she wanted.

She was starting to need him. It had been beyond sexy, the way he'd been with her parents—softly reminding them what they should already know about her, without the need for an altercation. His gentle, calming energy and easy-going nature was a balm to her stressful reality, so to hell with feeling insecure or needy. To hell with pushing him away.

Soon, they were both breathless with exhaustion, falling apart with stars in their eyes, letting out a laugh in awe as they lay side by side on their backs.

'We should probably talk about this,' he said after a moment, lightly tracing the curve of her waist with one hand while his other arm lay protectively across her body. He seemed to take a breath before speaking and Ana couldn't help but wonder if he felt the same way that she did—as if they were on the edge of something beautiful and terrifying at the same time.

'I don't want to,' she told him quickly, not wanting to break the spell.

'Really?'

'Really. We know all the reasons this shouldn't work, Gabriel…'

'But it does work,' he said under his breath.

She sighed softly, nodding a silent acknowledgement.

There were no words that would help this thing make any more or less sense. They had something incredible that seemed to run deeper the more she tried to deny it. So maybe it was time just to stop denying it, she decided.

# CHAPTER TWELVE

ANA PAUSED IN the clinic's doorway. The rain was picking up, not that it could dampen her mood in the slightest. No sooner had she wheeled her chair outside for a short lunch break than someone took her umbrella clean from her hands.

'A lady should never have to hold her own umbrella,' Gabriel said, appearing from nowhere and flipping it open over her head. Laughing, and feeling the familiar thrill of anticipation as he took her other hand, Ana followed his lead down the street and around the corner into the park, while he sheltered her from the rain all the way.

The last few days had started to blur for Ana. While Gabriel had started working with Bruno again this week, he'd still managed to put in a couple of shifts at the clinic as well. The droplets picked up in intensity, smacking hard at the ground and shaking the leaves in the trees all around them, but Gabriel didn't seem fazed, and at this point Ana knew she'd go anywhere with him. Well, within reason—she had a line-up of patients to see in less than thirty minutes, and so did he.

'You're early for your shift,' she said now, pulling out a bag of the tiny, delicious home-made empanadas Rosa had brought with her to her check-up this morning and offering him one.

'I was hoping to catch you at lunch,' he said, taking a bite and motioning her further into the park, where they stopped under her favourite tree, watching the rain.

'What is it?' she asked, suddenly suspicious. Things had been going so well lately, both with him and with work, and she had barely given another thought to the fact that they'd put their friendship on the line to pursue this. Was he having doubts now? The thought made her heart start to thump.

'Javi wants to know if you'll come to the 'pawrents' day' thing at the park,' he said, looking at her sideways. Between bites of his snack, he explained how Javi really wanted her to demonstrate the trick they'd been practising. Savio had learned to leap onto her lap in the wheelchair on command, as well as how to retrieve items from the fridge and bring them to her. Ana was pretty proud of her part in all this over the last few days, and spending more time with Javi as well as Gabriel and the dog had started to feel like a lot of fun. She'd never been part of a unit like this before.

'It won't be the same if you don't come,' he said.

'No pressure, then.' She smiled, while her heart continued its thudding, this time with joy and disbelief that, somehow, all of this was happening to her.

'I know it's happening when the clinic is open, but Ebony can cover now.'

Ebony was the part-time locum Ana had finally found who was able to cover whenever Gabriel's shifts with Bruno clashed with the clinic's.

'How do you know she can cover for us?'

'I already asked her.' Spinning her chair round so she was facing him, he bent to kiss her under the umbrella. Ana couldn't help the burst of laughter erupting from her throat as she tousled his hair, and the growing intensity of his kiss brought a soft moan to her throat. Soon her lunch was forgotten and they were feasting on each other in the rain.

It was so hot, kissing in the rain. So was the way she completely forgot where they were whenever she was with him, as if she were a teenager again. Wherever they were, her whole body felt filled with a sense of longing, but also total security, the likes of which she'd never asked for and hadn't known she'd needed. But how nice it was that he provided it anyway.

Come to think of it, she thought now, running her hand up and down his shoulder, admiring the feel of his impressive muscles, Gabriel was more emotionally available than anyone she'd ever dated. Yes, sometimes he still got waylaid by Ines and her demands, but it was nothing they hadn't been able to handle up to now.

'I'll come,' she told him quietly, breaking away for a second and gazing up at him as he stood tall.

He feigned shock. 'Already?'

'To the pawrents' day with you and Javi!' Ana pretended to slap him but he dodged her and took the umbrella with him, making her call out, laughing. Quickly he resumed his protective position over her and kissed her again, even more passionately than the last time. They were only forced to break apart when a lump of bread landed at Gabriel's feet. They stared at a cheeky bird, who pecked at the ground around her chair as if she was entirely in its way, and they turned to find a grumpy-looking old woman in a long red raincoat staring at them, shaking her head under a giant umbrella.

Quickly the woman deposited the rest of the bread on the ground and a flock of pigeons descended from the sky, momentarily blocking her from their view.

'Let's go!' Ana cried, still giggling as she sped back the way they'd come before the woman could chastise them again. Gabriel made pace with the umbrella close behind her.

'Why are you so wet?' Maria asked when they pushed their way back into the clinic.

'It's raining, Maria, that's what happens,' Gabriel quipped, winking at her as he pulled his white coat on and threw Ana hers.

Maria took her arm as she went to roll past and leaned down to her. 'Is everything OK?'

Ana's eyes were still on Gabriel's firm backside as he disappeared into the consultation room, but she drew them away quickly. 'Mm-hmm,' she mumbled. 'Why?'

Maria just frowned, as if deciphering all the things Ana's flaming cheeks must've been hinting at. 'Well, your mother was just in here. She said she's worried about you…you haven't been answering her calls.'

'Oh. Well… I had my phone on silent for lunch,' Ana replied heavily, yanking her phone from her pocket. Sure enough, there they were: six missed calls from her mother. Her heart sank on the spot. Why did she always feel like an incapable child the second one of her parents did this to her? Surely one call was enough, unless…unless something bad had really happened.

Feeling guilty, she called her mother back, following

Gabriel into the consultation room. His eyes never left her face as she spoke, and she was quite sure the mounting shame she felt was evident.

'She wants to know if she can cook for me tonight, and you and Javi too. All of us,' she explained when she hung up.

Gabriel perched on the desk, smirking.

'What?'

'I told you—they just love you. You're always so defensive.'

'Can you blame me?' She huffed, although he was right, she supposed. 'It's just, every time they call, I assume they're going to offer to help me do something I can do perfectly well by myself.'

'I know. We all know how much you're capable of doing,' he said, his voice turning low and gruff and ten times sexier as he scooped her out of her chair and held her close against his chest, running his thumb along her lip. 'It's not like *I* can forget *exactly* what you're capable of doing.'

'Very funny,' she said, clutching his shoulders and marvelling at how her raised hackles seemed to calm instantly under his kisses. 'So, can you come?'

'What, now?' he teased, nibbling her ear.

She thwacked his shoulder. 'Stop it!'

'Can't. You're too sexy.'

Sighing, she ran her tongue along his lower lip, forgetting where she was again until…a knock on the door.

Gabriel swiftly placed her back into her chair and almost flew to the other end of the room, smoothing out his coat. He was pretending to study a file when there in the doorway, alongside Maria's, was a face she recognised. Ana felt her eyes bulge cartoon-style at the long red raincoat, before quickly regaining her composure. The elderly woman from the park… Of *course* it would be that particular woman who had just seen them kissing in the rain!

Gabriel adjusted his coat again in an effort to resume normality as Ana ushered their patient to the table, introducing herself. Ana's face was flushed, her lips slightly swollen. It was obvious they hadn't really stopped kissing till just now. He almost wanted to laugh, but he knew it wasn't particularly funny. The woman must think them both entirely unprofessional.

'You have pain in the stomach area? When did it start?'

Ana was examining her now, trying not to meet his eyes, although as she spoke the woman, whose name was Edith, kept flashing her cynical gaze between them, as if she really didn't trust them.

Ana cleared her throat and told them both she suspected it could be Edith's gallbladder.

'We need to do some tests to confirm my suspicions,' she said in her usual gentle but authoritative tone. Gabriel recognised this tone as a sign that she was struggling internally to feel the way she wanted everyone to believe she felt, when in truth she felt the exact opposite. Her mother had got to her, even without offering to do anything besides cook dinner, and now this. Maybe he shouldn't be kissing her in the clinic. As if he could help himself!

'First we'll do a physical examination, then Ana will run an ultrasound of your abdomen,' he said, grabbing his pen light and moving into position, brushing Ana's sleeve accidentally with his as he shone it into Edith's eyes.

'No sign of jaundice, no other signs of infection,' he said next, realising Ana had pulled away a little too fast and wheeled to the other side of the table where they couldn't touch, even if they tried. 'We'll also want to take a blood sample to check for certain enzymes. Anything that may suggest inflammation or blockages, Edith.'

Edith simply nodded. With her raincoat now dripping from a nearby chair, she was turning something that was tucked just behind the collar of her blouse, studying each of them as though they were detailed paintings on a gallery wall. He stood taller under her scrutiny, but Ana was growing increasingly flustered and trying not to show it.

As reassuringly as he could, Gabriel continued his explanation as he inserted an IV line into Edith's arm and then watched as Ana injected a mild sedative into it. 'This will make you a lot more comfortable during the tests,' he told her, noticing Ana's hands were slightly shaking.

'Doctor,' he said quickly. 'Would you mind getting Edith some water? She needs to stay hydrated.'

Ana looked at him gratefully and rolled her chair to the sink. The woman seemed oblivious to the tube in her arm. Her gaze stayed fixed on Ana the whole time, before she interrupted Gabriel mid-speech and asked, 'Are you two married?'

Gabriel bit back a laugh. Then he saw what Edith was fiddling with behind her blouse collar. Around her neck a golden chain glinted importantly under the clinic lights. Fixed to that, currently getting his bare torso rubbed in devout adoration, was a pendant of Jesus.

'We're not married…yet…but we're planning on it,'

he said quickly, forcing a smile to his face as Ana spun round in surprise, almost spilling the water. Eyebrows raised, he nodded subtly towards the pendant. Luckily Ana caught on.

'Forgive us for what you saw earlier, in the park,' she muttered.

'We're just deeply in love,' Gabriel followed, unable to stop the way his heart felt as if it was pumping an extra pint of blood around his body, lighting up his nerve-endings as he said it.

It was kind of strange, saying it out loud. He had never said it till now. He wasn't completely sure if he even felt it. He was still getting his head around the change in their relationship—enjoying it, loving the invites that were now coming in for both himself, Ana and Javi, even though Ines would of course have a say about dinner tonight at the Mendezes' place, seeing as it wasn't technically supposed to be his night with Javi.

For the most part he was still breathing it all in, loving the way Ana's mere touch sent electricity running through his veins. Of course what he felt was love. What else could it be? It had a wonderful ring to it, too. He should say it more often, say exactly what he felt. Life was short and the passion he felt even being in the same room as Ana was unprecedented. He would have shouted from the rooftops if he could have, from that stupid antenna his dad wouldn't take down, how proud he was to be with a woman like…

*Oh. Hell.*

Ana and Edith were both staring at him.

He'd gone off inside his own head again.

'I'll wait outside, doctor,' he told her quickly, leaving

the room. Minutes later, after Edith was gone, he stepped back in to apologise.

'That wasn't ideal…' he started, but Ana drew a deep breath. There was no way to interpret her expression at all. It seemed to shut down and turn cold right in front of him. Then, to his horror, she gathered her clipboard abruptly, excused herself and left the room.

# CHAPTER THIRTEEN

To Gabriel's surprise, Ines happily agreed to let him have Javi for the evening. She even drove him to his place herself, though left quickly, without even exiting the car.

'I need him back by nine p.m.!'

'OK.' Gabriel watched her go, scratching his head. Something wasn't right with her, and it hadn't been quite right for a while, but he couldn't put his finger on it. She'd given him Javi's usual bedtime curfew but she hadn't asked much about their plans for tonight, nor given him an extra set of socks for Javi, as usual.

'Are we going to Ana's?' Javi said now, as he led him down the street under the lamps.

'We're having dinner at Ana's parents',' he explained, trying to ignore another bout of dread that had been over-shadowing his mood ever since he'd opened his big mouth in front of Edith this afternoon about being in love with Ana. She had been distant with him ever since. Whether he was still welcome for dinner or not in her eyes wasn't clear, but her mother had asked him personally in a text message, and he could hardly say no to Mrs Mendez. Besides he'd already cleared it with Ines.

The rain had dried up now, and they sat out on the deck, candles and fairy lights flickering across the big courtyard the Mendezes shared with their neighbours. He hadn't been aware till now that his parents had been invited too, but soon the Romeros were joining the rest of them around the table. One big, happy family, he thought in a moment of contentment, even though things were still somewhat strained between himself and Ana.

'Are we OK?' he asked her quietly, catching her arm as she went to pour him sweet, cold tea from a pitcher. 'You've been very careful not to talk to me since I said… that.'

She paused in her chair, and that cool look claimed her eyes again. '*That* what—that we're *deeply in love*?'

Gabriel's next words dried up in his throat. He got the distinct impression suddenly that he shouldn't have said it, even to appease an old woman's religious views.

'She wasn't happy that she caught us kissing in public when we're not married,' he explained in a hush, as if she didn't already know why he'd done it.

'I know that. That's not the point,' she snapped. 'We shouldn't have been so obvious at the clinic, Gabriel. We shouldn't be doing anything at all besides work! I've worked so hard for this opportunity and I need to be taken seriously.'

Her voice caught on the last few words and Gabriel took her hand.

'Ana. You know I wouldn't do anything that purposefully threatens your integrity, or anything you've worked for. You *know* that.'

'Well, you already did,' she said.

He felt himself stiffen. 'We both did.'

'Fair enough. But it has to stop now.'

'What do you mean, "stop"?' Gabriel clamped his

mouth shut. He could feel their mothers' eyes on them now and he retracted his hand, realising his passion had completely consumed him yet again. He was about to demand she meet him out front so they could talk alone, but Javi let out a squeal from where Ana's father was teaching him to spear sausages over at the grill. 'Look, Papa!'

When he turned back, his mother had taken Ana hostage with another conversation at the end of the table. Their intermittent piercing glances burned into his cheeks as they talked.

Annoyed, he scowled into his drink.

OK, so she was worried about looking unprofessional—understood. She had indeed worked very hard for the clinic, to get where she was, and she already had a thing about needing to prove herself. Maybe he should have been more careful in what he'd said to Edith. But what was he supposed to have done under the circumstances? They couldn't just stop this now, could they?

The smell of charred meat blended with the aromas of herbs and spices in the balmy air as Ana's father, along with Javi, prepared the cuts of beef for their dinner. His nose twitched at the paprika, oregano, garlic and parsley as it released its aromas on the open flame, the fat sizzling, popping and shooting even more tantalising odours into the night.

Usually he would have been up and dancing with his mother or Ana's mother by now. But now he could only sit and watch Ana doing her best to avoid him in her own parents' courtyard—talk about awkward. He'd probably scared her off, he thought in dismay, coming on too strong, getting over-excited about where this was going.

Idiot! Trust him to get completely carried away with a romance when he should be focusing on his son.

Ines had been pretty relaxed about him having Javi tonight, but he was still in her bad books for… He couldn't remember what for now; there always seemed to be something. Oh yes, apparently the other day Javi had gone home asking Ines if he could have a Ouija board to contact the dead spirits in the cemetery. He supposed that was kind of *his* fault. Javi had overheard Ana and him laughing about how they'd tried it once, never mind that they'd failed to pick up any messages at all. And, now that he finally had Javi on a rare week night, without Ines firing texts at him every second, he was still getting distracted by a woman!

Eyeing Ana from across the courtyard, Gabriel sobered as he pondered their situation. Perhaps he'd pushed too hard, too fast with her. He should probably back off. Standing up, he crossed to the grill and spent the rest of the night helping Ana's father show Javi how to man an asado while, as if reading his mind, Ana disappeared to the kitchen with their mothers to help prepare salads, roasted vegetables and sauces.

Gabriel took a break to chase fireflies with Javi. The little bugs always came out at dusk, and Javi was obsessed with them. Every now and then, he'd catch Ana watching them through the window, their eyes would meet and his head would reel all over again.

There was something between them that could not be ignored—something electric and undeniable every time they were in close proximity. From their open conversations about careers and obligations one minute, to passionate whispers about their dreams and desires lying next to each other in one of their beds the next—every moment they spent together felt as if it was charged with an energy all its own. But, right now, she wouldn't come outside until Javi literally ran over and urged her to come by holding her hands.

'Ana, Ana, come see what we caught.'

Her wheelchair got stuck on a patch of weeds for a few seconds on her way over. Gabriel saw her father put down the asado utensil he was holding and start to head towards his struggling daughter. The look on Ana's face was a warning, but her father hadn't noticed.

Quickly Gabriel held up a hand to stop him. 'Don't,' he mouthed, stopping him in his tracks. All the man saw was his beloved daughter in trouble, and as a father himself Gabriel understood that much, but the last thing Ana needed was everyone rushing to help her all the time. She noticed his little warning gesture, just as her chair came unstuck and her face softened somewhat as she mouthed, 'Thank you.'

The tension lifted a little, but he pretended nothing had happened as she studied the fireflies in the jar Javi was showing her.

'Your father and I used to do this as children,' Ana said to Javi, looking at Gabriel through the other side of the glass as she held it up in the glow of the fairy lights. 'There used to be more fireflies than this, though. Thousands of them.'

'I remember,' Gabriel said, picturing her as a girl in this very garden, running around with him, catching fireflies. If only he'd known to run with her even more while they could, or to warn her not to get in the damned car that day.

'Really? Thousands?' Javi was staring into the jar, mesmerised by the tiny glowing bugs. 'I can't imagine you being young, Papa. Or you, Ana.'

'Well, we were.' She smiled, sighing softly. Without thinking, Gabriel put a hand to hers and squeezed it tightly. Straight away, the adrenaline coursed up his arm and around his brain. What he really wanted to do was wrap her fully in his arms and run away with her.

Somewhere by the table he heard their mothers gasp and immediately start gossiping. He dropped Ana's hand, dragging his fingers over his hair. Stupid him, thinking they'd 'just been invited for dinner' again. Javi seemed oblivious to the undercurrents, content to hang out with Ana and him wherever they were, but it was clear that their families were all keeping tabs on what was proving to be a pretty obvious relationship. At least, he thought now, glancing at Ana, it *had* been pretty obvious to him till today.

Ana was trying to relax under the stars and fairy lights with all this love surrounding her, but somehow she just felt torn. As Javi practised his bowling skills with a set her parents had bought, she struggled not to feel as if this unit was probably the nicest thing she'd been a part of for years. It was, it was amazing. But what if it cost her everything else she'd worked so hard for? Love was nothing but a distraction and love for Gabriel… Well, she'd already learned the hard way years ago how much *that* could hurt.

It wasn't Gabriel's fault he wore his heart on his sleeve—in fact, that was one of the things she loved most about him. Of course he hadn't meant to make things weird by telling Edith they were 'in love'. She'd been angry at herself more than him today, for putting her own career and reputation in jeopardy. His confession, whether it had been just for Edith's sake or not, *had* felt pretty wonderful to hear…

'Ana, Ana, it's your turn,' Javi called now, urging her to the makeshift bowling ground and handing her a ball.

'Do your best, Ana,' Gabriel quipped, and when she caught his eye a spark sent her heart beating harder in a flash. Why could she not just turn this thing off between them—this thing that now seemed to claim her mind, body and soul whenever he so much as said her name? She had no doubt it was mutual; she could practically feel the heat of his every glance brush against her skin, making her heart race even faster. Yet here they were, both trying to maintain some kind of distance for everyone else's sake. Well, mostly for her sake, she realised now.

Just today, they'd been caught, properly caught making out like teenagers, and all of it had been entirely unprofessional. What was she doing, risking everything she'd worked for? If this all blew up in her face, she'd have nothing left. People talked around here—not that they didn't talk about her enough already, being the only doctor in the barrio confined to a wheelchair with her very own practice.

With a deep breath, Ana took aim and threw the ball with all her might. It was a strike, to her surprise. The whole group cheered behind her and she grinned back at them, feeling a little bit victorious, especially in front of her parents. Taking another look at Gabriel, she didn't miss his proud smile. *Curses!* She had been all ready to take a step back from it all, but here Gabriel was, doing everything right. He had even somehow stood up to Ines and managed to get Javi here this evening when it was supposed to have been her time with their son, something he'd never been able to do till now. Ines always seemed to have plans for Javi on their nights at home together. But here they all were, and it felt so good.

'What do you think, Ana?' Javi stopped in front of her, hands on his hips, lips pouting.

'Sorry, what was that, honey?' She'd zoned out again, lost in her own thoughts. Gabriel eyed her uncertainly as he rearranged the balls on the lawn.

'I said, maybe I can sleep at your place tonight? Papa says I can't stay at his.'

Ana frowned. 'Why can't you stay at your papa's?' she said, more in Gabriel's direction.

'Your mother wants you at home tonight, you know that,' he said sternly and, as if on cue, he pulled out his phone, no doubt to check for her messages. Ana sighed and refrained from an eye-roll, which wouldn't have been entirely fair. Of course Ines wanted her son at home, just as Gabriel wanted him at *his* home, but Ines always got her way. She supposed it was too good to be true that they might be allowed to have him for more than a few hours on one of 'her' nights.

'Well, if your mama wants you home, I can't very well let you stay at my place, can I?' she reasoned gently with the boy. Javi looked upset. His lip quivered for a second as he stared at the ground and she saw the same raging emotions in him that she often saw in Gabriel, before he managed to curb them one way or another. It would have been cute if it wasn't slightly concerning. Gabriel was still at Ines's beck and call, after all, worried about putting so much as a toe wrong in case she went for full custody. But what about what Javi wanted?

'I don't want to go home,' he said now, balling his little fists.

Gabriel was at his side in a second, crouching on the grass. 'Why not, *mijo*?'

'I just don't.'

Ana was well aware of her father's and Gabriel's eyes on her, but she had to focus on Javi. She didn't want him feeling bad, not tonight when they'd all had such a lovely time together. How could she make this right?

'Javi, I can't let you stay tonight, but how about this? I'm free the night before your pawrents' day, so why don't you both come over with Savio for a sleepover? We'll order a takeaway and watch movies all night long and eat popcorn till we're stuffed.'

She smiled at him in encouragement and the little boy's face lit up as he nodded eagerly, all tears forgotten. 'I'm sure your mama won't mind that,' she added, glancing at Gabriel. He was looking at her slightly in awe now, as if he was both perplexed and grateful that she could wipe his son's bad mood away so easily. Javi's face was still shining with excitement as he took his turn at bowling. While she knew she'd got herself into something else with Gabriel when she'd just been questioning whether it was right to even keep this thing going—whatever it was—it wasn't fair to let Javi down.

She was starting to love him being around, actually. Already she could picture him in the cute giraffe onesie she'd seen in the kids' shop around the corner. Maybe she shouldn't get so excited just yet, she thought when, as predicted, Gabriel started saying his goodbyes and bundling Javi up, ready to take him home. It wasn't even eight o'clock.

Ana feigned a smile, but she could feel her shoulders tense, watching the way the boy slowed his steps again, taking longer than necessary in the bathroom while Gabriel stood outside, urging him to hurry up. Javi didn't want to leave, and she didn't want him to go either. A sudden tightness in her chest told her that, no matter what either of them did or said, she was caught up in a situation that was increasingly out of her control.

'Ines wants him…' he started to say to her on the driveway after Javi had reluctantly hugged everyone goodbye, but she didn't let him finish.

'I know,' she said quietly. 'It can't be helped. Go, get him home.'

He shot her an apologetic look over his shoulder before they finally left.

Later, alone in her bed, she couldn't fight the inner turmoil from raging as it kept her from another night of decent sleep. She was getting all caught up in this when she had important work to focus on, when Gabriel had his son, his work commitments and Ines to placate around the clock. Wasn't this all getting far too complicated?

It was hard to imagine actually calling things off, though. Maybe she just needed a little more time, she reasoned with herself and the bedroom ceiling. Maybe she was starting to need Gabriel and Javi in her life more than she'd realised, which was why all this was affecting her more than any relationship ever had before. And that, right there, was the problem.

Since when had she *needed* anyone except herself? Well, OK, since always…but it wasn't something she particularly enjoyed admitting; in fact, it sat well outside of her comfort zone. What if Gabriel went all in with her and then something else happened, besides Ines, to make him decide it was all too much?

She simply had to call things off before she…before *anyone*…got badly hurt, including Javi, who seemed quite besotted with her already. It simply had to be done now while they could still go back to being friends.

# CHAPTER FOURTEEN

THE PARK WAS flooded with sunshine as Ana stopped her chair beside Gabriel and Javi. She was a little late getting to the pawrents' day event from the clinic, after Ebony had arrived late herself, but it was even more nerve-racking waiting for Javi's turn to demonstrate the tricks he'd been teaching Savio. The kid didn't look fazed, though. His grin spread from ear to ear as he waved at her excitedly around Gabriel, stroking Savio's soft head next to him, watching the other dogs and his school friends on the agility trail.

Ana felt a flush of pride, watching the sun catch in the kid's cute black curls, and then another flurry of nerves as Gabriel pressed his hand over hers, a sign that he was glad to see her.

'He's up next,' he said.

'Mmm.' She kept her eyes on the canine activities, wishing she wasn't such a coward. It was just that she liked him too much for her own good. Even his hand on hers in public made her want to grab him by the collar and pull him astride her, like she had last night in her living room before he'd carried her up to bed. How could she listen to her head about breaking things off when her heart was still pounding for him around the clock?

Infuriatingly, she hadn't yet managed to have that important discussion with him; she hadn't even come close! In fact, Gabriel's overnight bag was still in the car, after the fun night they'd all had last night at her place. They had stayed up late watching old black-and-white films and eating popcorn as promised, with Javi in between Gabriel and her on the sofa, and Savio sprawled lazily on the floor. She'd felt so happy, content and at peace with life, sitting there with candles flickering on the coffee table, listening to their laughter and joining in with their happy father-son banter. Javi had looked so cute in the giraffe onesie, too. She hadn't been able to resist picking it up for him.

After they'd put him to bed in the spare room, she and Gabriel had made love till the early hours. They were getting good at it. Too good: it was highly addictive. She had hoped that she'd be able to suggest an amiable departure from this new-found couple status of theirs, but this need to call it off, while justified, was starting to feel a lot like self-sabotage.

Over the last few days, whenever she'd made her mind up to put an end to what would surely only go wrong sooner or later, Gabriel had done something so right it had turned her stomach into a flock of butterflies. Maybe she'd let her own stupid fears of rejection get in the way of going all in, she decided now as Javi was finally called into the arena with Savio. And who could blame her? Not all men had it in them to handle her independence and her ambitious, unstoppable nature, let alone her disability, but somehow all that seemed easy-breezy to Gabriel.

And now, here they were at the pawrents' day. She was actively abandoning her duties at the clinic to be with them both again: did that make her a stand-in parent of sorts? It was everything she'd always said she would never do—put a man between herself and all she'd worked for, and a child too for that matter—but secretly she was absolutely loving it. So what was she supposed to do?

Pretty soon, Javi and Savio were performing the tricks they'd practised nightly like a well-oiled machine. As soon as the whistle blew, they dove straight into their routine. She watched in awe, listening to Gabriel's proud fatherly words of encouragement as Savio responded to each of Javi's commands with speed and accuracy. The dog leaped gracefully through an obstacle course of hoops and tunnels, then stood up on his hind legs while Javi commanded him to salute, do a barrel roll and then a paw-shake, much to the roar of the adoring crowd.

'Woo!' Gabriel let out the hugest cheer when Savio's fluffy paw touched Javi's hand, and Ana couldn't help going one better by wolf whistling. Several people turned to look, including Gabriel, and she shrugged.

'Something you have to learn when you can't move very fast,' she told him. 'Sometimes I need attention.'

'Like the attention you demanded from me last night?' he whispered seductively into her ear, and her whole ear turned red and tingled. He left a hand resting on her shoulder and she sighed in contentment. She had definitely been over-thinking this whole thing—why could she not just be happy to be in this new, wonderful situation?

With each trick that Javi and Savio performed, the audience clapped and cheered even louder. Savio started to spin round in circles, and Javi kept up with every twist and turn, till they were doing their own orchestrated dance. Ana's eyes widened as she watched this display of teamwork between boy and dog; it was almost too cute for words! Then, before she knew it, she was being called to demonstrate the trick they'd all mastered together.

'I believe in you,' Gabriel said now, feigning total seriousness before dropping a kiss to her lips. Suddenly a little nervous, she almost latched onto him like a monkey, but Javi was looking on and clapping in encouragement, so she broke away and made her way into the circle. Soon, Savio was running across the grass from Javi straight onto her lap in the wheelchair, and Javi was pretending to control her chair to reel them both back towards him on an invisible rope.

When they'd finished their routine, the audience erupted in more applause, and she bowed from her seated position, half-embarrassed at all the attention, but proud of Javi. Ana could see the tenderness in Gabriel's gaze when it wandered from Javi to her especially when, moments later, the judges announced he and Savio the winners and placed a huge, shiny gold medal around his neck in the shape of a paw.

'Amazing!' Gabriel enthused at them both, high-fiving Javi, then her. She was just about to suggest he join them for the team photo with the other parents, the kids and their dogs when she realised his phone was buzzing with the sound reserved for Ines. Watching him reach for his pocket at lightning speed, her heart sank on the spot, but this time she just couldn't hold her tongue…

Gabriel knew he'd messed up just from the look on her face. 'You don't have to always pander to her! She knows Javi is fine,' she said.

'I know that.' He frowned, retracting his hand, surprised at her acerbic tone. 'She just wants to…'

'To what? To remind you of something you already know, like the fact that she's collecting Javi in twenty-five minutes in the car park by the basketball court? We all know that.'

Gabriel bit his cheek and sighed through his nose. OK, so it annoyed Ana that he was constantly answering to Ines, but this was the first time she'd been snappy about it—not that he could blame her.

'I'm not answering,' he said as his phone continued to demand his attention. He could almost picture Ines scowling in annoyance at the other end of the line, probably in the car somewhere. She loved to call from the car. Ines would hold this against him as being a mark of disrespect. Maybe she'd use it later as evidence for her keeping Javi in her full custody.

'I'm not answering,' he told her again, and she nodded, even though she still seemed upset.

'Hey,' he said, reaching for her hand. 'I'm sorry.'

'I know you are,' she said, and her ensuing silence burned. They'd been having such a nice time, but of course this must have been getting on her nerves for a while. He always put Javi first, and with that priority came a whole lot of Ines. But Ana had to come equal first now. This new relationship was just as important to him. Ines did probably just want to remind him that she was due to pick up Javi soon, as if he didn't have the place and time drummed into his skull already. He was increasingly embarrassed at how he was always forced to talk to her and reconfirm all these arrangements in front of Ana.

'Your mama's going to come get you soon,' he told

Javi, feeling Ana's eyes on him, as if she knew damn well he was itching to pick up the phone still buzzing angrily in his pocket.

'What? Already?' Javi didn't look pleased. He bunched his red T-shirt at the bottom in his fists and his eyes clouded over with a sudden frustration and helplessness that jarred Gabriel.

'You must be excited to show her your medal? She'll be so pleased you won,' Ana assured him. She pulled out a treat for Savio and petted his fuzzy head affectionately. 'She'll want to see Savio, too.'

'No, can't we stay with you again?' Javi pouted, playing with the medal around his neck.

'Not tonight, but soon,' she said kindly, and Gabriel felt the dismay behind her words as she looked at him. Damn; his phone was ringing *again*.

'Yes, we'll do that again soon,' he confirmed.

'When? Why can't I stay tonight? I don't want to go home!'

Gabriel looked at his son in despair. Javi had been saying this quite frequently lately, but had never said why. On one hand, it was nice, knowing Javi wanted to spend more time with him, but what the heck was going on with Ines? He would have to talk to her, but not today. Ana came first, before his issues with Ines, he decided. He was going to take her out to dinner tonight and ask her to be his girlfriend officially. The thought filled him with nerves, but *that* was what he had to focus on now. He thought about the cosy, candlelit restaurant he had chosen and how romantic it would be—as long as she said yes.

Flustered, he said, 'Javi, how about we go for an ice-cream before we leave? Come on, I bet they have chocolate mint. Ana, do you want one?'

'I'll stay here with Savio,' she said, and on hearing his name the dog leapt for her cheek with a big lick. She laughed and Gabriel instantly felt better. 'We don't want to tempt him with ice-cream, he might knock the stall over. He's not *that* well trained yet, are you, boy?'

He left her talking to some of the other parents and ordered their ice-cream at the stand, trying to imagine what might happen this evening at the restaurant. Maybe he would wait till after the starter, so he could ask her before the mains arrived. Then they could toast each other with champagne.

Glancing back at her, he watched her laughing with a woman in a blue dress, patting Savio as though the dog had always been hers. She loved that dog as much as Javi did, he thought, unable to stop the silly grin from taking over his face as the guy behind the ice-cream stall handed him his cones.

'Mint choc-chip for you, sir,' Gabriel said, swinging round to Javi. But Javi wasn't there. *What?* He'd been standing right next to him just seconds before and now… where the heck was he? He couldn't have simply disappeared. Anxiety seized Gabriel's heart as he frantically scanned the crowd for his son. Stumbling forward, he promptly handed both ice-creams to a bewildered young boy and headed for Ana, fear taking over his confusion as he imagined all the 'what if?'s. His mind spinning a million miles a second, he couldn't help imagining the reaction Ines would have if anything happened to Javi on *his* watch.

Ana seemed to sense something had happened and rushed up to him in her chair, her eyes wide with concern. 'What's wrong? Where is he?'

Gabriel tried to keep it together. 'He's gone—I don't see him. Did you see him?'

'No, he was with you. Try not to panic, Gabriel, he can't have gone far. Savio, can you help find Javi?' she said to the dog, who was still trailing them, wagging his tail as if they were embarking on some grand, exciting adventure. Unfortunately, though, Savio hadn't been trained to locate missing people any more than he'd been trained not to beg for ice-cream.

'Oh God, Javi…' Gabriel groaned, gripping his hair, every muscle tense beneath his shirt. All around them people were enjoying themselves, kids running here and there, but he felt as if his heart was going to burst out of his chest with panic. All he could feel was the coldness of mounting dread as he and Ana searched every corner of the park for Javi's small figure, calling out his name.

'Where did he go, Ana?'

'I don't know.' He felt a chill run down his spine as she said it but just the look on her face kept him together. She was concerned, but still dead calm. Despite what was happening, she carried herself with a confidence that he drew from as he sucked in breath after breath after breath. People came to him with emergencies every day and he couldn't deal with theirs fast enough…but this was Javi.

The minutes passed like hours, until finally Ana grabbed his arm. 'Let's split up. You go that way, I'll go this way with Savio. Keep your phone close.

'Come, Savio boy, let's find Javi!'

# CHAPTER FIFTEEN

ANA'S HEAD WAS spinning faster than her wheels as she found herself scanning the periphery of the park, looking for Javi. 'Where are you?' Through clenched teeth she found herself murmuring prayers that hadn't left her mouth in years. Javi had only been gone a matter of minutes but she'd never seen Gabriel so distressed and it tore at her heart to see him that way. Javi was his whole world. Her heart had started beating a strange kind of warning back there, when he'd clutched at his hair as if he wanted to break something or...well...run away. There had never been a maternal bone in her body, but she knew this little boy very well by now. There was something important that he wasn't telling them.

A motion from the play park caught her eye, and Savio was alert now too. His ears pricked up, then he darted like a lightning bolt ahead of her towards the swings. At first she saw only the empty swings swaying on their chains in the breeze but, as she pulled closer, a flash of red alerted her to the bushes behind the climbing tower. *Javi?*

Savio got to him first, and Javi tried to push the dog off as he nuzzled his shoulder and cheeks. Javi was crouched down in a bush, his tiny body trembling as he hugged his knees. He was clutching his left arm to his body protectively.

Instincts primed, Ana leaned over him. 'Oh, honey, what happened?' She could see that he was trying to muffle his sobs, but still they escaped from him in short, painful bursts as he winced.

'My arm!'

'What's wrong with your arm, *mijo*?' Reaching for her phone, she called Gabriel.

'I fell from the tower!' Javi wailed.

Ana stroked Javi's hair soothingly, murmuring words of reassurance as she helped him up. Already she could see Gabriel sprinting towards them from the other side of the park.

'We're getting you some help. Why did you run away, honey? Why did you try and hide in the tower?'

'I don't want Mama to take me away!' he cried, just as Gabriel reached them and swept the little boy up into his arms. Ana's heart hammered as she explained what had happened. Savio did his best to lick Javi's tears away as Gabriel put his son down again, tearing at his own shirt to make a makeshift sling for the boy. Why didn't Javi want Ines to collect him?

Gabriel, now a picture of sculpted perfection in just his faded jeans, stood with his back turned to her. His tanned flesh rippled with each movement as he held his phone to his ear and spoke to Bruno, his muscles flexing beneath the skin. The lines on his face were etched deep when he turned back to her.

'Bruno's coming with the ambulance,' he said, before crouching down on his haunches, all his attention on Javi, who was still whimpering in pain. He called Ines next. It wasn't good, Ana could tell: the woman's voice was audible down the line, even as Ana sat three feet away with Javi, still holding his arm in the shirt sling. Ines sounded furious with Gabriel, as if this was his fault!

'It's not your fault, you know,' she tried to tell him, but he didn't seem to hear her.

All Ana could do was stay there, watching the distress cloud Gabriel's eyes. In this moment she wanted nothing more than to take away his emotional pain, but the anguished expression on his face broke her heart, and she realised she'd never felt this helpless. Of course he would blame himself.

Eventually the ambulance rumbled onto the road beyond the hedges, and in seconds Bruno and one of his young trainees were hurrying into the play park with a first-aid kit and a stretcher, while a crowd gathered around behind the fence. The young paramedic checked Javi's vital signs before examining the arm with ultimate diligence. She tapped and prodded gently, conferring with Bruno and Gabriel, and Ana watched the creases around Gabriel's eyes deepening again when Javi winced in pain. They all knew it was broken.

'It's definitely broken,' Bruno confirmed, ruffling Javi's hair gently. 'You're very brave, bud; I know it hurts. Let's get you to the hospital.'

'I'll come too,' Ana said before she could think, but Gabriel looked at her, then Savio.

*Oh, right.*

'You're right—we can't bring the dog,' she said as Savio licked at Javi's fingers while they helped him onto the stretcher. The distress mounted inside her as she felt increasingly redundant, but she sprang into action as best she knew how, summoning the dog. 'I'll take him home, then catch you up,' she told them, trying to keep her eyes as well as her hands from his exposed chest. More than anything she itched to pull him closer, or offer some kind of extra reassurance, which she was becoming increasingly aware that she could not provide. He didn't want her support. Gabriel merely nodded at her and quickly followed the others towards the ambulance.

A&E was as busy as ever, and Gabriel sat stiffly in the shirt Bruno had lent him. His friend Sofia, the trauma surgeon, had found him. Being as fond of Javi as she was, she'd been worried and had rushed to check on him. 'What's going on with our little *mijo*?' she asked now. 'And you? You look… Oh, Gabe.'

Gabriel accepted her comforting hug, realising he'd missed her since he'd been combining his shifts with the ambulance staff and the clinic. Not that she needed his friendly ear as much, now that she and Carlos Cabrera were an item.

'Things are OK,' he said. Javi's arm was now in a cast and, instead of crying, he'd seemed quite intrigued by the hospital once the painkillers were doing their job. He kept asking what this instrument was for, and what that machine did. 'How are you and Carlos doing?' he asked her, unable to stop a little sly nudge and wink.

Sofia bit back a smile, looked around her and leaned in conspiratorially. 'We are doing better than great,' she said, her pretty mouth breaking out into a fully fledged grin. He was about to ask for more juicy gossip when Ines swung through the door like a hurricane.

'I came as soon as I could, but the traffic was terrible… Oh, Javi!'

She rushed straight through to her son, speaking rapidly, checking his arm and then looking for any other injuries, dropping a flurry of kisses to his face and head. Then she stepped back and locked eyes with Gabriel. Sofia made her swift departure with a squeeze of his hand and he stood, bracing himself. Ines was a formidable woman—as tall as him, and statuesque, with the kind of beauty that drew attention wherever she went. Today being no exception as she glowered at him from beneath her heavy black fringe, causing the nursing assistant to excuse herself from the room.

'You were supposed to be watching him,' she admonished. Her dark eyes glinted with anger and indignation as she crossed her arms over her chest. 'What if something worse had happened?'

'I'm OK, Mama,' Javi insisted groggily, wiping lipstick from his cheeks. He was still wearing his medal, which glinted in the harsh lights above. Ines tapped her nails on her arms and shifted in the silk trousers that accentuated her curves. It was clear where Javi had inherited his fiery temperament from; Ines wanted answers and she wanted them now.

He was about to ask her why Javi hadn't wanted to go home to her in the first place when the door opened and Ana appeared. His heart leapt to his throat.

'Sorry to interrupt,' she started, before Javi called out to her.

'Ana! Look at my cool cast. Bruno and the nurse said I can get people to sign it later.'

'Very cool,' she said, though she was frowning in Ines'

direction now. He watched the two women size each other up. Suddenly he was more aware than ever of how different they were. Of course, they had met before, on that beach trip to Pinamar when Ines had been pregnant while they'd been trying to make things work. It only just struck him now how Ana had always made some kind of excuse as to why she couldn't stick around with them for long.

'Good to see you again,' Ana said politely. 'It's been a long time.'

'Hmm,' was Ines' cool reply. She stared at Ana, who was still holding a wrapped gift she had bought for Javi. 'I see now why Gabriel has been so distracted.'

Ana bit her lip and turned away and a surge of rage thundered through Gabriel that he had to suppress. He stood between them, lowering his voice so Javi couldn't hear. 'Ines, that's enough. Ana has nothing to do with this. What's going on with you?'

Ines blew air through her nostrils and looked between them. Her voice hardened as she glared at them. 'I just worry about Javi, that's all.'

'I know you do, but he's fine,' Gabriel told her, shooting a sideways look at Ana. He felt so bad at the way Ines was acting, and for dragging Ana into this mess. Hearing that Javi was fine wasn't enough for Ines, clearly. No sooner had the nurse arrived to discharge him, than Ines was whisking him away, insisting on carrying all his things to her parked car. Gabriel followed with Ana close behind, telling Javi he would see him later as Ines helped him carefully into the car. Once the door was shut, she turned to him, glaring again.

'This should not have happened—you're his father.'

'What's that supposed to mean?'

Ines just glowered at him a second longer before stalking to the other side of the car. In less than thirty seconds he was watching her pull out of the hospital car park. Ramming his hands in his hair, it was another moment before he remembered Ana was behind him. She was watching him closely, Javi's gift still on her lap.

'That went well,' he said drily. He crossed to her. 'Ana, I'm so sorry you had to witness all that.'

'It's not all your fault,' she replied as he took her hand.

'But she was right—I'm his father. I wasn't paying close enough attention to him.'

Ana sighed deeply, and to his shock she gently pulled her hand away from him. In the background he caught Bruno loading some supplies into the ambulance, watching them carefully, pretending he wasn't. 'I'm sorry, Gabriel.'

The look on her face sent his pulse to his throat. *Sorry?* 'Why are you sorry?'

She shook her head, her expression flashing with pain for just a second. 'Ana?'

'I have to go,' she said, her voice strained now.

'Can't we talk?'

'What about, Gabriel? This isn't going to work. There's just too much going on with you and Ines, and Javi, and you don't need me complicating things further.'

Dread coiled in his stomach at her words. 'How are you complicating things?'

She inhaled sharply. Sadness and regret flared around her irises as their eyes locked. 'I haven't been paying attention either, Gabriel, and we've both been distracted and preoccupied lately. We've both forgotten what really matters. I think we should just go back to being friends, don't you? I know you have a shift at the clinic tomorrow, but I'll ask Ebony to come in.'

The words felt like a punch to his chest, not what he wanted to hear at all. He stood taller, feeling his composure start to wane the more he searched her eyes for a hint that she didn't mean it. But she was clearly deadly serious. How long had she been feeling this way? Suddenly he could tell she'd been having these reservations for a while—he'd just been too stubborn to admit it to himself. Ana didn't need all this drama in her busy life, and this was her polite way of excusing herself from a difficult situation before she became even more tangled up in it all.

'I don't think I can go back to just being your friend,' he admitted with a frown. It was the truth. 'But don't bother Ebony. I won't let the clinic down.'

'I'm sorry,' she said again. Before he could so much as take her hand, or tell her how much he regretted dragging her so deeply into this mess, she turned away from him and sped her chair towards the exit faster than he'd ever be able to keep up.

# CHAPTER SIXTEEN

ANA HAD ALWAYS prided herself on her ability to stay focused in the face of chaos. But there was something about the way Gabriel's eyes met hers across the brightly lit examination room that threatened to shatter her composure. The tension that had been simmering between them all morning was still there, humming beneath the surface, and now it crackled in the air as they prepared to discuss expat Evelyn Sinclair's case.

'Mrs Sinclair, thank you for coming in today,' Gabriel began, placing the medical chart down on the bed, his voice steady and reassuring. It was the opposite to how he'd been yesterday, when he'd been wracked with despair over the missing Javi, and then consumed with guilt and dread in the face of his ex's fury.

'Can you tell us about your symptoms—when they started and how they've progressed?'

The room was filled with the soft hum of medical equipment and the faint scent of antiseptic mingled with Gabriel's fresh, familiar scent as Evelyn started recounting her fatigue and her achy limbs. Ana made notes, but her mind kept drifting as she tried not to look at Gabriel. He'd been so cool with her since she'd called things off. He hadn't even tried to talk to her about it, almost as if he knew they'd be better off as friends. Maybe he'd change his mind about not wanting to be friends, she thought hopefully, though it didn't feel right to her either any more. How on earth could they put something so wonderful into reverse so quickly?

They would just have to try.

She had slept with his scent surrounding her in bed last night despite the absence of him. Clutching the pillow he'd last slept on, she had let the tears fall, agonising over what she'd done. She had to let him go, though. She was doing the right thing, wasn't she? Surely he realised she was simply getting in the way? Javi was everything to him, and now, after the incident in the park, Gabriel was probably even more terrified that Ines was going to go for full custody. He had always been Ana's rock, had always been there to support her, even when she'd insisted he and everyone else leave her alone. It was only fair that she release him now and let him focus fully on his son.

Evelyn's voice wavered as she continued, looking at Gabriel. 'It started about six months ago. First the tiredness, no matter how much rest I got. My muscles felt so weak, and my skin…it became so sensitive that even the slightest touch was painful. My hair started falling out and my nails turned brittle. I've lost weight, despite eating more than usual, and I have trouble sleeping.'

'That's quite the list,' Ana said, catching Gabriel's eye.

'Not being able to sleep is the worst,' Gabriel said directly to Ana. OK, so that was a dig. She had clearly kept him from sleeping, as much as her abrupt decision to end things had kept her from nodding off until well after three a.m.

'The last clinic I went to didn't know what was wrong

with me,' Evelyn continued. 'Lately, I've been having trouble swallowing, and my voice is hoarser than it should be. Can you hear it?'

Ana nodded. 'Have you experienced any mood changes or emotional symptoms?' she asked.

Evelyn hesitated, her eyes dropping to her lap. 'Yes, I've been feeling depressed and anxious. It's been hard to concentrate and remember things. I just haven't felt like myself lately.'

'I know what you mean,' Ana muttered under her breath as she made for the store cabinet, letting Gabriel explain that they would have to run some tests, including blood work and imaging. It was getting near on impossible to ignore the way her own emotions were fraying around him, but the clinic came first, as did her reputation. She was not about to let a brief love affair ruin anything for her, any more than she was willing to complicate things for Gabriel and Javi.

Ana was still fighting her own wavering emotions by the time they were alone again. It was just herself and Gabriel, analysing tests, discussing symptoms and reviewing Evelyn's case, while the big fat elephant still stood unaddressed in the middle of the room.

Gabriel sat on the examination table, staring at her over the edge of a medical chart. Her pulse quickened when their eyes met but she kept her voice calm. 'It appears that Evelyn has an auto-immune disorder that's attacking her thyroid,' she said. 'We'll put together the treatment plan, starting with…'

'This is so weird,' Gabriel said suddenly, slamming the file on the bed and gripping the edge of it. His dark eyes bore into her as she felt the sweat prickle on the back of her neck 'Don't you think it's weird? I'm not sure, now I'm actually here, that I can work with you any more, Ana. This should be my last day.'

His words felt like a gut punch. She sucked in a breath as he jumped from the bed, slowly spinning her chair round to him. 'I thought we could at least try and be friends, Gabriel…'

'I told you, that's not going to work for me,' he said curtly, and for a moment, the tension between them felt too strong to be contained. She thought he was about to grab her face, kiss her doubts away and remind her that they could and *should* never be platonic again, but his emotions stayed behind his eyes before he strode to the window and heaved a sigh at the glass.

'Well, Ebony's told me she can probably start coming in full-time,' she offered matter-of-factly, afraid that she was about to follow him and demand he kiss her, and that she'd been wrong to call things off.

*Don't be weak, Ana, this is what you wanted!* Didn't he see how this was best for him and for them? Somehow, though, the words wouldn't leave her mouth.

'Right, then,' he said, unbuttoning his coat while she felt the panic rise in her throat. 'If Ebony's free, that would be best.'

*Ugh.* He was being so cool now, it was sending an icy blast through her bloodstream, chilling her to the bone. She'd come to want him here at the clinic, she realised, overcome by her own selfishness suddenly as he stared out of the window with his back turned. To think she'd always thought she was the strong one, the independent warrior ploughing onwards, over anyone in her path. Now, the thought of him not being here any more, not being anywhere in her day-to-day existence, was really sinking in.

Later, at home, Ana sat in silence, prodding at a plate of pasta spirals. Her appetite was non-existent; all she kept thinking was how she would ever be able to go about her working day at the clinic without Gabriel, and without knowing she'd see Javi at the end of it.

What was wrong with Javi, anyway? It seemed as though he was increasingly frustrated about having to be at home with his mum and stepdad. The way Ines was reacting to the smallest things… OK, some of the bigger things too—the broken arm wasn't exactly a mother's dream, but it all spoke volumes about the other woman's unhappiness.

Her doctor's instincts were on alert. It was very clear when someone was stressed, and Ines was definitely highly stressed. Her mood swings were giving poor Gabriel whiplash. But it wasn't Ana's place to do anything about it.

The next day, Ana was eating lunch alone in the clinic's small staff room, watching the rain falling outside. Naturally she was thinking about Gabriel and Ines. She could hardly believe it when a cough behind her drew her attention back to the door, and there was the woman herself. Spinning round, she almost dropped her salad into her lap. 'Ines?'

'Your receptionist let me back here—I hope that's OK. I think we need to talk.'

'Yes…'

Ana studied Ines as she stepped fully inside, glancing

warily at Ana from head to toe as Ana touched a hand to her flowery headband. Ines was the opposite of her when it came to style. She wore a crisp white blouse tucked into dark-washed high-waisted jeans and wore cream-coloured ankle boots. Her hair was loose, framing her face in long waves that reached down to her collarbone. She was stunning but there was an air of sadness about her.

'I'm sorry for how I reacted yesterday,' Ines said, taking a plastic seat at the small table. 'I know you've grown quite close with Javi, and he's very fond of you too. I just thought, maybe I owed you an explanation. Things have been a little off lately.'

Ana nodded, debating with herself whether it was right to do this or not. Would Gabriel think this was gossiping, or her sticking her nose in where it wasn't wanted? What was the point of getting involved when she had already excused herself from their lives anyway? Hadn't she decided just last night that it wasn't her place to get involved in this…whatever it was? But, then again, whatever was up with Ines affected Gabriel and Javi too and, the more she thought about it, the more guilty she felt at doing nothing but walking away—so to speak. She'd done nothing to help Gabriel, when he'd *always* gone out of his way to be there for her.

'Javi's in reception—he wanted to see your children's toys,' Ines said. 'They're looking after him for me. Your staff are lovely, by the way.'

'They're the best.' Ana offered to make Ines some tea and she accepted.

'How is Pedro?' Ana asked, filling the kettle from the tap, hoping it didn't sound too much as though she was probing.

'He's working, as usual, locked away in his study,' came her cool reply, followed by a deep, resounding sigh.

Ana nodded. OK, then, so that was a pretty big hint as to why Ines might be unhappy. Something was going on with Pedro and her.

'It's mint,' Ana said a couple of minutes later, putting a cup of steaming tea down in front of her visitor and positioning her wheelchair at the opposite end of the table. Ines thanked her and sipped the sweet tea, and Ana wondered if it was acceptable to ask about the state of her marriage.

Ines sighed again, no doubt seeing the question in Ana's eyes and probably realising that there was no point in denying it. She put down her cup with a slightly trembling hand and looked away for a few seconds before finally speaking.

'We've been arguing a lot recently,' Ines admitted reluctantly. Her face dropped and she seemed to become smaller in her chair, as if someone had let out all of the air inside of her. Ana felt a pang of empathy for the woman.

'I'm sorry to hear that.'

'Javi has picked up on it, though we've tried not to argue in front of him. I feel so guilty…'

'Oh, Ines,' Ana said, suddenly torn. Tears began to well up in Ines' eyes as she started going into details about how busy Pedro was with his work, how they'd turned into strangers in the same house and how he never even bought her flowers any more. Ana felt overwhelmed. She reached out a hand across the table and clasped her fingers. Ines squeezed hers back. She hadn't expected Ines to open up so fast to her, but it seemed as if she'd been bottling this agony up inside for too long now, just waiting for someone to notice and listen.

'I suppose I can understand why Javi wants to stay with his papa, and you,' Ines conceded. 'I just feel so helpless, knowing I might lose him.'

Ana balked. Did Ines even know that Gabriel constantly worried that *he* might lose his son—that Ines would ask for full custody? 'You won't lose Javi, Ines. You are his mother—he loves you.'

'Ana?' A small voice from behind the door made her start. Suddenly Javi appeared, his little hand in Maria's.

'Sorry, ladies, he was asking for you,' she said, releasing him into the staff room. Ana smiled at him as he walked to them in his cast, wearing a loose cotton shirt printed with robots and matching dark-blue trousers.

'What are you doing?' he asked them.

'I'm just talking with your mama.' Ana smiled. Ines promptly got up to refill their tea cups, and she felt Ines watching them as Ana asked how he was and finally handed over the gift she'd been keeping for him. Luckily, she'd had it stored there at the clinic in her locker. Ana's heart melted as he pulled out the stuffed toy—a dog that looked rather like Savio.

'I love it, thank you, Ana!' Javi hugged it tightly under his good arm as Ines put her refilled cup down and asked to see the toy.

For a second Ana thought a gift from her might have been a little unwelcome, but Ines shot her a look of gratitude over Javi's head as she swiped at her own tired eyes.

'Right, Javi, we didn't finish inspecting the fire engine out there,' Maria said, beckoning the boy back outside again with her. Ana knew she could tell they needed to talk. Ines dropped a kiss on his head. Javi kissed his mother's cheek and then, to Ana's surprise, turned to kiss hers too before heading back outside with Maria and his toy.

Ines watched him go. 'He likes you a lot,' she said.

Ana smiled. 'I like him a lot too.'

They both sat in silence for a moment and then Ines turned to her. 'I'm so sorry for how I've been acting lately,' she said, her voice barely above a whisper.

Ana shook her head. 'I think Gabriel feels like he's failing you,' she said, feeling empowered now and determined to make things right. 'But the truth is, Javi getting his arm broken in the park was just an accident. It wasn't Gabriel's fault, it wasn't anyone's fault.'

'I know.'

Ana reached out and squeezed Ines' hand once more. She could hardly imagine how difficult it must be to be a full-time parent, juggling a thousand things, always blaming yourself when things went wrong. Ana could understand now where Ines had been coming from—she'd never meant to blame Gabriel for anything, she'd just been frustrated at her own situation, feeling guilty and stressed.

Ines sat up straighter and composed herself. 'I appreciate you seeing me today, Ana, I do.'

'That's OK. And I know you'll talk to Gabriel soon and reassure him that this wasn't his fault.' Ana looked at her hopefully, hoping her message was coming across.

Ines nodded. 'I'll talk to Gabriel. I just didn't want him to think I wasn't doing my best as Javi's mother, you know?'

'You're doing your best as his parents—you both are,'

she told her, relieved that Ines had come to see her and that now, hopefully, Ines would finally explain to Gabriel what had been going on.

'You're good for Gabriel, you know,' Ines said when Ana walked her to the door. 'You're together, aren't you, finally?'

*Finally?* Ana realised she must have be frowning in confusion. Ines smiled.

'I think I always knew Gabe and I wouldn't work out. I always thought he was in love with someone else.'

'You mean me?' Ana heard herself say, surprised at how it just came out of her so easily, and how the giant knot in her stomach reformed on the spot, tighter than ever.

Ines laughed. 'Yes, you!'

'Well, we're not together,' Ana told her, flustered suddenly.

Ines looked surprised. 'You're not? Why not?'

Ana drew her lips together and shook her head. 'We're just focusing on other things,' she said, although the second she said it she realised how hollow her words must sound to Ines, who'd come here because she had eyes and could tell something was going on between them. She was right, of course. The only thing Ana had been able to focus on for the last few weeks was Gabriel but, just as she did with everyone, she had pushed him away. Because of her, they were over.

Ines kissed her cheek and said she'd see her soon. Her insides were swirling with this new information. Ana couldn't help thinking that maybe, in another world, she and Ines might even have been friends.

# CHAPTER SEVENTEEN

ANA WATCHED FROM across the room with a heavy heart as Carla helped one of the elderly patients out of her seat in the waiting room. Her returning assistant, now fully recovered from her Carnival injury, was a petite woman with short, dark, wavy hair and a warm smile who, like Ebony, had a calm presence that put many of the patients at ease right away. But neither of them was Gabriel. It felt wrong, not having Gabriel there beside her, helping out in his own unique way. It felt like for ever since she'd seen him, even though it had been less than a week, and she missed him more than she'd ever thought it was possible to miss anyone!

Her stomach tightened in a knot of longing and she struggled to contain her emotions. His cheerful personality had been like sunshine in the clinic, everyone had said so, and she couldn't help thinking that, without him, the place she had been dreaming about for so long lacked the one special something it needed most.

'Where's Gabriel?' she heard Evelyn ask Carla some time later. Evelyn directed the same question to her once she was seated in the consultation room. Of course, Gabriel had been here for her first visit, when they'd run the tests and discovered her thyroid was causing her complaints, so she wanted him to see to her this time too.

'He's not working here any more,' she said sadly, forcing a smile at the look Maria threw her as she put down a file, then closed the door. Maria knew how much Ana missed him; she had told her many times.

Carla was doing an amazing job, but they all knew it didn't compare with what Gabriel had brought to their team of healthcare providers. Every patient he had treated seemed to light up when they saw him walk into the room—even if they'd been feeling down or unwell when they'd first arrived. He had such a natural way of making everyone feel comfortable and reassured. And, as for her, she missed him at night. She missed the way he had made love to her. She'd probably never find that with anyone again, but he was clearly already over her. She'd not heard from him since he'd walked out.

The rain finally cleared later that day as Ana ran a small yellow duster over the leaves of her favourite fern. Everyone else had left for the day and it was just her here now, wrapping things up before they closed. She was taking her time. It was important to show her plants as much care as they showed the patients in this place, and she took pride each time she wiped the dust away from their delicate leaves.

But today, if she was really honest with herself, she just didn't want to go back home to her lonely, quiet apartment. Before starting this relationship with Gabriel, she hadn't felt lonely. It had just been normal for her, going home, reading her books, working, working some more, pretending to cook whilst heating up her mother's leftovers which she was still kindly leaving on Ana's doorstep, unasked for but much appreciated. Now, she spent most nights staring blankly at screens and pages, each one stretching ahead of her like an eternity.

She was just telling herself that there was no point in dwelling on what was over and done with, and that she'd be just fine with heating up another slice of lasagne and getting an early night, when a noise at the glass entrance door caught her ear. Wheeling herself round the corner, she stopped short in her chair.

'Savio?'

There was something on the little dog's collar. Moving forward and opening the door, she realised it was a beautiful, voluptuous orange marigold, just as the dog leapt for her lap, as if he couldn't wait to do his half of their well-practised trick. He sat there proudly, looking at her with his intelligent black eyes, and she stared back at him, not sure what to think.

'Did you escape, *mijo*?' she found herself asking the animal.

'He's with me,' came the voice. Peering over the dog's head, Ana's eyes widened as Javi stepped into view. He was also holding marigolds, a small bunch, which he held out to her as Savio leapt from her lap. She took them, breathing in their soft, subtle scent, too surprised to speak for a second.

'Javi, these are beautiful, but what are you doing here, and where's your…?'

The word 'papa' got stuck in her throat. Her question was answered before it even left her mouth. Stepping out from around the building, walking towards her, was Gabriel. She stared at him in disbelief. He was holding a bigger bunch of marigolds, so big it engulfed the top half of his body, before he moved them aside to reveal his handsome face.

'Gabriel.' Her hand flew to her mouth as he stopped in front of her. He was wearing a crisp white shirt, unbuttoned at the top to reveal his strong collarbone and gleaming dark skin. Oh, how she'd missed him. The deep-navy suit jacket paired with black trousers was complemented by the unruly mop of dark hair, as if he had been running his hands over it with nerves.

'Hi,' he said simply, holding out the flowers to her. 'These are for you.'

Taking them, her hand brushed his, shooting sparks right to her heart. As he fixed his penetrating gaze onto hers, she couldn't help but think that he was, without a shadow of a doubt, the most handsome man she had ever seen. But what was all this about?

He smiled at her, dimples peeking out on either side of his face, and all the days and nights she had spent apart from him melted away in an instant, even as the nerves settled back in. 'What is all this?'

He motioned for her to wheel her chair along next to him, and she let him help her lock the clinic doors. As they started down the street, with Javi talking to Savio just up ahead, she could feel her heartbeat in her throat.

'So, Ines got in touch…' he started, pressing his hands into his pockets. Ana clutched the flowers to her lap, wondering what had been said. She'd contemplated that maybe Gabriel would be angry with her for sticking her nose in, seeing as she hadn't heard from him till now.

'Thank you for talking to her,' he said, and she sighed in relief. 'I know you were worried about Javi.'

'I just knew something was going on,' she admitted. 'I was worried about you too.'

'Well, I appreciate it. Ines has agreed to let me have Javi more often while she and Pedro work things out. I have you to thank for that.' He sighed and she realised he looked more anxious now than he had before when he'd showed up. 'I shouldn't have just quit on you, Ana, as a friend or co-worker…'

'Neither should I!'

'Working at the clinic with you, that's given me more than I ever knew I needed or wanted. Maybe some day, if you'll have me, I can work with you full-time?'

*If you'll have me?* Ana's mind was reeling now.

'It's not the same there without you,' she admitted, as the idea took seed in her mind and started sprouting in every direction. Of course she would take him on full time—everyone adored him.

'My *life* isn't the same without you,' he said. Gabriel stopped, glancing at Javi quickly. 'There's something I have to ask you.'

Ana sucked in a breath as he took her hand, turning it over in his, studying her fingers. Oh…he wasn't going to propose, was he? Suddenly her heart was a riot. This was something she had not been prepared for at all, not that she could imagine a future with anyone else. Of course, she would probably say yes if he asked, and maybe even move into his place if he didn't mind always carrying her to the bedroom…

'Will you be my best friend, now and always?' he said, cutting into her frenzied inner monologue.

*What?*

She stared at him, searching for words as the smile

she knew and loved stretched out across his handsome face. Gosh she could look at those dimples for ever, but… 'Friend?'

'I want that, with you. But I also want you to be my girlfriend. Will you be both, Ana? I'm madly in love with you—you know that, don't you?'

Ana blinked, her mouth opening and closing several times before the words came tumbling out. 'Girlfriend? I mean…yes! Of course! I've wanted to be your girlfriend for so long, Gabriel.'

She felt her cheeks heat up with a blush as he smiled down at her, obviously pleased with her answer, even though she'd blurted it out at a million miles an hour. Luckily, there were no more words needed. Gabriel bent down to her slowly and closed the distance between them, his lips brushing hers ever so gently till she looped her arms around him and kissed him back even harder. Suddenly there was another brush of wetness on her cheek and she shrieked with laughter, pushing Savio away.

'Off, boy! This is not a kiss you can take over!'

Javi was giggling and clapping his hands in glee. 'Yay, Papa!' He ran up to greet them both with a huge hug that threatened to squish all her flowers, but she could hardly see a thing through the tears in her eyes.

She realised she was grinning like a teenager now as she looked from Javi to Gabriel. How could she not feel blessed, being here with two of the most important people in her life? And now she not only had her best friend back, she had an incredible, loving, kind, hotter-than-hot boyfriend too—not to mention his adorable son. Oh, and a dog, she thought, laughing again as Savio went in for another lick…

*One year later*

'Gabriel, come and try the cake!' Ana called out.

Gabriel disentangled himself from the increasingly knotted bunch of strings dangling around him. 'One second,' he called back from the top of the ladder. His house was already filled with decorations for Javi's birthday party but he needed to tie the last of the colourful balloons to the curtain poles. They were bobbing from every corner, as if they wanted to escape through the window and take flight in the sky, and it wouldn't do to release them before Javi and his friends had even seen them.

The smell of freshly baked cake had been wafting in from the kitchen all morning as Ana cooked, and the sweet vanilla essence already had him feeling hungry as he stepped into the kitchen. He couldn't help smiling at the sight of his beautiful girlfriend. Ana was covered in flour and her colourful patterned shirt was coated in a layer of fine dust as he leaned down to kiss her.

'My floury maiden,' he teased, and she laughed, handing him a small cupcake.

'Taste it! I made the main cake from the same mix.' She looked at him hopefully while he took a huge bite and chewed it, his eyes never leaving her face.

She wrinkled up her nose. 'Oh no, is it too sweet?'

'They're kids, they live on sugar,' he replied. 'It's perfect!'

Ana still looked nervous as she dabbed at her face and seemed only just to realise she was covered in flour. 'I should shower; Ines and Pedro will be here soon with Javi.'

'Want me to join you?' he asked, cocking an eyebrow, and before she could even answer he was swiping her giggling body up from her chair and making for the bathroom.

By the time they emerged from the bedroom, hot and sweating after their shower, they were even later for the start of the party. Gabriel watched her dress in amusement. He didn't miss how she swiped up items of clothing from the drawers he'd cleared for her and put them back again straight away. When she decided on a floral printed dress with a green headscarf covered in peacocks, she promptly spilled the rest of her scarves and headbands from their box onto the floor.

'Hey, what's going on with you?' He laughed, racing to help gather them up. 'It's just a children's birthday party!'

Ana couldn't seem to look him in the eye. Something was wrong. He pressed a kiss to her lips, as if to calm her, and she sighed against his mouth. Then thankfully she smiled, but he could tell she was nervous about something.

'Everything's going to be great. The cake is delicious, the decorations are amazing and Javi will know how much effort you've put in,' he reassured her.

Ever since she'd moved into his place last year and they'd adapted the house for her wheelchair, she'd been going out of her way for Javi and him, and he was very much enjoying working more at the clinic. He did just three shifts a week with the ambulance team at the Hospital General de Buenos Aires, and the rest of the time he spent with her and the patients at the clinic was the perfect mix of action and calm for him at this stage in his life—but this was still Ana, of course. Everything had to be perfect. Most of the time now she let him help her, if only by calming her down. Hopefully she'd relax before Ines arrived…

Too late—the doorbell was ringing. They were here, and Javi's friends would be arriving in less than half an hour. Pressing another kiss to her lips, he said, 'You're perfect—I love you,' and hurried down the stairs.

Ana took a deep breath, staring at her reflection in the bedroom mirror. The peacocks on her headband seemed to be smirking at her. Why was she suddenly losing the ability to think straight? Gabriel—dear, sweet, wonderful, unsuspecting Gabriel—had no idea why she was so antsy. In fact, only Ines knew. Ines was her accomplice, her co-conspirator and…dared she say it?… friend.

She met Ines downstairs in the kitchen, where she was admiring the robot-shaped cake Ana had made, her arm looped through Pedro's. They both smiled warmly at her before Ines leant to kiss both her cheeks. Ana didn't miss the look in her eyes before she whispered, 'You've got this, Ana.'

Gabriel popped his head in. 'Are you guys coming? We're about to start "pass the parcel"!'

Gabriel had hung streamers from the windows to the doorway, and she felt as though she was floating as she entered the party with Ines and Pedro. Javi had invited ten of his closest friends over. Music filled the air and laughter echoed through the house as he ran around excitedly with his friends, dressed in an adorable sailor costume complete with captain's hat. He'd insisted on a fancy dress party. Even Savio had on a special costume—the poor dog was sitting a little grouchily on the floor in the corner, no doubt feeling sorry for himself, dressed as a giant watermelon.

Everyone else was enjoying themselves and, for a moment, she simply watched them all, drinking in their faces and listening to their conversations and laughter as the parcel went round and round the circle, stopping with the music to let another child tear off a layer, revealing a little gift inside.

It all felt like a dream, even though her nerves were now sky-high. Since Gabriel had asked her to move in a year ago, things had been pretty much perfect. As the most talked about couple in the district, not least because of their hugely successful practice, she was proud to be seen out and about at events and functions, and even prouder to be invited to couple's gatherings and family fun days with Gabriel and Javi. No more loneliness! She no longer felt the sting of sad nights by herself, and she'd even taken up cooking, much to her mother's delight.

Ana's mother had developed the special knack of arriving early at the weekend with a bundle of fresh ingredients and her recipe box. She would take over the kitchen, bustling to and fro as she chopped vegetables and simmered sauces, explaining every step as she worked.

Ana had felt awkward at first, but she had gradually come to understand that everything her mum did was out of deep love, respect and pride for her other more professional achievements. Accepting her parents' help every now and then didn't feel so suffocating, now that she had Gabriel to bring his light-hearted presence and sense of humour into every situation—she was happy to need him. She was even happier that he seemed to need her just as much in return.

The time had come. Ana steeled herself; there was no going back now. When the last layer of the parcel had been snatched up and torn into even smaller pieces by the watermelon dog, she wheeled herself to the front of the room, her heart beating a million miles a minute as she shifted slightly in her chair. Taking a couple of deep breaths, she reached into the pouch by her right thigh and called for Gabriel. She could see Ines was fighting a smile, while Pedro and Gabriel, who'd been chatting in the corner, just looked confused.

'Gabriel, you've made me think a lot this past year,' she started, as he dropped to the couch just by her side and ran his hands through his hair. Looking straight into his gorgeous brown eyes, she felt the chattering children and the music fade away and had to fight an enormous wave of emotion just to get her next words out. Clutching the box containing the ring to her heart for a moment, she took his fingers.

'Ana, what is it?' he whispered. She almost giggled at the concern and confusion on his face, but Ines was encouraging her, nodding for her to continue, as they had planned when they'd chosen the ring for him.

'Being your friend was wonderful,' she said. 'Being your girlfriend is even more so. But, Gabriel, I want more than anything to be your wife.' She opened the box up slowly and swallowed a last flurry of nerves as an audible gasp travelled around the room. 'I love you. Will you be my husband? Will you marry me?'

Gabriel's eyebrows shot to his hairline. He seemed nearly as taken aback as everyone else, and he just stared at the ring for what felt like for ever. Then finally, in a soft voice, he said, 'Yes.'

He stood up, letting her push the ring onto his finger, a grin breaking out on his face. 'Yes!' he exclaimed loudly, lifting her clean from her chair and spinning her around. Pandemonium broke out among the children as they laughed and Gabriel kissed her. Everyone was clapping and cheering, no-one louder than Javi, and she even caught Ines crying softly as she leaned into Pedro's shoulder.

'You're crazy, but I am in love with you,' Gabriel whispered, just as a giant fuzzy watermelon jumped up for one more group kiss. This time Ana didn't push him off. There was enough love here for everyone, however they wanted to show it.

* * * * *

*Look out for the next story in the*
Buenos Aires Docs *quartet*

Secretly Dating the Baby Doc
*by JC Harroway*

*And if you enjoyed this story, check out these other great reads from Becky Wicks*

Melting the Surgeon's Heart
Finding Forever with the Single Dad
South African Escape to Heal Her

*All available now!*

# SECRETLY DATING THE BABY DOC

JC HARROWAY

MILLS & BOON

To all the mums, working mothers and single parents—
great job!

# CHAPTER ONE

CONSULTANT NEONATAL SURGEON Emilia Gonzales strode along the indistinguishable hospital corridor, her head held high as if she knew exactly where she was going. No one would guess it was her first day—new job, new hospital, new country.

Battling nerves and a raft of other unsettling emotions, she followed the signs for Theatre, scanned her security pass and entered the operating suite. Faced with another corridor, she tried to orientate herself to her surroundings.

She'd been given a tour when she'd come to the Hospital General de Buenos Aires for her interview earlier in the year. She was used to working in leading tertiary referral hospitals in her native Uruguay, but the General was four times the size of its counterpart in Montevideo. And she couldn't help but be distracted by the painful dull throb of her heart.

Her late husband, Ricardo, had been born in this very hospital. Despite five years of widowhood, Ricardo was always in her thoughts. How was she supposed to work here, be back here in Argentina, and not be constantly reminded of the loss of the love of her life?

Emilia breathed through the now familiar grief, pulling herself together. This new job represented a fresh start for her and her daughter, Eva. Eva had wanted to attend the same university as her father, and Emilia was happy to facilitate and support all of Eva's dreams. She just wished this particular change could be less triggering.

'Are you lost?' A man spoke from behind Emilia, making her jump.

She turned, and found herself eye to chest with his tall, athletic frame and looked up. With dark hair sprinkled with grey and deep brown eyes, her rescuer's friendly smile immediately set Emilia at ease.

'Is it that obvious?' she asked with a smile of her own. 'I was hoping to hide it better. It's my first day.' And she had a surgery to get to.

The tall and helpful stranger glanced at her brand-new name tag, his expression shifting from mild curiosity to pleasant surprise.

'Ah, you're Dr Gonzales,' he said, his smile widening. 'Our new neonatal surgeon. I've been expecting you.'

'Sorry if I'm late,' Emilia said with a wince. That was no way to make a good first impression.

'Not late at all.' He offered his hand. 'I'm Felipe Castillo. Welcome to the General.'

Emilia shook his hand, momentarily thrown by his welcoming manner and the confidence of his relaxed smile. They'd never met before, but she knew Felipe Castillo was a senior neonatal surgeon there. Not only was he jointly responsible for the patient Emilia was in Theatre to meet, he was also Emilia's clinical supervisor, until her full registration with the Argentine Medical Council was granted.

'Please, call me Emilia,' she said, sliding her hand from Felipe's warm and sure grip, her nerves intensifying.

They were a similar age, both in their fifties, but Felipe

would be overseeing all her surgeries for a probationary period of three weeks. As a mother, Emilia had taken a little longer to train, what with maternity leave, years of part-time work while Eva had been small and then time off on compassionate leave during the two years Ricardo had been ill.

Only she hadn't expected her clinical supervisor to be so…attractive—setting her heart aflutter and raising her body temperature. After losing Ricardo, she'd assumed herself immune to physical desire, but no, her body seemed to be fully back in business. Her stare furtively dipped to his left hand, confirming the absence of a wedding ring, but his marital status was irrelevant.

As she'd told Eva again and again, she wasn't interested in dating. It seemed too hard and pointless as well. She'd had the great love of her life, and she had no intention of looking for love again.

'I'm looking for Theatre Six, the Lopez case,' she said. 'I assume that's where you're heading, too, seeing as we're going to be working together for a few weeks.'

'I am.' Felipe nodded and gestured with an outstretched arm. 'Allow me to show you the way.'

Emilia gratefully fell into step at his side, ignoring the sexy surgeon's swagger and how good he looked in the hospital's shapeless, green scrubs. She rarely noticed a member of the opposite sex, but when she did it still somehow felt as if she were cheating on Ricardo.

But then, they had been married for over twenty years. Sometimes, when she remembered that he was gone, she had to catch herself. It was as if half her heart was missing.

'So you're from Uruguay?' Felipe asked, glancing

her way with obvious interest. 'What brings you to Buenos Aires?'

Emilia sucked in a breath. She'd known this line of questioning was inevitable. Consultants her age, the wrong side of fifty, rarely shifted hospitals, unless it was for personal reasons. And there was nothing more personal to Emilia than her beloved daughter, Eva.

'My late husband was Argentine. He was born in this hospital in fact,' she said, her voice tight. It often was when she talked about Ricardo. 'Our daughter wanted to go to university here, so I thought I'd make the move, too, as it's just the two of us. My parents died a few years ago, so there's no family keeping me in Uruguay.'

She trailed off, aware that she might be viewed as an over-protective mother. She had no intention of smothering Eva, but her eighteen-year-old daughter was all the family Emilia had left. It made sense to at least reside in the same country in case of emergencies, and to emotionally support Eva.

But she was thrilled that Eva would be able to spend more time with her father's side of the family. Losing her father at the age of thirteen, Eva had been through a lot. There'd been times during the past five years where Emilia had worried for her daughter's mental health—she'd seemed so sad and withdrawn.

'And why not?' Felipe's easy smile widened. 'Why should the youngsters have all the fun?'

'Quite.' Emilia heard herself laugh, the sound high pitched and a little strained. Since Ricardo's death, there'd been little time and even less inclination for *fun*. What with raising a teenager solo and maintaining her busy and demanding career, Emilia often reached the end of another week exhausted and faced with the realisation that, yet again, she'd inadvertently put herself last.

'Buenos Aires is a great city,' Felipe continued, with enthusiasm. 'You'll both love it here, I'm sure, once you've settled in.'

Emilia stayed silent. Settling into a new life, a new home and new job would be no mean feat. But as long as Eva was happy, she'd be happy.

Just as they rounded the corner to Theatre Six, their pagers sounded in unison with an urgent call.

'Looks like we made it in the nick of time,' Felipe said, silencing the alarm.

They hurried into Theatre Six's scrub room and passed their pagers to a theatre technician. Felipe reached for a theatre hat and mask and Emilia did the same.

'Nothing like a little excitement to start your first day,' he added, switching on the water over the sinks and vigorously washing his hands.

Emilia laughed. 'If you say so.'

Tamping down her adrenaline with some deep breaths, she glanced into the theatre as she joined him at the sinks. Through the glass, they had a bird's eye view of the brightly lit obstetrics' theatre. Isabella Lopez was already gowned up and surrounded by the delivery team, and a man Emilia assumed was Sebastian Lopez, her husband.

'So, a few weeks ago, the smallest of the Lopez triplets was prenatally diagnosed with a congenital diaphragmatic hernia, using foetal MRI scanning,' Felipe said, bringing her up to speed on the case as they scrubbed up, side by side.

Emilia nodded, working a scrubbing brush under her nails. 'I came in early to read the case file. I understand you performed a fetoscopic endoluminal tracheal occlusion at twenty-seven weeks. That's impressive in a multiple pregnancy.'

He raised his eyebrows over his mask. 'You'll see I'm not a shy surgeon. But the parents, Isabella and Sebastian, are both emergency doctors here at the General, so they were happy to consider the procedure. They want the best possible outcome for all three babies, so together we weighed the pros and cons of the FETO. Hopefully the gamble paid off.'

'I met Isabella Lopez when I came for my interview in January,' Emilia said, briskly scrubbing her hands and arms.

She'd immediately clicked with the other woman, who, along with her husband, ran the emergency department at the General. And after their difficult fertility journey, she knew how much the couple wanted these three miracle babies that were about to be born. At nearly thirty-one weeks gestation, all three Lopez triplets would need to spend some time on the neonatal intensive care unit, or NICU, and the smallest baby also faced surgery to correct the defect in the diaphragm.

'Right, let's go meet the Lopez triplets,' Felipe said, turning off the taps and using his back to push through the door into the operating room.

Three resuscitation tables for newborns were set up to one side of the room, each warmed and awaiting a baby. A cluster of neonatal registrars and nurses waited nearby, expressions tense.

Emilia glanced over at Isabella, trying to send her calming positive vibes from behind her mask. The birth of a child was always emotional, but when the babies were premature and one needed surgery, it might be overwhelming for the couple.

After being assisted by scrub nurses into surgical gowns and sterile gloves, Felipe and Emilia nodded to the Lopezes and joined the obstetrician performing the elective caesarean section.

The first two babies were delivered, one after another. Their umbilical cords were clamped, and they were quickly whisked away by the neonatal team. Each baby was placed on the resuscitation table's heated mattress. The neonatal nurses gently dried the newborns with a towel and cleared their noses of mucus with a small suction tube.

'Apgar is nine,' the registrar caring for the first triplet said.

Emilia breathed a sigh of relief and glanced at Felipe, who nodded. The oldest Lopez baby had a low birth weight but was breathing spontaneously, had a good skin colour and normal reflexes, his condition stable enough for transfer to the NICU. The baby was wrapped up and carried over to Mamá and Papá for a quick cuddle.

At the next resuscitation table, triplet number two was being assessed by a second registrar. While slightly smaller than his brother, baby two was mewling loudly, his tiny pink face scrunched up in outrage.

'Apgar is ten,' the neonatal nurse said, wrapping him in a sheet and scooping him up for a few seconds of skin-to-skin contact with his parents.

Emilia smiled under her mask at Isabella and Sebastian's joy. But there was still one more baby to deliver. As the obstetrician delivered the head of the third and smallest baby, the atmosphere in the room changed.

'Syringe,' Felipe asked, holding out his hand.

The tube blocking the baby's airway, which had kept the lung expanded as the baby developed in utero, needed to be removed before the umbilical cord was cut, as it was essentially breathing for the baby via the placenta.

Emilia had only seen the FETO procedure a handful of times, so she was glad for Felipe's greater experience in this instance. Felipe quickly deflated the balloon and removed the endotracheal tube from the baby's mouth. The delivery of the third Lopez baby was completed and the cord clamped as usual. Except unlike his brothers, baby three was limp and silent, his skin grey with cyanosis—a lack of oxygen.

Moving quickly, Emilia and Felipe carried the baby to the third resuscitation table, which had been set up in a screened off area with dimmed lighting.

While a nurse suctioned mucous from the mouth and nose, Emilia gently dried the baby with a towel to stimulate spontaneous respiration. Urgency shunted her pulse through the roof. She reached for the neonatal resuscitator, just in case the third triplet failed to start breathing on his own.

Those couple of seconds, during which the baby made no respiratory effort, felt endless. Emilia willed him to make it, her stare flicking to Felipe's.

'There's a heartbeat,' Felipe said, removing his stethoscope, 'but little respiratory effort. We already know from the scans that the left lung is hypoplastic.'

Emilia nodded, quickly but gently inflating the baby's underdeveloped lungs with the resuscitator. The third Lopez baby was struggling to breathe unaided. Because of the hole in the diaphragm, abdominal organs had herniated into the chest and prevented the left lung from growing. Felipe had mitigated some of the pressure on the developing lungs with the FETO procedure, but the underdeveloped lung was still smaller than normal.

Emilia placed electrodes on the newborn's chest, her relief mounting when the heart monitor picked up a normal trace.

Their eyes met over the tops of their masks. 'We still have sinus rhythm,' Emilia told him.

Felipe nodded, his thoughts likely matching hers. For the time being, the smallest Lopez baby would need to be ventilated until they could close the diaphragmatic defect and give his lungs the space to grow.

'I'm going to intubate,' Felipe said, reaching for a laryngoscope and endotracheal tube. 'Then we'll transfer him to the NICU.'

With the intubation complete, Emilia passed a nasogastric tube into the baby's stomach to empty it of any contents and take the pressure off the baby's tiny lungs, which were already compromised by the herniation of small bowel loops into the chest.

As the baby's oxygen saturations climbed into the normal range, Felipe inserted an umbilical vein catheter into the cord so they could administer fluids, drugs and easily take blood samples. They worked together as if they'd been doing it for years, each of them anticipating the other's moves and assisting where required.

Once they had the third triplet stabilised, Emilia glanced at Felipe. 'A quick hello to Mamá and Papá and then up to NICU?'

Felipe nodded, peeling off his gloves and mask. 'Let's reassess him this afternoon, but he's booked for surgery in two or three days, as long as he remains stable. The sooner we can close that hole in his diaphragm the better.'

As Isabella was still on the table being sewn up from her C-section, Felipe and Emilia carefully wheeled the mobile resuscitation table over to the parents.

'We knew from the scans that the left lung was small,' Felipe explained to Isabella and Sebastian, who were understandably tearful and overwhelmed, 'so I've placed baby three on a ventilator, to help him breathe.'

'We've decided to name him Luis,' Sebastian said, gently taking his wife's hand so together they could reach out and touch their son's tiny curled fist.

'We're taking Luis to the NICU,' Emilia said, trying to sound reassuring, although they all knew the situation was serious. 'As soon as you're ready, you can see him and his brothers there. Try not to worry.' She met Isabella's stare. 'We'll take the best of care of them.'

Isabella nodded, tears seeping from the corner of her eye as she reached out and squeezed Emilia's hand. From one mother to another, Emilia heard what was being left unsaid: *Take care of my babies while I can't.*

'Congratulations on the birth of your sons,' Felipe added, resting his hand on Sebastian's shoulder, as if he too was aware of the turmoil and concern of the new parents. 'What a blessing.'

While the registrar and neonatal nurses whisked Luis upstairs to the NICU, Felipe and Emilia de-gowned, tossing the garments into a dirty laundry bin outside Theatre Six.

Emilia sagged a little, releasing an audible sigh as most of the adrenaline left her system. 'Well, that *was* an eventful first morning.'

Felipe nodded, one side of his mouth curling up in a charming smile. 'Now that the excitement is over, let me show you the most important room in the department, in case you get lost again.'

Emilia ignored the return of the silly flutter in her chest at how attractive and charming he was. It made no difference. That Felipe was so friendly and welcoming was nice, given they'd be working so closely together, but it also left her strangely unsettled. She wasn't used to male attention, not that he was overtly flirting. Would she even know what flirting looked like, having been off the market for so long?

'I hope it's the coffee room.' She laughed, smoothing her hat-flattened hair back from her face. 'I may not know my way around the rest of the hospital yet, but when I came for my interview, I made sure to ask for directions to the nearest coffee machine.'

'A woman with priorities,' he said with that confident smile that put her at ease, but also sped up her pulse. 'Although there's only instant in the break room. For the real thing, espresso, the best place to go is Café Rivas, upstairs in the foyer.'

'Oh, I definitely need the real thing to get through my first day.' Instant coffee just wasn't going to cut it.

'In that case,' he said, 'why don't I show you the way?'

'Great, thanks.' She followed him from the suite of theatres and up the stairs. She'd have to find her way around the hospital without his help soon enough. But, for now, there was no harm in accepting a guided tour from a supportive and approachable colleague.

'Café Rivas has an app so you can pre-order drinks without waiting in line,' he said, pushing through double doors at the top of the stairs.

'Uh-oh,' she said, waggling her eyebrows, 'that sounds dangerous.'

'Very,' Felipe agreed, holding the door open for her to pass through. 'Although I won't tell if you don't. It will be our little secret.'

Emilia couldn't help but smile, even as she felt her barriers rising. Charming, a fearless surgeon and hot. Never mind the easily accessible coffee being dangerous—she'd have to be very careful around Felipe Castillo.

# CHAPTER TWO

FELIPE OFTEN HEADED to Café Rivas for a fix before a routine Theatre list. But with Emilia's fascinating company, there seemed to be an extra spring in his step today that was in no way related to the promise of caffeine.

'So what can I get you?' he asked as they entered the sun-filled café, which was situated at the front of the main hospital foyer and serviced both staff and visitors alike.

'A cappuccino,' she said, 'but *I* can get it.'

'Please, allow me,' he insisted, noticing the appealing slope of her exposed neck and the rich brown of her tied-back hair. 'Until you've had a chance to download the app,' he pressed, hoping to convince her. 'That way we can bypass the queue at the till.'

That the new neonatal surgeon was so stunning had caught him completely off guard. The hospital scrubs were forest green, a colour that complimented her skin tone and the golden brown of her eyes. As standard issue, they weren't that flattering, but he didn't need to be medically qualified to know her slender athletic build ticked every box for him. She was exactly his type.

'Okay, thanks,' she said. 'I owe you one.'

Felipe inclined his head, hoping there'd be plenty of opportunities to share drinks in their future.

'So, I realise that I bombarded you with questions earlier,' he said as they loitered near the espresso machine. 'Now it's your turn to ask me anything while we wait.'

'Okay…' She smiled, her studied observation raising his body temperature a few degrees.

'What drew you to neonatal surgery?' she asked. 'Do you have your own children?'

'No, I don't.' Felipe shook his head, loving her directness—a woman who knew her own mind. She didn't strike him as someone who would play games. And after fifteen years of casually dating, Felipe had seen every game in the book.

'Luckily I love kids,' he continued, 'given our work. I just never quite got around to having one of my own. My ex-wife didn't want children, and I was content to see them every day here.'

He shrugged, thinking of his younger brother, Thiago, and Castillo Estates, the family vineyard business that Felipe had refused to take over in favour of selfishly pursuing his medical career. Now that Felipe was committed to staying single, and had just turned fifty-five, the burden of producing the next generation of Castillo children was solely down to Thiago and his soon-to-be wife, Violetta.

The same single-mindedness that had driven Felipe to pursue his own profession had probably also led him to neglect his marriage, while he worked to prove to his family that he'd made the right decision in pursuing medicine. Not that his divorce was solely his fault…

'How about you?' he asked, shoving his ex-wife of fifteen years, Delfina, from his mind. 'Just the one daughter?'

He'd rather talk about the fascinating and sexy new consultant than think about his failed marriage. Or how he'd also let down both his brother and his parents. Emilia Gonzales was surprisingly down to earth, clearly intelligent and utterly gorgeous. He couldn't help but wonder if she was seeing anyone…

'Yes, Eva.' Emilia smiled, maternal pride shining in her eyes. 'She's just started law at UBA.' Her smile deepened to reveal a charming dimple in one cheek.

'Not medicine?' he asked, surprised. 'The University of Buenos Aeries has an excellent medical school. That's where I trained.'

Emilia laughed, shaking her head so her ponytail swung. 'No—I managed to somehow put her off. Instead, she's following in her father's footsteps. He studied law at UBA, too.'

Felipe could instantly tell that she and Eva were close. No wonder she'd made the shift to Buenos Aires when her daughter moved there to study. But starting over in your fifties could be…isolating.

'Eva sounds scarily smart,' he said, newly intrigued by the woman with whom, at first glance, he had heaps in common.

'Oh, she is,' she agreed, tilting her head to observe him in a way that saw him clenching his abs.

Now he was grateful that he worked hard to keep in shape. There was obviously a spark between them, a mutual attraction.

'So, how long have you been divorced?' she asked.

'Fifteen years,' he confessed, wincing when her eyebrows shot up with surprise. 'It was a perfectly amicable split,' he continued, feeling, as he always did, that he needed to justify his divorce. 'We'd just drifted apart.'

And over those fifteen years, he'd carved out a great life for himself, finding the perfect balance of work and social life, punctuated by the occasional casual date. Only no matter how many years passed, he couldn't seem to shake off the guilt that, because he'd pursued his career so diligently, he'd been a second-rate husband. No wonder he was content to date casually. Unlike Thiago, who was about to walk down the aisle.

Emilia eyed him a little more closely, as if trying to figure him out. 'Do you have a new partner?'

It was a logical next question, but he couldn't help hearing a hopeful curiosity in her voice.

'No, I'm single. I date, but nothing serious. What about you? Do you mind me asking how long it's been since your husband died?'

The curiosity was mutual. If she was on the market, he'd definitely be interested in something casual.

'Ricardo,' she said, supplying her husband's name as pain dulled her stare for a second. 'He's been gone five years.'

'I'm sorry.' Why had he asked? They'd only just met and now he'd made her sad. 'Starting again at our age is an adjustment,' he added, trying to repair the damage, 'and that's without moving to a new country the way you have.'

It was difficult enough to meet new people, especially the *right* people. He knew. He'd had fifteen years of experience.

'Oh, I'm not starting again apart from this new job.' She self-consciously toyed with her long hair, avoiding his stare. 'I'm too focused on making sure that Eva is settled here to worry about myself.'

Felipe's stomach fell. So she *wasn't* dating. He could understand why she put her daughter's needs above her own. Her situation was very different from his. She'd clearly loved her husband to the end, and probably still did. That didn't mean she was immune to loneliness though, especially given that her daughter was all grown up and would presumably be leaving the nest one day soon.

Maybe they could simply be friends?

'Well, there's no shortage of things to do in Buenos Aires,' he said, hiding his disappointment that he couldn't ask her out. 'What do you like to do when you're not working?'

Although given that he had to supervise her surgeries and make a report to the Argentine Medical Council, it was probably for the best that she was off limits. He didn't want Emilia to be at the centre of any hospital gossip.

'Gardening, reading, walks in the park with the dog. Nothing exciting.' She laughed. 'I get all the adrenaline I need from work.'

Felipe chuckled in agreement. Everything about her so far was seriously attractive.

'What about you?' she asked, watching him again.

'The same, actually, minus the gardening. I live in an apartment, and I usually *run* in the park with the dog. He's a border terrier. Dante.'

Excitement lit her eyes. 'Mine's a springer spaniel—Luna. Although she's really my daughter's dog, I always seem to be one doing the walking…'

'Funny that,' he grinned, knowingly. 'So do you know anyone here in Buenos Aires?'

Emilia shook her head, a slight flush to her cheeks. 'No. My husband's family are from Córdoba.'

'In that case, we should get the dogs together sometime for a doggy date at the park.' Felipe held up his hands. 'That's not a line, just a friendly invitation.'

Emilia offered him a watery smile, failing to hide her horror at the idea.

Before she could politely decline, he jumped in. 'But I'm sure you'll have no trouble finding the best dog parks in the city without my help.'

He'd heard the message—she *really* wasn't interested. Just then, the barista called out Felipe's name and held out their takeaway order.

'Here you go,' Felipe said, passing Emilia her coffee.

'Thanks,' she said, heading with him towards the exit. 'I'm going to meet my registrar on the NICU and do a quick ward round, acquaint myself with the patients I've inherited from my predecessor.'

They paused at the top of the stairs where he'd be heading down to Theatres, while she went up to the third floor.

'Page me if you need any help,' Felipe said. 'I'll see you back in Theatre. We have a full list this afternoon.'

Before they could part ways, Emilia touched his arm, stalling him.

'Sorry about just now, Felipe,' she said, looking mildly embarrassed. 'I'm just a little sensitive about the whole dating thing. Eva thinks it's high time I got back out there and I'm really not keen. It's something of a touchy subject at home.'

She'd just moved to a new country, a place that must hold painful memories of her husband. That would make anyone feel bewildered and reluctant to date.

'No need for an apology.' Empathy tightened Felipe's chest that they had yet another thing in common. 'I understand the well-meaning pressure from family. My younger brother is soon to be married, and my entire family think I too should remarry before it's too late.'

He widened his eyes, mock horrified, and she smiled. He knew all was forgiven.

'I'm glad I'm not the only one being...*encouraged*.' She rolled her eyes. 'At our age, we can't possibly look after ourselves, can we?'

'One of the best things that comes with reaching half a century is that we know our own minds, right? You'll date when you're ready.' He shrugged. 'Or not.'

'I agree.' She smiled, gratitude sparkling in her eyes. 'But try telling that to my teenage daughter.'

They parted ways and Felipe headed downstairs, his spirits a little deflated. So he'd imagined the way she'd checked him out. Mistaken her friendliness for flirtation.

They could still be friends, though.

Except the dull throb of disappointment stayed with him for the rest of the day.

# CHAPTER THREE

THAT NIGHT, AFTER a busy first day, Emilia and Eva met at an authentic Argentinian restaurant near the hospital. Eva ordered some sweet-sounding cocktail and shot her mother a familiar glare.

'You're too set in your ways, Mamá. You should try something new. We're celebrating the start of our new life.'

'You're right.' Emilia nodded, feeling a hundred years old. Part of her wished that she didn't need to start a new life. She'd liked her *old* life, when it had been the three of them: Ricardo, her and Eva. Starting over seemed monumental, not that she'd ever confess as much to Eva.

Emilia offered the server an apologetic smile. 'Actually, cancel the Chardonnay and make that *two* pomegranate gin fizzes, please.'

Trying new things kept life interesting, that's what she and Ricardo had always taught Eva. It was just that, for Emilia, *everything* in her life at the moment seemed new and mildly terrifying. New home that Ricardo hadn't ever lived in. New job in a place with bittersweet reminders at every turn. New pressures to put herself back out there—on the *meat market.*

She hid a shudder. Now wasn't the time to dampen the mood by voicing her unpopular reflections.

'It sounds delicious,' she said to Eva as the waiter left. At least this concession over a drink was easier to grant than the ongoing battle over how long was too long to grieve for her husband.

'So how was your first day at work?' Eva asked, pushing her long brown hair over her shoulder.

Her dark eyes were so like Ricardo's that sometimes it hurt Emilia to look at her beautiful daughter.

'It was good,' she said, brightly. 'Busy and eventful. We had newborn triplets admitted to the NICU today.'

Eva's eyes rounded with empathy. 'Oh, I hope they'll be okay.'

'So do I.' Emilia nodded, sharing Eva's sentiment. She'd spoken to Isabella and Sebastian Lopez on the NICU before she'd left the hospital that evening. They were understandably concerned about all three babies, but were putting on brave faces.

But thinking about the tiny Lopez babies brought to mind her sexy surgical colleague, Felipe Castillo. Another new thing to contend with, the shock reawakening of a badly timed and inappropriate sexual attraction. Of course, it was just Emilia's luck that her supervising consultant would be hot, divorced and, with fifteen years' experience, an expert in casual dating.

Yes, he'd made her first day a little less daunting with his easy camaraderie and professional support, but the undercurrents of attraction between them had also set her alarm bells ringing. He was the first man she'd truly noticed in *that* way since Ricardo, and she wasn't certain she was ready yet to open that particular can of worms.

She'd loved her husband of twenty-one years. She loved him still, despite him losing his battle with grade four brain cancer. Even after five years alone, being attracted to another man felt…somehow disloyal. But, she had no intention of acting on that attraction.

That was why she'd freaked out when Felipe had suggested a harmless walk in the dog park together…

*What was wrong with her?*

'How was university?' she asked Eva, changing the subject.

'Good. It was clubs day,' Eva said, her eyes bright with excitement. 'I've signed up for social volleyball and the Modern Feminist's Society.'

'Sounds great.' Emilia's heart warmed that her daughter seemed to be embracing their new life much better than her mother. 'You'll soon be making more new friends.'

And Eva deserved a little happiness. After some rocky times over the past few years, when Eva had struggled with understandable bouts of sadness and anger over her father's untimely death, it was a relief to see her daughter energised about her university life.

'What about you?' Eva pressed. 'Did *you* meet anyone interesting at the hospital?'

Just then, the waiter returned with their drinks, placing the fussy pink concoctions on the table with a flourish.

'Of course not,' Emilia mumbled, a flush brewing, making her neck itchy. She pounced on her drink, taking a generous gulp to calm her nerves and hide her reaction from eagle-eyed Eva.

She didn't want to talk about Felipe Castillo and his confusing friendliness. She didn't want to examine her body's unexpected reaction to the man. She just wanted to feel like her old self, to remember that she was here in Buenos Aires primarily for Eva. She was focused on her daughter's happiness, rather than probing the soft, vulnerable spots of her own emotional and physical well-being.

Eva regarded her mother with suspicion. 'I hope you're not walking around with your eyes closed, Mamá. In a hospital as big as the General, there must be at least *one* single man your age.'

'I'm sure there is,' Emilia said, picking up the menu and scanning the delicious-sounding dishes, rather than thinking about the sexy, talented Felipe again.

Only everything was blurry—she needed her glasses.

'So...what are you having?' she asked, steering the conversation back to the menu. 'They have empanada, which look good.' Emilia fished around for her glasses from the bottom of her bag, aware of the loaded silence. She looked up to find Eva watching her with a clear and telling sympathy.

If she'd hoped to avoid this topic tonight, Emilia was out of luck.

'You know that Papá wouldn't want you to be alone forever, don't you?' Eva said, unfairly playing her winning argument.

Emilia had nowhere left to hide. She and Ricardo had even discussed this very situation, near the end, when it had become obvious that all treatment options had been exhausted. He'd made her promise to be happy. To take care of herself as well as their daughter.

But the execution of her promise wasn't straightforward. It meant overcoming her grief, being honest about her needs as a woman, stepping out of her comfort zone and putting herself out there into the terrifying ether of dating some...stranger.

Emilia blinked away the sting in her eyes and closed the menu in defeat. 'I know, I just...' Her throat tightened. She couldn't simply switch off her feelings for the man she'd loved most of her adult life. And deep down, what scared her most was that her dating again would be the final confirmation that Ricardo wasn't coming back.

Of course, she already knew that in her head, but her heart was much slower to adjust to this harsh new reality.

'*I* want you to be happy too,' Eva pressed, 'especially as we're starting over in a new country. I know I've encouraged you before, but perhaps now that we're here it's the perfect time to start dating.'

Would there ever be a perfect time for *that*? Emilia hadn't been single since her early twenties. Even if she wanted to get back out there, the rules of modern dating were a total mystery. There were apps and confusing terminologies. It was a steep learning curve.

'I'll think about it, okay?' She took another swallow of her overly sweet cocktail, hoping to put an end to the uncomfortable but familiar line of questioning. In desperation, Emilia scanned the restaurant's elegant and dimly lit booth-style layout for a glimpse of their server to take their order.

That was how she spotted Felipe Castillo a few tables away.

Emilia froze with shock.

He was casually dressed in dark chinos, a blue shirt open at the collar and a linen sports jacket. He looked cool and sophisticated—and he was pulling out a chair for a beautiful, statuesque brunette woman.

Emilia's body flooded with uncomfortable heat.

*He* was on a date, while she sat there mooning over how nice he'd been, making excuses for why she could never be interested in him, or any man, even casually. She made a crestfallen squawking sound in her throat.

As if he'd heard her from across the room, he looked up and their eyes met.

The full body flush turned anticipatory. He looked so dashing in his regular clothes. More approachable, taller, hotter. It wasn't fair. They smiled at each other, then Emilia ducked her head, but not before she saw him murmur something to his date, who smiled up adoringly and touched his arm as he left her side.

'Oh, no…' Emilia whispered under her breath as she saw him head their way in her peripheral vision.

He was coming over. Now she'd have to act natural in front of Eva. She'd have to contain her surprise at how good he looked out of scrubs, *and* manage her disappointment that, despite what he'd told her in the hospital café, he was obviously taken.

But of course he was, a man like him…

She scrabbled for the menu again, opening it blindly while she tried in vain to control her blush.

Eva looked around, her eyes wide with curiosity. 'Who's that?' she whispered.

Emilia grimaced, her cheeks flaming. 'Just a colleague from the hospital.' She'd barely uttered the words when Felipe arrived at their table.

'Emilia. Good to see you,' he said, his smile wide and genuine, as if they were already old friends. 'I see you've discovered Buenos Aires's best kept secret. The tamales here are delicious.'

Emilia laughed nervously, pushing her reading glasses up on the top of her head so he came back into focus.

'Felipe,' she said, her voice emerging embarrassingly high pitched, 'this is the daughter I was telling you about, Eva.' She glanced at her delighted daughter, reluctantly completing the introduction. 'Felipe Castillo is a senior neonatal surgeon at the General. We're working together.'

Eva held out her hand and Felipe shook it with another warm smile.

'So you're the scarily smart law student,' he said.

Eva accepted the compliment with a shrug for Felipe and an intrigued glare for Emilia.

'I was telling your mum about the dog park in the city,' Felipe continued, easily charming Eva. 'It's a great place to take Luna. There's a pond and an obstacle course. My dog loves it.'

'Oh, thanks,' Eva said. 'I'll have to check it out, although Mamá loves to walk Luna, too.' She stared at Emilia, her excited eyes practically on stalks. 'Perhaps you could give her and Luna a tour sometime,' she added to Felipe.

Emilia glanced up at Felipe, apologetically, while inside she curled in upon herself with embarrassment. 'Felipe and I have already discussed that, Eva.'

Her face flamed as she turned to Felipe. 'But we won't keep you from your *date*.' She stumbled clumsily over the last word as if she didn't even want to say it, let alone *do* it. 'Thanks for the menu recommendation and enjoy your evening.'

'You too,' he said with an easy-going shrug. 'See you at work tomorrow. Eva, it was a pleasure meeting you.' With another devastating smile for Emilia, he made his way back to his table, to the woman who watched him approach with obvious adoration.

Emilia lowered her gaze to the tablecloth. She didn't want to witness Felipe sharing a romantic dinner with his glamorous date. Slowly, she exhaled the breath she'd been holding, an unexpectedly hollow sensation in her chest. But of course he was taken. He was single and hot, in or out of the scrubs, and a surgeon. Plus he had that smile thing going on, the one that came from his eyes and made you feel like the only person in the room…

Except she hadn't anticipated seeing him with another woman to trigger such an intense return of her loneliness. Maybe Eva was right; maybe she *did* need to address the gaping hole in her personal life. She didn't want to turn into one of those older women who lived only through their grown-up child.

Eva deserved better than to have to worry about her poor sad Mamá.

'I thought you said you didn't meet anyone interesting at work today,' Eva said, dragging Emilia back into conversation. 'You two seem to have really hit it off.'

If only she could share Eva's obvious excitement. If only it was as simple as meeting a sexy man at work—one she had heaps in common with—and enjoying a few easy, confidence-building dates, nothing serious.

'Oh…? Not really,' Emilia bluffed, recalling how effortless and relaxed her and Felipe's few conversations had been, until she'd freaked out. 'I was lost on my way to Theatre this morning and he showed me the way.'

Her explanation fell flat, dragged down by her dampened spirits. Fifty-two was no age to abandon companionship, even sex, altogether. Maybe she was overcomplicating the issue simply because she was terrified of taking the first step—a date with a man she'd never met.

'*And* he remembered your daughter's degree and the name of your dog,' Eva pointed out. 'He's obviously interested in *you*.' Her eighteen-year-old rolled her eyes as if Emilia was utterly clueless. And she wasn't wrong.

Unlike Felipe, who'd been single and dating for fifteen years, Emilia was seriously out of practice.

She flushed at the very idea of Felipe Castillo finding her sexually attractive. Perhaps he also simply needed companionship, someone to laugh with, to enjoy a meal or a movie with. Maybe what Emilia needed the most was someone to remind her that, after the death of a beloved spouse, life went on.

Only one look at him all dressed up and smelling delicious, the way his date drooled at him, and instinct told her that Felipe's night was going to end with some pretty steamy sex.

'I don't think so,' she said, primly sliding on her glasses again so she could study the menu in earnest. She needed to stop thinking about Felipe Castillo's sex life. 'Anyway, he's obviously taken. In case you haven't noticed, he's on a date with a beautiful woman. He was just being polite.'

Eva scoffed. 'A date he abandoned to come over and say hello to *you*.' Then her expression softened with another of those sympathetic looks that made Emilia wince. 'But I'm sorry that he's taken. He seemed really nice, and you two obviously have heaps in common. You know what they say, though—*plenty more fish in the sea*.'

'No need to be sorry.' Emilia shooed away her daughter's well-meaning concern. 'I'm fine. I'm too busy with work and settling into our new life here, making sure you have everything you need, to worry about meeting men.'

'Mamá… What about what *you* need? Papá's been gone five years now.'

Emilia hid her sigh. As if she wasn't aware of every single one of the two thousand and eighty-six days she'd woken up without her husband, her best friend, her rock.

Eva reached for Emilia's hand across the table. 'I saw the way you smiled at Felipe. I think it's time you at least consider dating. Please… For me?'

Emilia winced, powerless in the face of her daughter's pleading. 'Okay, fine. I'll consider it.'

'Great.' Eva reached for Emilia's phone, scooping it up from the table.

'What are you doing?' Emilia spied the waiter heading their way and sagged with relief. If they passed on starters and dessert, they could be out of here in under an hour, and that way they'd avoid watching Felipe's romantic date unfold.

'I'm signing you up to a dating app,' Eva said with a stubborn expression. 'There are specific ones for the over forties, so you should have no problem finding someone you have things in common with.'

'Yay…' Emilia said sarcastically, surreptitiously glancing Felipe's way as he and the brunette clinked wine glasses in a toast.

'This is how you meet people these days, Mamá. You have to move with the times.'

Emilia smiled at her daughter, silently addressing her beloved Ricardo in her head: *Why, oh, why is our daughter so headstrong? And why did you have to go and leave me to this utterly daunting fate?*

# CHAPTER FOUR

EARLY THE NEXT morning Felipe entered Café Rivas and instantly spied Emilia waiting in the coffee queue near the espresso machine.

His pulse galloped with the kind of excitement that had been totally lacking from his date the night before. Emilia looked sensational, smartly dressed in a grey blouse and black skirt, her hair clipped back at the nape of her neck and small gold hoops in her ears.

What was it about her simple, sophisticated elegance he found so appealing? Was it just that they had so much in common? That he admired her intelligence and sense of humour? She even had an obviously close relationship with her delightful daughter, and it couldn't have been easy raising a teenager alone.

She was so intent on her phone that she didn't notice him approach.

'Did you enjoy your meal last night?' he asked, startling her so she placed one hand over her heart and laughed up at him with shock.

'Oh… Hi. Yes. It was delicious, thanks.' She pushed her glasses up onto her head the way she had last night. 'Eva wanted us to celebrate the first proper day of our *new life*.'

'Eva has her priorities set right, I think. Casa Comiendo is one of my favourite restaurants.'

She tucked the phone into the pocket of her skirt, a sheepish look on her face.

'Are you having trouble with the coffee app?' he asked. 'I'd be happy to help you set up a standing order for your favourite drink if you want. Cappuccino, right?'

'No… I, um…' She flushed prettily, glancing away so he noticed the berry-coloured sheen of gloss on her full lips. 'Well, the truth is, Eva signed me up to a dating app last night, and I was trying to turn off the notifications. My profile has only been live for fourteen hours and I keep getting hits or swipes or whatever they're called. It's very distracting and I have clinic this morning.'

Felipe's stomach took a disappointed dive, but he kept his smile fixed in place. So she *was* dating?

'I'm sure it shows,' she said, inclining her head in his direction and lowering her voice, 'but it's my first time on a dating app. I had no idea it would be so…overwhelming.'

Another wave of disappointment struck. No wonder her phone was going nuts. She was gorgeous and smart and sophisticated. She'd be beating men off with a stick. He swallowed the bitter taste in his mouth, wishing *he* could be the one to take her out and show her the best Buenos Aires had to offer. But he was supervising her. And her personal life—who she dated—was none of his business.

'If you want my advice, and I've been doing this for fifteen years,' he said, sticking his nose in because he felt somehow protective of her, and she was looking up at him expectantly, 'is to take your time. You don't have to feel pressured to meet anyone unless it feels right.'

She'd been off the market for what, over twenty years? Things had changed in that time. He knew exactly how it felt to relearn all of the dating rules.

At her relieved smile, a fresh surge of protective impulses shook him. Crazy. She was an intelligent grown woman with an adult child. She could take care of herself. Although they *were* colleagues, and she didn't yet have any friends in town…

She nodded, her brown eyes curious, as if she was appraising him every bit as much as he was her. 'Try telling Eva that. She seems to think that five years alone is long enough, which is why, despite my better judgement, I'm meeting some stranger called Santino tonight.' She stared at him, imploring. 'Help—what should I expect?'

Felipe stood a little taller, happy to take her under his wing, both in and out of the operating room.

'Things have certainly changed since we were in our twenties,' he said, trying not to think about this lovely woman with some lucky guy named *Santino.*

'Tell me about it.' She rolled her eyes and then sobered. 'I'm tempted to cancel, but I worry about Eva. She's been through a lot, losing her dad and now moving away from all her old friends. I don't want her to worry about *me.*'

Felipe nodded, his heart going out to her and her daughter. 'Well if you *do* meet this guy, make sure it's in a public place.'

She nodded intently, urging him to continue.

'A bar or a café is good, but not one that you frequent regularly,' he said. 'If you don't like him, or it doesn't work out, you don't want him showing up at your favourite haunts all the time.'

Emilia's eyes widened in horror. 'I didn't think of that,

thanks.' She looked at him as if he'd just rescued her from a burning building. 'Anything else?'

Felipe fought the urge to tell her to forget other guys and date him instead, but he already felt invested in her happiness. 'It's better to suggest drinks rather than dinner for a first date. That way, if it's not going well, you can just cut the night short.'

'Another awesome tip,' she said, looking, if anything, a little *more* nervous.

'I'm sure it will be great,' he said, hoping to boost her confidence. If Santino had any sense, he'd realise what a great catch Emilia was and hold onto her, tightly. She was beautiful and intelligent. She had everything going for her.

She shrugged and then changed the subject. 'So, how was *your* evening last night?'

Felipe considered sugar coating it, but he didn't want to lie to her when she'd asked for his advice. 'Not great, to be honest.' He sighed, wishing he'd gone to his favourite restaurant alone last night. Who knew how the evening might have unfolded differently if he hadn't been on a date.

Her eyebrows rose with surprise.

'The food was delicious,' he said with a shrug, 'as it always is at Casa Comiendo. I ordered a world-class bottle of malbec—my family own a vineyard in Mendoza so I'm a bit of a wine snob, I'm afraid—but I won't be seeing my date again.'

Emilia paled a little. 'Oh…that bad, huh? I'm sorry.' Her expression was genuinely sympathetic, but he wanted to convince himself that he saw a flicker of excitement in her stare.

'Now I'm regretting the impulse to be brave and give

dating a try myself,' she added with a wince. 'You have way more experience and there's still the possibility of failure. What hope do *I* have, a complete beginner…?'

'Don't be put off.' Felipe said, internally cursing fate that he was encouraging her to date other men when he was so attracted to her. 'I'm sure you'll have a great time.'

Why couldn't he meet someone like Emilia? Someone on his wavelength who wanted the same things—just some casual, fun dates. Although some instinct warned him that Emilia might only want that for now, but once recovered from her grief, she might one day want more.

'It's just that the trouble with dating apps,' he continued, 'is that someone can seem great on paper, but when you meet in person, you realise you have less in common that you thought.'

Emilia nodded vigorously. 'That's what worries me. I'd much rather meet someone the old-fashioned way. You know, face to face.'

'I agree.' Felipe nodded, thinking of how *they'd* met, instantly clicked, effortlessly got along.

'I'm not interested in commitment or marriage,' he continued, 'but no matter how many ways I make that clear on my profile, I still seem to attract women who want something serious after two dates.' Last night's second date had asked him *where this was going* over dessert.

'Hmm… That *is* tricky.' Emilia's lips twitched playfully. 'I guess some women look at you and see the whole package—good job, tall, handsome…' she peered closer, mischief in her eyes '…your own teeth and hair.'

He laughed, shooting back, 'As opposed to someone else's.'

She chuckled and, once again, Felipe railed against

the fact *Santino* had beat him to Emilia. She really was easy to talk to. Perhaps he should ask what app she was using and do a little swiping himself…

He sobered, dragging in a breath. 'I just wish people were honest about what they're looking for from the start. I have no time for game playing.'

Emilia tilted her head, regarding him thoughtfully. 'Maybe you'll meet someone at your brother's wedding. Apparently, weddings are, according to my daughter, a great place to meet people.'

'Yes…' he drawled sarcastically. 'Flirting with someone while my entire family eagerly looks on. Talk about overwhelming.'

She pressed those full lips of hers together, hiding a smile. 'Yes, I can see how that might be awkward. Poor you.'

Felipe grinned, decidedly pleased with himself that yet again their conversation was light and playful. Except she was going on a date with some other lucky guy.

'Have you reviewed Luis Lopez?' he asked, changing the subject to one that didn't twist his gut with envy. He didn't want to think about some guy named Santino enjoying Emilia's sense of humour and her sparkling smiles. He definitely didn't want to think about her going home with the man…

'Yes,' she said, taking her takeaway coffee from the barista. 'I came in early and popped up to the NICU. He's stable. He's lost a little weight, but that's only to be expected. I spoke to Isabella and Sebastian again and they seem as happy as can be expected with the way things are going.'

Felipe's coffee arrived. He scooped it up and they left Café Rivas together.

'Do you want to review him together tomorrow morning?' he asked, pausing at a fork in the corridor as they were headed in opposite directions. 'First thing, before we take him to Theatre?'

He'd only known her a day, but it felt as if they'd been friends and colleagues for years. Except he couldn't ignore that unrelenting attraction…

'Sure,' she said taking a sip of her coffee and holding out her phone with her number displayed. 'Here's my number, text me when you arrive and I'll meet you on the NICU.'

Felipe stored her contact in his phone, an excited flutter in his gut. They had a date. A work date, but he'd take it.

'I'm on my way to the ED now,' he said. 'I'm on call today. Good luck tonight, with your date.'

'Thanks.' She winced. 'Somehow it feels like sitting an exam I haven't studied for.'

Forcing himself to step away from her easy and enchanting company, Felipe said, 'Just be yourself and you can't go wrong.'

She shot him a dubious look and walked off in the opposite direction.

He watched her depart for way too long. Why couldn't he meet a woman a bit more like Emilia Gonzales? Not exactly like her, because if her grief was any indication, she was obviously a lifelong commitment type, whereas he was a steadfast bachelor. Maybe the best plan of action was to forget his attraction to her and focus on their professional relationship—and what could be a highly rewarding friendship.

# CHAPTER FIVE

THE NEXT DAY in Theatre, Emilia stood opposite Felipe while they operated together on tiny Luis Lopez.

Having met Isabella Lopez before the triplets were born, and now that she considered the younger woman a friend, she couldn't help her nerves. That Felipe was there helped boost her confidence as she gently guided the loops of small bowel through the defect in Luis Lopez's diaphragm, drawing them back into the baby's abdominal cavity.

Across the operating table, Felipe shifted his weight, his hand remaining steady on the small retractor, which held open the laparotomy incision in Luis's abdomen. Despite operating alone in Uruguay, she'd already grown used to Felipe's calming presence. Unsurprisingly, he treated her with respect, stepping back and merely observing to allow her to make the critical decisions. After only a couple of days at the General, she already felt like a valued member of the neonatal surgical team, and it was largely down to Felipe.

'Let's see what we're dealing with,' Felipe said, as Emilia exposed the two-centimetre hole in the baby's diaphragm.

'The scans measure the defect at twenty-eight percent,' she said, her mind weighing up the two possible surgical approaches. They could suture the defect closed, like sewing a hole in a jumper, or they could put a synthetic patch over the defect.

Felipe peered inside, assessing the situation. His stare met hers. 'Looks too big for a primary closure. Are you happy to patch the defect?'

'Yes, I think that's the best approach in this case,' she said, glad that he'd asked her opinion.

The scrub nurse opened the sterile synthetic patch and passed it to Emilia, who positioned it over the defect in the diaphragm. She'd only sutured half the patch in place when the heart monitor alarms sounded, shrilly disrupting the quiet.

Emilia paused what she was doing, her adrenaline spiking. All eyes turned to the anaesthetist.

'We have a bradycardia,' he said, while checking Luis's ventilation, oxygenation and blood pressure.

Emilia paused, her own heart rate frantic. Having her work there supervised, her every move and technique scrutinised, naturally led to a wobble of confidence. But she worked hard at her job, and she was good at it. There was no need to panic.

'Probably just a bit of vagal stimulation,' Felipe said, glancing at Emilia, encouragingly.

The vagus nerve innervated part of the diaphragm, so inadvertent irritation of the nerve during the surgical repair was the most likely explanation. Only Emilia wanted to be sure.

'I'm just going to thoroughly check for bleeding anyway.' She'd performed this procedure many times before in Uruguay, but never on a baby as small at Luis Lopez. She really appreciated Felipe's presence as a senior, more experienced surgeon.

'Are you happy for me to proceed?' she finally asked the anaesthetist after making her checks, taking in some deep breaths to slow down her own heart rate. The sooner they successfully completed the surgery, the happier she'd feel for baby Luis and his family.

At the anaesthetist's nod, Emilia continued suturing the synthetic patch over the hole in the diaphragm, the remaining surgery passing without a hitch.

'Would you like to close up?' she asked her registrar, who was close to sitting her final surgical exams and would soon be eligible for her own consultant post.

The younger woman nodded and swapped places with Emilia as Felipe did the same with his registrar. They would review Luis back on the NICU. His recovery and prognosis would depend on his weight gain, lung development and the lack of both surgical and medical complications. For now, Emilia and Felipe had done all they could.

'There's a new admission to the NICU,' Felipe said, tossing his gloves and mask in the bin. 'A case of oesophageal atresia. Want to come and examine the baby with me? I'll probably add her to our Friday operating list.'

'Sure,' Emilia said, dumping her gown and hat into the used linen bin outside Theatre.

They washed up and headed up to the third floor together.

'Thanks for all your support back there,' she said, glancing his way. 'Before I moved here, I was nervous to be supervised, but I'm glad they chose *you* to oversee my work.'

Operating alongside Felipe had become second nature so quickly. They shared a similar surgical style, and Felipe was generous with his advice and knowledge, always looking out for her. It made her feel protected and valued, reminded her of how she'd felt the same within her marriage to Ricardo, who had always been her number one supporter, despite knowing nothing about medicine.

'You're welcome.' Felipe smiled at her compliment. 'I can understand your nerves. *I'd* feel the same. Speaking of nerves, how was your exam last night? Your date?'

She laughed at his joke and looked up at his expectant face, searching for his feelings on the change of subject. Was he just being friendly, or was he genuinely interested in her sad dating life? But given that she'd asked for his dating tips, she was happy to share her experience.

'Honestly?' she asked, mentally comparing the man she'd met last night, Santino, to both Ricardo and Felipe, unfavourably so.

'Always the best policy,' Felipe said with a wince, as if already anticipating her bad news. He held open the door to the stairwell and Emilia passed through. He was such a gentleman.

'It was awful,' she confirmed, amused to see a hint of surprise in his expression, as if he'd truly been rooting for her. 'Right from the get-go,' she continued, warming to her horror story, 'I could tell all he wanted was for me to go home with him.'

Felipe scowled and Emilia nodded and went on. 'He wasn't interested in getting to know me at all. He clearly just wanted a hook up. So, it turns out that men play games, too.'

'I'm sorry that it didn't work out,' Felipe said, the excitement hovering in his eyes saying the opposite.

Emilia shrugged. She wasn't offended. She and Felipe obviously fancied each other. Eva was right… Oh, how it stung to admit that. But just because there was attraction didn't mean they should act on it. They were work colleagues. He was supervising her. She couldn't simply date him instead. She sighed, even more averse to the idea of dating now that she'd had a bad experience.

'I still need your advice,' she pleaded. 'You're my dating coach.'

He nodded, proudly, and Emilia continued. 'Blind dating seems fraught with potential disasters. How do I tell the good guys from the bad from their brief profiles?'

Felipe inclined his head in sympathy. 'I know it seems risky,' he said, obviously trying to make her feel better, 'but for every bad date there are a bunch of good ones. I promise you, next time will be better.'

He offered her that easy smile of his, the one that made him look approachable and trustworthy, and made her even more aware of how in sync they were. Emilia shook her head dubiously, wishing she'd trusted her instincts and stayed the hell away from the stupid dating app in the first place.

'I don't know if I have the patience for the bad ones though,' she said as they paused outside the NICU. 'Mr Horny—that's what I'm calling Santino—knocked back his drink in two swallows, offered to *walk me home*,' she made finger quotes, 'and when I refused, he made excuses and left. He'd pulled out his phone even before he'd walked away. Probably had another date lined up, just in case ours was a bust.'

'What a jerk,' Felipe said, his frown deepening as his stare traced her face.

He seemed genuinely outraged on her behalf, which was flattering. It was certainly nice to have an ally. For the first time in so long, she didn't feel quite as alone.

'Thanks for being on my side,' she said, smiling. If only there were plenty of Felipe Castillos out there. 'But

I'm so out of practice with the whole dating thing that there's enough to consider without trying to figure out what the other person is thinking. At least you've had enough experience to know when it's worth persevering with someone. I've had *one* date and I'm just about ready to give up on the whole idea and delete my profile. If it wasn't for my promise to Eva, I would,' she added emphatically.

'I can totally see why you might feel that way.' He tilted his head, his deep brown eyes soft with empathy. 'Unless...'

His index finger tapped his lips in a way that made her acutely aware of their pleasing shape and apparent softness. 'Why don't *we* go out, strictly no strings.'

Emilia held her breath, her heart going crazy behind her ribs. Wasn't that exactly what she'd been thinking only moments ago? But they worked together. Was it a professional conflict? She didn't want to be the source of hospital gossip.

'I'll take you to another of my favourite restaurants,' he continued, enthusiastically, 'teach you all my top dating tips, and you can practice your dating small talk on me. It will give you a bit of confidence for the real thing.'

Emilia dithered, her stomach swooping excitedly. She already knew that five minutes of Felipe's easy and platonic company was worth at least ten excruciatingly awkward dates with horny strangers. Only there was that undercurrent of attraction to consider... Could she ignore that and simply enjoy his company? At least with Felipe there'd be no pressure to have a relationship. Like her, he just wasn't interested in anything serious.

But what would she tell Eva, who already thought Felipe fancied her?

'Oh...that sounds too good to be true,' she said, thinking how a casual date with Felipe under the guise of building up her confidence might actually appease her daughter. 'But we work together. Won't it be...awkward?'

Felipe shrugged his broad shoulders nonchalantly. 'Only if we have undeclared expectations.'

He glanced along the corridor as if making sure they were alone, and then dropped his voice. 'So you know exactly what you're getting with me, I'll come clean,' he said, casually folding his arms over his chest. 'I *do* find you attractive, but I also like you. We have a lot in common. I'd be happy to be just colleagues and friends, so it's just dinner. No games.'

Hearing his honest declaration seemed to light some kind of fuse inside her, the fizz and hiss of anticipation for their non-date date a hundred times greater than what she'd experienced during the real thing last night.

'I like you too,' she said, her throat tight with nervous energy and her cheeks warm, 'and we've already established that you're easy on the eye and in possession of your own hair and teeth.'

His delighted grin gave her courage.

'But if we *do* go out for dinner,' she added, 'that would be my second *date* in twenty plus years, so no-strings suits me just fine.'

She wasn't looking for a relationship. Her heart still belonged to Ricardo. But if she had to do this, put herself out there and get used to the idea that one day she might want to date for real, wasn't it better to practice with a man like Felipe? A man she knew and respected and had heaps in common with.

'Great,' he said, his eyes sparking with excitement. 'Then we're on the same page. You can try out your dating moves on me, knowing that I'm not trying to get you into bed, and I'll enjoy your company knowing that you're not hoping to move into my apartment by the weekend. We both win.'

His smile broadened and Emilia laughed, already looking forward to it. Perhaps she could wear that new dress in her wardrobe…

'I'll book us a table,' he said, 'and pick you up at seven tomorrow night. Does that work?'

'Seven it is,' she said with a smile, gently shaking her head.

He really was too self-assured for his own good. Some women couldn't help but find that irresistible. No wonder they fell for him hard. But Emilia wasn't looking to be one of those women. For one thing, they had a professional relationship to preserve, and for another she'd done her falling twenty-five years ago. Now she had other priorities, like building a stable life here in Buenos Aires for her and Eva.

'Only one more thing,' she said, pausing as they entered the NICU to meet their new oesophageal atresia patient, who'd been born earlier that morning. 'This stays just between us.'

'Of course.' He smiled, winked and paused at the sink to wash his hands.

Emilia joined him, slowly exhaling an excited breath.

A non-date date. Whatever would Eva think? But perhaps Emilia should keep it to herself. After all, it was only a practice date between two people uninterested in dating seriously. No use raising Eva's hopes unnecessarily.

# CHAPTER SIX

THAT FRIDAY EVENING Felipe smiled across the table at Emilia and poured the last of the wine between their glasses. Unlike his last date, when most of the conversational burden had fallen to him, tonight's conversation had flowed non-stop from the minute he'd collected her from her neat two-bedroom house in a taxi.

He couldn't recall the last time he'd felt so excited by a new connection. Maybe it was because they were on the same page when it came to their relationship expectations, but he and Emilia seemed to just effortlessly click, the invigorating camaraderie they shared at work spilling over into their *date*. Except he needed to remember that it wasn't a *real* date, that they were just friends and colleagues.

'So what type of wine does your family's vineyard grow?' she asked, her deep brown eyes accented by the sapphire blue dress she wore, the neckline showing a tantalising glimpse of her tanned and freckled chest.

He was having a hard time keeping his stare from her sensational body. She looked elegant and relaxed, her make-up subtle and her long, dark hair swept over one tanned shoulder. Felipe forced his gaze away from the curve of her lovely lips back up to her playful stare. She really was stunning. And intelligent and interesting.

And a *friend…*

'We specialise in Syrah and Malbec, of course,' he said, naming the most famous of the Argentinian grape varieties, 'but we also grow Chardonnay and Semillon. My parents are retired now, so my brother has taken over and also added a sparkling wine to the estate's production line.'

'Ooh…' Emilia said, impressed. 'Do they have an open cellar door? I might have to visit the region sometime. I haven't been to Mendoza since my twenties.'

'Of course.' Felipe smiled, eager to give her a personal tour of the Castillo Estate Winery. 'There are tastings and wine tours and, thanks to Thiago's vision and hard work, a brand-new restaurant with a world-class chef.'

'Sounds amazing,' she said, licking her lips in a distracting way that, despite his best intentions, made him desperate for a taste of that lovely mouth.

All night he'd secretly toyed with the idea of how to say goodnight. A cheek kiss, as was standard among Argentinians, seemed too impersonal, but if he brushed her lips with his, he might not be able to stop himself taking it further. Perhaps it was best to let Emilia dictate their goodbye.

'So Thiago is the brother who's getting married?' she asked.

'That's right. He's ten years younger than me,' Felipe said, grasping the topic of conversation to distract himself from how badly he wanted to kiss her—right there and then—but couldn't. 'Fortunately for me,' he continued, 'Thiago wanted to work for the family business when my parents retired.'

Why had he suggested a platonic date when they'd admitted they were attracted to each other? Yes, he'd friend zoned her and wanted her to feel comfortable after her first date failure, but enjoying her sparkling company knowing he couldn't take it further was like a form of self-inflicted torture…

'You didn't?' she asked with a curious frown, twirling the stem of her wineglass as she watched him thoughtfully.

She seemed genuinely interested in his personal life and the feeling was mutual. They'd been at the restaurant for almost two hours and hadn't once talked about work.

Felipe shook his head, the old familiar rumble of guilt lodging under his ribs like a stitch.

'At the time, when I told my parents I wanted to go to medical school at UBA,' he said, glancing down at the table, 'that caused quite the upset, as you can imagine. I think my parents dreamed of both their sons running the family business together, but I was drawn to the big city lights and to medicine. I'm not sure they've ever quite forgiven me.'

He grinned, his light-hearted tone hiding how his career choice still felt like a bone of contention between him and his family. Felipe had always felt protective of Thiago, and the pursuit of his surgical career had inadvertently placed a responsibility for the family business on his younger brother's shoulders, especially as their parents grew older.

The consequences of Felipe's decision had also spilled into his private life. He'd felt compelled to make his career a success, almost to prove to his family that he'd made the right choice. And while he'd worked long hours to build up his professional reputation in Buenos Aires, he'd unwittingly neglected his marriage.

'I'm sure they're proud of you both,' Emilia said, her

stare moving over his face as if she was figuring him out and somehow knew that, for him, this was a touchy subject. 'How often do you get home for a visit?'

'Not as often as I'd like,' he admitted. 'You know how demanding our work can be, but Thiago and Violetta's wedding will be a chance to catch up with all my family in one hit. Every cloud has a silver lining and all that…'

Emilia eyed him intently. 'You're really dreading the wedding, aren't you?'

Felipe added fearless and intuitive to her growing list of positive attributes.

'Not the wedding itself…' He shrugged, sitting forward to rest his forearms on the table. 'Just the look of disappointment in my mother's eyes. She's desperate to be an *abuela*, and I'm afraid I've failed her miserably.'

He smiled, his regret that he wasn't a father only momentary. He had a great life—a comfortable home, a full social life and a challenging job he loved.

'But at least Thiago has time to redeem himself and produce a grandchild,' he added. 'His wife-to-be is younger than him and has already told him she wants at least two children, so it seems my mother will get her heart's desire after all.'

His smile widened with mischief. 'And I'll get to be cool uncle Felipe who spoils them with sweets and inappropriately expensive gifts.'

Emilia's tinkling laughter eased the restless ache in his chest that came when he thought about Thiago, the wedding and his family's expectations.

After dinner, they headed outside. The restaurant opened onto the buzzing Plaza de Luco, a favourite gathering place for Argentinians keen to enjoy the abundant nightlife on offer. It was a balmy autumn evening with lots of people out and about, frequenting the city's many restaurants, cocktail bars and dance clubs.

'So, what did you think of your second date in twenty years?' Felipe asked, casually strolling at her side across the square. 'Please tell me it went better than the date with Mr Horny.' He'd definitely made Emilia relax and smile tonight, and hopefully negated her bad experience with that other guy.

'A hundred times better.' She laughed, her stare sweeping over him from head to toe. He walked a little taller. 'Tonight's date lasted two hours instead of twenty minutes, for one,' she said, stepping a little closer.

'Good food and wine are worth savouring,' he said, desperate to take her hand or offer her his arm, but he held back. He didn't want to make any moves on her, given how he'd promised they could be just friends.

'Secondly,' she added, 'you've asked me plenty of personal questions and seemed genuinely interested in me.'

'I *am* genuinely interested,' he said, trying not to appear too smug that he'd bested Mr Horny.

'And thirdly,' she concluded, her twinkling gaze full of playfulness, 'you didn't once stare at my chest.'

Felipe kept his expression neutral as he nodded. Oh, he'd looked all right. He'd simply been subtle about it.

'But seriously, thanks for suggesting tonight.' She smiled up at him, her eyes sparkling. 'You have no idea how much you've set my mind at ease.'

'You're welcome,' he said, glad he could restore her faith in men. 'Take it from your dating coach—a date shouldn't feel like a trip to the dentist.'

'Well, you're the expert,' she said with a curious expression on her face. 'Fifteen years is a long time to date without falling into a serious relationship.'

'I guess,' he said with another shrug, because he'd never before considered how his lifestyle choices might appear from the outside. 'What can I say—I enjoy the company of beautiful, intelligent women.'

And until Emilia had walked into his life, he'd never once questioned his behaviour. Dating was a means to an end. He enjoyed socialising and eating out and had a healthy sex drive. But now that he'd met her, he realised how many of his other dates had been empty somehow, although it was his choice to keep things superficial. There was something special about her that left him unsettled, as if he knew he could be happier. But perhaps it was just this inconvenient attraction to her that he had to constantly battle.

'Plus, what's a single person too young to be all alone supposed to do?' he asked, playfully. 'I'm always safe and responsible, and I think I show my dates a good time. I've certainly never had any complaints.'

'I should hope so.' She laughed, stepping aside as they passed a large group of people—her arm brushed his.

Felipe reflexively offered her his arm, and to his relief, she accepted, sliding her hand through his elbow. He hid his body's shudder of excitement.

'At least now you have some tips and pointers for the next time you go on a date, and can easily dismiss anyone who doesn't make the grade.' Hopefully, he'd set the bar nice and high. Except the idea of her dating other men only intensified that restlessness in him.

*He* wanted to take her out again, but it was complicated. As she'd pointed out they worked together. He'd have to provide a report on her for the Argentine Medical Council. She was still grieving, vulnerable and he genuinely wanted to be her friend.

'Shall we take a taxi,' he asked, as they arrived at the taxi rank. 'If you don't mind, I'd like to see you home? No strings, I promise. I'm just a bit old fashioned like that.'

Emilia looked up at him, an enigmatic look in her eyes that gave nothing away. 'Isn't it out of your way?'

Her teeth dragged at her distracting bottom lip as if she was waiting, thinking, maybe even plotting. Felipe couldn't stop staring, still arguing back and forth with himself if he should kiss her goodnight. Would their chemistry be as hot as he imagined, or would a harmless kiss ruin their budding friendship?

'It's worth it for a little longer in your company, if you don't mind,' he said, holding up his hands in supplication. 'But it's totally your call.'

She hesitated, wrapping her arms around her waist as if she was cold. Felipe shrugged off his sports jacket and draped it over her shoulders.

She smiled up at him. 'Thank you.' She blinked, something conflicted shifting behind her eyes. 'I'd like your company for a little longer too, but I have a nosy teenager at my place.' She stepped closer, vulnerability in her eyes that told Felipe how uncertain and out of practice she was when it came to interacting with men. 'You could, um… invite me back to your place for a nightcap?'

Felipe froze, his heart racing with excitement, but his head applied the brakes. Just because she wasn't ready for their evening to end just yet—and the feeling was definitely mutual—didn't mean she wanted more than just his company. If anything more was ever to happen between them, he would need very clear signals from her. Except it was taking all his strength to resist the temptation to kiss her. Having her in his apartment would test him further, but more than anything he wanted her to be comfortable with him, his protective urges flaring to life.

'I'd love that,' he said, 'but I only live a five-minute walk from here and it's a beautiful night. Shall we walk?'

Emilia nodded, seeming to relax. They set off at a leisurely pace, side by side. This time she spontaneously looped her warm hand around his arm, her touch electrifying his skin through the thin cotton of his shirt, as her perfume wafted on the cool evening air.

Just like that his restless feeling evaporated.

But he needed to be so careful with this woman. Unlike the strangers he often dated while also keeping at arms' length, there was so much more at stake: their working relationship, their budding friendship, Emilia settling into an unfamiliar city where she had no other friends. They couldn't allow lust to cloud their judgement, and Emilia was new to casual dating. He didn't want to hurt her somehow or inadvertently let her down after everything she'd been through.

'So, tell me about your husband,' he asked after a moment's silence, the subject a timely reminder of another obstacle he needed to be mindful of. 'What kind of lawyer was he?'

Emilia glanced up at him as if surprised by his interest. 'He specialised in commercial law,' she said, a small half-smile on her lips. 'He and a friend from university started their own firm in Montevideo. He was very successful.'

Felipe nodded encouragingly and she continued.

'Then, at only forty-seven,' she said, 'he was diagnosed with glioblastoma multiforme.'

Felipe winced, regretting that he'd made her feel sad. GBM was the most aggressive form of brain cancer.

'I'm sorry. That must have been hard on all of you.

What a tragic waste.' He squeezed her hand between his elbow and his side, letting her know that he understood her grief, which was so evident in her beautiful eyes.

She shrugged but then swallowed, as if with effort. 'Within two years, he was dead. Eva was only thirteen, a real Papá's girl, so of course, it hit her the hardest.'

Her voice fell. She ducked her head and Felipe wished he'd chosen a lighter topic of conversation. But a part of him wanted to know everything about her, even this.

'And you lost the love of your life,' he pointed out. 'It's hard on both you *and* Eva.'

As a solo parent, she was probably used to putting her needs last, but her grief was every bit as valid as Eva's.

'Yes,' she admitted, watching him for a few seconds. 'But I just got on with things. I had a teenager to raise, so I couldn't afford to break down. I didn't want Eva's young life to be derailed by my grief. Besides, wallowing wouldn't have brought Ricardo back.'

Felipe rested his hand over hers on his arm. 'That's understandable. You felt you had to set aside your own grieving process to focus on Eva. It's not surprising that dating has been a low priority for you until now.'

She nodded, her eyes alight with what looked like gratitude. 'Thanks for asking about Ricardo. It means a lot to me. Many people are scared to ask about him in case I find the reminder too upsetting, but that means it can sometimes feel as if there's no one I can talk to about him.'

'You're welcome, Emilia. Any time you need to talk, I'm here.' Out of nowhere, a fresh surge of protectiveness built inside him.

She was amazing. She had a busy and emotionally demanding career, she'd raised her daughter alone for the past five years, while also grieving, and now she'd moved to a new country.

'This is my building,' he said, pausing in front of a modern apartment block facing the park in Palermo, a fashionable central city district. 'Dante and I are in the penthouse.'

She smiled, flashing her dimple. 'Of course you are.' But her teasing seemed to break the tension.

'Hey, it has the best views,' he said, scanning the building's electronic lock with his key fob.

'Another of your dating moves?' she asked, pushing inside to the building's foyer. 'Wow women with your penthouse apartment?'

Felipe reached for her hand and tugged her towards the lift. 'That's rookie dating mistake number one.' He winked, enjoying the laughter in her eyes. 'Never invite a first date back to your place. If she turns out to be too clingy, then there's no escape—she knows exactly where you live.'

Emilia shook her head as if in wonder. 'Oh, well done you. But see, I didn't even think of that. I have so much to learn.' She stepped inside the lift at his side.

Felipe gently squeezed her hand and pressed the button for the top floor. 'Well, that's why we're here. This is a practice date, remember?'

Only right then, he was struggling to think about anything but how much he wished it was the real thing.

# CHAPTER SEVEN

AS FELIPE RETOOK his seat in the living room, after taking Dante out for a quick toilet break and then settling him in the spare bedroom, Emilia sipped her brandy, the warmth sliding through her stomach and infecting her limbs like a much-needed dose of liquid courage.

He smelled so good… She could hardly believe that she'd boldly suggested coming back to his place, but his charming, unthreatening company was so easy to enjoy. Tonight he'd made her feel safe and attractive. Light-hearted. He'd been funny and attentive and considerate, his assurances that they could just be friends completely removing the pressure from the situation. He'd even asked about Ricardo, giving her the space to talk about her husband beyond the illness that had stolen him from her.

She hadn't wanted the evening to end and couldn't have asked for more from a first date.

Only this was a *fake* date. A practice run. And unlike Emilia, committed bachelor Felipe was the expert at dating.

'So,' she said, gulping another sip of brandy to abolish her regrets that she'd been so brave to suggest this nightcap, 'your ex-wife got the house and you ended up here?' A stunning penthouse apartment in central Buenos Aires. She glanced around, appreciatively, finding the space modern, minimalist and very masculine. The spectacular city views alone would most definitely wow any single woman who set foot in the place. And with fifteen years of casual dating, there must surely have been many women to impress.

Jealousy, hot and shocking, slid through her veins. But she didn't want to think about Felipe's *other* dating moves, the ones that led to tangled, sweaty sheets and very satisfied women…

This close to him, lured by the romance of his views, and with his earlier talk of a healthy sex life fresh in her mind, she was already struggling to think about anything else beyond how much she wanted to kiss him. But the staggering strength of her attraction aside, was she ready for such a momentous step?

He shrugged, his eyes steady on hers as they had been all evening. 'I offered Delfina the house, but in the end we split everything fifty-fifty and each moved on. Only fair. I didn't want to squabble over *that's mine, this is yours* and there were no children to consider.'

Emilia watched him in rapt fascination. She liked the respectful way he spoke about his ex-wife, with courtesy and mild indifference. It was obvious he had no lingering feelings, not that it was any of *her* business.

'So where is she now, your ex?' she asked, her inhibitions lowered by the way he'd made her feel—as if her body and desires were coming back to life. He seemed like such a catch, such a gentleman and a good listener. She couldn't imagine what might have gone wrong in his marriage.

Felipe glanced out at the lights of Buenos Aires below. 'She lives on the other side of the city, although we hardly ever see each other. I wish her well. We were married for fifteen years, and I played my part in the demise of our relationship.'

'Did you cheat?' she asked, intrigued. She couldn't imagine him being unfaithful. He was too honest.

'No, but I spent a lot of time at work.' He turned back to face her, his stare bold and steady, as if he owned his mistakes. 'I can't blame my ex for making a separate life for herself.'

'Did *she* cheat?' Emilia realised the moment the question was out that she was being nosy. But she was too relaxed, too focused on the self-generated heat of attraction making her languid. And what kind of woman would let Felipe escape?

His lip curled as he placed his glass on the table. 'Not as far as I know. But we woke up one day and had nothing to talk about. I think we both realised there should be more passion, more fire to a relationship than that, even after all those years together.'

Emilia nodded, aware that she and Ricardo had had their challenges in their marriage too, but had loved each other passionately to the end, maybe because they'd also been best friends.

'So, what brought you two together in the first place?' She was pushing, but she wanted to know what kind of a man he was outside of work, where he was a dedicated, well-respected surgeon. He'd mentioned letting his family down over his choice of career, but what intense passions, what fire had driven a younger Felipe?

'Sex.' He grinned as he stared intently into her eyes.

Emilia's body went up in flames and she dragged in a shuddering breath. Was everything about sex tonight?

Felipe turned serious. 'We also shared drive and ambition, and a desire to leave our small town for the thrill of

Buenos Aires. But when passion cools, and if that drive takes you in different directions, you suddenly realise that you're married to someone with whom you have little in common.'

'I'm sorry it didn't work out for you,' Emilia said, sensing his regret. A high-achieving man like Felipe would likely baulk at any form of failure. 'What does Delfina do?'

Talking about his ex-wife was helping her to rationalise her own body's reaction to him. It was understandable that after so many years of grief and loneliness her physical desires would eventually reawaken. Especially as she felt safe with Felipe. Respected.

'She works in fashion,' he said. 'She's a buyer for the fashion brand Hermoso.'

His stare moved over her face as it had several times tonight. Was he wondering if he should kiss her? Was that usually the way his dates ended?

'That explains why you're always so stylishly dressed,' she said, the last word emerging a little strangled as lust swept through her at the idea of kissing Felipe Castillo.

But was she seriously considering it after only kissing one man for so long? Imagining the previously unimaginable, her heart thumped and her mind went crazy with questions.

Would it be as exciting as she imagined, life-affirming? Or would it leave her riddled with embarrassment, regret and guilt? Would kissing Felipe be a betrayal of her beloved Ricardo, of his memory and everything they'd shared during their marriage? Or was she overthinking it, terrified by how badly she wanted to find out the answers?

As if aware of the direction of her thoughts, Felipe

stilled. 'I think you look beautiful in that dress,' he said in a tight voice. 'That's a great colour on you. Makes your beautiful eyes shine.'

Emilia swallowed hard, blinked at the intensity of his eye contact. Stunned by the honesty of his compliment.

He thought she was beautiful. She dragged in a breath, tired of her mind's back and forth. Tired of fighting the demands of her body. Tired of having this fear of being intimate with anyone else hanging over her like a storm cloud. Sometimes you just needed to take a chance and try new things.

'I don't know if it's the brandy,' she said in a whisper, her heartrate flying, 'or maybe your apartment's spectacular views, but I really want to kiss you.'

The air left her in a rush, as if she'd jumped from a plane but her parachute had opened. There was a second's pause that felt like an hour where he simply stared at her, immobile. Had she judged it wrong? Was it a terrible idea given they were colleagues? But surely no one else needed to know—

'Thanks goodness for that,' he said, exhaling harshly and glancing down at her lips with hungry eyes. 'I was starting to get desperate over here. I've wanted to kiss you all evening.'

Without hesitation and before she could second guess her impulse, he cupped her face between his palms, then slowly and deliberately leaned in and brushed her lips with his. A soft teasing swipe that tasted of brandy, and elicited a low sigh in the back of his throat.

Her lips tingled, her adrenaline spiking. Long-forgotten need roared to life, hijacking her body and obliterating her thoughts.

She blinked, dragged in a shuddering breath for courage as she looked up at him. She hadn't done this in so long, but as thrilling and tantalising as that whisper of a kiss was, she didn't want it to end. It had been alien but wonderful and far too brief.

As she sensed him pulling back, she raised one hand to his cheek. She sighed as their lips met again. This time, Felipe lingered, his lips softly gliding over hers again and again as if slowly and thoroughly learning their shape and savouring their taste.

Despite the frantic galloping of her heart, Emilia relaxed into it. Felipe was obviously taking it slow, giving her time to adjust, a chance to dictate the pace or maybe to apply the brakes. Her eyes stung with emotion. He was so thoughtful. He must have guessed that a huge part of her, the part that still felt married to Ricardo, was crushed with guilt for kissing another man. But Ricardo was gone, and ignoring the physical demands of her body, staying faithful to his memory, wouldn't bring him back.

Because she wanted a night off from feeling sad and alone. Emilia closed her eyes and allowed herself to enjoy kissing Felipe. As if it was natural, she parted her lips, tentatively touching her tongue to Felipe's. Her body melted as his arm came around her waist and his lips turned more insistent, commanding their kiss, the passion building until it was all she could do to forget about breathing for a while, clinging to his toned body and strong arms and kissing him back.

Disorienting forces tugged her in opposing directions. This felt both wrong and wonderfully right. But if she had to get over this intimacy hurdle with anyone, she'd much rather it be mature, considerate Felipe than some unpredictable stranger she'd met on a dating app.

At last, Felipe pulled back, his breathing harsh. 'I have

a confession to make.' He pushed her hair back from her warm face, his stare flitting over her as if checking she was okay.

She nodded for him to continue, her lips desperate for more.

'I *did* look at your chest earlier.' A sexy flash of excitement lit his eyes. 'I just did it discreetly.' His gaze swept lower now, to her lips, her cleavage and back. Emilia felt scorched, restless, needy. 'You have a great body,' he said, resting his hands on her shoulders, his thumbs swiping back and forth over her bare skin.

She swallowed, thrilled and electrified by his simple touch. 'So do you.'

He was so sexy. And nice and decent and dedicated. She instinctively knew she could trust him. Kissing him didn't have to be a big deal.

With a shaking hand, she placed her glass aside and reached for his waist, leaning into him and kissing him again. She wanted the liberating pleasure of their undeniable chemistry.

The second kiss was even better, as if they'd learned the shape of the other person and everything instantly and effortlessly slotted exactly where it should. Only now that it was more familiar, it was also more intense.

His fingers slid into her hair, urging her closer. She gripped his shirt at the waist, her lips and tongue bolder against his. He slanted his mouth over hers, deepening their kiss, and she moaned, the sound forced from her throat by the euphoric excitement of being kissed properly again—with heat. Being this in sync with another person. Being desired.

Maybe she could let go of her doubts and reservations and embrace her desire for this man. Neither of them was looking for anything serious, and they were mature enough to stop their personal lives bleeding into their professional relationship.

Heat pooled in her pelvis as the embrace turned more passionate. He hauled her close, his strong arms banded around her waist so her breasts grazed his chest as their tongues surged together. In an instant, she was too hot. Achy. She couldn't seem to get close enough to Felipe. She wanted more.

'You are so incredibly sexy,' he groaned, shifting back against the sofa and tugging her with him, pressing kisses to her jaw and neck. 'I'm so glad you moved to Buenos Aires.'

Emilia smiled as she sat astride his lap, holding his face between her palms. 'That's very flattering.'

'Do you realise how rare this is, just clicking with someone so effortlessly?' He smiled softly, cupping her face tenderly as if he understood how she must be feeling—both exhilarated and guilt-ridden.

'Is it?' she asked, knowing he was right. She had a sneaking suspicion that she'd have to date a lot of guys to find one as perfect for her on paper as Felipe.

But this was about physical desire, nothing more. To remind herself of that, she leaned in and kissed him again. She wanted to feel, not to think. She wanted to set everything else aside and focus on *her* needs for once. To admit that while she would always love her husband she was human. A woman. A sexual being.

Distracting her from the sudden spike of fear, his hands gripped her hips, and he crushed her close. He was hard, his stare dark with arousal as he looked up at her, letting her dictate the pace of whatever this was. Both scared and desperate, Emilia shifted on his lap so their bodies aligned, the steel of him and the heat of her as she pressed kisses down the side of his neck.

This felt too good to stop. It was as if he'd awoken every cell in her body and they urgently wanted the same thing.

'I want you,' she whispered, pulling back to look at him. Her pulse buzzed in her ears, but it felt right. Felipe wasn't some stranger. He'd shown her the kind of man he was these past few days. She felt safe with him, safe to explore the ferocious arousal he'd inspired in her.

'Are you sure?' He watched her face, his hands guiding her hips into a hypnotic rhythm that seemed to appease them both.

But the friction wasn't enough. After so many years of denying her sexuality, need built inside Emilia like a tornado.

'I'm certain.' She nodded, her fingers undoing the top few buttons of his shirt, exposing his bronzed chest that was dusted with manly dark hair. 'Only it's been so long for me,' she said, a second of doubt gripping her like a cold fist.

What if she'd forgotten the moves? She'd loved one man most of her adult life. Her hesitance to be intimate with someone new made sense. But now wasn't the time to think about her husband.

'I know...' Felipe groaned, his hands fisting the fabric of her dress at her hips, as if he was holding back. 'That's why I want you to be sure.'

Emilia nodded, panic squeezing her lungs. What if it was horrible and they ruined their working relationship and their friendship? What if she chickened out and missed this chance? 'I am sure, if you are. Just tonight.'

She was a mature woman who knew what she wanted.

With Felipe, she felt seen and understood and respected. That was enough for her.

'Deal—then we go back to being friends.' His eyes darkened with arousal. 'I wanted you the first time I saw you,' he said, his hands moving slowly from her hips to cup her breasts. 'I know, very inappropriate at work… and me your supervisor…'

Emilia gasped as his thumbs rubbed over her nipples through her dress, sending dizzying waves of pleasure through her entire body. 'Don't forget dating coach,' she said with a smile, before leaning in to kiss him again.

He was right. A connection like theirs was rare, made all the more perfect by the fact that they wanted the same things—no strings. Just one night of passion.

His hands caressed her breasts, the delicious friction dragging a moan from her throat. 'Felipe…' She dropped her head back and closed her eyes, awash with sensation. She was going to do this. Sleep with a sexy work colleague and have no regrets.

'I want to make you feel good,' he said, while Emilia leaned over him, lost in kissing his chest, the side of his neck and the angle of his jaw. His warm hands skimmed along the length of her thighs, raising the hem of her silky dress over her hips.

'Me too,' she said, too far gone to hesitate as she lifted her arms overhead so he could quickly remove the garment.

He tossed it aside, his stare feasting on her near naked body with thrilling hunger. His hands followed the path of his stare, gliding over her hips, her waist and her breasts.

Watching his hands on her skin, Emilia bit down on her bottom lip, trying to contain the firestorm of need coursing through her veins. She couldn't wait any longer—she'd waited long enough. Overcome with urgency, Emilia popped the remaining buttons on his shirt and hurriedly tackled his trouser fly, her fingers clumsy in their haste.

As if reluctant to simply be undressed, Felipe dragged her mouth back to his and expertly unclasped her bra with a single pinch. As he removed it, his mouth sought out one nipple and then the other. She shuddered against him as if she'd never before been touched.

He groaned, sucking her nipple until she gasped and her head swam. She ached from head to toe, her heart banging wildly and fire scorching her every nerve.

'Yes…' she moaned, sliding her fingers through his thick hair and watching his mouth on her breast.

Breaking free, Felipe threw off his shirt and trousers and laid her back against the cool leather of his sofa. His gorgeous, toned body covered hers so she was engulfed by heat and steel and flexing power. It was so good to feel desired again, to feel that neglected part of herself—her sexuality—unfurl and come back to vibrant life.

His tongue dipped inside her mouth, his hips grinding against hers so they groaned in unison, the wildness building. Emilia shoved at his boxers, cupping his erection. He thrust his tongue against hers with a throaty growl, and the urgency ramped up a notch. There was a frantic scramble while they removed their underwear and he reached for a condom from his wallet.

Gripping Felipe's shoulders as he rolled on the condom, she pulled him down on top of her, kissing him deeply. She was burning up, awash with arousal, desperate for the release building inside. Felipe's hand slid between her legs, his fingers stroking her so there was no room in her head for anything but pleasure and passion. As he touched her, he pulled back from their kiss to peer down at her, need stark in the set of his jaw and the depths of his dark eyes.

'I want you,' Emilia said again, because she didn't want there to be any doubt in his mind.

She spread her thighs and hooked her legs around his hips, drawing him closer. He reared back, braced on his arms, and with their stares locked he pushed inside her, watching her gasp with pleasure. Triumph and excitement darkened his eyes to almost black.

Emilia gripped his face, bringing his mouth back to her kiss. He was such a good kisser. She couldn't seem to get enough. He moved inside her, his fingers teasing her nipples and his tongue thrusting against hers so every part of her felt electrified, alive. Emilia slid her hands over the taut muscles and smooth skin of his shoulders, his back, his buttocks, her senses flooded with the scent and feel of him and the sound of his sexy groans.

Her orgasm built swift and strong. She cried out his name and he reared back, watching her disintegrate, his thrusts speeding up so sweat slicked his bronzed skin. With a hoarse shout he came, burying his face against the side of her neck, clutching her so tightly through the body-racking spasms she almost couldn't breathe.

But who cared about breathing after sex that good?

Emilia lay still as he slipped from her body, her heart still racing against his.

'That was amazing,' she said, initially feeling a massive weight off her shoulders. Just what she'd needed to get her confidence back. But now that it was over, awkwardness rushed in, smothering down all the lovely endorphins.

Her mind unhelpfully produced fresh doubts. What

was the one-night stand protocol? Should she dress and leave straight away? Thank him and say, *'See you Monday'*?

'It was.' Felipe stirred, raising his face from the side of her neck and looking down at her with a soft, slightly dazed smile. He brushed the hair back from her face and pressed languid kisses to her lips. 'How do you feel?' he asked, sliding to the side but keeping his hand on her waist.

His question was so unexpected that her eyes started to sting with the release of pent-up emotion. Silly—it was only sex. But for so many years, sex for Emilia had been about love.

'Good,' she said, her hand stroking up and down his strong arm, from elbow to shoulder, as if seeking comfort. 'How about you?'

His smile widened. 'I feel fantastic. So, no regrets?' he pressed, his intent gaze moving over her face as if he really cared that she was okay with her decision to sleep with him.

'Not one.'

'I'm glad.' He pressed one final kiss to her lips, then reached for a tissue from the end table and dealt with the condom. Then he stood and took her hand, pulling her to her feet.

For a few seconds they stood naked, facing each other with goofy smiles on their faces. Then he slid his stare down her naked body and started to get hard again.

'Wanna see my bedroom?' he asked with a sexy flick of his brows, letting her know he was up for round two if she was. 'The views are even better.'

Emilia laughed, nodded, her breath snatched away

by excitement. ‘Yes, but then I have to get home. Parental curfew.’

He reached for her hand and led the way. ‘I don’t want to get you into trouble.’

Emilia stood on tiptoes and pressed her body and mouth to his. ‘Then stop talking.’

# CHAPTER EIGHT

EARLY MONDAY MORNING, Felipe strode onto the NICU to find Emilia already at Luis Lopez's bedside with both her registrar and his. They'd agreed to review the baby's post-op progress together, but now that the moment had come to face her and act as if Friday night hadn't happened, he felt an uncharacteristic shudder of apprehension.

'Dr Gonzales,' he said, his stare meeting hers across their tiny patient while his heart banged with excitement. She looked beautiful as usual, only now he knew exactly how every part of her body looked and felt and tasted.

'Good morning, Dr Castillo,' she replied, her expression neutral, giving nothing away.

Was it just his imagination, or did she seem a little subdued this morning? Friday night, she'd reassured him that she had no regrets, but maybe with the whole weekend to ponder what they'd done she'd changed her mind. He'd considered calling her over the weekend to make sure she was okay, but she'd been on call at the hospital, and they'd agreed to put that one night behind them.

Not that he could blame her if she did feel derailed. The events of Friday night had certainly taken him aback. They'd had a great date, they'd opened up to each other about their pasts, and as for the sex… He hadn't expected their easy connection to turn so heated, nor had he anticipated how much he'd want to see her again outside of work, like for that walk in the dog park perhaps…

Deciding it was best that he *hadn't* succumbed to the impulse to call her, Felipe turned to his registrar, Dr Ruiz. He listened to the latest blood results on Luis, while simultaneously trying to come to terms with that insanely hot night with his new colleague.

Now that they'd slept together, his awareness of her was finely tuned—the subtle scent of her perfume, the length of her dark eyelashes, the visible softness of those lovely full lips. Only he needed to put the amazing sex into perspective and act normally. He didn't want any awkwardness to ruin their friendship and, as her supervisor, he needed to show discretion at work.

'Luis has had multiple apnoeic spells this morning,' his registrar said, thankfully oblivious to the tension between Felipe and Emilia.

Felipe nodded, gently pressing his stethoscope against the baby's tiny chest, listening to the rapid beat of his heart and the whoosh of air in and out of his lungs.

'Chest is clear. Heart sounds normal,' he said, glancing at Emilia for her input.

Apnoea, when breathing stopped for a significant period of time, was common in pre-term infants, but Luis Lopez was only three days post-op. His left lung was still small and underdeveloped because of the diaphragmatic hernia. The last thing they needed was for his recovery to be hampered by a chest infection or some other post operative complication. He watched as Emilia gently palpated Luis's abdomen.

'It's soft,' she said. 'No evidence of peritonitis or a collection and the wound looks good.' Their eyes met as they each pondered the likely cause of Luis's apnoea.

Felipe's heart rate spiked with excitement and uncertainty. He wished he knew how she felt after their date. He didn't want that night to ruin the easy working relationship they'd developed, and he still valued her friendship.

'We could repeat the scan to make sure the internal repair is sound,' Felipe suggested, concerned for the smallest Lopez triplet. 'The chest drain is patent, so it's unlikely to be a haemothorax.' Only they didn't want to miss something.

'Surgically everything seems stable,' Emilia agreed, and then turned to face her registrar. 'Have we run a blood glucose recently? Hypoglycaemia can cause central apnoea.'

Very low birth weight babies often suffered low blood sugar, especially when feeding was interrupted by surgery, as in Luis's case. One registrar made a note in Luis's file, while the other organised the blood work.

'While we're checking that,' Felipe said to them, 'let's retest electrolytes and blood gases too.'

'Are you happy to recommence nasogastric feeds?' Emilia asked him as the neonatal nurse switched out the intravenous saline for glucose. 'Feeding will help stabilise blood sugars.'

'Sounds good,' he said, glancing back down at Luis. 'Let's leave our team to sort all that while we speak to Isabella and Sebastian.'

Together, they found the couple in the family room and explained Luis's progress to them.

'From a surgical standpoint,' Felipe told the Lopezes, 'everything looks good. There's no sign of complications, but we're concerned that his blood sugars might be a little low. We'll test for that, and re-establish the nasogastric tube feeding regime today and wean Luis off the oxygen. Keep bringing in your expressed breast milk.'

Isabella nodded and glanced at Emilia, as if for her confirmation. But of course, the women had met before the babies were born, and mother-to-mother, they shared a bond.

'The surgery went very smoothly,' Emilia confirmed, looking to Felipe to include him in the conversation. 'But to be on the safe side, Dr Castillo's registrar is going to order some blood tests and repeat the scan.'

After a few more questions, the couple seemed relieved and headed back to the NICU, hand in hand.

'Can we talk for a second?' Felipe asked Emilia as they left the third floor and took the stairs down to Theatres.

'Of course,' Emilia said, glancing his way as they entered the surgical department. 'Is everything okay?' Doubt flickered across her eyes, and Felipe offered her a reassuring nod.

'Of course.' He indicated his office and followed her inside, closing the door behind them.

She turned to face him with an expectant smile. Felipe hesitated. Perhaps he'd misjudged her withdrawal. Perhaps she'd put Friday night well behind her and was simply getting her head into another working week after the weekend. Perhaps it was only *him* who'd been rocked to the core by what had happened.

'I just wanted to make sure you were okay after Friday night?' he said, diving straight in to dispense with any awkwardness. 'You were gone when I woke up. Sorry that I fell asleep. Not very gentlemanly of me…'

Emilia shook her head, a delicate flush on her cheeks as she reached for his arm and gave it a reassuring squeeze. 'It's no problem. I had to sneak home before

Eva realised I wasn't back. I felt like a teenager again, creeping into my own house.'

She grinned and Felipe's doubts settled, his entire body relaxing for the first time since he'd walked onto the NICU earlier. She was a capable, mature woman who knew what she wanted. There was obviously no awkwardness between them this morning. But a niggle of unease lingered. Was he disappointed to return to just being friends?

'You called a taxi?' he asked, a part of him wishing she hadn't needed to rush off. He usually tried to avoid having women sleeping over in favour of keeping things casual, but she'd felt far too good in his arms, warming his bed.

She shrugged. 'I didn't want to wake you.'

The second time, after a shared shower, they'd taken things slower. In his king-sized bed, he'd kissed every part of her body, bringing her to climax with his mouth before pushing inside her once more.

She dropped her hand to her side, and he quickly snagged hold of her fingers.

'So we're good?' he pressed, peering into her eyes. 'No awkward feelings? No regrets?'

Why was he so invested in making sure she'd had a good time? And why was he still dazed by how hot they'd been together? Emilia was a passionate, experienced woman.

Her smile softened and she inched closer, keeping her fingers entwined with his. 'I had a lovely night, Felipe, although it went a bit further than I expected for a first date...'

'Then it's a good thing it wasn't a *real* date,' he said with a smile, 'just a practice run.'

She laughed and the sound lifted his spirits, any reservations he had about them sleeping together and working together dissolving. But, despite thinking they were done, that everything would return to their pre-sex vibe, he found himself desperate to kiss her again, if only to make sure it was as good in the cold light of day. Not that he truly needed the experiment. Their chemistry was as strong as ever, which was maybe the main reason he *shouldn't* kiss her again. They'd promised each other—just one night.

'I wanted to thank you, actually,' she said, a little hesitantly, looking up at him. 'You can imagine how apprehensive I was to be intimate with anyone else. No matter how illogical it might be, part of me still felt guilty, as if I was…cheating.'

Empathy gripped him. 'I can understand that,' he said, a lump in his throat that she felt comfortable enough to confess such a personal detail.

'But you were so considerate and thoughtful,' she added, squeezing his fingers. '*Definitely* a gentleman.'

She stepped closer, looking up at him with that open expression, and his body instantly reacted, desire and protective urges flaring, every muscle tensing, his temperature shooting through the roof. He still wanted her, just as much as before. Only they'd agreed to one night. His head should be on their working relationship, not sex…

Only with Emilia, it was more than just great sex. They were friends, too.

'I had a really good time,' she went on, sincerely. 'I want you to know that, thanks to you, I feel as if a weight has been lifted from my shoulders, somehow.' She closed the distance between them and raised her face to his, pressing a swift kiss beside his mouth.

Felipe froze, his first instinct to forget their working relationship, forget friendship, to spear his fingers through her hair, crush her body to his and drag her mouth back to his. It was a natural urge after their red-hot night. But Emilia was different to the other women he'd dated, and he needed to stay professional.

'You're welcome,' he said, his stare snagged on her parted lips and the soft gust of her rapid breaths. 'I had a really good time, too.' The best time he'd had in years. Maybe that was why he had an uncharacteristic urge to see her again.

For a handful of seconds, they stared at each other, smiling, as if suspended in time. Emotions flitted across her face: excitement, hesitation, that telling flicker of desire.

Felipe snapped. To hell with their working relationship. He'd been denied that goodbye kiss when she'd left his bed in the early hours of Saturday morning. It would be almost rude not to take the opportunity to do it now.

Done wrestling with his thoughts, and because she was still holding his hand, he scooped one arm around her waist, cupped her cheek with his other hand, hauled her close and kissed her. Emilia met him halfway, surging up on her tiptoes to cement their kiss.

As if they'd both been holding back, the first touch of lips to lips unleashed a torrent of arousal. She moaned—he released a low growl in the back of his throat. How was he expected to resist this amazing woman who was now a friend, a colleague, a passionate lover?

Without breaking contact, he spun them around and pressed her back against the closed office door so he could align her body to his in all the places that mattered. She whimpered a sexy little sound that inflamed him further, her fingers tangling in his hair.

He pinned her to the door with his grinding hips, their bodies touching from shoulder to thigh, moving restlessly together as if to deepen the friction and seek out release. Her hands gripped his neck, keeping their lips locked together, their tongues surging, teasing, tasting. Drugged with desire, Felipe cupped her breast through her shirt, his thumb toying the nipple erect until she moaned and dropped her head back against the door.

'Felipe…' she gasped, staring up at him, her teeth snagging her bottom lip, which was swollen from their kisses.

'That's the goodbye kiss I would have given you if you'd woken me before you left,' he said, dragging his lips over her throat and sucking in the heady scent of her skin.

'Then I'm really sorry I missed it,' she panted, palming his erection through his trousers as she pulled his mouth back to hers.

He needed to stop this. They couldn't be caught making out in his office. They had a full morning of surgeries about to begin and they were supposed to be done with the physical side of their relationship.

Only his head and his body were in direct conflict.

Finally, with a strength he hadn't known he possessed, Felipe dragged his mouth from hers and let his hands slip to her waist. 'Sorry about that. I got carried away. I felt as if I'd been cheated out of that one last kiss by falling asleep.'

She smiled sheepishly, smoothing down her blouse. 'I'm sorry, too. You're very good at kissing.'

He smiled and they stepped away from each other, as if physical distance would squash further temptation. While Felipe dragged in some calming breaths, Emilia glanced at the door and sobered. 'That night was just between us, right? I wouldn't want anyone here to know.'

'Of course.' Felipe brushed a hand down his shirt and straightened his tie, shrugging off disappointment. While he was still reeling over how much he still wanted her, in spite of their promise to each other, she was more pragmatic. 'But do you really need to ask?'

She was right to reset the boundaries. They were professionals. He was her supervisor. And he respected her as a friend.

'No,' she said, shaking her head. 'Sorry. Perhaps I just needed to remind *myself* that we're at work. You're kind of irresistible.' Her stare flicked to his groin, where he was still tenting the front of his trousers. For an agonised second, he couldn't tell if she was about to kiss him again or leave.

Then she rested her hand on the doorknob at her back, her intentions clear. It was time to shelve their chemistry and put work first.

'I might need a second,' he said with a wince, stepping behind his desk to put a piece of heavy furniture between him and Emilia.

Shooting one last almost wistful glance below his belt, she nodded. 'I'll um…go and get changed. See you in Theatre.'

It took him a solid five minutes to calm down.

# CHAPTER NINE

'I'M HOME,' Emilia called later that night, closing the front door behind her, kicking off her shoes and bending to give a welcoming Luna an ear-rub.

After a day with back-to-back surgeries, her feet were killing her. But the throbbing helped to keep her mind off Felipe and that incredibly reckless but raunchy kiss in his office. What had she been thinking? Anyone could have walked in and caught them getting steamy against the door, and they'd promised to return to being just friends. But she hadn't been able to help herself after their seriously sexy night together.

She'd spent the entire weekend with a dreamy smile on her face, reliving every steamy second. Their *date* had given her back her confidence. And today he'd been so thoughtful and considerate, checking that she'd had no regrets. She had no hope of resisting one more kiss. But it had taken all her strength to walk away. If they hadn't been at work, if they hadn't made it clear it was a one-off thing, she would have absolutely slept with him again. He was just so good in bed…

Fanning her face to cool down, she shrugged off her coat and tried to shove aside the memories. It was done. Time to move on. No more thinking about his sexy smile, or the way he touched her face, or that soft groan he made whenever he crushed her in his strong arms…

'I'm making dinner,' Eva called from the kitchen, sounding cheerfully upbeat.

Emilia joined Eva in the kitchen, pouring herself a glass of red wine, trying to appear like a fifty-two-year-old woman who hadn't had mind-blowing sex at the weekend.

*And almost again at work today...*

'Smells delicious,' she said, stirring the pot to distract herself from thinking about Felipe's skill as a lover. 'Thank you for cooking. My last surgery ran overtime.'

Eva batted her mother's hand away, so Emilia took a seat at the breakfast bar to sip her wine and watch dinner progressing.

'So how was your second date on Friday night?' Eva asked, hope shining in her big brown eyes. 'I didn't hear you come in and we've hardly seen each other since.'

Eva had played social volleyball on Saturday and spent most of Sunday at the law library, while Emilia had been on call, spending much of the weekend at the hospital.

Emilia took another sip of wine and prayed that she wouldn't blush and give herself away. It should be *Eva* sneaking home in the early hours after a hot date, not the other way around.

'It was nice,' she said evasively, uncomfortable with why she hadn't told Eva about the non-date date before now. But a part of her hadn't wanted to answer questions about her and Felipe, and Eva had already considered him interested in Emilia.

'Better than the first one, I hope,' Eva pressed, shrewdly watching her mother for more details.

Emilia nodded. 'Yes. Although it wasn't a *real* date.

Felipe, the guy you met that night at Casa Comiendo, invited me to one of his favourite restaurants. His family owns a vineyard in Mendoza so he's really into wine. But the evening was a good confidence boost for me and the opposite of the dating app disaster.'

She was babbling, but she couldn't admit to her daughter that she'd gone home with Felipe, and she didn't want Eva to get the wrong idea about them. It wasn't like she and Felipe were going to see each other again. They were just friends and colleagues.

Nothing to explain.

Colleagues who'd had passionate and steamy sex. *Twice.* Her stomach quivered at the memories.

Eva looked up from slicing tomatoes and capsicums with surprise. 'So you're *not* seeing him again?' Her mouth turned down in a frown of disappointment.

'No, apart from at work.' Emilia shook her head and stole half a cherry tomato from the chopping board, popping it into her mouth, a twinge of regret pinching her stomach. 'We're just friends. He's a committed bachelor who's been casually dating for fifteen years since his divorce, so I desperately needed his advice on how to spot a bad date after my first disaster.'

Funny that they hadn't talked much about dating tips though. They'd been too busy sharing stories of the places they'd travelled and the books they liked and the movies they wanted to see. And now that she'd taken that terrifying leap and overcome her fear of being intimate with another man, maybe the next time she wanted to be social she could embrace online dating once more.

She sighed. Meeting a random stranger still held little appeal.

'Oh…' Eva looked away. 'Well at least you're actually putting yourself out there, Mamá. I'm proud of you. I know it's not easy. But surely the first few dates are the hardest. You'll soon get into the swing of it.'

Emilia's heart sank. Eva obviously still expected her to persevere with the wretched dating app. Emilia hadn't expected that meeting new men would be *easy*. Except with Felipe, of course. It had been such a relief to go out with someone honest and mature and with no hidden agenda. Not to mention sexy as sin. And today had proved that their insanely passionate night wasn't going to affect their working relationship in the slightest. She should feel relieved, and she did, but there was also a wistful edge to her thoughts, most likely due to how comfortable she felt around him.

Now she needed to keep her hands off him at the hospital.

'So, what about you?' Emilia asked, trying to change the subject so Eva wouldn't worry about her sad, single mother. 'Any social plans in the pipeline?' Since starting UBA, Eva had only mentioned a couple of friends. Emilia knew it took time to settle in and find your tribe, but she couldn't help but worry after the upheaval of moving to a new country and leaving behind all her old friends.

'Actually, yes,' Eva said, tossing her long hair over one shoulder. 'I'm hanging out with Paloma at the weekend, a girl I met at volleyball.'

'Oh, that's great.' Emilia's heart swelled with pride. 'I'm so glad that you're making new friends.'

Eva shrugged. 'Paloma lives on campus, and there's a party for first years at the student's association. We might swing by.'

'Great,' Emilia said, her stomach clenching painfully at the idea of Eva leaving home like her peers. She wanted the best for her daughter, of course. Eva needed to live her own life and not worry so much about her mother. But Emilia couldn't help the secret stab of loneliness that crept up on her. Her little girl was a woman. She'd soon be flying the nest, and Emilia would have to get used to living all alone.

Her breath caught on a wave of grief. Ricardo should be there. They were supposed to grow old together after their daughter was all grown up. Just because Emilia had had sex again didn't mean all of her problems were miraculously resolved.

'If I'm out this weekend, perhaps you should organise another *real* date,' Eva suggested, sliding the salad ingredients into a bowl from the chopping board. 'That way you won't be at home by yourself.'

Emilia smiled, forcing herself to practice her brave face for when the time came for Eva to leave home. 'I don't mind being alone, *mija*, but you're right,' she added, seeing the look of concern on Eva's face. 'Maybe I will.'

Maybe now that she'd dispensed with her nerves over the whole dating thing, now that Felipe had provided a frame of reference for comparison, she could move on to more dating successes. The trouble was that Felipe Castillo had certainly set the gold standard. Their non-date date would be a tough act to follow.

For the rest of the week following his date with Emilia, a busy routine developed. Felipe's team were on call, which meant sleepless nights, several emergency surgeries and plenty of new surgical admissions. He and Emilia had spent hours together, operating and reviewing patients, building on their growing friendship.

However, every time they had five minutes alone in the

surgical staff room, there was a palpable tension between them—knowing looks and the accidental and electrifying brush of a hand. It was driving him insane. There'd been no time for any more heated kisses though, and he should be okay with that sad state of affairs. Except Felipe couldn't seem to scrub their night together from his mind, nor could he convince himself that it would be foolish to do it again.

It was torture.

That Friday, on their final surgery of the day, Felipe and Emilia worked on a patent ductus arteriosus—or PDA—case.

'Do you have a good view?' Felipe asked, retracting the thoracotomy incision in the left third intercostal space to expand the surgical field.

'Thank you,' she said.

He glanced at Emilia across the table. Only her eyes were visible between her mask and her theatre hat, but now that he knew her so much better he could read her emotions in her stare. Their mutual professional trust and respect were obvious.

Operating together they'd quickly learned each other's preferred style. While Emilia was now performing simple routine surgeries unsupervised, they were still doing the more complex cases together. This routine heart surgery to close a PDA, an abnormal connection between the aorta and the pulmonary artery, would be relatively straightforward, but Emilia seemed a little tense.

'Adjust the light, please,' she asked the theatre technician, who angled the overhead light, directing the beam into the wound.

'So we have the aorta and pulmonary artery trunk,' she

said, pointing out the major blood vessels to and from the heart. 'The vagus nerve and recurrent laryngeal nerve.'

Taking a forceps and scissors, she carefully opened the pericardium, the sac around the heart, to expose the abnormal connection. The structure normally closed soon after birth, but in cases where it remained patent, the mixing of oxygenated blood form the aorta and deoxygenated blood from the pulmonary artery placed undue strain on the heart and lungs.

'Haemostatic clip, please,' Emilia asked, reaching for the forceps while Felipe watched, confident now in her abilities. She was a meticulous surgeon. Careful and thorough. He had no concerns about her competence.

She isolated the fistula and placed two metal clips across the ductus.

'Looking good,' Felipe said, letting her know that he used exactly the same technique.

She'd finished sewing the pericardium closed when the cardiac monitor sounded an alarm. All eyes swivelled to the heart monitor, which spewed out a paper rhythm strip.

'Looks like sinus tachycardia,' the anaesthetist said with a frown of concern.

'Blood pressure?' Emilia asked, checking the operative field for evidence of haemorrhage or other serious complications.

'BP looks good,' the anaesthetist confirmed, silencing the alarm.

'I can't see any bleeding or pneumothorax,' she said, her worried stare meeting Felipe's. 'Am I missing something?'

It was natural to doubt yourself when those alarms sounded. They were designed to prompt action in an emergency. Only that sometimes there was no obvious explanation for an elevated heart rate.

'I don't think so.' He shook his head, repeating the same checks that Emilia had made. Cardiac arrhythmias were relatively common in neonates, and this one didn't appear to be associated with hypovolaemic shock, which would indicate blood loss.

'Are you happy for us to close?' Felipe asked the anaesthetist, quickly shaking off the false alarm. He tried to communicate reassurance to Emilia through his eyes, but she seemed intent on checking again. For some reason, despite her assuring him she had no regrets, Felipe sensed an extra tension between them today.

At the all-clear, Emilia resumed the surgery, closing the chest and siting a drain in the pleural space to prevent the build-up of any air or fluid around the lung.

'Well done,' Felipe said as they left Theatre. 'I couldn't have done that better myself. One more week of supervision and you'll be all set to go it alone.'

He wanted to reassure her that he had no professional hesitations when it came to her surgical abilities, that the two of them succumbing to their mutual attraction would in no way affect his recommendation for her full registration with the Argentine Medical Council. Only he'd kind of assumed that it went without saying.

'Thanks,' she said, tossing her gown and hat into the laundry bin and heading for the sink. 'Nothing like an alarm to keep you on your toes, keep your adrenal glands working.'

'The perfect end to a long and busy week.' He smiled as he flicked on the taps and began sluicing his hands and arms with water. 'So, any plans for the weekend?' he asked, keeping his tone light. He was fishing, yes, and he didn't want her to feel as if she had to tell him about her personal life. Only a big part of him wanted to ask her out again. They could take the dogs to the park, stop for an ice cream, perhaps catch that new movie they both wanted to see.

Except they were together all the time at work, and neither of them had suggested a repeat of that night. Maybe for Emilia one night had been enough.

'Um…well, Eva is going to a party on campus with a new uni friend,' she said, focusing on washing her hands and not looking at him. She yanked a couple of paper towels from the dispenser and dried her hands. 'And I'm… um…going on another date tomorrow, actually.' She looked up at last and sheepishly met his stare. 'I thought I'd give the app one more try.'

Felipe swallowed down his jealousy and disappointment, plastering a bland expression on his face. 'Sounds good. But is everything okay? You seem a little tense.'

She sighed and shrugged, turning to lean back against the sinks with her arms crossed over her chest. 'Well, I'm not really looking forward to meeting another stranger to be honest. And I guess I feel a little awkward discussing it with you, after…' She tilted her head. '…you know.' She glanced down the deserted corridor, ensuring they were alone.

Oh, *he* knew exactly what she meant. They'd agreed it was a one-off, but the part of him that still fancied her like crazy, that frequently relived every minute of their night together, couldn't forget how good they'd been. He didn't want to hear how she was dating another man.

But he also wanted her to be happy. She *deserved* to be happy after everything she'd been through. Who knew, perhaps her *Mr Right* was out there waiting for her.

'No need to feel awkward,' he said, tossing his balled-up paper towels in the bin with a little too much force. The idea of there being a *Mr Right* for Emilia shouldn't bother him. He'd happily abandoned the idea of being that for anyone many years ago. Perhaps it was just Thiago's looming wedding putting romance in the air.

'I too have a date tonight, as it happens,' he said, leaning beside her, his shoulder a few inches from hers. 'I arranged it weeks ago.' He held her stare. He had no idea why that last detail was important, especially as they weren't seeing each other and she also had a date, but he wanted her to know that he'd organised his date *before* they'd slept together.

'Oh...' Her face coloured and she looked away. 'That's great. Are you going anywhere special?'

Did he imagine her flash of disappointment? Was she jealous, too? Maybe they should both admit that this wasn't over and date each other again. Only that seemed...complicated.

One, she didn't really want to date and was only doing it for Eva. Two, they were colleagues and needed to keep *them* a secret. And three, Felipe rarely dated the same person more than two or three times. Longer represented something serious, and he'd spent the past fifteen years shying away from that. It was just that he'd never met anyone he got along with as well as Emilia.

'Just drinks,' he said with a casual shrug. 'Maybe dancing if it goes well.' Although he'd much rather take Emilia dancing. But he owed it to tonight's date to make an effort.

'Well,' she said, as they headed for the theatre changing rooms, 'I took your advice about only meeting for drinks. Even so, I'm a little nervous about meeting another complete stranger. But that's normal, right?'

'Of course,' he said, his voice full of reassurance as they paused outside the staff changing rooms. She was going out with another man, but he still wanted her to have a good time and feel confident, and she still clearly needed his *dating coach* advice. Only witnessing her uncertainty, he also wanted to take her in his arms, hold her, whisper words of encouragement until she smiled that beautiful smile of hers. But she was a grown woman. She didn't need him to hold her hand no matter how badly he wanted to.

'Just be yourself and have a good time,' he said, forcing himself to inch towards the male changing room on the left. 'I'll see you Monday.'

'You too,' Emilia called, her smile looking a little forced as she ducked through the opposite door marked *female*.

Inside the changing room, Felipe yanked off his scrubs and slammed open his locker, frustration an itch under his skin. He had no right to feel jealous. He and Emilia weren't exclusive, or even dating. *He* definitely wasn't her *Mr Right*. He should be looking forward to his own date tonight. The woman was a successful accountant with a love of good wine and a divorcee, like him. They had heaps in common.

Except she wasn't Emilia.

# CHAPTER TEN

THAT SATURDAY EVENING Felipe met with Thiago in Bar Armando, a popular casual bistro not far from the hospital. They had heaps of wedding plans to discuss, including Felipe's important role as best man. Only all Felipe could think about was Emilia. She'd even been on his mind last night, throughout his decidedly average date with the accountant.

Jealousy soured his mouth, so when the barman placed two tall, sweating glasses of golden beer on the table, he barely even noticed. Somewhere, right now, out there in the city, Emilia was meeting another man. Was she okay? Still nervous? Having a horrible time? He had the irrational idea to text and check in with her, before he pulled himself together and focused on his brother.

'So, I'm giving you the rings now,' Thiago said, handing over two velvet boxes. 'Obviously remembering to bring them to the ceremony next weekend is your most important job.'

Felipe pocketed the ring boxes and took a sip of beer, trying and failing to forget about Emilia. 'I thought my most important job was to tell embarrassing stories about you in my best man speech.'

Thiago shook his head and ignored the jibe. Felipe grinned, looking up from his brother to see Emilia enter the bar. His smile slid from his face while his heart went crazy. She looked sensational in a sexy black dress with a low back.

Then, his stomach dropped. He watched as if in slow motion as she approached the busy bar. She was meeting her date there, at Bar Armando. He felt as if he'd been punched in the gut, but he couldn't look away as Emilia greeted a guy wearing a shiny grey suit who'd been sitting at the bar when Thiago and Felipe had arrived ten minutes ago.

The man appeared to be on his third or fourth shot already, and he didn't even stand up to greet Emilia properly. He simply waved his hand at a vacant barstool, motioning for Emilia to join him.

Felipe fumed on Emilia's behalf. What a jerk. She deserved so much better.

He'd completely zoned out of the wedding talk, barely hearing his brother's comments on the burgeoning guest list and the hire company they'd engaged for the extra tables and seating required.

His insides twisted with jealousy as he watched Emilia order a glass of wine and then turn her lovely smile on her date. Stupid, because he and Emilia weren't a couple. They weren't exclusive. They weren't even dating. They were just friends, and like Felipe she was free to see whoever she chose. Except, his feelings didn't seem to give a damn about any of that. *He* wanted to be the one on a date with her tonight. *He* wanted to pull out her chair and offer her his arm and kiss her goodnight.

Disgusted with the possessive direction of his thoughts, Felipe knew he shouldn't watch her date unfold. But his stare was glued to Emilia. She'd only just sat down, but the creepy guy in the shiny suit kept touching her—her arm, her hand, even her bare shoulder—and she clearly wasn't into it. Felipe could see her flinch away from this distance.

'…and the band we wanted has become free so Violetta is excited, but—' Thiago finally broke off, the sudden silence drawing Felipe's attention away from the woman who'd occupied his thoughts since the moment they'd met.

'That's fantastic,' he said, faking it, one eye on his brother and the other on Emilia.

The man she was with slid his stool closer, leaning in to whisper something in her ear. Felipe looked down, feeling nauseous. He had no claim to her. He himself had gone on a date last night, as previously arranged. And while the woman he'd met had been perfectly nice and clearly only interested in dating casually, he hadn't even taken her up on her offer to go back to her place. It was as if now that he'd slept with Emilia his heart wasn't interested in dating anyone else.

'You haven't heard a word I've said for the past five minutes,' Thiago complained. 'Have you?'

Felipe winced and fought the urge to check on Emilia again. 'Of course I have. The band. Great news.'

Thiago scowled, unimpressed. 'Don't pretend that you've been listening.' He jerked his chin in the direction of the bar. 'Who is she anyway?'

'Who is who?' Felipe said, playing dumb as he stared down at his drink without taking a sip.

Thiago grinned, knowingly. 'The beautiful woman you can't keep your eyes off. I assume you know each other, perhaps intimately if the daggers you're shooting at the man she's with are any indication.'

Felipe waved his hand, evasively. 'We work together.

She's a fellow consultant at the General, and my sex life is none of your business, baby brother.'

Thiago raised his hands in surrender and relaxed back in his seat, wearing *that* look on his face. A younger brother knew exactly how to needle on older one, and vice versa. 'If you're so hung up on her, old man, why is she over there fending off that idiot, while you're over here, mooning and lovesick?'

Felipe kept his face impassive, no mean feat considering he wanted to tie the touchy-feely hands of Emilia's date behind his back with his own shiny tie.

'I'm not lovesick,' he said. 'I'm just looking out for her, that's all. She's just moved here, and she's been single since she lost her husband five years ago. She's new to dating, and there are some real creeps out there.'

He glanced Emilia's way once more, appalled to see that the guy she was with was now knocking back red wine and talking about himself loudly, drawing attention.

'Maybe *you* should be the one dating her,' Thiago said, smugly. 'That way you can save her from the creeps and also focus on an important conversation with your one and only brother.'

'Sorry,' Felipe said, resolutely turning his back on Emilia. 'I *am* listening, I promise. The wedding—I can't wait.'

But Thiago had made an excellent point. Why couldn't he and Emilia continue to date, in secret, of course? After all, Felipe's last date had been as tedious as Emilia's current one seemed to be. Perhaps what they needed was to casually date each other until this thing between them fizzled out. It made perfect sense.

Thiago shook his head dismissively. 'Okay, cut the sarcasm. I hope you're going to put on a better show of enthusiasm than this on the day of the wedding, if only for the sake of my bride. Perhaps you should invite your friend over there to be your plus one,' he suggested. 'You might actually enjoy the event then...'

Felipe froze, a thrill snatching at his breath. Why hadn't he thought of that? It was the perfect solution. Not only would he love to have Emilia's easy and enjoyable company at the wedding, but he could also show her the family vineyard. Not to mention that her presence as his *date* would deflect the inevitable questions from well-meaning relatives about Felipe's long-time single status.

'That's not a bad idea actually...' he said slowly, thinking it through.

Emilia would have no expectations of their date. She'd made it clear that, like him, she wasn't interested in anything serious. They could just focus on their friendship and having a good time—dance a little, sample some world-class wines, enjoy the stunning setting of Mendoza's Uco Valley where he'd grown up. He'd wine her and dine her and put that smile back on her face. Everyone loved a good wedding.

'I do have them from time to time,' Thiago said dryly.

Felipe checked his watch, wondering how long it might be until he could invite her to the wedding as his plus one, deciding he'd give it until her date with the creep was over, but not a second more.

Emilia abandoned her unfinished wine, fixed her tense smile in place and ducked her shoulder yet again from underneath her date's over-familiar and slimy touch. 'Well, thanks for meeting up. I think I'll be going now.'

She'd forced herself to try another date tonight, predominately for Eva. And she'd also wanted to prove to herself that she could have a good time without Felipe guiding her through the process. But no matter how hard she'd tried to make the effort, this guy, Marco, was definitely no Felipe Castillo.

'Don't go,' Marco whined, rudely clicking his fingers to attract the attention of the barman. 'Let's have another drink.'

'Not for me, thanks,' Emilia said, pushing back her barstool and clutching her bag like a shield. She should never have sat down. Marco had been drunk when she'd arrived, and during their brief conversation he'd also downed most of a bottle of red wine. She'd only stayed for the half a drink she'd managed out of some warped sense of politeness. But she couldn't tolerate a second longer of his loud and obnoxious company, not to mention the vile pawing.

She shuddered, sliding from her barstool—she was going straight home for another shower.

'Of course you will,' Marco said, rudely ignoring her as he summoned the barman over. 'Another bottle of red, please,' he said to the young guy. 'And a fresh glass for the lady.'

Emilia caught the barman's eye and shook her head, inching away between the cramped barstools so no part of her accidentally brushed against Marco.

'Is everything okay?' the barman asked Emilia, ignoring Marco's order.

'Yes, thanks,' she said, clenching her jaw with determination. 'I'm just leaving.' She hadn't signed up for *this*. She wanted a little fun, some light-hearted company, maybe a little flirtation, not to run the gauntlet of lecherous creeps who thought themselves entitled to sex simply because she'd shown up.

'No,' Marco cried, coming to his feet and swaying slightly. 'We haven't swapped numbers. I want to see you again, unless you want to get out of here now, together.' He raised his eyebrows hopefully.

'No,' Emilia said firmly. 'I'm leaving, *alone*.'

'She's not interested, mate,' the barman said quietly to a belligerent Marco. 'Don't make a scene.'

Emilia was about to turn away and head for the exit when Marco turned on the young barman.

'Mind your own business and get my wine,' he spat, raising his voice so several people turned to stare.

Emilia hesitated, her face aflame. She wanted to escape this disastrous date, but she couldn't abandon the young barman who'd come to her rescue. He didn't look much older than Eva, and Marco had now turned the full force of his disgruntlement onto him.

Before she could intervene, someone touched her elbow. She was so jumpy, she yelped. But it was Felipe.

She almost sagged with relief to see a friendly face.

'Are you okay?' he asked, guiding her a short distance away while the bar staff dealt efficiently with the drunken Marco, escorting him outside to hopefully put him in a taxi.

Emilia nodded, touching Felipe's arm with gratitude. She was so pleased to see him. 'I'm fine,' she lied, feeling close to tears. 'He'd had too much to drink.' She sniffed, glancing down while she tried to manage her humiliation. 'It seems my third date was even worse than the first one. You promised me they would get better.' She forced herself to smile and met his compassionate stare, dragging her eyes away from the open neck of his shirt and the tantalising glimpse of dark chest hair and golden skin.

She shouldn't drool over one man while her date with

another was barely over. But even if Marco had been sober and charming, she wouldn't have given him her number or agreed to a second date. They'd had zero sexual chemistry, unlike her and Felipe…

'For me, the bad dates seem to outnumber the one good one,' she said with a humourless laugh. 'You must tell me your secret.' No doubt his date last night had been a resounding success, especially if he'd looked even half as hot as he did tonight. But she couldn't think of that, or she'd want to ask if he'd slept with the woman, if he planned to see her again, none of which was her business.

Felipe pressed his lips together and glanced over his shoulder, looking torn. Emilia stepped back, mortified. Was he on another date? A second date, perhaps, with the woman from last night, because it had gone so well. Oh, no….

Not only had Felipe witnessed Emilia's *date from hell*, but she'd probably also dragged him away from some glamorous and entertaining beauty. It was Saturday night after all.

'I'll be fine,' she blurted, desperate now to run home. 'Don't let me interrupt your evening. I'm going to wait until he's definitely gone—' she glanced at the door '—and grab a taxi.'

'Look,' Felipe said with a frown, his hand lingering on her bare elbow, which was enough contact to send her entire body up in flames, despite her humiliation. 'I'm having a drink with my brother. Why don't you come and say hello.'

Emilia nodded, too confused by the relief coursing through her veins to speak. So he *wasn't* on a date. Should she be this relieved? Except Felipe hadn't simply set the standard against which her other dates could be measured, he'd also set Emilia's expectations sky high.

But why shouldn't she hold out for a kind, smart and thoughtful mature man who was also a great lover? At her age and stage in life, she absolutely refused to settle.

'Thiago,' Felipe said as the other man stood, 'this is Emilia Gonzales. We work together at the General. Emilia is from Uruguay.'

Emilia shook Thiago's hand. He looked just like his handsome older brother, the same deep brown eyes, only with longer hair.

'Nice to meet you,' she said, feeling less self-conscious than if Felipe had been with another woman, although his brother had likely witnessed her terrible date, too. 'I hear you're soon to be married. How are the preparations going?'

Thiago smiled a charming smile. 'I'm largely keeping out of the way, as any sensible groom would. But I'm looking forward to it. Having hosted so many other people's weddings at Castillo Estates it will be great to enjoy my own wedding there.'

'Why don't you join us for a drink?' Felipe urged, smiling, his hand sliding to the small of her back—she shivered with delight rather than revulsion, as she had at that other man's touch. Thiago nodded in agreement.

'Oh, no, thanks.' Emilia blinked, her eyes stinging again, this time with emotion at their kindness. The Castillo family had raised two exceptional sons. 'That's very kind, but I'm heading home, now.'

Confused by her reaction to Felipe's touch, she wanted to hurl herself into his arms, to feel safe and respected. They were so good together. But she needed to remember that, A, they were just friends and colleagues and,

B, Felipe was a committed bachelor, himself still dating other people. She couldn't rely on him for emotional support, no matter how tempting.

'Then let me see you home,' Felipe said, stepping closer and lowering his voice. 'You seem understandably shaken up.'

Emilia fought the urge to beg him to hold her, to feel his strength surround her, to hear his murmured reassurances as she had that night they'd slept together, when he'd been so considerate of her feelings and treated her like he truly cared. Instead, she vigorously shook her head and backed away from the dangerous temptation of him. 'No, please don't interrupt your evening on my account. I'll be fine. Eva will probably be back from her party and waiting for me at home, anyway.'

Felipe likely *did* care. He was a considerate person. But they weren't a couple, only friends who'd slept together. No doubt there was some new fandangle term for that, but the important thing was that she was fine alone.

She swallowed, a new resolve straightening her spine. 'It was a good thing that my date was a disaster, actually. It's helped me to decide that I'm absolutely done with dating apps.'

Felipe frowned in concern and Thiago winced.

'Enjoy the rest of your night,' she said, smiling as brightly as she could manage before heading for the door.

Outside the cool breeze caressed her heated face. What a horrible evening, the humiliation of her date made more obvious by the contrast of Felipe's soothing presence, not that she'd needed rescuing. It was only that for a second, when he'd first touched her arm, it had felt so good to have an ally, to know that she hadn't been as utterly alone as she'd often felt these past five years.

But one thing was certain—she wasn't putting herself through any more mystery dates, not even for Eva. She'd meet someone the old-fashioned way or not at all.

# CHAPTER ELEVEN

LATER THAT NIGHT, after saying goodbye to his brother, Felipe tapped on Emilia's front door. He took another glance at his phone and the text he'd received in response to his, which had enquired if she'd made it home safely and how she was feeling.

I'm okay. Eva is staying the night at her friend's place. Come over and keep me company if it's not too late.

After witnessing her demoralising date tonight, wild horses couldn't have kept him away. She didn't need him to look out for her, but he hated the idea that she might be feeling vulnerable and alone. Seeing her out with another guy tonight, all dressed up and hopeful only to be so badly let down, had sent his protective urges into overdrive.

They weren't an item, but he hadn't expected to feel so…jealous, so possessive and invested in her happiness. He'd even abandoned his beer and switched to soft drinks after Emilia had left the bar, just so he could drive to her place and check up on her.

The door swung open and she stood on the threshold. His heart thumped excitedly. She'd changed out of her dress into jeans and a sweater. She looked relaxed and welcoming and unbearably beautiful.

'Hey, how are you feeling?' he asked, leaning in to brush her cheek with a kiss.

'I'm good. Come in.' Her smile for him was just the ego boost he needed. It lit her eyes as if, right then, he was the only person she wanted to see.

But he was fantasising, and he couldn't afford to over-think his possessive feelings. They were understandable, as he'd said to Thiago, considering how well they got on and after everything Emilia had been through—losing her husband, raising their daughter alone and moving countries. And of course the amazing sex had complicated things, distorting his perspective.

Felipe followed her into a modern living room filled with comfy sofas, contemporary furniture, lamps and potted houseplants. A dog, he assumed Luna, greeted him with a thumping tail before sloping back off to her faux-fur dog bed.

'Coffee or wine?' Emilia asked, the wide neck of her sweater slipping to reveal one tanned and freckled shoulder and the lacy strap of her bra.

'Better make it coffee. I drove here.' Felipe released an internal groan of frustration. He was so drawn to her brand of effortless sophistication and unassuming sex appeal. Only he'd come to support her, not to seduce her. But resisting her now that they'd been intimate and knew each other so much better would not be an easy task, especially if she kept looking at him in *that* way.

'Thanks for coming over,' she said as she prepared his coffee. 'I think I was still a little in shock when you texted. When I got home to find Eva's message and an empty house, I almost burst into tears. Thank goodness for Luna.' She glanced gratefully at the dog, who thumped her tail in response.

'I'm sorry you had such a bad experience tonight,' he said, removing his jacket and taking the cup of coffee from her. 'Although you handled yourself impeccably. You were firm and classy. But forget about that guy. He wasn't worth your time,' he added as they sat side by side on the sofa.

Emilia had obviously been sitting there before he arrived. Her half-full glass of wine sat on the coffee table next to an open book. Felipe placed his mug on a coaster and turned his attention to Emilia, taking her hand in his. 'Are you truly okay?'

She nodded, vulnerability clouding her stare. 'But I just can't do it any more,' she said with a shudder. 'I was going through the motions of dating for Eva's sake. Ever since her father died, she worries so much about me being alone, and the last thing I want is to be any sort of burden to her. I want her to be young and carefree like her contemporaries.'

'Of course you do.' Felipe nodded in understanding even as he processed his disappointment that she was done with dating. 'You're a wonderful mother. A role model, not a burden. I'm sure your strength is inspiring to her.'

She blinked, gratitude shining in her eyes. Her fingers curled tighter around his. 'Thanks Felipe. What would I have done without you these past couple of weeks?'

Felipe's heart soared that she valued his friendship, except a huge part of him wanted to be more than her friend. Was that just his over-protectiveness at play? He still wasn't looking for a serious relationship, but that smile of hers was addictive. He wanted to be the man to put it on her face.

'I'm sorry that you've been unlucky with your dates,' he continued, sliding his thumb back and forth over the back of her hand—touching her was second nature. 'You deserve so much better. It's not supposed to be *that* hard.'

And if she was finished with dating, where did that leave them and his hopes that they could spend more time together?

'Right?' She nodded in agreement. 'I mean I'm not even looking for love. I've had that once.' Her eyes landed briefly on the framed photo on the table—her and Eva and a man that was obviously Ricardo. 'I was just hoping for a little fun,' she said, 'like the night *we* went out—nice food, great conversation, no games. That was easy. You made me feel uplifted. But I can't go through another date like tonight's. Not even for Eva. I know she'll be disappointed with me, but it's just not worth it.'

She looked down at their clasped hands and compassion swelled in his chest. He would be her friend if that was all she wanted.

'She'll understand,' he said, resting his index finger under her chin and tilting it up so their eyes met. 'You two are wonderfully close. But the downside is that you know each other so well emotionally. Talk to her and explain how you feel. Just because you're not ready to date now, doesn't mean you won't be one day.'

Although a huge part of him had hoped she might want to date *him* again…

She nodded and glanced at the photo once more. 'Eva and I *are* close. Losing her father hit her so hard. She was very withdrawn for a long time.' She sighed and Felipe squeezed her hand. 'Of course, I worry that I'm messing her up even more because I'm the only parent she has now...'

Felipe shook his head adamantly. 'I'm no expert when it comes to teenagers, but if it's any reassurance, she seems like a very intelligent and switched on young woman.'

A soft smile touched her lips. 'Thanks for listening, Felipe.' She snagged her bottom lip with her teeth, drawing his attention back to those soft, kissable lips. 'Sometimes I forget that Ricardo isn't here. I'll have a bad day at work or a parental worry and my first thought is to discuss it with him. Then, with sickening shock, I remember that he's gone and that, whatever the dilemma, I need to deal with it alone. It sounds silly, but it can be so tiring.'

'Not silly at all.' Felipe took her hand in both of his, his offer spoken before he could overthink the impulse. 'I know it's not the same, but you can call me any time and I'll listen, help out if I can. I'm alone too, so I get it, only I don't have the responsibility of a child of my own. But seriously, just call me.'

'That's very thoughtful of you.' She blinked and swallowed as if struggling to find the words. 'I hope I didn't ruin your evening, too. What must your brother think of me?'

Felipe made a dismissive sound, wishing he could hold her in his arms, kiss her and chase away all her fears and doubts. But she was strong. And fortunately she didn't need him to take care of her, because he was no good at that.

'I'm not particularly happy about him noticing,' he said about Thiago, 'and I let it slide because he's getting married, but he thought you were beautiful, which you are.' He grinned, partly joking about his brother and partly serious. It seemed where Emilia was concerned, the possessive feelings, the jealousy, no matter how unfounded, were here to stay.

She stared, her eyes flicking between his as the tension between them seemed to crackle. Oh, how badly he wanted to seduce her again, to show her just how beautiful and amazing she was, to worship her body with his until he'd replaced her humiliation from earlier with memories of passion. But he needed to tread carefully. Emilia was feeling understandably vulnerable and alone, and he'd really only come here to check on her. She didn't need a saviour and he couldn't be one. He was no longer serious commitment or husband material.

'Tell me more about Ricardo,' he said instead as he glanced at the picture of them together, steering the conversation out of danger and deliberately bringing up the man who *had* been everything to Emilia.

She eyed him curiously, some of the tension leaving her. 'You really want to know?'

'About the man you loved?' he asked. 'Sure.' Felipe didn't see Emilia's husband as competition. Strangely he wasn't jealous of Ricardo Gonzales. Their marriage and their history was theirs and theirs alone. He certainly wasn't looking to replace the man, even if he could have. It was just that Ricardo Gonzales had excellent taste in women.

'You might have liked him, actually,' Emilia said with a soft smile. 'He was a runner too. He completed the Montevideo marathon six times, before Eva came along.'

'Impressive.' Felipe nodded, urging her to continue. 'How did you meet?'

She relaxed back into the sofa and placed her other hand over his in her lap, so now his hand was sandwiched between both of hers. 'He was travelling after graduating from UBA. He was sleeping on the floor of a friend of mine before taking off to backpack around Brazil. I knew after our first date that he was *the one*, but we were also great friends.'

She smiled fondly. 'I'd been planning to go travelling too, so I changed my itinerary and we explored Brazil together. You really get to know a person when you share a two-person tent.'

Felipe smiled in agreement. 'I can imagine.'

Still clinging to his hand, her expression changed, as if she was no longer seeing the past, but was firmly in the present. 'Your brother looks a lot like you. Are you close?'

Felipe shrugged, relaxed in her company, as always. 'We are surprisingly close, although sometimes I overdo the protective big brother thing. He's a good man. I'm glad that he's met Violetta and that she makes him happy.'

Only Thiago's happiness and the wedding plans, combined with his jealousy over Emilia's date, had accentuated Felipe's restlessness, his loneliness. It was as if his career and his string of deliberately casual dates were no longer enough to keep him content. And the only thing in his life that had changed was him meeting Emilia.

'The family business sounds very successful,' she continued, dragging him away from the unsettling thought. 'How many weddings do you host a year?' She reached for her wine glass from the table and took a sip.

'I believe it was over thirty last year. Not that *I* can take any credit. The success is all down to Thiago.'

She eyed him over the rim of her glass, placing it back on the table. 'I've touched a nerve?'

While Emilia was a great listener, Felipe hesitated. 'Not really...' He didn't want to expose his worst flaws to this woman, but Emilia didn't play games. She wouldn't use his regrets against him, and she'd opened up to him about all sorts of things tonight.

'It's just that sometimes when I see Thiago,' he continued, 'I still feel a little guilty that I abandoned Castillo Estates to follow my surgical career. He's never thrown it back at me, but he had no choice in having to step up and take over the business from our parents after they retired.'

Emilia frowned, her dark stare full of empathy. 'We all have a choice, Felipe. Thiago doesn't strike me as a pushover. I'm sure that he'd have followed a different career if he'd really wanted one. Your parents could have employed a manager or sold the business.'

'That's true.' She was so understanding. 'I guess the guilt comes from in here.' He rested his balled-up fist over his sternum. 'So it's not particularly logical.'

She leaned closer, the passion building in her voice. 'Because you're a decent man who cares about people. But it's like my wise daughter says—*you* deserve to be happy too. It's okay to have your own ambition and dreams, and you've worked long and hard for your career.'

'Yes…'

She eyed him sadly. 'Yes, but…?' she pressed with a question in her voice.

Felipe dragged in a deep inhale. 'But I'm aware how my ambition, my career, has also cost me my marriage in addition to burdening my brother with the family business.' Why was he telling her this? It was as if she'd popped the lid on his deepest vulnerabilities and he couldn't seem to quell the outpouring.

Her stare softened with understanding. 'Nothing is ever that straightforward in a marriage,' she said, knowingly. 'It's the most complex and rewarding relationship we enter into. Two people, often from different walks of life, sharing everything—a home, a life, a family. Marriage takes work and commitment and compromise on both sides, and even then that's sometimes not enough to make it last.'

'Look at us,' he said with smile, hoping to lighten the mood—after all he'd come over to make her feel better. 'If only we'd had all this wisdom in our twenties.'

She chuckled. 'Indeed.'

Because he desperately wanted to kiss her, he raised her hand to his mouth and pressed a kiss there. 'Thanks for listening. I was supposed to be the one doing the comforting. That's why I came over.'

Emilia shrugged, her eyes bright. 'I like that it's mutual. And I can't take all the credit. You're easy to talk to, too. You make me feel safe and understood, so thank you.'

Felipe looked up from her mouth, his stare latched to hers. He didn't want to look away. He didn't want to miss one second of the way she was looking at him, because he recognised the desire in her expression and it matched the urgency pounding through him in time with his rapid heartbeat.

But he didn't want to cross the line.

'Your coffee's probably cold,' she whispered, her tongue touching her lush bottom lip.

'Who needs coffee?' He shrugged, willing her to make the first move, willing her to want him as much as he wanted her in that moment.

He couldn't promise her for ever, but he definitely

wanted more than one night. They could have a good time while they continued to explore this intense chemistry.

It made so much sense. He just hoped she wouldn't take too much convincing.

# CHAPTER TWELVE

EMILIA DRAGGED IN a shuddering breath as they stared at each other. She couldn't look away. That he'd driven over after his night out with his brother, that he'd not only listened to her express her concerns for Eva and talk about Ricardo, but also shared *his* feelings with her—it was humbling. At work, he was so controlled and driven and confident, she hadn't expected him to voice such deep-rooted doubts over his failed marriage and his relationship with his family.

He had so many positive attributes, but he was also a complex man with fears and regrets, just like her. The more time they spent together, the closer they became. And right then, the only thing she was certain of was how stupid it would be to ignore their continuing connection.

'You think I'm beautiful,' she whispered, her pulse tripping.

'I do,' he said, his grip tightening on her hand.

Silently, she leaned forward. He moved too and their lips met in a rush. Desperate, she whimpered. Felipe gripped her neck and her waist and commanded the kiss, which went from zero to ten in a second, as if they'd both been holding back for too long.

'I can't stop thinking about you,' he said, kissing a

path down her neck as his hands slid inside her sweater to caress her skin. 'I can't stop wanting you.'

'Me neither,' she moaned, tilting her head to expose the sensitive places on her neck to his lips.

Why had she bothered with the dating app when she didn't even need to think about her relationship with Felipe? They just understood each other. Clicked. It was always easy, always uplifting and, if she was honest, she'd never stopped wanting him since the first time they were intimate.

'Come with me.' She stood, tugging him to his feet and leading him to her bedroom, closing the door to keep the dog out. They pulled at each other's clothes, their lips moving frantically together as they inched towards the bed, their tongues surging wildly to assuage the burning desperation of every touch.

This felt so right, it was almost terrifying. Only it wasn't about feelings or for ever. Felipe made her feel safe and accepted, so she could almost glimpse the old, resilient, grief-free Emilia, a woman who'd had it all: a husband she loved, a daughter, a career. Was that woman gone for ever, or was she there somewhere, licking her wounds, ready to one day make a comeback?

Because she was tired of thinking and wanted only to feel, she fumbled with Felipe's shirt buttons, exposing his bronzed chest, pressing her lips over his pecs and the valley between as her hands reached for his belt. She looked up as she stripped him. His stare was almost black with desire, as he removed her sweater and cupped her breasts, thumbing the nipples.

'I hated seeing you with him tonight,' he said, his voice breaking with the depth of his passion.

His jealously inflamed her, matching her own for the

woman he'd taken out the night before. She crashed her lips back to his and slid her tongue into his mouth, as he unclasped and then removed her bra.

She didn't want to think about him being intimate with anyone else, even though she knew if he'd been single for fifteen years that he'd had his fair share of lovers.

Felipe gripped her upper arms and tore his mouth away. 'Ask me. I know you want to.'

She froze, her heart raging. She could pretend she had no clue what he was talking about. But what was the point? They were clearly frantic for each other.

'Did you sleep with her last night?' she asked, her jealousy a shocking sting in her veins. She'd never been the possessive type and Felipe wasn't *hers*, but she wanted to know that he was as consumed with her as she was with him.

'No,' he said, hauling her lips back to his. 'I only want you.'

His dark head swooped and he captured her nipple between his lips, his tongue flicking over the bud. A deep ache settled in her belly. His hands unbuttoned her jeans as he sucked, pushing them over her hips until she'd wriggled free. Then he cupped her backside in both hands, grinding his erection between their bodies.

'Why haven't we been doing this all week?' she asked, slipping her hand inside his jeans.

She stroked him, smiling when he crushed her to his naked chest and groaned. 'I have no idea. Because we're stupid?'

Emilia laughed, pressed her lips over his neck, his jaw, his chest. Felipe fumbled with his wallet, removing a condom, and Emilia shoved at his jeans and boxers, sliding them over his hips so he could kick them off.

When he stood before her, gloriously naked and erect, and before he could put on the condom, she dropped to her knees and took him into her mouth. She wanted him as wild as she felt. She wanted to imprint the memory of tonight, of their undeniable passion, in both their minds. She wanted to banish any trace of her disastrous date and Felipe's previous lovers.

'Emilia,' he growled, watching her take him, his hands cupping her face, fingers tunnelling into her hair. 'You are so sexy.'

Power surged through her as his hips jerked and his skin flushed and his breathing turned harsh and ragged. He was so male—honourable and honest and trustworthy. He'd come to her rescue tonight in his own respectful way, not that she'd needed him. But it was good to know she wasn't totally alone, that she had a champion, someone on the same wavelength, someone who cared.

Before she could get carried away, he jolted his hips back and dragged her to her feet, kissing her soundly while he rolled on the condom and removed her underwear. His hands caressed her breasts as he walked her back towards the bed. She sat and he leaned over her, tonguing first one nipple and then the other. Emilia sighed, leaning back on her elbows as Felipe trailed the tip of his tongue down her body, until his mouth covered her sex.

She gasped, her head light with delirium, the waves of pleasure scalding her, hotter and hotter. 'Yes,' she cried, tunnelling her fingers through his hair as he worked her higher and higher, his hands splayed across her backside, holding her to his mouth.

Just when she thought she might come, he surged to

his feet and covered her body with his, grasping one thigh over his hip as he pushed inside her.

'Look at me,' he said, entwining their fingers together as his hips moved in slow, deep thrusts.

Emilia held his stare, her body alive from his touch, her heart thudding against his as heat consumed her.

'I want to take you dancing, I want to pull out your seat and see you home safely,' he said, the sincerity in his stare a confirmation of Felipe's passionate nature.

'Yes…' Emilia nodded, chasing his lips with hers to satisfy the need burning her up.

He pulled back, his hips thrusting in a steady rhythm that took her higher and higher. 'I want to hold your hand and listen to your concerns and laugh with you.'

She nodded, too choked and turned on for speech. He was everything she needed in that moment, his words soothing her soul, his body driving her closer and closer to blissful release.

'I want you, Emilia,' he ground out, picking up the pace, shunting her higher and higher.

'Felipe,' she cried as her orgasm struck.

He kissed her, thrusting through every spasm until she was spent, and then he too let go, groaning against the side of her neck as his body stiffened in her arms.

Emilia held him as they each caught their breath, her heart a wild flutter behind her ribs and her throat tight with emotion. Their intense passion was difficult to deny, but after the emotional rollercoaster of the evening, now that they'd satisfied their physical need for each other, she wasn't sure how to feel apart from unsettled, as if she were being chased in the dark.

She lay still, her heart banging against his. This time

had been different, more intimate, especially after their heartfelt talk.

But *nothing* had changed. They weren't making a commitment to each other. Felipe had managed to avoid serious relationships for fifteen years—Emilia was still very much focused on making sure Eva's life was stable, and was clinging to the precious memories of Ricardo. Not to mention that they worked together. If they didn't handle this physical side of their relationship like mature adults, it could damage their professional relationship when it ended. And given Felipe's commitment avoidance and her fear of opening up her emotions, it *would* end, probably sooner rather than later.

'Are you okay?' he asked, raising his head to peer down at her.

She nodded, still overcome by what tonight meant. 'I wasn't expecting that to happen.'

He offered her a small smile. 'Me neither, but we don't need to overthink it. You wanted me, I wanted you. We're both single.'

Emilia nodded, the simplicity of his explanation not quite dispelling her unease.

'I should go,' he said, pressing a soft kiss to her lips. His smile touched his eyes and she knew that he too was feeling a little caught off guard by what they'd just done. 'But first, I wanted to ask you something.' He rolled to the side and drew the covers over her body. 'Would you like to be my date at Thiago and Violetta's wedding next weekend?'

Emilia stilled, her heart racing with panic. A wedding date felt more serious than a regular date.

'We can make a weekend of it,' he added, perhaps sensing her hesitation. 'I'll even give you a personal tour of the estate, show you the vines and the cellar, and the very vat where I crushed my first vintage by foot when I was six years old.'

His excited smile was hard to resist. And where was the harm? He wasn't suggesting they become an item or even asking her to date him exclusively. As long as no one at the hospital got wind of it, it might be fun. A chance to dress up and dance and relax in a stunning part of Argentina, with a man who understood and respected her and had done so much for her confidence these past two weeks.

'I'd love to…' she said, chewing at her lip. 'But I don't know… I'd have to tell Eva if I'm away for the whole weekend, and I don't want to confuse her about us. Especially when I keep telling her that we're just friends.'

'Of course.' He nodded, the sparkle in his eyes dimming. 'We *are* friends, but I understand if it's too hard to explain. It's your call.'

Emilia touched his face, stroking her fingers through his luxuriant hair. 'Won't your family get the wrong idea, too? You said they're keen to see you settle down again. Won't me turning up as your date make them mistake us for a couple?'

That would only put pressure on the situation and *she* wasn't even sure herself what it was they were doing. *Friends with benefits? Casual sex? Secret fake dating?* It was all a messy blur.

Felipe took her hand and kissed the centre of her palm so her toes tingled. 'They know me well enough to understand that just because I bring along a date it doesn't mean I'm in a serious relationship. They know I'm done with those.'

Of course, his family knew him best. If he'd managed

to stay single for fifteen years since his divorce, there was little risk of anyone, including Emilia, changing his mind.

'And anyway,' he added, 'it was Thiago's idea that I invite you. We can make it clear to anyone who asks that we're just friends.' He drew her lips back to him and pressed a whisper-soft kiss there, coaxing. 'Say yes. I want to show you where I grew up.'

Emilia dragged in a shuddering breath, berating herself. Felipe was a committed bachelor. It was much more likely that his family would see her as the *woman of the moment* rather than a serious contender for his heart.

'Okay. In that case, I'd love to go,' she said, ignoring the prickles of possessiveness that once more reared their head. So there would be lovers after her—that suited her just fine. If she wasn't ready to date strangers, she certainly wasn't ready to open her heart up to feelings. She might never be ready for that…

'But please don't mention that I'm going with you to anyone at work,' she urged. 'I don't want the hospital rumour mill to start up, and you *are* still my supervisor.'

After this fling or whatever it was ended, they still had to work together. Neonatal surgery was a small specialist field. They couldn't afford to allow their personal lives to damage the professional relationships they'd built up. And she highly valued his friendship. She wouldn't want to lose that either.

'Of course not,' he said with a small frown, stealing one last kiss before leaving her bed to deal with the condom.

They dressed and returned to the living room, collecting up the wine glass and coffee cup and stacking them in the dishwasher.

'I'll see you at work Monday,' Felipe said. 'We have

that Hirschsprung's disease pull-through surgery first thing.' He drew her into his arms for another searing kiss that stole her breath. She'd barely released him when there was the sound of a key in the lock and Luna hurried into the hall, her tail wagging.

'Eva…' Emilia froze, staring in horror at Felipe, who was fully clothed but had that arousing post-sex look going on—tousled hair, rumpled shirt, slumberous eyes.

Panic snatched at her breath. What had she been thinking inviting him here? She could have met him at *his* apartment. She didn't want Eva to feel threatened or confused by her and Felipe's relationship. And aside from great sex, which was the one thing she *couldn't* discuss with her daughter, there really was nothing to tell.

Felipe nodded, stepped aside and ran his fingers through his hair while Emilia guiltily adjusted the neck of her sweater.

'Hello?' Eva called, appearing in the doorway with Luna a second later, her surprise at Felipe's presence evident.

'Mija, I thought you were spending the night at your friend's place,' Emilia said, praying that it wasn't obvious that her and Felipe had just got out of bed. 'You remember Felipe Castillo from the hospital, don't you?'

Her voice was too high pitched. She sounded guilty, as if she'd done something naughty. She took some calming breaths, reminded herself she was a grown woman who deserved a sex life, and forced herself to appear nonchalant.

'Hi,' Eva said to Felipe, barely looking his way as she tossed her bag on the sofa and stooped to give Luna an ear rub. 'Paloma's boyfriend came over,' Eva said, her voice flat with disappointment. 'I didn't want to play gooseberry, so I thought I'd leave them to it. Besides, I have heaps of studying to do tomorrow. I'm going to get up early and tackle my essay.'

'Oh…okay,' Emilia said, feeling flustered. 'Well, Felipe was just leaving. He rescued me tonight from a horrible date, but I'll tell you all about that tomorrow.'

'See you,' Eva said before heading towards her own bedroom with the dog in tow.

Emilia sighed, relieved that Eva hadn't suspected a thing, but also guilt-ridden that she'd been so careless. She crept outside onto the doorstep with Felipe, gently pulling the door behind her.

'That was close,' she said, wincing. 'Imagine if she'd come home five minutes earlier. How would I have explained that!' She'd have to be more careful. Her daughter was her priority, and she'd almost put herself and Eva in an embarrassing situation simply because she found Felipe Castillo irresistible.

Felipe frowned, a flicker of hurt in his stare, although she might have imagined it. 'It's okay for her mother to have a healthy sex life,' he said, gently raising her chin and kissing her softly. 'I'm sure she'd understand that you have your own life, your own needs.'

Emilia said nothing. The trouble was she wasn't a hundred percent convinced that it *was* okay for Eva to know those things, not when so much of her young life had been upturned by grief and confusion. Felipe wasn't Eva's father. Emilia certainly didn't want to discuss with her whatever it was that she and Felipe were doing, especially when they were just fooling around.

And what if Felipe was wrong? What if the idea of her mother with another man *did* upset Eva? What if she saw Felipe as some sort of threat for her mother's attention? What if she thought Emilia was trying to replace Ricardo? The poor kid had already been through so much. Emilia didn't want to put any kind of strain on their close relationship.

'Hmm,' she said, 'I'm not sure *I'm* ready for that particular parent–child conversation.' She knew he meant well, but they weren't a couple.

He accepted her excuse with a casual shrug, stepping back. 'Goodnight, Emilia, sleep well.'

'See you at work,' she said, holding onto his fingers until the last possible moment as he reluctantly stepped away and headed for his car.

She stayed on the doorstep to watch him leave, her head all over the place. Felipe's words rang through her mind. A big part of Emilia was scared to admit her own needs even to herself. Because admitting them meant acknowledging the hole in her life. She couldn't smother Eva, or live vicariously through her daughter, simply because she was too scared to open herself up to a fulfilling relationship. No one could replace Ricardo—she'd have to reiterate that to Eva. But did Emilia truly want to be alone for the rest of her life?

As she headed to bed, the scent of Felipe's cologne lingered on her sheets. Being brave enough to put her needs first and meet new people was one thing, but finding someone who she could connect with, trust and maybe open up her heart to was a whole other ballgame.

Even Felipe, who was head and shoulders above those dating app guys she'd met recently, wasn't without risk. After all, he'd successfully and resolutely avoided a serious relationship and love for fifteen years.

Even if she wanted to, how could she put her bruised and terrified heart in the hands of a man like that?

# CHAPTER THIRTEEN

EARLY MONDAY MORNING, at the request of his registrar, Felipe strode into the emergency department to review a new admission and saw Emilia already with the patient.

His blood heated at the sight of her, the memories of Saturday night as fresh as if she were still in his arms. They'd really opened up to each other that night. Her about her concerns for Eva's happiness, and him about his guilt over letting his family down. For a moment, as he lay in her bed, his heart pounding against hers, he'd felt so close to her.

Joining her now, excitement fizzed in his veins. He couldn't wait to show her off to his friends and family at the wedding that weekend. Of course, he'd need to downplay their relationship, as promised. He didn't want to upset her or spook her away with any awkward questions or misguided assumptions from his overzealous family.

Emilia looked up, spying him. Excitement flared in her dark eyes, gone in a blink. 'Good morning, Dr Castillo,' she said, with a tight, professional smile.

'Dr Gonzales,' he said, wishing he could kiss her breathless until she moaned his name. 'Who do we have here?' He glanced at the grizzling baby and the anxious parents expectantly.

'This is Bruno,' Emilia said. 'Two days old, born at

thirty-nine weeks gestation by uncomplicated vaginal delivery. Bruno's parents became worried by a red swelling in the groin. He's pyrexial and not feeding, and on examination has an incarcerated left inguinal hernia.'

'Mind if I take a look?' Felipe asked the parents, quickly washing his hands at the sink.

Bruno's mother laid her fractious boy down on the bed, and Emilia and Felipe examined the newborn together as the parents worriedly looked on. As well as a painful, irreducible swelling in the left groin, Bruno also had a slightly distended abdomen and absent bowel sounds, all signs that a loop of intestine had become trapped inside the hernia, which required urgent surgical repair.

'As Dr Gonzales explained,' Felipe said, addressing the couple, 'it seems that Bruno has developed a small hernia.' He refastened the baby's nappy and handed him back to Mamá. 'The concern is that a piece of bowel is trapped inside the hernia. The longer it stays there the greater the risk that its blood supply is restricted. That can lead to necrosis of the bowel, so I'm afraid we need to surgically repair the hernia and, while we're there, have a look at the bowel to make sure it's all healthy. If we do find a necrosed segment of bowel, we'll also need to remove that, but this won't affect Bruno's ability to feed and grow as normal.'

'When did Bruno last feed?' Emilia asked as she and Felipe rewashed their hands.

'About eleven last night,' his mother said, 'but he also vomited some bile around five am.'

'We're about to head into Theatre,' Felipe explained, 'so we can add Bruno to our list and operate this morning. Dr Ruiz, my registrar who you've already met, will be along soon to consent Bruno for the surgery and run some blood tests.'

'The procedure shouldn't take more than an hour,' Emilia added, 'but we'll need to keep Bruno in hospital for a couple of days until he's feeding and his bowel starts working properly. You're welcome to stay with him, of course.'

'Any questions for us?' Felipe asked the couple, who glanced at each other and then shook their heads. 'Dr Ruiz can also answer any questions you think of after we've gone.' Felipe opened the curtains around the bed.

Emilia left the emergency department at his side, her demeanour somewhat distracted.

'Is everything okay?' he asked quietly as they headed for the surgery department.

'Fine,' she said, not quite meeting his eye. 'I came in early and saw Dr Ruiz. Thought I'd review the patient before Theatre in case he needed to be added to the urgent list for today, which as it turns out he does.'

Felipe nodded, frustrated that she was talking about work when he'd really been enquiring about *her*. 'I meant is everything okay with you?' He paused outside his office, inclining his head and inviting her in.

She hesitated for a split second and then followed him into the room. Felipe closed the door and immediately reached for her, scooping her into his arms as their lips met in a frantic breathy kiss of desperation. To his relief, she curled her arms around his neck and pressed her body against his. Felipe gripped her neck and deepened the kiss, his fingers curling into her hair as arousal flooded his veins.

'I missed you,' he breathed, pulling away from the kiss

that had turned way more heated than he'd planned. He just couldn't seem to keep his hands off her, even at work.

Emilia shuddered, her eyes glazed with desire as she looked up at him. 'I missed you too…but we need to be careful. I don't want anyone to think that I didn't earn my job here, fair and square.'

Felipe winced—she was right. He didn't want to make her uncomfortable or let her down simply because he was crazy about her, and couldn't seem to keep his hands to himself.

'I'll try to control myself,' he said, stepping away. 'But there's nothing wrong with two colleagues talking before they head into a full day of surgeries. What happened after I left on Saturday? Was Eva suspicious because I was there so late?' he asked, wondering if concern for her daughter was the reason Emilia seemed a little out of sorts.

Emilia sighed. 'I don't think she suspected anything, which I'm relieved about. I know I'm entitled to a personal life,' she glanced down, 'but I don't want to do or say anything that might affect my relationship with her at the moment. She's still settling in at uni and trying to make new friends, she still misses her father terribly…'

It was the same message as Saturday night. Emilia obviously still had reservations about relationships. She clearly wasn't ready to put her own needs first, and Felipe could totally understand how she might be scared to upset her traumatised and vulnerable daughter.

That didn't stop the stab of doubt and disappointment though. He was so excited about her being his date for the wedding. He wanted to dance with her, show her the place he'd grown up, hold her all night long and sleep at her side. They would have the other person all to themselves for two whole days, a chance to really cement their growing connection.

'Did you tell Eva about the wedding invitation?' he asked cautiously, desperate for Emilia to commit to visiting Mendoza.

He wasn't a parent. He had no right to tell Emilia how to manage her relationship with Eva. And now clearly wasn't the right time to discuss them dating each other. Emilia was obviously holding back to focus on Eva, and he didn't want to push her further away. And part of him was terrified to over-commit, to give Emilia the wrong idea about them and hurt her. He wasn't sure where that left them—he just knew he wanted her.

'Yes, I did.' She looked down to where her hands were clasped together and his trepidation grew.

'How did she take it?' He didn't want to stop and analyse just how upset he'd feel if she changed her mind about being his date, especially when he wasn't offering her anything serious.

'She seemed okay about it.' Emilia frowned, obviously concerned and suspicious about Eva's reaction. 'She said that it sounded fun, and she hoped I'd have a great time,' she added, nibbling at her lip. 'I thought she'd be more pleased that I'm being social, but she was a little subdued. Perhaps she's stressed by her course workload.'

Hoping to appease her concerns, Felipe gripped her upper arms, pulling her close so she rested her head against his chest. 'You could always see how she seems as the week progresses. If you decide you need to stay at home with her, Thiago will understand. And I do too. Eva comes first.'

But the swoop of his stomach told him exactly how

much he would miss her company now that the idea of her being his date had solidified.

'Thank you.' She looked up at him and blinked, the gratitude in her stare all the confirmation he needed about where Emilia's head was at, not that he could blame her.

He brushed her lips with his. 'That being said, I'd love you to be there as my date, but I also want you to have a good time and feel comfortable. You won't be able to do that if you're worried about Eva. Just let me know so I can book our flights to Mendoza.'

'I'm sure she'll be fine. She hates me fussing anyway.' Emilia smiled up at him, putting on a brave face. 'I'm really looking forward to the wedding. It will be nice to dress up and relax with you, and not have to rush home like I've missed my curfew.'

She kissed him again, her lips parting on a sigh and her tongue gently sliding against his. His doubts disappeared. Just because there were complications, their relationship—their friendship and their physical connection—was important to him and, therefore, still worth pursuing.

Felipe lingered over their kiss, his mind snagged on how him and Emilia being together like this was bigger than just the two of them. It also involved the memory of Ricardo and the welfare of Eva. The ghost of his failed marriage and his fears of letting Emilia and Eva down. Their working relationship and their professional reputations. So much more at stake than simply two people having a good time.

And in many ways, he was wholly unprepared for such a complex relationship. He'd spent the past fifteen years avoiding serious entanglements, predominantly thinking only about himself. He needed to be so careful not to make Emilia any promises he couldn't keep. The last thing he wanted was to hurt her and, by extension, her daughter.

'That Hirschsprung's case is calling,' he said finally. 'We'd better head to Theatre. We have a busy day ahead.' Maybe they just needed to take their fling one day at a time. He would continue to support Emilia emotionally as her friend, without placing any pressure or expectations on her. It wasn't his place to interfere when it came to Eva anyway.

She nodded and stepped back, out of his arms. 'And I'm on call tonight, and you're on call tomorrow night.'

'Is there any chance we could get together mid-week after work?' Felipe asked, missing her already. 'I'm not sure I can wait until the weekend to be alone with you.'

Her sexy stare shone with mischief and promise. 'I'll see what I can do. Maybe I could sneak around to your place after work Wednesday night. Eva has a Modern Feminist's Society meeting, so I guess I could be a little late home without her noticing.'

'It's a date then,' he said, willing away every second of the next two days so he could kiss her freely. 'A *secret* date.'

Two days later, just as she was about to leave the General for the night and swing by Felipe's place as promised, Emilia was urgently called to the NICU to review Luis Lopez. The baby had been recovering well from his surgery, and had been weaned off his ventilator, but earlier today he'd taken a turn for the worse.

'He's been vomiting and passed some bloody stools,' Felipe's registrar Dr Ruiz said. 'His bloods are deranged and he's had a few apnoeic spells.'

Emilia examined the baby's abdomen, which was soft

but slightly distended, her apprehension building. Her first instinct was to call Felipe, but he'd been on call last night and she could handle this without him, even if Luis was under their joint care. They weren't attached at the hip.

'Obviously the greatest concern is necrotising enterocolitis,' she told Dr Ruiz, fearful of the potentially life-threatening diagnosis, which comprised inflammation and bacterial overgrowth of the intestine. 'Let's stop the nasogastric feeds, start broad spectrum antibiotics and get an urgent abdominal X-ray,' she instructed the younger doctor.

The registrar made a note in the file. 'Dr Castillo has already left for the day,' he said, fatigue and concern in his eyes.

Emilia nodded, her poker face in place. She knew exactly where Felipe was. She was supposed to be at his apartment as they spoke. But kissing him, holding him, sharing her rough day with him would have to wait.

'I'll talk to the team on call tonight,' she said, 'and ask them to review Luis later this evening. Dr Castillo and I will review him first thing in the morning. Hopefully we can avoid surgery.' Although if the necrotising enterocolitis or NEC worsened, they might have to resect the involved segment of intestine.

Emilia asked Luis's neonatal nurse to contact Isabella and Sebastian. Then she turned back to Felipe's registrar. 'Once you've ordered those tests, you should go home and get some rest. You were on call last night. I'll speak to his parents, let them know what's going on.'

By the time she'd checked the results of the abdominal film, which indeed confirmed distension and thickening of the bowel wall—the early stages of NEC—and had spoken to Isabella, Sebastian and the neonatal surgical team on call, it was close to eight p.m.

Herself tired after a long day, Emilia considered texting Felipe that she couldn't make it to his place and going straight home, but she wanted to see him. Eva had dropped a bombshell that morning about moving out, and Emilia was still reeling over the timing. She couldn't seem to shake the helpless feeling that her daughter was hiding something.

'I thought you'd changed your mind,' Felipe said with relief after swinging open the door to his apartment and reaching for her.

Emilia walked into his embrace and buried her face against the side of his neck, breathing his comforting masculine scent. 'I had to review Luis Lopez,' she said, looking up. 'He's developed stage one NEC.'

'Oh, no.' Felipe frowned and closed the door. 'Why didn't you call me? I'd have come back in.' He guided Emilia inside his apartment and they sat on the sofa.

'Dr Ruiz and I dealt with it, and I've spoken to Jose,' she said about their neonatal surgical colleague, who was on call that night. 'He'll review him overnight and we can see him again first thing tomorrow. Hopefully he won't need a second surgery.'

Felipe nodded, his concerned frown lingering as his stare moved over her features. 'Are *you* okay? You seem...distracted.'

'I'm fine.' Emilia swallowed the sudden lump in her throat. He was so intuitive and thoughtful. 'Maybe I shouldn't have come. You must be tired after your on-call, but I wanted to see you.'

His smile softened. 'I'm glad that you came by. I'm not too tired for you.' He pressed his lips to hers and all of her troubles—work, Eva, the secrets she was keeping—seemed to dissolve. Only the taste of fear lingered. Was she too reliant on Felipe emotionally? It made sense after having to rely on him professionally while she was still under his supervision. But she couldn't lean on him the way she'd leaned on Ricardo. They weren't a couple, and a part of Emilia felt as if she had to shoulder her fears for Eva alone.

'Something else is wrong,' he said. 'Tell me what it is?' His stare offered the support she was scared to depend upon. Felipe was a wonderful doctor and a caring person, but he obviously enjoyed his carefree, single life. He didn't have his own children, and he had no need for the kind of committed, emotionally supportive relationship she'd had with Ricardo.

Except maybe she was overthinking it. He had said she could talk to him about anything…

'It's silly,' she said, resting her head over the thump of his heart.

'Tell me anyway,' he gently urged, his hands stroking her back.

Emilia surrendered with a small sigh. 'I'm just a bit thrown. This morning, Eva said she's thinking about moving out next semester. She wants to share a flat with some friends.'

She looked up and then away from the compassion in his eyes. 'She's finally had enough of living with her over-protective old Mamá.'

It was perfectly normal to outgrow your parents and want to be independent. Many of Eva's peers had already left home, but the house would be so quiet without her daughter. And Emilia would be truly alone, with only her memories for company.

Felipe tilted his head in sympathy, his palm cupping her cheek so she felt cherished and understood. 'Just because you care doesn't make you over-protective. I can understand how you must feel,' he said, brushing his thumb over her cheek, 'but leaving home is only natural. We've all been there.'

That he understood the complexities of having a grown-up child to consider and put first warmed Emilia's heart. Felipe would have made a wonderful father.

'I know.' She swallowed, her mind going to Ricardo. He'd always had a way of saying the right thing, too. What would he have thought of Felipe? And when had she started thinking of the two men in the same sentence?

But just because she needed a bit of support didn't mean anything. It was just a sign of how close she and Felipe had grown. No wonder, given they were working together and sleeping together and had become friends.

'No matter how much you prepare for your child leaving home,' she said, emotion straining her voice, 'when the time finally arrives it still feels as if it's crept up on you from nowhere, especially when it's your *only* child.'

Felipe drew her close and pressed his lips to the top of her head. 'You'll support Eva's decisions just as you've always done, but be gentle with yourself, okay?'

She nodded, snuggling back into his arms. It felt so good to lean on someone again, to share her troubles and not have to shoulder things utterly alone. Except what would she do when this came to an end? Would their friendship end too? Would she have to go back to hearing about his current date, or would they slowly stop confiding in each other and simply drift apart?

'Can you stay a while?' he asked, pulling back to press his lips to hers.

Oh, how she wished she could say yes and spend the evening with Felipe, cooking, eating, talking. But domestic bliss was something she'd only shared with her husband. Could she risk replacing those memories with new ones of her and Felipe, especially when their fling, their closeness, was obviously temporary?

Emilia shook her head. 'I'm sorry. Because I was delayed getting here, I really should get home now. I told Eva that I've given up on the dating app, so I've no excuse to be out late.'

She didn't want to tell Eva she was having a casual sex relationship with her work colleague. It would be different if she and Felipe were seriously dating—then she'd *have* to tell Eva. But Felipe didn't do serious dating.

Felipe pressed his lips together as if he was holding back on what he wanted to say. 'Of course,' he said finally, standing and pulling her into his arms for a final kiss. 'I've just booked our tickets to Mendoza. Assuming all is well with little Luis, we leave Friday night after work.'

Emilia forced her concerns for Eva to the back of her mind. 'Thank you. I can't wait.'

Except lately, every time she gave herself permission to be excited about being Felipe's date for the wedding, a sense of foreboding rushed in too.

## CHAPTER FOURTEEN

THAT SATURDAY FELIPE stood at his brother's side beneath the antique wrought-iron gazebo under an arbour of mature trees on the Castillo Estate. The autumn sun shone as the celebrant pronounced Thiago and Violetta husband and wife, and the bride and groom kissed. Felipe clapped and cheered along with the rest of the congregation, and then breathed a sigh of relief.

The simple ceremony had gone without a hitch. The bride looked stunning, and the pride and love shining in Thiago's eyes had sent a stab of envy through Felipe on more than one occasion throughout the vows.

His stare flicked to Emilia, who was seated with his cousins. Like the rest of the congregation, she too seemed overcome by the romance of the ceremony. She looked breathtaking in her simple emerald-green dress and matching heels, her hair casually pinned up to expose her elegant neck and dangling earrings.

For an unguarded second that niggle of doubt settled in his gut. Emilia's maternal concern for Eva's welfare was natural, but observing from the outside a part of him worried that, by always putting herself last, Emilia was indefinitely delaying facing up to her own grief. Not that it was any of *his* business. Only if she constantly set her needs aside, where did that leave them? Because his need for *her* grew stronger and more insistent every day. But that was because they had so much in common, he told himself, including a passionate sex life.

Her eyes met his and she smiled. Something inside him reached for her, wished he was at her side, holding her hand. The urge to wrap her in his arms and tell her how beautiful she was, how happy he was that she'd come along as his guest, flared to life. Except his best man duties and their circumstances meant he would need to bide his time.

At Emilia's request, and to avoid the inevitable questions from his family, they were playing this weekend very low key. He'd need to avoid the public displays of affection that now felt like second nature around Emilia to keep up the *just friends* pretence. The last thing either he or Emilia needed was an inquisition from his well-meaning relatives. His aunts in particular considered themselves the family matchmakers, and he didn't want speculation over his and Emilia's relationship to detract from the bride and groom.

'Congratulations,' he said, embracing a delighted Thiago, before he kissed Violetta on both cheeks. 'Mrs Castillo, you look beautiful.'

Violetta laughed, her eyes shining with tears as she turned to hug her bridesmaids. Felipe relaxed for the first time that weekend, the most important part of his best man duties successfully completed: *ensure the groom arrives at the ceremony on time and remember the rings.* As the bride and groom made their way down the aisle, Felipe took his place in the wedding party, escorting the chief bridesmaid, his stare drawn to Emilia.

Reassured that Luis Lopez seemed to be recovering from his latest setback and would avoid a second surgery, they'd arrived at the Castillo Estate late last night. The minute they'd closed the door of the estate's two-bedroomed guest house they'd rushed into each other's arms. Having to keep their relationship secret from people at work and from family was certainly adding to their desperation for each other.

The reception was being held on the two-hundred-year-old bottling barn on the estate, a place of many Castillo family celebrations and countless guest weddings over the years. Having escorted the chief bridesmaid there and temporarily released from his best man duties, Felipe immediately headed back outside to find Emilia.

Pride filled him as he strode her way. That such a beautiful, kind and intelligent woman was here with him made him feel ten feet tall. The weekend stretched out before them, plenty of time to show her around the estate, to coax out her wondrous smile with dancing and good wine, to worship her body as he'd done late last night and again first thing this morning. The *one day at a time* plan seemed to be working out.

She looked up from her phone as he approached, a small frown pinching her eyebrows together.

'Is everything okay at home, with Eva?' he asked, pressing a chaste kiss on each of her cheeks as he'd done to countless relatives that morning, then offering her his arm. He'd grown attuned to Emilia's maternal concern, found himself increasingly invested in Eva's well-being in the same the way he cared about Emilia. And he wanted her to relax and have a good time today. They worked hard, they deserved some downtime and a wedding was the perfect occasion.

'I think so,' she said, her voice hesitant. 'She finally replied to my text with an *"I'm fine"*, which is a little terse for Eva, if I'm honest. Perhaps she's just a bit lonely. Unless I'm at work, I'm usually always at home.'

Felipe rested his hand over hers. 'Do you want to give her a call before the reception? You have plenty of time.' He was dying to introduce Emilia to his extended family and his parents. By the time they'd arrived last night from Mendoza Airport it had been too late for introductions.

Emilia shook her head, pasting on a bright smile. 'No. She'll only accuse me of fussing. I'm sure everything is okay. Let's go have some fun.'

She squeezed his arm and Felipe smiled, wishing he could kiss away that last glimmer of concern in her eyes. He understood the pressures on Emilia. Raising a child wasn't easy, but doing it alone was twice as challenging. Because they'd been getting closer and closer, he knew that Emilia doubted herself as a solo parent, and he wanted to be there for her, but it was fine line to tread without crossing it. He wasn't Eva's father. He didn't know the first thing about raising a child, and he didn't want to get in the way of her close relationship with her mother.

'So, did you enjoy the ceremony?' he asked, changing the subject as they ambled back towards the barn.

'It was so beautiful,' she said, her hand resting on her chest. 'I might have shed an emotional tear or two.'

'Me too,' he said, laughing. 'I'm so proud of my little brother. By the way, you look utterly beautiful. I wanted to tell you earlier but Thiago was a bundle of nerves before the ceremony and wouldn't allow me to leave his side.' He'd almost drooled when he'd spied Emilia taking her seat in the rose garden for the ceremony.

'Thank you.' She smiled. 'You look very smart. And very hot,' she added in a whisper. 'I'm a huge fan of the relaxed wedding attire look,' she said, eyeing his beige linen sports coat and his powder-blue shirt, which was open at the neck.

When her stare returned to his, it carried that secret look he'd now come to expect, the one she gave him when they kissed passionately or when they were intimate, as if she trusted him. He never wanted to lose that trust.

'Are you ready to meet my parents?' Felipe asked as they reached the short line of guests entering the barn, who were being greeted by the bride and groom and both sets of parents. A big part of him wished he could whisk Emilia away somewhere private. It was torture being unable to act naturally, to touch her or kiss her the way he wanted.

'As ready as I'll ever be,' she whispered, giving him a small, nervous smile.

Except Felipe had no doubt that Emilia would charm every single member of his family. If he could keep the intrusive but natural questions about them at bay this weekend it would be a miracle.

Sliding his hand to the small of her back, they entered the barn. 'Mamá, Papá, this is a friend of mine, Emilia Gonzales, a fellow doctor at the General. Emilia, meet Carolina and Gabriel Castillo.'

Pride bloomed in his chest as Emilia greeted his parents warmly, shaking their hands.

'Thank you so much for inviting me,' she said. 'What a beautiful home you have and what a stunning ceremony that was.'

His father beamed and kissed both Emilia's cheeks. His mother's eyes lit up with surprise and predictable speculation as she glanced Felipe's way. He'd have some more explaining to do later, but for now he wasn't ready to answer probing questions about them or put a label on what they had, which was something special but also new and fragile for them both. For now, he simply wanted his beautiful date to forget her worries and have a good time.

They moved away from the line up and headed for the bar. Felipe took two glasses of Castillo Estate bubbles and handed one to Emilia. 'A private toast, just for us,' he said, clinking his glass to hers and enjoying the excited sparkle in her eyes. 'To you, Emilia. To our secret weekend and to family, big or small, here or departed.'

Family was so important to them both, and obviously Ricardo was always in Emilia's thoughts. He wasn't threatened by that, but he hoped to spend the rest of the weekend making her smile.

Emilia swallowed, blinking up at him, her emotions clearly on display. 'That's a beautiful toast, Felipe. To family,' she replied, her eyes sad but hopeful.

They took a first sip, their stares locked together. The rest of the room seemed to fade out, as if they were alone. Felipe stiffened, restless. How would he get through today without holding her the way he wanted to, without kissing her and showing everyone here how passionately he wanted this incredible woman, who had also become a great friend?

Her stare shifted over his face, as if she too felt the same impulses. Then she blinked and the moment passed. 'I hope you're keeping some of that good stuff for your best man toast.'

Felipe grinned, recalling how he'd promised to play down their connection—he'd need to stop looking at her as if he couldn't wait to strip off that dress. 'I'll try to pull something out of the hat.'

Emilia took another sip of wine and glanced around the

crowded room, where the party was already in full swing, the music playing, the drinks flowing, joy and laughter a loud din. 'Do you know everyone here?' she asked.

Felipe shrugged, stepping closer because she felt too far away. 'My father is one of five brothers.' He indicated the huddle of uncles in the far corner, drinking and laughing and generally staying away from their wives—his aunts—probably in case they were tasked with some job or other.

'I have fifteen cousins,' he added. 'I'll introduce you to a few more, but don't worry—you don't have to remember everyone's names.'

Emilia smiled, looking relieved. 'And all the children are little Castillos?'

'The children of my cousins,' Felipe confirmed. 'Oh, I forgot. Speaking of children, I wanted to show you something. Come with me.'

He guided her out of the rear door of the barn, taking her hand as they crossed a cobblestoned courtyard, which later would be lit with a thousand twinkling lights as dusk settled.

'This is it,' Felipe said, pausing at the foot of a set of stone steps, where a huge concrete planter spilled over with flowers. 'This is my vat, where I trod my first vintage.'

Emilia's eyes lit up.

'See,' he said, running his finger over the brass plate engraved with his name and a date. 'I was six years old. Come—I'll show you.'

He opened the door to another barn used for storage and office space, locating the framed photograph on the wall. 'That's me.' He was treading the grapes for the first time and was so small that he barely reached over the side of the vat.

Emilia peered closer, her smile full of wonder. 'Oh, you were an adorable little boy. And look at that cheeky smile.' She beamed up at him and he slipped his arm around her waist, pulling her close because they were alone.

'It's the same as this one,' he said, smiling down at her. 'I haven't been able to wipe it off my face today, because you're here.' He brushed her lips with his, tasting lipstick and wine and Emilia. 'Thank you for coming. I know my big noisy family are a bit overwhelming. But say the word and we'll duck out for a break. I know all the best hiding places around here.'

'I'll remember that,' she said breathily, her stare dipping to his mouth so he once more captured her lips in a kiss.

Fire raced through his blood and their kiss turned passionate. Emilia slid her arm around his waist, inside his jacket, as she parted her lips and touched her tongue to his. Felipe forgot where he was, forgot that as far as anyone else here was concerned, they were *just friends*, forgot that he'd spent fifteen years keeping the women he dated at arm's length.

Emilia was different. She was special. He wanted her too much to keep a lid on his feelings, even though they were terrifying. But as long as he kept them to himself, as long as he didn't pressure her to consider them dating exclusively for a while, he could examine them more closely after this weekend.

'Felipe...' she moaned as he pressed kisses down the side on her neck, hitting all the spots that made her gasp when he moved inside her. His hand roamed the body he now knew so well, cupping her breast, her waist, her hip and her backside as her fingers slid through his hair, bringing him back to their kiss.

They were like a flame and oxygen—one touch, one look, one word setting off a chain reaction of desire until they surrendered and quenched it in each other's arms. Emilia pressed her body to his, moving against him so he grew painfully hard, his only thought to wonder if they had time to slip back to the guest house.

'I can't wait to get you alone later,' he whispered against her lips, his hand fisting the fabric of her dress over her hip. 'I'm going to peel off this beautiful dress, cover your body in kisses, spend the whole night pleasuring you, making you come so many times you won't ever forget this weekend.'

Emilia licked her lips, her eyes glazed over with passion and she gripped the lapel of his jacket as if for balance. 'I can't wait. But we should get back. You're the best man. They'll start looking for you soon.'

'Party pooper,' he teased, pressing one last chaste kiss to her smiling lips.

'I'll make it up to you later,' she said seductively, batting her long eyelashes so he almost groaned.

Felipe stepped back and reached for her hand. 'I guess I can keep my hands off you for a few hours longer. Come on, let's introduce you to even more people.'

It promised to be a wonderful party, but for Felipe it would also be a very long day.

# CHAPTER FIFTEEN

AS DARKNESS FELL the sultry beat of the tango music began, the band striking up the famous intro to *La Cumparista* which, while linked with Buenos Aires, had originated in Emilia's native Uruguay.

On the dance floor, Emilia smiled as Felipe drew her close into his arms, their bodies scandalously close. Her heart, already skipping from dancing all night long, fluttered to new heights as they moved provocatively around the dance floor. Felipe was a great dancer.

Emilia breathed in the scent of his warm body and his spicy cologne, the memory of that searing kiss in the barn making her bones melt. Romantic, seductive Felipe was dangerous, and she had a hard enough time resisting regular Felipe. But in a couple more hours they could retreat to the guest house and finally be alone.

Smiling up at him, she released a contented sigh. Everything about today—the wedding, the reception, the dancing—had been magical. Maybe it was how hot he looked, or the delicious wine that had flowed all day, or the excessive romance of both the location and occasion, but Felipe had made Emilia feel beautiful and cherished. It had been a long time since she'd been so joyous and content.

Was it wrong that she'd only thought about Ricardo

a handful of times today? She would always love him deeply, but being here with Felipe, having such a fun time, it was as if she'd finally given herself permission to find new ways to be happy.

She dragged in a breath, her head swimming with fear that such feelings couldn't possibly be trusted. The last time she'd felt happy and content, Ricardo had fallen sick. Could the universe be cruel enough to steal this feeling from her a second time? And was she wrong to associate happiness with a man who was all about having a good time, but when it came to feelings never thought about tomorrow?

Because she didn't want to tempt fate, she cleared the doubts from her head with a shake and leaned back to look at Felipe. 'Are you having a good time now that your best man duties are behind you?' she asked, intentionally spoiling the moment of intense intimacy created by the dance.

His entire family were watching. They couldn't perform the tango, the most seductive dance on the planet, as freely and naturally as they wanted to. If they did, everyone would know they were sleeping together. Their pretence of *just friends* would be exposed. And if they weren't friends, what were they? What did she even want them to be?

Felipe stared down at her, his feet gliding over the floor, carrying her along. 'I'm having a wonderful time, and it's all down to you.' His stare lingered on her lips and she held her breath. Would he kiss her in front of everyone? 'Thank you for being my date,' he said instead, perhaps sensing her withdrawal.

Emilia's cheeks heated at his caution when there was stark passion in Felipe's eyes. But he was a passionate man. Combined with the way he was holding her, as if he'd never let her go, she was having a hard time remembering that they weren't alone, not to mention that he deliberately kept his passion superficial.

'Thank you for inviting me,' she said, grateful. 'I've had a lovely day. Your family is as charming as you are. They've all made me feel so welcome.' She couldn't recall the last time she'd enjoyed herself so much or felt so light-hearted.

He shrugged and smiled. 'That's the Castillo way. Perhaps next time we visit we could also bring Eva. There are plenty of my cousins' children her age.'

Emilia nodded vaguely, her pulse flying. What was happening here? Return visits, bringing Eva along, the way they'd made love late last night and again early this morning, as if reaching for each other had become second nature.

Before she could examine the terrified lurch of her heart, Felipe said, 'My parents loved you by the way. They dragged me aside earlier and asked if we're more than friends.'

Emilia scoffed, that carefree part of her that he'd brought back to life desperate to know if they could ever be more, and the rest of her rejecting the idea flat out. She still loved *Ricardo*. There was no room in her heart for Felipe. Except since she'd first met him a few short weeks ago she'd changed, grown somehow, learned new things about herself and found fresh resilience.

She'd spent so many years putting herself and her needs last out of necessity. Two parents raising a child while holding down full-time jobs was hard enough. Raising a grieving child solo, while also grieving herself, had put Emilia into survival mode. But the past few weeks had shown her that she wanted more for her future. She didn't want to be alone as Eva built her own life. She would always be there for her daughter, but she also wanted things for herself. To enjoy the good things in life, to laugh in good company and maybe even to love again one day.

Immediately dismissing the possibility, she shuddered. It was probably just a romance hangover from the wedding.

'Don't worry,' Felipe said, reading into her pensive silence. 'I told them to relax. They'll be the first to know if I ever decide to once more embark on another serious relationship.'

Emilia pulled a watery smile. It didn't matter how much *she'd* grown. Felipe, the only man she'd met recently who she could see herself in a relationship with, was a staunch commitment-phobe who'd been single for fifteen years. She needed to remember that he might be a passionate lover and a considerate friend and colleague, but he clearly wasn't thinking about them having any sort of lasting relationship. If she wasn't careful, if she didn't hold back and protect herself while this fling ran its course, she could get badly hurt.

'By the way,' he asked, 'did you hear back from Eva?'

Emilia had texted earlier, checking in that all was well back at home. She shook her head, fingers of concern creeping up her spine now that he'd reminded her. 'No, she must be busy. She said she might go to social volleyball, so perhaps she's hanging out with friends.'

Felipe nodded and the song came to an end. Emilia stepped out of his close embrace, her head all over the place, as if the spell of the wedding and that feeling of contentment had been broken. 'I think I'll get a glass of water,' she said. 'All this dancing has made me thirsty.'

'I'll get it for you,' he offered. 'Why don't you sit at our table and I'll bring it over?'

Emilia returned to their table, gratefully sank into a chair and kicked off her heels to ease her aching feet. She hadn't danced so much in years. But now that the seed of doubt had germinated, she wondered if she was making a fool of herself with him, just like those other women he dated who saw his wonderful attentiveness as a sign of commitment he just wasn't into, or maybe even capable of given his regrets over his marriage. As she watched Felipe at the bar, she probed her feelings, tasting fear. Was she already falling for Felipe Castillo?

Just then someone sat beside her. 'Are you having fun, dear?' the elderly woman asked.

She was one of Felipe's aunts, but Emilia couldn't for the life of her recall her name.

'Yes, I am. What a beautiful wedding and a great party.' Emilia smiled broadly. 'I'm sorry. I've forgotten your name.' She'd drunk too much wine and met too many people to risk getting it wrong.

'I'm Lucia,' the other woman said with a smile, 'Felipe's oldest and favourite aunt.' She winked playfully. 'So you and Felipe work in the same field at the hospital?'

Emilia nodded, happy to talk about her work rather than analyse her jumbled and scary feelings. 'Yes, we're both neonatal surgeons, although Felipe is senior to me. He's been mentoring me while I get my Argentinian practising certificate.'

'How smart you are,' Lucia said, impressed. 'And my nephew tells me that you have a lovely daughter.'

'Eva,' Emilia said, wondering again if Eva was okay

at home alone. 'She's eighteen and has just started law at university.'

'Ah...clever, like her mother. My grandson is eighteen. That's him on the dance floor, the tall one.'

'He's very handsome,' Emilia said.

'That's Castillo men, for you.' Lucia's shrewd eyes filled with mischief. 'But I don't need to tell *you* that. You and Felipe make a very attractive couple.'

Emilia flushed from head to toe—she'd known the tango was a mistake. 'Oh, no...we're not together. We're...just friends.' Only a part of her—that secret, locked away part that was scared to open her heart to love—had maybe foolishly started to imagine them as more.

Lucia shooed away Emilia's lame explanation. 'Oh, nonsense,' she said with all the authority of a veteran matchmaker. 'The family aren't fooled. Felipe's clearly in love with you. And about time too. He deserves to find happiness again. And if the way you look at him is any indication, you're in love with him too.'

Emilia froze, her blood running cold. 'In love...?'

*No, no, no...* She couldn't be in love with Felipe.

'Yes, love,' Lucia said, oblivious to the fear and turmoil flooding Emilia's entire body. 'The other aunts think we might soon have another wedding at Castillo Estates.' The older woman winked suggestively.

Emilia lips twitched automatically, although she'd never felt less like smiling. Her blood rushed with panic. She sought out Felipe who'd been waylaid on his way back from the bar by a group of male relatives. He glanced her way and their eyes met, locked—his were smiling.

With her stomach twisted into knots, Emilia looked away quickly, confused by what she saw in his expression and by the painful turmoil in her chest. Could it be true that he had feelings for her? No, Felipe's aunts must be mistaken. Felipe didn't want a serious relationship, he'd literally *just* told her that on the dance floor. And as for her...had she missed the signs? Did her feelings for Felipe go beyond respect, friendship and passion? Was that why their relationship, their growing closeness, seemed less like a betrayal of Ricardo and more and more natural? No, she couldn't forget her husband so easily. She would hate herself if that happened and Eva would never forgive her.

'But maybe I'm getting ahead of myself,' Lucia admitted sheepishly, patting Emilia's arm affectionately. 'Don't listen to me, dear. I'm an old romantic at heart.'

Emilia tried to smile, except the damage was already done. The floodgates had opened and Emilia was swamped by her feelings. Overwhelmed.

Just then a small huddle of children rushed over and interrupted. 'Abuela, Abuela...' they called, dragging off their grandmother.

Shaking inside, Emilia slipped on her shoes and headed for the bathroom. She wasn't ready for an emotional realisation. Not now, not with all these people watching her and secretly commenting. She needed a moment to herself to process that conversation and what it had unearthed, away from prying eyes and more importantly away from Felipe. If she had fallen for him, she couldn't tell him. Unless her feelings were already obvious to him? Was that why he'd made his point about avoiding serious relationships on the dance floor? To warn her off?

Ducking into the bathroom, she locked herself in a cubicle and leaned back against the cool wood of the closed door, her heart thudding wildly. Her head was all over the place, but she tried to think rationally. Her fear and panic every time she thought about having more than what they had now was understandable. If she thought seriously about her own needs, about moving on, about opening her heart up to another man and falling in love again, it felt like a betrayal of Ricardo and everything they'd had for over twenty years.

But she *did* have feelings for Felipe. How could she not? He was a great man—caring and compassionate and romantic. That didn't make it *love*. Was she even capable of love again, after losing her beloved husband? She'd grown so used to shoving down her own feelings and concentrating on Eva that now she wasn't sure which way was up.

She didn't want to embarrass herself by putting herself out there and telling him how she felt. She'd only be risking further heartache if Felipe didn't feel the same way. And what did all this mean for Eva? Emilia didn't want her relationship with Felipe to hurt or upset her daughter in any way. Eva would always be her main priority.

Pulling her phone from her purse, Emilia checked for a reply to the text she'd sent to her daughter earlier.

I'm okay. Feeling a little sad for some reason. Talk tomorrow. Eva xx.

A chill of foreboding raised goosebumps over her bare arms. How could she have become so carried away enjoying herself that she'd neglected to check in with her daughter? What if Eva wasn't *okay*? And why was she feeling sad?

Emilia dialled Eva's number but the call went straight to voicemail. It was past eleven-thirty—maybe she was already asleep. Or maybe she *was* upset, while Emilia had been dancing and putting her own irrelevant feelings first. She was a mother, a mature woman. Why was she hiding in the toilets, agonising over her feelings for a man who might never return them?

Ashamed of herself, Emilia left the cubicle and washed her hands. Coming to the wedding had been a mistake. She'd put her own needs first and made a fool of herself, acted like a love-struck teenager in front of Felipe's family.

With her temples throbbing and her insides a trembling mess, she headed back to the party to find Felipe.

# CHAPTER SIXTEEN

BY THE TIME Felipe wound up his conversation with his cousin Mateo, Emilia seemed to have disappeared. Felipe scanned the barn, a vague rumble of unease in his gut. Then he came face to face with Thiago.

'My best man—are you enjoying yourself?' Thiago asked jovially, slinging his arm around Felipe's shoulders.

'Absolutely,' Felipe replied, his smile for his brother genuine. 'It's been a great day. But more importantly, are *you* happy?'

Thiago released Felipe and spread his arms wide. 'I'm a married man. Of course I'm happy.'

Felipe laughed, thinking back to his own wedding day, so many years ago. He'd been so young, full of optimism and confidence that his marriage to Delfina would work out. But somehow, as the years had passed, they'd grown in opposite directions, and Felipe had lived with the consequences ever since. Felipe prayed for his brother's sake that Thiago and Violetta would last the distance. At least Thiago had maturity on his side, and a partner who seemed to share his dreams and goals as much as he shared hers.

'Everyone loves Emilia,' Thiago continued. 'She's a real hit.' He slapped his brother's back. 'Nice work.'

'Thanks.' Felipe laughed good-naturedly, his stare

seeking her out once more. If he'd been on the marriage market, Emilia would indeed be a very good catch. They shared so much—their world views, their careers, their personal aspirations. Not to mention intense physical passion. The more time he spent with her the closer he felt to her. It was no surprise to him that Emilia was the reason he currently felt so…content.

'So what's the plan?' Thiago asked. 'Are you two still casual? Please tell me you're not going to watch her date any more idiots? Maybe you should think about popping the question.'

Felipe laughed nervously, prickles of unease creeping up his neck. His family meant well, but he could sense the pressure building. Emilia had stiffened in his arms earlier when he'd mentioned his parents' questions. And she obviously had a lot on her mind with Eva. The last thing he wanted to do was transmit any of that pressure to Emilia and scare her off.

'Listen,' he said, turning serious, 'things are…delicate between us. We're not in our twenties. We both have our pasts to deal with and Emilia's daughter is her priority, quite rightly.' Felipe winced. 'Please don't say anything to scare her off. I really like her.'

Thiago was right in one thing. Felipe didn't want to watch Emilia go on any more dates. *He* wanted to be her date. He wanted more than just great sex and friendship. But his family were unaware of the fine details of his relationship with Emilia. He didn't want one of them to inadvertently put their foot in it or spook her. And as his feelings for her deepened there was already enough pressure within himself to ask her where their relationship was headed.

After fifteen years of staying single, he couldn't simply

rush in and make her any promises. Maybe they could continue to build on their connection, one day at a time. Maybe he should ask her to be exclusive but take things slowly.

'Of course,' Thiago said, resting his hand over his heart. 'You have my word. I understand how it's more complicated second time around. But if you really like her…'

Thiago's voice drifted off as he peered over Felipe's shoulder, his eyes widening. 'Here she comes.' He embraced Felipe, spoke briefly to Emilia, kissed her cheek and wandered off.

'There you are,' Felipe said with smile, handing over her glass of water. She looked pale and distracted. 'Are you okay?' he asked, alarmed.

Had she overheard any of his conversation with Thiago? Felipe had no idea how Emilia felt about them having something more than casual sex, and she was obviously still grieving for Ricardo. But perhaps they could enjoy each other's company while it lasted. Suddenly, the idea felt hollow, as if he already knew it wouldn't be enough for him.

When she said nothing, placing her drink on a nearby table without touching it, Felipe's alarm grew. Had she received bad news? 'Is it Eva?' He ran his hands down her bare arms, chasing away her goosebumps. 'Is everything okay at home?'

'I'm not sure…' She shivered, dragging in a deep breath, but she couldn't quite meet his eye. 'I don't think it's anything serious, but she said she's feeling a bit sad and now she's no longer answering my texts.'

Felipe's mind reeled. Of course she'd be distracted by

concern for Eva while being so far away. He was a little worried, too.

'Have you called the house?' he asked, snagging his jacket from the chair and draping it over her shoulders to ward off the chill.

She shook her head vaguely. 'No… But I tried her cell phone.' She raised her hand to her temple. 'I… I'm sorry. I'm not feeling that well. I have a headache, suddenly. Probably stress. I might call it a night if that's okay.'

A swell of compassion engulfed him. He wrapped his arm around her and held her close. 'Of course it's okay,' he said. 'Let's get you some painkillers. I'll walk you back to the guest house.'

'Oh, no…' Emilia pulled back, her stare flitting everywhere but at him. 'Please don't interrupt your evening on my account. It's your brother's wedding.'

He winced at his automatic display of affection. Of course Emilia wanted their relationship to remain a secret, but he couldn't help his feelings. He cared deeply about this woman. It was second nature to touch her and comfort her, to try and be there for her.

'Emilia, it's no problem,' he said in a low voice, trying to be discreet. 'Let me look after you. I can run you a bath if that will help with the headache.'

She shook her head, a determined tilt to her chin. 'Actually, I think I might go back to Buenos Aires on the first flight tomorrow morning.'

Stunned, Felipe all but gaped. 'Is that really necessary? I'm sure Eva is fine. I had plans to show you the estate tomorrow.' Her concern for her daughter was understandable, but taking an early flight home seemed like a bit of an overreaction. Unless there was something else going on…

'If I don't go,' she continued, 'I'll just spend the rest of the weekend worrying. And I don't want to make a fuss or be a bother to your family at this happy time.' Her stare flicked around the room, where the other guests were still in high spirits, then she looked at him, imploring.

'Of course…' His mind scrambled to catch up. Had he upset her in some way? 'Why don't you get some rest?' he urged. 'I'll change our flights to the morning.'

She shook her head, already backing away, as if she feared he might try to hold onto her. 'No, I don't want to interrupt your weekend celebration with your family, and you're the best man. I've already called a taxi to take me to a hotel near the airport for tonight, so I don't disturb anyone when I leave early. Can you please thank your parents from me and wish the bride and groom farewell? I'll just quietly slip out now.'

That was when he spied her overnight bag at her feet, his stomach sinking. She'd already been back to the guest house and collected her things. There was clearly no persuading her to stay. Confusion settled like a weight in his chest. What was happening? Had he inadvertently moved too fast? Spooked her? They'd been having a great time, and now it seemed she couldn't wait to get away from him.

Her phone pinged with a text and she shrugged off his jacket, handing it over. 'I'm sorry Felipe. I really have to go. My taxi is almost here.'

'I'll walk you out,' he said, feeling numb and a little stupid, as if he'd done something wrong but had no idea what. 'Will you call me, when you get to the hotel?' he asked, reaching for her hand as they walked towards the estate's gate at the top of the driveway.

'Okay,' she said, her voice devoid of any warmth.

'And if you hear from Eva. I'm concerned, too.' How could he enjoy the rest of the party with everything between them up in the air? Couldn't she understand that he cared about her and her daughter?

A hundred questions stuck in his throat at the sudden change in Emilia. He'd thought they were growing closer, but now he was filled with doubts. Maybe he'd misjudged things. Maybe she was still grieving too much for a new relationship, even a casual one. Maybe she still wasn't ready to put her own needs first.

'Listen,' he said as they paused at the top of the drive. 'I understand that you must put Eva first, but I want you to know that I loved every minute of you being here with me this weekend. It's made me realise that we might be able to have something more than just a casual fling.'

She opened her mouth to speak but he held up his hand. 'No pressure, nothing serious, but maybe we could be exclusive, only dating each other. That way you wouldn't have to experience any more bad dates, and I wouldn't have to worry about clingy women looking for a proposal.' He tried to smile, but it felt like his face was made of rubber and Emilia looked horrified. As he'd talked, her eyes had widened, as if with growing fear, and a pulse ticked frantically in her neck. Not the reaction he'd hoped for.

'You don't have to answer now,' he added, deflated. 'Just have a think about it.' Felipe sucked in some breaths, feeling as if he'd just run a marathon and then ripped his racing heart out of his chest and held it out to her as a gift. How had he misjudged this so badly?

She gripped both his hands, looking up at him and held his stare. 'I've really enjoyed getting to know you, and this weekend has been wonderful, the most fun I've had in years.' She paused, looked down at her feet, and Felipe heard the *but* coming as if from a mile away. His stomach sank.

She looked up, smiled sadly. 'You've helped me to move past my grief, and I'll always be grateful to you for that.'

Internally, Felipe recoiled. He didn't want her gratitude. He wanted her passion. He knew it was there—he felt it every time they touched. But maybe she was holding out for more. Maybe when her heart had healed she'd go searching for someone she could love again. Someone without his track record for failing when it came to relationships. Someone who could be her *Mr Right*.

'But we agreed to keep it casual,' she went on, calmly delivering the final blow. 'I'm still finding my way as a single parent, still acclimatising to a new job and a new country. Still figuring out if I want to even be in another relationship in the future. I don't think I can devote energy to anything else right now.'

Felipe stiffened. This sounded like goodbye, not just from the weekend but from *them*. He glanced away and saw distant headlights slowly approaching in the dark. Emilia's taxi.

'So you don't want to see me again? Not even casually?' he asked, his throat raw. How could she just walk away after everything they'd shared? How could he let her go when it felt so utterly wrong? But he couldn't force her to care about him or want to date him. Maybe she was right. Maybe he'd never be what she needed. Maybe to try and cling onto something with her would only hurt her, and by extension Eva, in the long run.

'I can't risk having feelings for you, Felipe.' She tilted her head and squeezed his hand, but he was in no way comforted. She saw through him, saw how he might let her down. 'Maybe it's best to call it a day now,' she went on, 'before we both get our hearts broken. Neither of us needs that.'

Felipe nodded, his mind and body reeling. She was right to protect herself. The last time he'd tried a serious relationship he'd been a bad husband, and he'd spent years since then swearing off commitment. But now that she was ending it, now that there was a hole blown through the centre of his chest, he could clearly see that it was already too late for him. He already had deep, deep feelings for Emilia. Not that it was enough.

The taxi pulled up. Emilia pressed a brief kiss to his cheek, her soft and warm lips doing nothing to ward off the chill in his bones. 'Thank you for a lovely weekend. I'll always remember it.'

He frowned, silently watching her walk away. She handed her overnight bag to the driver and quickly ducked into the back seat without a backward glance. Felipe stood frozen, rocked to the core. Just like that, what had begun so passionately and unexpectedly was over.

As the taxi drove away—the taillights getting smaller and smaller, finally disappearing around a bend in the road—Felipe could only reel in shock and pain. It was a weekend he'd never forget either, a weekend he'd always remember as the time he had his wise old heart crushed to smithereens.

# CHAPTER SEVENTEEN

THE TRIP HOME to Buenos Aires without Felipe had taken a lifetime, beginning with the endless taxi ride down Castillo Estate's driveway. Emilia had forced herself to look straight ahead, rather than turn around to see if Felipe had watched her leave or simply headed back to the party. After a few sleepless hours in the airport hotel, the two-hour flight home had only provided her with more time to think and feel and tie herself into knots over the decisions she'd made.

She'd run scared, there was no dressing it up. But now she needed to own her choice, because it had been the right one.

Regardless of her feelings for him, Felipe's matchmaking aunts had been wrong. He wasn't in love with her. Of course he'd enjoyed the good time they'd had together, enjoyed the sex, but the only thing he'd wanted was for them to date exclusively.

And for Emilia, with so much on the line—*her* happiness, Eva's happiness, even her job—his underwhelming offer was too great a risk to her fragile heart.

Numbly opening the front door, Emilia dumped her bag in the hall. She poked her head inside Eva's room, finding her daughter safe and asleep, before stooping to greet Luna and letting her out into the garden.

Emilia shuffled into the kitchen and reached for the coffee, glancing at the clock. Ten a.m. Thank goodness it was Sunday. She had another twenty-four hours before she had to face Felipe at work. How would they act with each other now that they were returning to being just work colleagues? Would there be awkwardness, bad feelings, regret? Could they still be friends when she'd obviously confused him and hurt his feelings?

No, they were mature adults. They'd manage their working relationship as they always had: with mutual respect and collaboration. Except no matter how much she tried to convince herself that all would be well, Emilia couldn't seem to shake the terrible feeling in the pit of her stomach that she'd done something terribly wrong.

'You're back,' Eva said sleepily, coming into the room still wearing her pyjamas. 'I thought your flight was this evening.' She stepped automatically into her mother's embrace and Emilia held her too tight for too long.

'Good morning, *mija*.' She pasted on a bright smile as Eva stepped back. 'I came home early. I have some admin to catch up on.'

'That sounds dull.' Eva frowned, reaching for the kettle to make herself some tea. 'So how was the wedding?'

Emilia's breath caught—*confusing, painful, one big mistake.*

'It was lovely,' she said, her stomach taking another sickening dive. If she kept talking, she wouldn't have time to reflect on the look of disappointment and hurt on Felipe's face when she'd told him they were done. 'Very romantic and such a stunning location.' Emilia took a sip of coffee, her eyes stinging at the way the weekend had ended. 'But it's good to be home.'

Yes, *home* was where her focus needed to be. Away

from Felipe she could gain some perspective. And surely, with a good night's sleep behind her, she'd soon see that her choice to end things was for the best. She couldn't go on being heartbroken at her age. Only her chest ached every time she thought of him and what she'd done. His pain and confusion had been so difficult to witness.

'Mamá, you weren't even gone forty-eight hours,' Eva scolded.

'Never mind about that,' Emilia said, shoving her own feelings aside. 'How are *you*? Do you still feel sad? I was a little worried when I saw your text last night.'

Eva gasped, turning to face her mother. 'You didn't come home early for *me*, did you?'

'Not really…' Emilia waved her hand dismissively as she sipped her coffee, downplaying her concern. 'I mean of course I was concerned. You seemed very distracted when I left Friday, and then you said you were feeling sad, and then you stopped answering my texts…'

'Only because I fell *asleep*,' Eva explained, her eyes wide and shining with tears. 'I'm sorry if I ruined your weekend.'

'Don't be silly, mija. You didn't ruin anything.' She drew Eva into another hug, uncertain which of them needed it the most. 'Are you sad because of Papá?' Emilia whispered into her daughter's hair.

Eva nodded, her face crumpling. 'The truth is,' she said with a sniff, 'that I *have* been struggling these past couple of weeks.'

Emilia nodded for her to continue, brushing away Eva's tears. 'That's okay. I'm always here for you, you know that.'

Eva blinked, looking uncertain. 'It's just that everything is new. Everything seems to be changing so fast.'

She winced, crossing her arms over her waist defensively. '*I* was the one who encouraged you to date, but then when you did I panicked, because I suddenly thought about Papá.' She raised tear-reddened eyes to Emilia and whispered, 'What if we forget him? I never want that to happen.'

'Oh, Eva,' Emilia cried, cupping her daughter's face so she couldn't hide her emotions from her mother. 'We'll *never* forget him. Never. He'll always be in our hearts.'

Emilia wiped the tears from her daughter's cheeks, the way she had when Eva had been a little girl, feeling choked herself. 'I see him every time I look at you,' she continued. 'I feel him smiling when you do something that makes me proud, I even talk to him in my head about how well you're doing at uni and the new friends you've made.'

Eva nodded uncertainly.

'Come on.' Emilia grabbed their drinks and they sat on the sofa. She turned to Eva. 'I know we've been through some big changes recently, but now that we're settled here in Buenos Aires nothing else is going to change, I promise.'

Of course Eva felt overwhelmed after everything she'd been through.

'My full registration with the Argentine Medical Council is almost through,' Emilia said, 'so my job is secure, and I've decided that I'm not dating any more, so there'll be no more distractions. In fact, I came home early from Mendoza because I ended things with Felipe last night. From now on my focus is back where it should be, on you and me and building our new life.'

'No, Mamá,' Eva said, horrified, fresh tears spilling

over her lids. 'Why did you do that? Felipe makes you so happy.'

'I...' Emilia trailed off, lost for words. She had no idea Eva had intuited so much about her relationship with Felipe. But it was too late now. She'd made her decision and the damage was done. She shook her head. 'It doesn't matter how he makes me feel. *You* are my priority. I've had my chance at happiness with your father, that's why I won't ever forget him. I'm happy to be alone, really I am.'

Eva gripped Emilia's hands. 'No... I've seen you smile more since you met Felipe. You deserve to be *truly* happy, not just going through the motions.'

'I *am* happy.' She smiled, but the expression felt unconvincing.

'But I don't want you be alone because of me,' Eva insisted. 'I'm just taking a little longer than anticipated to adjust, that's all.'

Emilia nodded. 'I understand. I'm struggling to adjust too.' She dragged in a shuddering breath, laying herself open and being completely honest with her daughter, who wasn't a child any more and deserved the truth. 'But you're right,' she said. 'I *have* felt lighter and happier since meeting Felipe. Only I'm not sure I'm ready to fall in love again. It's terrifying.'

Eva reached for her hand, her gaze sympathetic.

'What if it doesn't work out?' Emilia continued. 'What if my relationship with Felipe hurts you? What if I *do* fall in love with him and I lose him too?'

At that final question, her own eyes stung with tears, and she hung her head. This was the deepest root of her fear. She was scared to make herself vulnerable again, fully open to love, because of the pain she'd experienced from loving and losing Ricardo. She'd never survive it a second time.

'I know nothing will bring him back,' Eva said in a hushed whisper, 'but if you could do it all again with Papá, knowing what was to come, would you?'

'Of course,' Emilia said without hesitation, her own tears spilling freely down her cheeks. How was her eighteen-year-old so emotionally intelligent? So wise when Emilia had been so foolish as to run scared?

'Because loving him all over again would be worth the risk,' Eva said. Emilia nodded.

'Worth *any* risk,' Emilia confirmed, realising now how she'd been standing in her own way of experiencing happiness again. Loving someone carried massive risks, yes, but also even greater rewards.

'So if Felipe makes you so happy,' Eva urged, 'after everything we've been through, all the sadness and loss and change, don't you think you owe it to yourself to see where your relationship with him could go, regardless of the risks? What if you *do* fall in love again? Wouldn't it be worth it, the way it was with Papá?'

'Maybe,' Emilia said in a choked voice, ashamed of herself. 'I just got scared,' she admitted, 'at the wedding.'

Her daughter squeezed her hand. 'I can understand why,' Eva said. 'I'm scared too, because change is hard, and when Papá was well our lives were so wonderful.'

'Yes, they were.' Emilia nodded, her heart clenching with love for Eva. As a little family, they'd had it all. But could she have it all again?

'I love Papá and I'll always miss him,' Eva said, 'but I think it's time that we let him go a little and start over properly with open hearts. We both need to be brave and embrace all the new changes in our lives. Don't you think?'

'You're right.' Emilia sniffed, taking a tissue from the box on the coffee table. Could she set aside her fear of losing someone she loved and open her heart fully?

Eva was right. If she found love it would be worth any risk. To have someone who understood you, cherished and supported you, and you them in return—it was rare and precious. And she was falling in love with Felipe.

'But you're already so brave,' Emilia said, sniffling into a wad of tissues. 'Whereas I wasn't brave. One of Felipe's aunts said something to me at the wedding, how she thought Felipe and I looked like we were in love and it spooked me. So I allowed my fear to make my decisions and I ran away.'

She had cut Felipe off without giving him a chance because she was scared to open her heart fully to him. Scared that, because of their pasts, any serious relationship between them would be doomed to failure and she'd be hurt again. Scared to love and to lose.

Eva frowned. 'Maybe he *does* love you. But that's a good thing, isn't it?'

Emilia shrugged, her heart sore. 'If it's true, it's good. Because I think the aunt might be right about me. I *have* fallen in love with him, the way I fell for Papá. But would that upset you?'

Eva smiled, fresh tears glittering on her long dark lashes. 'You never needed my permission to move on, Mamá. I want you to be happy. But I think you need to tell Felipe that you love him. It's the brave thing to do, and he deserves to know.'

Emilia dragged in a breath and nodded. 'You're right.

He does.' Even if he didn't love her in return. 'I'll tell him first thing tomorrow morning.'

She didn't want to tell him something so important by text, and he would be leaving Mendoza soon for the afternoon flight they'd been supposed to take together.

As she held her daughter until the tears dried, Emilia silently spoke to Ricardo. *'I'm so proud of our girl.'*

She would always love him, always prioritise Eva in her life, but it was time for Emilia to finally put her own needs first. It was time to be brave. It was time to love again.

# CHAPTER EIGHTEEN

LATER THAT SUNDAY evening Felipe emerged into the domestic terminal of Buenos Aires airport after his flight from Mendoza, his frustration and impatience an itch under his skin.

The flight home had seemed endless.

He checked his watch. Seven-thirty p.m. Not too late to call Emilia. She'd probably be at home, alone or perhaps with Eva. She'd texted him earlier today to let him know that all was well. But it wasn't, not with him. His stomach lurched with fear. He should never have let her leave.

Turning to Thiago and Violetta behind him, he dropped his overnight bag and held open his arms. 'Well, have a wonderful honeymoon, you two.' He kissed Violetta on the cheek and hugged Thiago, pasting on a fake smile.

The couple had been on the same flight from Mendoza—the one Emilia and he were supposed to take together before she'd run out on him Saturday night. The newlyweds were heading to the international terminal to take their connecting flight to the Caribbean island of Aruba for two weeks.

'We will,' Violetta said, stepping back, but Thiago hesitated.

'Darling,' his brother said to his new wife, 'could you give me a second? I just need some brotherly advice.'

'Of course.' Violetta smiled encouragingly at both men and ambled a short distance away to give them privacy.

'What's up,' Felipe asked, impatient to be on his way. Maybe he'd forget calling and simply knock on Emilia's door. He had to do something to make things right before he lost his mind, because the last time they'd spoken his words had come out wrong, his feelings tripping him up. He needed to make her want him again. 'I hope you're not going to ask me what to expect on your honeymoon, because you're a little old for the birds and bees talk.'

His joke masked the painful hollow feeling in his chest. All he'd wanted to do since he'd watched Emilia drive away was chase her down and beg her to reconsider. It had taken her leaving him stranded in the dark to realise that he'd fallen madly in love with her, and he had no idea what to do about it. But missing her was a physical pain all over his body. He needed to see her, to beg her to give him another chance.

'I was going to ask *you* what's up, actually,' Thiago said, ignoring Felipe's attempt at humour. 'You haven't really been present since Emilia left last night. I know you tried to convince everyone that you two are *just friends*, but it's time to be real.' Thiago tilted his head sympathetically. 'Especially because you're acting as if she cut out your heart when she left.'

Felipe gripped the back of his neck and exhaled noisily. He was fifty-five years old. He didn't need love-life advice from his little brother. Except maybe he did. Because Thiago was right. His heart had been ripped out. Maybe he should hear his brother out, seeing as on his own he'd made such a mess of his relationship with Emilia.

'If you must know,' Felipe said with a sigh, 'we *were* more than friends, but it's over. She broke things off before she left the wedding. Said she couldn't risk having feelings for me.'

Thiago frowned, looking as confused as Felipe felt. 'Sounds like she already has feelings for you, just like you have for her. She was probably just running scared.'

Felipe glanced at the floor, impotence a heavy weight on his shoulders. 'You've been married a day and you're already an expert on relationships?'

Thiago shrugged, nonplussed. 'I *am* an expert on some relationships. I know, for example, that you still have some warped big brother over-protective streak when it comes to me, and a sense of guilt because you didn't want to run Castillo Estates.'

Felipe pressed his lips together. He didn't want to have this conversation, least of all in a public place. But he couldn't let Thiago go on his honeymoon with this accusation unresolved.

'It wasn't your calling,' Thiago added before Felipe could interject. 'The rest of the family accepted that years ago. You're a much better doctor than you are a winemaker anyway. We're all proud of you. You're the only person who can't let it go. It's like you're scared to let yourself be happy again.'

Felipe shook his head. Having discussed it with Emilia, he had begun to let it go. She'd already pointed out his flawed thinking about his family. She'd given him a reason to question the status quo of his life. But Thiago was right. *Again*. Felipe had punished himself long enough for the things he saw as his failings.

'I *can* let it go,' he said, meeting Thiago's stare. 'And I'm proud of you and what you've achieved with the business. You're right. I wouldn't have been half as good as you at running the estate because it's not my passion.'

Thiago slapped Felipe's arm with enthusiasm. 'Whereas I'm excited by the challenges. I can't wait to watch my family grow up surrounded by the ancient vines. And Violetta feels the same way. It wasn't your calling but it's *ours*.'

Felipe nodded, his throat tight with emotion. Had he spent so long feeling guilty about his career choices and his failed marriage that he'd overlooked what made *him* excited? His career, for sure, but also someone to share all the good things in his life with. *Emilia.*

'But back to Emilia,' Thiago pressed. 'Did you tell her how you feel about her?'

'No.' Felipe winced, feeling stupid. 'I tried, but that just seemed to make things worse.' Because instead of telling her he had feelings for her, instead of telling her he'd fallen in love with her, he'd held back out of fear that he couldn't be what she needed, that he'd somehow let her down. Only now, it was so obvious. Even if she still didn't want him, even if she was still protecting her vulnerable heart, Emilia needed to know that he'd fallen head over heels in love with her anyway.

'So you let her run scared?' Thiago pointed out.

'Like I said, it's much more complicated second time around,' Felipe said, absolutely gutted that he'd allowed her to walk away without telling her how he felt. 'I was trying not to scare her off. She'll always love her husband, and I've no desire to make the same mistakes I did with Delfina.'

'Just because Emilia loves her husband doesn't mean that she can't love you, too,' Thiago said, making it all sound so straightforward.

Felipe shook his head, speechless. Could Emilia love him back? Was that what she'd meant when she'd said *'before we both get our hearts broken'*? He needed to go to her—right now—and sort this out.

But Thiago hadn't finished. 'And you can't take all the blame for your divorce. I've heard that Delfina has moved on, so why can't you?'

'That's a great question.' Why couldn't he move on? Why was he punishing himself? Didn't he also deserve happiness?

As if he'd heard the unasked question, Thiago said, 'The family want to see you content, that's all. We love you. We want what's best for you, whatever that is. But don't let fear, either yours or Emilia's, stop you from being honest about your feelings. Tell her how you feel and what you want and take it from there.'

Felipe nodded, pulling Thiago in for one final hug. 'Thanks for the pep talk, little brother. Now go and enjoy your honeymoon. I have to go to Emilia.'

Because, just like Emilia, he *did* deserve to be happy. Only to achieve that he needed her. With a fresh sense of urgency, he grabbed his bag and took off running towards the taxi rank.

# CHAPTER NINETEEN

A SUNDAY EVENING on the sofa with Eva watching a chick-flick was just what the doctor ordered. So Emilia jumped in surprise when the doorbell rang halfway through the film.

'I'll get it,' Eva said, pausing the movie. 'My friend Paloma said she might swing by.'

The dog jumped down from beside Emilia and followed Eva into the hall.

Seconds later, Eva called out, 'I'm just heading out to get some frozen yoghurt with Paloma. Don't wait up.'

*What? That was sudden.*

'Okay, *mija*,' Emilia called, feeling a little abandoned. She rose from the sofa and shuffled out to the hall to say goodbye.

'Felipe…' She gasped at the sight of him standing just inside the front door. He looked tired, a little rumpled, but wonderfully familiar, and Emilia's heart reached out to him. She'd hurt him last night and she needed to make it right.

Eva took her coat from the hook, winked at her mother and pulled the door closed as she left. Emilia and Felipe were alone. For a few seconds they only stared at each other. Emilia held her breath, everything she wanted to say trapped in her throat by the surge of love she felt for this man.

'What are you doing here?' she finally asked, bewildered, her pulse fluttering with excitement. Then she remembered what she'd said and done yesterday and how she'd most likely already ruined her chances with him.

Felipe placed his overnight bag on the floor and stepped closer, his stare searching hers as if he was thinking of something to say. Emilia had a fleeting thought that perhaps she'd left something behind in Mendoza and he was simply there to return it. Her stomach sank, her second chance evaporating.

Then he reached for her hands. 'I'm sorry to come around uninvited, but I've been dying inside since you left yesterday.'

Fresh hope bloomed in her chest. 'I'm so sorry if I hurt you, Felipe.' She swallowed, her eyes smarting with tears that she'd caused him pain.

He shook his head, his stare growing more intense. 'It's my own fault,' he said with the passion that was a massive part of his personality. 'I was stupid enough to let you go last night, when I should have told you how I feel instead. I love you, Emilia.'

She gasped at his miraculous words, the floor tilting under her bare feet. Could that be true? Were his aunts right? Did he love her, after everything?

'I messed up,' he rushed on, his expression wreathed in sincerity, his vulnerability heartbreaking. 'I've always felt like I let my family down, and like I'd messed up my marriage, and I was scared that if I tried to have a relationship with you I'd only let you down, too. And I never, ever want to hurt you. There was so much more at stake for us, after everything you'd been through with Ricardo and with the added responsibility of Eva, who of course must always come first in your life.'

Too choked to speak, Emilia shook her head. There was finally space in her heart for love again—for *him*. He was just as important to her, too.

He released one of her hands and cupped her cheek, wiping away a tear she hadn't even known had escaped. 'But I'm not scared any more. You deserve to know how madly I've fallen in love with you, even if you can't love me back. I won't pressure you if you're not ready for a relationship, but I want to be in your life in any capacity you'll allow. To be there for you, always. As a friend and colleague if that's all you want, but I hope that one day you might want more...'

'Felipe...' Emilia released a sound, half sob, half exclamation of joy as she reached for him, her hands finding his waist. 'I was scared, too. But I *do* want more. I love you, too.'

'You do?' He frowned, staring so intently into her eyes it almost hurt to look at him.

'I do.' She nodded, tears spilling free.

He stepped closer, cupped her face in both hands and kissed her with fierce desperation. Emilia kissed him back, her heart soaring with love. He pulled back, holding her tightly as if he'd never again let her go—and that was fine with her. She was exactly where she wanted to be.

'I thought I was done with love after my marriage failed,' he said, pressing a kiss to her temple, 'but I was *so* wrong. I think I was scared to allow myself to be happy again, and I was obviously just waiting for *you*, wonderful you, without knowing it. Because you are everything I could ever want in a partner.'

Emilia looked up, blinking away the sting in her eyes.

'I'm so sorry I hurt you. I was scared that loving you meant I'd be betraying Ricardo, scared that I'd hurt Eva if I embarked on another relationship—although I'm sure that when she gets to know you she'll love you, too—scared that if I loved you as desperately as I do that I might lose you as well.'

He dragged her into his arms, pressing a kiss to her forehead. 'I'm here. Nobody knows what's around the corner, but I'll love you fiercely and passionately for however long we have together. You are so beautiful. I want you to be mine. Always.'

No one could promise for ever. But the important thing was that they valued the time they did have together. That they squeezed every drop of life and love and joy from every day they shared. That they felt the fear and loved each other anyway.

Emilia held him tight. 'And I'll love you back the same way. I know it hasn't even been twenty-four hours since I left you, but I missed you so badly. You feel like home to me.' Taking his hand, she led him into the lounge and the sofa where they sat side by side, Luna content at their feet.

'I can't quite believe that you're here,' she said, caressing his handsome face. 'I had a long talk with Eva this morning, and I realised that you deserved to know how I felt. I was going to find you first thing tomorrow and beg you to give me another chance. I'm so sorry that I hurt you, that I allowed my fear to push you away when you've brought me back to life.'

Felipe gripped her hands, pressing kisses over her knuckles. 'And I'm sorry that I wasn't brave enough to fight for you at the wedding. Part of me knew that I loved you then, and I regret letting you leave without fully realising it.'

'But you're here now,' she whispered, her heart bursting with love for this thoughtful and passionate man who was everything she wanted and needed.

He nodded, pressing his lips to hers. 'I'm here now.'

Holding both her hands, he stared into her eyes—she saw his vulnerability. 'I wanted to ask you something. Don't freak out.'

Emilia laughed, kissed him, pulled back. 'Okay, I won't.'

'Will you date me—just me—exclusively?' His grip on her hands tightened. 'I'll make us work. I promise.'

'I will, absolutely.' She nodded, laughing through her tears. 'And *we'll* make us work.' She leaned in and kissed him again. She couldn't seem to stop and realised with a soaring heart that she didn't have to.

'In that case,' he said, his beaming smile lighting his eyes, 'How would you feel if we delete our dating apps together?'

Emilia gasped with excitement. 'I think that's a brilliant idea.' She reached for her phone and he pulled his from his pocket.

'Ready?' he asked, his finger poised over the icon on the screen.

'Definitely.' Emilia nodded, never more excited to be rid of the horrible dating app. 'One, two, three.' They pressed the little x's in unison and the apps vanished back into the void.

'Good riddance,' Emilia said, her cheeks aching from smiling as she abandoned her phone and threw her arms around his neck. 'I only want *you*.' Her man, her friend, her lover.

'I only want *you*, for the rest of my life,' Felipe said,

tossing aside his phone and reaching for Emilia, dragging her into his arms.

It wasn't a proposal, but it was a commitment nonetheless. A promise to be there for each other, with fully open hearts.

'And to think we met the old-fashioned way,' Emilia teased, her arms tight around the man she loved. How had she been so lucky to be given a second chance at love? To have met not one but two amazing men in her life.

'I am such a good dating coach,' he said playfully, his hands in her hair and his eyes full of love. 'I told you it would all work out.'

'You did and you were right,' she whispered, sinking into his kiss.

His lips caressed hers, their kisses growing more and more passionate. They loved each other all night long and Emilia finally had everything she needed.

# EPILOGUE

*Two years later...*

THE CASTILLO ESTATE winery was even more spectacular in spring, the perfect season for a wedding celebration. Felipe once more stood under the antique wrought-iron gazebo with Thiago at his side, only this time *he* was the proud and nervous groom.

Only his nerves were more about excitement. After a long courtship—he'd asked Emilia to be his wife three months into their exclusive relationship—today he and Emilia would finally make it official.

The music began and Emilia emerged from the avenue of pink-blossomed Oleander trees that led back to the house. Felipe and Thiago had played under those very trees as boys, and to see the woman he loved in this magical place that was so close to his heart left him choked. He held his breath, his heart racing at the beautiful sight she made. Dressed in a simple sleeveless gold satin dress, with her hair casually pinned up, she looked breathtaking. Eva, wearing a deep blue dress, walked arm in arm at her mother's side.

His eyes met Emilia's, the small congregation of friends and family melting away for a second so they were alone in this intensely personal moment. Today was just about them and the love they'd found while neither of them had been searching.

Felipe grinned, the broad smile on his face impossible to stop. He probed his feelings, relieved to find no trace of the fear that had held him back for years. His relationship with Emilia wasn't perfect. They'd had their tests and trials over the past two years, like any couple. But every day they woke up together and showed up for their relationship, willing to work at it, to stay committed and to act with the unstoppable love and passion they shared.

When she reached his side, Felipe took her hand, leaning down to press a brief kiss on her lovely lips. 'I love you,' he whispered. 'You're beautiful.'

'Me too,' she replied, laughing as family members cheered at their sneaky pre-vow kiss.

But neither of them cared. Today was *their* day, a day of love, and the celebration of two families—one big and one small—coming together.

Felipe held Emilia's hand throughout the entire ceremony, his heart swelling with so much love he thought it might burst. As they exchanged vows, promising to love and care for each other, he'd never felt more content or more certain of them as a couple. Of his ability to care for this woman and her daughter, and to make Emilia happy.

'Emilia and Felipe are now husband and wife,' the celebrant declared to raucous cheering from the audience.

Felipe held Emilia's face, slowly dipping his head to hers and bringing their lips together. Thoroughly and passionately he savoured their first kiss as a married couple. Emilia sank into his arms, her hands gripping his neck as she kissed him back with equal passion.

Kissing Emilia should never be rushed. Kissing his wife, likewise.

'I love you,' he said when he pulled back, staring down into her beautiful deep brown eyes. 'I'm never letting you go again.' He squeezed her hand to prove his point and she laughed.

'I love you, too.' She smiled that secret smile of hers and his heart soared.

Second time around wasn't without its challenges, but the rewards when you made that commitment were magnified tenfold. He and Emilia would cherish every moment they had together—a little older, hopefully a little wiser, but no less in love.

As they were swallowed up by well-wishers, engulfed in hugs and kisses and congratulations, Felipe kept his promise and kept a hold of his wife's hand.

As the entire wedding party moved to the barn, which was festooned with swathes of romantic flower garlands and twinkling lights, Emilia couldn't seem to stop smiling. With Eva at her side as maid of honour, and Felipe holding on tightly to her hand, she felt cocooned in love.

'It's so beautiful,' Emilia whispered to Felipe as everyone poured into the barn and the party began—the wine flowing, the music playing and their loved ones smiling.

Felipe motioned to a waiter, who handed them each a glass of special sparkling wine, a vintage that had been specifically created by Thiago for Emilia and Felipe's wedding. It even had their names on the label.

'A toast, just for us, before the partying begins,' Felipe said, touching his glass to hers. 'To you my beautiful wife. May our marriage be long and full of passion. I will love you and take care of you and Eva every day of my life.'

'And to you, my dashing husband.' She smiled, blinking away the sting in her eyes as she stared at him over the rim of her glass. 'I'll love you and support you and care for you and our marriage with all of my heart, always.'

They both took a sip of the delicious wine and then Felipe drew her into his arms, kissing her once more. Emilia melted into the kiss, indulging in her husband's lips for far longer than was decent. But she didn't care. Life was too short to deny yourself the good things it had to offer.

When they pulled apart there was another cheer from the guests, punctuated by the odd wolf-whistle and cry of, *'Get a room!'*

Felipe dipped his head to whisper, 'All in good time.'

His promise for their wedding night sent shivers down Emilia's spine. But she forced herself to act with decorum and welcome her guests. She and Felipe worked the room hand in hand, stopping for a chat with each friend and family member in turn. By the time they reached their work colleagues from the General their glasses had been refilled several times.

'I hear you're both going to be working part-time when you return from your honeymoon,' Isabella Lopez said, her husband Sebastian at her side. The triplets—Sergio, Lorenzo and a happy and healthy Luis—were toddling around, kept safe with the helping hands of their friends from the hospital and nearby clinic, Carlos, Sofia, Gabriel and Ana.

'We are,' Felipe confirmed, his arm around Emilia's waist, holding her close. 'We have too much life to enjoy living to work full-time. I don't want the hospital to be the only place I see my wife.'

Emilia smiled up at him, excitement for their future a flutter in her veins. With Eva in her penultimate year at law school and living in a flat with her uni friends, she and Felipe had sold Emilia's house and moved in together to Felipe's apartment. There was a spare room for Eva, if she ever needed it, and Luna and Dante kept each other company, enjoying daily walks with the dog-walker while they were at the hospital.

Life was good again, and Emilia would never take one second of it for granted.

Later that night, after the best party ever, Felipe swung her up into his arms and carried her over the threshold of the estate's guest house.

'Congratulations, Mrs Castillo,' he said as he kicked the door closed and placed her on her feet, making sure that her body slid down his so her every nerve was electrified.

'Congratulations, husband,' she said, undoing the top few buttons of his shirt to press kisses to his chest, his jaw, his smiling lips.

'Now, stop talking,' she said, taking his hand and dragging him to the bedroom.

And he did.

* * * * *

*If you missed the previous story in the*
Buenos Aires Docs *quartet, then check out*

Daring to Fall for the Single Dad Doc
*by Becky Wicks*

*And if you enjoyed this story, check out these*
*other great reads from JC Harroway*

Her Secret Valentine's Baby
Phoebe's Baby Bombshell
Breaking the Single Mum's Rules

*All available now!*

# MILLS & BOON®

Coming next month

## REUNION WITH THE ER DOCTOR
Tina Beckett

Her whole being ignited.

It was as if Georgia had been waiting for this moment ever since she'd come back to Anchorage. Eli's mouth was just as firm and warm as she remembered. Just as sexy. And it sent a bolt of electricity through her body that morphed into some equally dangerous reactions. All of which were addictive.

And she wanted more.

Her hands went behind his neck and tangled in his hair as if afraid he might try to pull away before she'd gotten her fill of him. Not that she'd ever been able to do that. No matter how many times they'd kissed, no matter how many times they'd made love, she still craved him.

Despite the three years she'd spent away on Kodiak, that was one thing that evidently hadn't changed.

She pulled him closer, relishing the feel of his tongue pressing for entrance—an entrance she granted far too quickly. And yet it wasn't quick enough, judging from the way her senses were lighting torches. Torches that paved the way for an ecstasy she could only remember.

How utterly heady it was to be wanted by a man like this.

*Continue reading*
REUNION WITH THE ER DOCTOR
Tina Beckett

*Available next month*
millsandboon.co.uk

Afterglow Books is a trend-led, trope-filled list of books with diverse, authentic and relatable characters, a wide array of voices and representations, plus real world trials and tribulations. Featuring all the tropes you could possibly want (think small-town settings, fake relationships, grumpy vs sunshine, enemies to lovers) and all with a generous dose of spice in every story.

@millsandboonuk
@millsandboonuk
afterglowbooks.co.uk
#AfterglowBooks

**For all the latest book news, exclusive content and giveaways scan the QR code below to sign up to the Afterglow newsletter:**